MOON TORTURED

(SKY BROOKS SERIES BOOK 1)

MCKENZIE HUNTER

This is a work of fiction. Names, characters, businesses, places, events, and incidents are either the products of the author's imagination or used in a fictitious manner. Any resemblance to actual persons, living or dead, or actual events is purely coincidental.

McKenzie Hunter

Moon Tortured (4th Edition)

McKenzieHunter@McKenzieHunter.com

ISBN: 978-1-946457-90-5

ACKNOWLEDGMENTS

It is humbling to have such wonderful people take the time out of their schedule to not only read my manuscript, but also offer constructive criticism, invaluable feedback, and support throughout the process. I am truly thankful for my mother, Shawn Arroyo, Gregory Caughman, Tiffany Dix, April Franks, London Gibbs, and Marcia Snyder. This book is not solely my creation but a result of the time you all gave to improve it from the original.

I would like to offer a special thanks to Sheryl Cox and Stacy McCright. Sheryl, I can never truly express how grateful I am that you made the time between working full-time and going to school, to read each draft, coach me, and offer your skills and experience selflessly. You treated my manuscript as though it were your own, and worked tirelessly to support and encourage me throughout the process. I can never repay you for that level of dedication. Stacy, I don't believe you have the same twenty-four hours in your day as everyone else. You didn't hold your punches and gave freely of your compliments as well as criticism, which after developing thicker skin, I learned to appreciate. I developed a love/hate relationship with each critique you e-mailed me and quickly learned to accept them for what they were—a challenge to improve.

I would also like to thank Wayne Purdin, my editor and and Orina Kafe, for the cover art.

Last but definitely not least, I would like that thank my readers for giving my book a chance and choosing to follow Skylar through her journey.

CHAPTER 1

I looked around the unfamiliar room, acutely aware of the light footsteps below me. This wasn't the first time I'd awoken in a strange place, naked and bloodstained. But it was usually in the woods with Bambi's or possibly Thumper's mutilated and half-eaten carcass lying next to me. Waking up in a stranger's house—naked—surrounded by a distinctive male musk was inconceivable. My life just wasn't that interesting.

Each time I moved, my body ached as it pressed against the hardwood floor. I tugged the blanket closer, brushing my sweat-drenched hair away from my face, slowly came to my feet, and looked around the meticulously neat room. The king-size bed across from me was covered by a henna-colored, paisley-patterned duvet that looked like it had never been used. Dark mahogany nightstands were placed on each side of it, meticulously aligned with the headboard. Even the bronze gourd lamps on the nightstands were perfectly centered. The room looked like a hotel room, but I had a feeling I wasn't in one.

Where am I?

I took a quick look at my reflection in the cheval mirror across from me: my hair was disheveled, a long scratch ran along my right arm, and plum-colored marks in the late stages of healing covered my shoulders and arms. Handprint-shaped bruises wrapped around my calves. I wasn't sure which was worse—the way I looked or the way I felt.

The scent of blood and spiced musk inundated and lingered in the large space. The walls were solid and reinforced. They would be damn hard to break through without tools. When the double-paned security windows opened with ease, I breathed a sigh of relief. I was on the second floor. *No problem. I've jumped from higher.*

Taking a seat on the small accent chair in front of the writing table, I looked through the drawers before delivering the same treatment to the dresser, nightstands, and walk-in closet. With the exception of the hangers I found in the closet, everything was completely empty.

I looked out the window. It was late afternoon and the sun would set in a couple of hours. I was surrounded by what looked like nearly twenty acres of dense woodland. I assumed I was still in Illinois, but for all I knew, I could be in any of the other flat states surrounding it.

Every visible area was covered by large masses of trees. There wasn't a neighbor in sight. If I screamed, it would go unheard. How far would I need to go before I ran into someone?

I was about to find out. I quickly braided my hair and tucked it into a bun, then I tightened the blanket around me.

Before I could do anything, I heard light footsteps approaching. I wondered if I should stay in the room or wait to see who was coming. I opened the door. It was so thick and heavy it was an effort to open it. That must have been to block out sound.

I poked my head out and saw him. I could never forget that tense, harsh grimace and his predacious movements. Forced to the surface was the memory of him standing in my living room covered in blood, four bodies lying at his feet. He had killed them so effortlessly and brutally that my only instinct now was to run.

I considered securing myself in the room, but it locked from the other side. Instead, I darted out of the room and down the hall, running past an oddly placed console and sprinting toward the stairs, nearly hitting the wall as the hall came to a dead end. Taking a sharp right turn, I kept running, barely holding on to the blanket. Saving my life trumped Midwestern modesty.

"Skylar!" His voice was like sandpaper. I continued to run, lunging for the stairs in a frantic rush. But I didn't make it before a firm grasp yanked at the blanket, pulling me back. Crashing to the floor, I skidded backward and slammed against the wall. When he reached for my leg, I kicked him. Spinning on my butt, I kicked him again. My legs thrashed out, trying to keep him at bay. It was the same way they showed me in my self-defense class.

Nothing seemed to deter him.

His cruel gaze and vicious movements made his declaration that he wasn't going to hurt me hard to believe. Werewolf strength gave me a physical advantage most of the time, but he had my five-eight frame by at least four inches. His lean, sinewy muscles flexed and tightened, holding exceptional power. With one swift movement, he grabbed my legs, immobilizing me, and pulled me into his arms. I was bundled so tightly that the only thing I could move was my head. His movements were so efficient and precise it was obvious he'd done this before—many times before.

I clawed at his hands. When his hold didn't give, I bit down into his shoulder, grabbing more t-shirt than skin. I stayed clamped to whatever I had, doing whatever it took to keep him from taking me back to that lockable room. Steel-like corded muscles flexed and distended, making it difficult to keep a firm hold. The unforgiving muscles fatigued my jaw and made my teeth ache, but I hung on.

Pounding down the hall, he seemed unaffected by my teeth embedded in his arm. He tossed me back in the room. When I wouldn't stop screaming, he leaned over me. "Shut up!"

I couldn't. Yelling at the top of my lungs, I hoped someone, anyone, would help. I needed to be heard, to stop him before he did to me what I had seen him do to those four other people.

He used one hand to cover my mouth and nose. His other hand snapped around my wrists, cuffing them over my head. "Stop it. If I wanted to hurt you, I would have. And you've given me more than enough reasons to do so." His fingers scorched against my skin as sharp, angry eyes demanded silence. Silence that didn't come easily but instead was whittled into a whimper as I tried to grab oxygen from any space his hands would allow. As soon as I stopped struggling, he removed his hand from my face.

His eyes narrowed as he examined mine. Frowning, he asked, "What—what *are* you?"

What am I? He doesn't know.

I stared at him for a long time, remaining silent, refusing to talk to the man I had watched kill so quickly and violently that it would haunt my nightmares for the rest of my life. He studied me inch by inch, crevice by crevice, imprinting my face, features, flaws, and markings to memory. "What are you?" he asked again, his curiosity belied by his aversion.

"Ethan, get off of her," commanded a firm, feminine voice from behind him. He stiffened at the sound. The woman's face, soft and round with small patches of freckles decorating her nose and cheeks, looked just as kind and gentle as her voice. Her deep auburn hair was pulled back into a ponytail, wisps of bangs angling across her face. Pale brown eyes cast a gentle gleam as she spoke. "Ethan ..." she urged again when he didn't move.

He stepped back, taking a position near the door as she inched closer to me. He continued to watch me, his thin lips twisted into a sneer. The glaring way he peered at me with his gunmetal gray eyes, in an odd state between revulsion and fascination made me feel the decision not to hurt me wasn't his own.

Noticing my reaction to Ethan, the woman turned to him. "Give me a moment," she requested warmly. "Please," she added when he was slow to respond. He gave me another chilling look before he walked out of the room.

I came to my feet, securing the blanket around me, keeping my distance from her. "Who are you?"

Her lips spread into a warm smile that was disarming and comforting. It was easy to imagine her standing in a classroom surrounded by small children who looked upon her dotingly.

"My apologies. I'm Joan." She pulled up a chair from the corner of the room and placed it in front of me. "Please, have a seat."

I remained standing. "Where am I?"

"You're in a retreat home."

Keeping my focus on her, I stepped behind the chair, creating a barrier between us. She was very calming, parrying my skepticism, distrust, and anger with ease. Whether intentional or not, she made me feel like surrendering, like an unwary and trusting child. I didn't like that. "What am I doing at a retreat?" I asked abrasively.

"I hoped you could tell me." She lowered herself to the edge of the bed, keeping the chair between us. "Skylar, what can you tell me about last night?"

The long uncomfortable silence didn't seem to bother her as she waited for me to speak. I took a seat at the head of the bed. "There was a break-in—four—no, five men came after us. It happened so fast, most of it's just a blur," I admitted, frustrated. I fidgeted with my braid. "We ran ... two men were up there ... one grabbed me, the other my mother." I stopped speaking, unable to go on.

The images were just erratic blurs bouncing around in my

head. I didn't know what came first or what really happened. I just knew the intruders were fast, strong, and hard to evade. It was as though they had anticipated every movement I would make. Their movements were so sharp and quick, I felt as though I were shuffling about in slow motion.

Then Ethan appeared with a massive animal, a large coyote, maybe a wolf, and a tall, dark-haired woman. Chaos ensued. Blood and bodies moved around me so fast that I labored to stay out of the way, to avoid the gore and dismembered body parts.

Then everything stopped—well, for me it did. The sounds of violence whirling around me—bones crunching, grunts of pain, muscle and tissue ripping—came to an abrupt stop. My mother lay near the stairs, motionless, covered in blood, face pallid, chest stilled. I ran to her and immediately started CPR. I continued for fifteen minutes. Ribs broke under my hands from panicked compressions and my rescue breaths were so hard, her chest distended unnaturally. It felt like I couldn't push hard enough or blow breath deep enough into her lungs. I couldn't make the life, which I refused to accept was gone, respond. Exhausted and tearful, I finally conceded and accepted the harsh truth: she was dead.

I was surrounded by three strangers covered in blood, four decapitated bodies, and my dead mother. I didn't want to be there to dwell in the intense emotions and violence. Escaping in the only way I knew, I changed. Usually I fought her presence, but now I welcomed her gratefully, because standing in front of my mother's lifeless body was definitely where I didn't want to be.

That is how my wolf functioned. When emotions ran so high that I could barely contain them, she showed up. I was never sure if it was to protect me or to offer an escape or reprieve; nevertheless, it liked to be present when mayhem occurred. At that moment, I didn't care.

"They weren't men," Joan finally stated quietly. I lifted my gaze to meet hers, waiting for her to continue. "They were vampires. Skylar, why are vampires after you?"

I had seen the onyx-colored eyes, the fangs and the pale skin, and yet I couldn't believe what she was saying. I turned into a werewolf every full moon, yet vampires still seemed to be folklore to me.

Taking in what she said and what I just relived, I did what all sensible people do when someone tells them something horrific, unbelievable, and life-changing—I ignored and avoided it.

"Do you know what happened to my mother? Is she still at the house?" I asked. My voice was hoarse and my lips trembled. The memory I had repressed so diligently surfaced with a vengeance, winding me: her lying on the floor motionless. Her pale blonde hair, which was usually pinned up, was fanned out around her face. She was frozen in a liminal state of shock and fear.

Joan bit down on her lips. Troubled eyes gazed at me briefly before they lowered to the ground. "The body is downstairs."

The body is downstairs. That same tight feeling that restricted my chest earlier had returned. It was debilitating. Heartbreak, it felt the way I imagined a heart attack would. You couldn't breathe, talk, or even think straight through the wrenching pain.

I pressed my eyes firmly together, forcing back tears.

"Would you like to see her?"

No, no, I don't want to see her. As long as I don't see the lifeless body, I don't have to accept it. I don't—I won't—I can't see the body.

When she reached over to touch my hand, I jerked it back. Her eyes roved over the room and periodically she looked in my direction. "Some of your clothes are in there." She nodded at the bag she'd brought in with her. "You should shower and get dressed. Maybe then you will be ready to see her."

"Where am I, the address?" I asked, peering out the window, briefly appreciating the crowning beauty of the autumn. Being around her was a hell of a lot better than Ethan, but I didn't trust her.

"The bathroom is over there," she said, pointing to my right.

"The address?" I repeated impatiently.

Her smile deepened, revealing a small dimple at the corner of her right cheek. "You're anxious, perhaps a warm shower and food will ease you," she continued, in that soothing voice that people often used with children during their tantrums. "I will be more than happy to answer your questions afterward." Her insolence was vaguely buffered by the mildness of her voice. It was apparent that until I did what she said, I wasn't getting any answers.

"Why do you change locked in a cage rather than the woods?" she inquired before I stepped into the bathroom.

Of course they went through my house. Did I really think they wouldn't?

She knew what I was and I didn't have the energy to deny it. I looked over my shoulder. "Because animals belong in cages."

The look eclipsed her face so quickly. It was a flash, easily missed. She looked aggrieved, perhaps even offended. "And the sedatives?"

"It doesn't like being caged, and I haven't found a way to put it down without killing me." I glanced down at my wrist. The years had faded the scar into a thin light line, but it was a constant reminder of how much I hated that part of me. At fifteen, the typical teenage angst, pimples, and a gangly body that didn't want to cooperate were further complicated by my horrid transformation into a wolf. The moon called and I responded. My body pulled and contorted to torturous limits, ripping at my humanity until the only thing left was the unfamiliar feral animal—a werewolf.

I gave in to the depression and the iniquity, but it refused to be put down. The only thing I accomplished that night was hurting my mother and realizing I wasn't as strong as I thought. That night, she vowed to make my life as normal as possible. I changed into a wolf every full moon. How normal could my life be?

I lifted my gaze to meet Joan's; it was just a beat as it dropped from mine. She saw the scar where I had slashed my wrist repeatedly with a silver blade. Too many assaults to the same area prevented it from healing well. It left me scarred with a constant reminder of what I had done. I waited, watching her reaction, anticipating the horror, the intrigue, even the concern. And there it was—concern. The same look my mother gave me when I spoke of the wolf as though it were a separate entity. My mother always wanted me to embrace it, but I couldn't. As far as I was concerned, it was an unwelcome guest that showed up once a month despite my objections. It was a plague, a betrayal of my humanity, and I refused to accept or embrace it. Instead, every full moon, I would lie locked in a cage, sedated, until it was all over. At least I could pretend my life was my own and I was somewhat normal.

"I'll be here with some food when you're done," Joan stated with a plaintive smile.

If taking a shower was supposed to calm me, she was mistaken. Instead, it heightened my anxiety; fight or flight egged me on to respond. On the countertop were *my* blow-dryer, *my* curling irons, *my* toiletries, *my* Sonic toothbrush, and *my* beauty products. I stared at the counter. These were *my* things placed neatly on a *stranger's* bathroom counter. I rummaged through the cabinets, the linen closet, and the medicine cabinet, not quite sure for what. My head was starting to ache as I tried to make sense of this.

Have I been abducted? If so, they sure are some thoughtful criminals to care about my comfort. I tried to make light of the situation because if I didn't, I was going to spiral into a panic. The woman who stared back at me from the vanity mirror didn't make things better. I looked terrible. My thick, curly hair was barely contained in the braid. Olive skin that usually looked vibrant was now dull and blanched. Desolate eyes reflected back at me, darkened to the point that they looked jasper rather than emerald. I quickly pulled my gaze from the mirror.

For a brief moment, I considered fleeing out the small window just above the garden tub. Instead, I sat on the edge of the tub, formulating a plan on how to make an escape. I could go through the bathroom window, but for some reason, I felt like I would be met with the angry psycho from my earlier attempt. If I could manage to get past Joan, could I get past the people I heard downstairs? I showered, taking an exceptionally long time. Part of me hoped Joan would have given up and left. I opened the overnight bag with *my* clothes in it and put on a t-shirt and a pair of yoga pants. I'd give it to them: they were oddly meticulous and thoughtful, which should have comforted me, but it didn't. Weren't psychopaths and serial killers usually meticulous?

When I walked out of the bathroom, Joan was seated in a chair next to the bed. A waiter's cart sat next to it with an assortment of sandwiches that filled the room with alluring scents. My stomach began to rumble.

"Please have a seat." She patted a spot on the bed near her. Slowly, I walked toward her, watching her intently as I sat farther away than the spot she pointed to, closer to the door.

"Why am I here?"

"Eat. You must be famished. You've had quite the night," she urged in that same gentle voice. It was still soft and warm but it no longer soothed me. Instead, I now found it irritating because I figured she was doing it to manipulate me. It was hard to break the social rule and be a raging jerk to someone who was being exceptionally kind. She slid the cart of food toward me. There were several roast beef sandwiches, bags of chips, and sliced fruit. I usually liked my sandwiches warm, but I was too hungry to let something like that stop me. Discreetly, I sniffed the sandwiches. They seemed okay. I hesitated for a moment before I took a bite. I was on my second sandwich when she inched toward the edge of the chair.

Studying me, she seemed distracted by her own thoughts. After long moments of intense silence, she asked, "Do you know why the vampires were after you?"

"No. But I'm sure you do," I challenged, waiting for her to explain why Ethan and his crew of hostile strangers were at my home. "Joan, is it?"

She nodded.

"Why am I here?"

Her smile broadened as her gaze wandered. I suspected she was getting her story together or establishing a believable lie. "The vampires have taken a special interest in you."

"And?" It came off harsh and ruder than intended, but I hated having to extract information question by question. Her thin lips curved into a demure smile, trying to defuse my growing exasperation. I continued, tone crisp, gaze jarring, "Ethan rushed in like they expected them to be there. As though they were just waiting for them to strike. What do you know that I don't?"

"Their attack was anticipated but the reason is unclear. We've been petitioned to keep you safe." Her tone and inflection were cooler now, more professional.

The tension that came off her made me uncomfortable. She

was withholding, but I wasn't sure how much. *Is my mother really downstairs?*

"I want to see my mother," I admitted. If she were really here, then I could determine how much trust I was willing to put in Joan. If she took me downstairs, I could explore the retreat and plan my exit strategy.

She nodded slowly, and I followed her out the door down the long hallway. As we descended the stairs, the footsteps and sounds of movement seemed to come to a hurried stop. They scattered at my approach. Now those noises were nothing but phantom sounds from people I could never identify. As I followed her to the left, we walked past the large great room decorated for function not design. Two solidly built sofas were at the opposite ends of the room, separated by muted geometric-patterned accent chairs. A large, dark leather ottoman was placed in the middle. If I were watching one of those design shows on HGTV, they would call the room something catchy like "modern chic meets functionality," as a bubbly designer fixated on the mundane details of the décor.

What I saw was furniture that was so durable it couldn't be broken. Two deep claret-colored sofas that could easily hide most stains, most likely blood. I smelled it in this room. Blood had been spilled many times throughout it. With a normal sense of smell, when blood is washed away, so is the scent, but for me, it was only dulled to the point that it could be ignored.

I stayed close to Joan as she took me around the corner and we passed another room, which I assumed to be the living room. In most households, the room's only purpose was to showcase elaborate decorative furniture, art, and collectibles. This room was slightly different. The sofas were a luxurious tan, more traditional, still durable. Instead of an ottoman in the center of the room, there was an ornate wool rug. Unique pictures of wildlife and nature covered the walls. The rust and cream paint were blended together in an intricate and charming faux finish. It was aesthetically pleasing, but it also hid the subtle markings and dents of a battered wall. I wondered who or what battered them. This might be the room they used to show a more refined side of themselves, but blood had been spilled here, as well.

I couldn't help but wonder why the people who resided in or visited this house had so many accidents, lost so much blood, bled so often. My curiosity was a weighted vest, making it hard to continue following Joan. I wanted to make a mad dash for the nearest door and probably would have, but I had to see my mother.

I trailed Joan down the lengthy hallway through plain white double doors into another hall. It looked like an addition to the house. After a left turn, I found myself in a hospital—rather a home version of one. The walls were white and sterile and the floors were the same high-gloss tile that you see in doctors' offices, hospitals, and clinics.

It's not that I had a lot of experience in doctors' offices or hospitals. My mother was a pathologist. When I needed a doctor, she was there. I rarely needed her in that capacity. As a child, I wasn't plagued with the same childhood problems as others. Broken bones? Not a chance. If I fell from a tree, I would walk away unscathed. A skinned knee was healed before you could get the bandages out of the box. I never had a cold, flu, or even the chicken pox, yet I had somehow built up the antibodies. My mother did the bloodwork. Things like that didn't just happen without her poking me with a needle and drawing blood to find out why.

Those things should have clued her in that something was very wrong with her daughter. Perhaps she knew and did an excellent job of hiding her *my-daughter's-a-freak* look.

Joan and I continued down the hall past three doors that were numbered. I assumed they were recovery rooms, but for all I knew, they could have been little prison cells. Each one was locked from the outside and two were padlocked. I decided then that as soon as I saw my mother, I was leaving. This beautifully decorated house was just camouflage for all the iniquities it hid.

Finally, we made a right down another hallway. I paid close attention to every turn, every loop, despite the fact the house was a maze.

When she opened another set of double doors, the room temperature dropped. Chill bumps rose along my arm. The open room smelled of disinfectant, sulfur, and medicine. There were seven beds, separated only by dividing curtains. Perhaps there were nine; two of the curtains were closed. Near the desk at the far end of the room was an examining table. At the other end of the room was a microscope with testing supplies. Multiple cabinets filled with medical supplies were placed throughout the room. *Why the hell do they have a hospital in their house, and why do they require so much medical attention?*

Joan pulled back the thin dividing curtains. My mother lay on the examining table. With pale skin and bluish lips, her face was peaceful, void of life and the jovial expressions that it always held. This was my mother, or rather, her body. The lifeless shell of the woman who took me into her life, her home, and raised me as her own after my mother died giving birth to me. She was the person who forced me to learn Portuguese in order to have some part of my birth mother with me, who did everything she could to give me a normal life, despite the circumstances that would deny me that.

I closed my eyes, reluctant to open them again and accept the reality that my mother was dead. "Skylar," said a deep sympathetic voice behind me. I turned slightly toward the tall, slender gentleman with silver hair with hints of dark gray. A congenial smile settled on his ruggedly handsome face. I didn't respond. Everyone seemed to know who I was, but didn't bother introducing themselves.

"Who are you?" I asked icily. I couldn't believe how incredibly rude I sounded. When your mother was lying dead in front of you, being impolite was acceptable or, at the very least, understandable.

"I'm Dr. Jeremy Baker. You are welcome to call me Jeremy." He looked down at my mother, his empathy and concern apparent. I felt like a jerk for being so rude to him. "I wish there had been something I could have done for her, but she was gone before she got to me. We couldn't even consider changing her." He ran his fingers through his thinning hair. Narrow, aristocratic features may have made him look cold, but I didn't think he was. After a few moments, he gave me a reassuring pat on the shoulder. He and Joan left the room, leaving me alone to grieve.

And grieve I did. First, shock made it hard to cry. Instead, I stared at her, in a frozen state of disbelief. *This isn't happening. No, this can't be happening.* Whether or not I chose to accept it, or live in a state of utter denial, it happened. There she was—or rather her body. All life was gone from her. The reassuring smile and gentle eyes that always made things seem less perilous and easier to handle were absent. The delicate lines of her face relaxed into an eternal sleep. Her skin was the palest I had ever seen, and her lips were cracked and a silvery blue. Now she was nothing more than a lifeless body.

She was dead soon after the attack. After I stopped the CPR, I tried to accept it; she was gone. Taking another look at her, I crumpled into the small space next to the bed. I cried until the urge to scream dwindled to a whimper. When I was done, my eyes were dry, tear ducts battered, and my throat parched from sobbing.

When I walked out of the room, Joan stood by the door waiting for me. Her lips curled into a gentle, sympathetic smile. As she guided me back to the bedroom, I aimlessly followed her in a dissociated state, barely noticing the new rooms she took me through. This wasn't a house; it was an estate, or worse—a compound.

I didn't see them but I could feel all eyes on me. They were skulking in the shadows, eerily watching me as I moved through the house. I wondered if they were hiding from me or if they didn't want me to see them. I wouldn't be able to name names or identify the faces of the people I hadn't met, if needed. Periodically I would look over my shoulder, hoping to get a glance at a face or catch a glimpse of the people who were so obsessively watching me.

As we walked up the stairs, the dark-haired woman who had accompanied Ethan into my home was descending them. Her gaze met mine briefly. She appeared hard and palpably unwelcoming, yet I couldn't drop my eyes from hers. There was something hauntingly intriguing about her. I stared at her as she passed us. Feeling my attention, she craned her neck to look back at me, and her deep hazel human eyes changed to ... *snake eyes?* Long vertical slits sharpened, making her pupils resemble those of a serpent. I stared at them, transfixed, unable to pull my gaze from hers.

"Winter, is everything okay?" Joan inquired, turning to focus on the woman with the peculiar eyes.

She ripped her gaze from mine to look at Joan, her eyes back to hazel but arctic cold. "Of course," she responded in a low terse voice. She glided down the stairs with soft purposeful movements, giving me the impression that I only heard her moving because she desired it. Any other time, she probably moved in silence, undetected, a predator on a perpetual hunt.

In the room, I sat on the bed trying to focus and gain perspective on what was going on. "What did Dr. Baker mean, that he couldn't 'change her'?"

"As were-animals, we have the ability to change others to our form. If the process is successful during the conversion, most, if not all, injuries are repaired." Her eyes roved over my face assessing me. "A change to a lesser species isn't as traumatic but the conversion doesn't allow the best physical repair. As you can guess, change to a greater species is far more aggressive and the survival rate is low, especially if the person is physically compromised. We were left without options for your mother."

Were-animals? Is that what they are? Humans forced to share their body, their life with an animal, like me? "You are all werewolves?" Then I remembered the animal that was at Ethan's side when he barged into my home. It wasn't a wolf. With everything going on around me, I thought my eyes were playing tricks on me when I saw a person in the phase of mid-change. By the time I focused on him again, he was a coyote. Well, I assumed the massive thing was a coyote. Its features resembled one, but it was larger than anything I had seen in the woods or zoo. It viciously ripped into the man—or rather—vampire, killing one of the four people who entered my home.

She nodded her head slowly. "More than just werewolves, were-animals."

"Why am I here?" I was hesitant to ask. The more questions I asked, the weirder things became: werewolves, or rather were-animals, vampires, and beautifully decorated compounds with built-in hospitals.

"Because you need help," she stated elusively.

"What if I don't want your help?"

The muscles around her neck tightened marginally, but she maintained the same pleasant smile. "I hope you will accept it and stay here. Then we can guarantee your safety." She was very cautious and deliberate in choosing her words. Despite the assertive undertone and my efforts to resist, when she spoke, it was soothing.

I was silent for a long time, looking around the room. Now there were more of my things in it, set up for an extended stay. "Why do I have a feeling that your request is just a courtesy and I really don't have a choice in leaving?"

"We will not keep you here against your will. However, it will make it much easier to keep you safe here. The vampires are wise enough not to come here," she continued, maintaining a professional yet gentle tone.

"If I choose, I can just take my things and leave, no questions asked?" My eyes narrowed, scrutinizing her. I was having a hard time believing that.

"We hope that you choose to stay," a baritone voice added. I swallowed a gasp. My body tensed. Some people have the ability to command a room, others to control it. When someone does both, it is consuming. He was a presence that occupied the large room, shrinking it to a quarter of its size. I felt the urge to find a small space that he didn't occupy, and cower.

His skin was a flawless deep espresso-brown. His full lips, which should have overwhelmed his face, did nothing but enhance it, despite the fact they were dipped down into a frown. Prominently defined cheekbones and a strong jawline made the look of reproach he gave me even more severe. My gaze fixed on his oval light brown eyes that were so imposing they trapped me where I stood. As he moved farther into the room, the waves of muscles that clung to his broad build moved in unison with each step.

"Skylar, this is Sebastian, the Alpha of the Midwest Pack," Joan explained with her brow raised as a warning. She nodded, or rather bowed, her head to him in a respectful greeting to acknowledge him.

I forced contact with the male whose mere presence left me wishing I could be anywhere else. "Nice to meet you, Sebastian," I lied.

Crossing his arms over his chest, he nodded a greeting. His eyes roved over me inquisitively. The frown remained. Whatever he saw, it left him either disappointed or unimpressed.

"I am extending an invitation for you to stay here for your own protection. You will not be safe in your home any longer," he stated firmly. "It would be advisable that you accept."

"But if I choose to decline your help and leave, I'm free to do so, right?" I challenged. Joan implied that I could leave at any time, but my gut was telling me otherwise.

His face tensed. I got the impression Sebastian wasn't questioned or denied often. "No one will stop you, but I doubt you will be gone long before the vampires come for you again, and your fate with them will be far worse than being a guest here," he responded in a crisp tone.

I tried to meet his gaze but it was too intense, scary. "Who petitioned you to protect me?"

The stern look remained as he spoke. "That's irrelevant. They want you alive. That is all you need to know."

"And the vampires? Why do they want me?" Now that I knew there were other were-animals—enough to form a pack—this had nothing to do with me being a werewolf. Except for being a werewolf, there wasn't anything else exceptional about me.

"At this time, we don't have that information," he admitted in a stiff voice.

"Let me see if I understand. The vampires have an interest in me. You were petitioned to protect me by someone who seems to want anonymity, and you have no idea what the vampires want with me, but still you have chosen to help me?" I asked incredulously.

It was obvious from the way the muscles of Sebastian's neck and jaw twitched with tension that he didn't like questions or being in the dark any more than I did. And pointing it out wasn't winning any favor with him, either.

"Why would you choose *not* to stay?"

I shrugged. "Let's just say I have trust issues and don't believe in altruism. I don't understand why you want to help me." That was a slight lie. I did believe in altruism but I surely didn't believe he was capable of such an act.

He nodded his head slowly, still assessing me with that penetratingly intense gaze. Sebastian didn't just share his body with his animal; he had bonded with it and become one with it. The primordial nature of his animal was so tightly interwoven with the man before me that he was something different—a "manimal."

There was a protracted silence. His brown eyes flickered to deep amber and I was faced with very familiar animal eyes. Sebastian was a wolf—like me. *Well, maybe not like me.* The animal that stared back at me projected a level of danger that left me shaken. I doubt even on my best day I could ever be that terrifying in human form.

"We saved your life, Ms. Brooks. I think we have earned your trust."

Have they? The only thing I knew about these people was they knew how to kill: savagely, effectively, and efficiently. They lived in a well-equipped compound that smelled of spilled blood. They were half-animals that gave into their primal urges gregariously. They hadn't earned my trust. The only thing they had earned was my innate wariness and self-protective urge to get as much distance between them and me as possible.

Impatient, waiting for me to respond, he directed his attention to Joan. "If she is too foolish to accept our help graciously, then she will have it begrudgingly. She can stay as our guest or our prisoner. I don't care about the spirit in which our invitation is taken." Then he stalked out of the room, leaving me staring at the empty space he once occupied.

Joan's lips trembled slightly before she swallowed hard and mustered that oddly pleasant smile. "Skylar, there isn't much more for you to understand. The vampires came to your house, killed your mother, and attempted to abduct you. Their intentions for you are unknown at this time. This is fact. It is in your best interest to stay here for the time being, until we have this situation under control." When I didn't respond, she continued taking small deliberate steps, pacing in the small space that separated us.

"Forcing me to stay isn't really helping to build my trust."

Her voice still had the gentle cadence, but now there was a hint of urgency and frustration that she was working to suppress. "Demetrius wants you alive. Never before has he orchestrated something so extreme for one person. He sent his best for you." Reading the confusion on my face, she elaborated. "Demetrius is the Master of the Northern Seethe, the strongest in the world. The vampires aren't usually a menace, choosing to spend most of their time whoring around and satisfying their lusts in varying degrees. But when Demetrius peeks his head out from his self-indulgences, he likes to flex his power. When he does, it's never good. He may want you alive for now, but I can assure you, it probably won't be for long."

If her intentions were to scare me, then she had won a gold star. "They will not stop until they have you—for whatever reason that may be. I can assure you that they will hurt and even kill anyone who gets in their way. You are under the Midwest Pack's protection. It is a responsibility not taken lightly. I assure you the pack does not enter situations foolishly or without adequate cause. Do yourself a great service and accept our help. You won't survive alone."

I chewed on my bottom lip, hanging on to her words. "I am sorry if I seem ungracious. It isn't my intention," I finally admitted, so softly I wasn't sure if my words were even audible. "I don't know if you realize it, but a lot is being asked of me. You want me to trust you with minimal specifics. I am forced or rather strongly encouraged to stay in a house with were-animals that are obviously dangerous. Until today, I didn't know were-animals existed." I let out a distressed sigh. That was a partially true statement. I never thought I was the only werewolf in the world, but I had no idea other types of were-animals existed.

"I'm not saying it's not a lot to deal with. But don't make it any harder on yourself. Our contact is out of the country right now; he is expected back in five days. At least remain our guest until then. Contrary to what you have seen, Sebastian is a fair and reasonable leader, and I am sure he will allow you to speak to our contact when he arrives. Okay?"

"Who is your contact?" I needed more information. They had to at least tell me who was so diligent about protecting me.

After a furtive glance at the door, she spoke, but it was barely audible. "Josh."

I had a name but I had no idea who it was. *Josh?* Who was he and why did he want me alive? Most importantly, how did he know I was in danger?

Joan was still waiting for an answer.

"Who is Josh, and why does he care whether I live or die?"

The pleasant smile returned and I knew she wasn't going to give me any more answers. "That is all the information I can give you. Will you at least stay with us the five days?"

Why was she asking me? Did I really have a choice in this matter? Sebastian made it clear: guest or prisoner, I was staying. Joan waited for a response that I was unable to give.

She gave me another congenial look before she left.

CHAPTER 2

Placing the messenger bag stuffed with clothes, wallet, and a few toiletries across my chest, I opened the window. I wanted to trust these people, but I couldn't. The idea that Sebastian and Ethan wanted to keep me safe was hard to believe when everything about them seemed primal, vicious, and lethal. And I couldn't get the disdainful way Ethan had glowered at me. And Winter? What was it about her that warranted trust? Was it the way she glided through the house unheard and barely noticed? Or the mesmeric way she held my gaze, leaving me paralyzed? *You don't trust people like this. You get a good look and make sure you can identify them in a police lineup.*

I couldn't place the responsibility of my safety and life in the hands of strangers I didn't trust. I was good at living under the radar, becoming invisible in a sea of faces. It was something I practiced all my life—never standing out, always unnoticed. Obscure to the point where I was anonymous. I could hide and never be found.

We had a home in Canada that we inherited from my grand-parents. I considered going there, but if the vampires were as good as the were-animals led me to believe, undoubtedly they would look there. Nevertheless, Canada was an excellent place to hide. My mother and I visited Nova Scotia a couple of years ago and I fell in love with the quaint province. It was a charming place, but too small to offer the anonymity I needed. The best way to hide was in a well-populated area like Toronto or Montreal, cities so heavily occupied you could hide in plain sight, virtually lost in a sea of faces. You become just one out of millions, not thousands.

I hated large cities; that's why I adored our suburban home. Just thirty miles outside of Chicago, it was close enough so that when you felt the urge, you could easily take part in the unique culture, arts, exceptional restaurants, and nightlife. Yet you were far enough away that you could still enjoy the subtle allures of the Midwest.

As I sorted out my plans, a sudden wash of sorrow engulfed me because it was then that I realized how utterly alone I was. My mother was an only child. I didn't have any aunts, uncles, or cousins I could contact for assistance. My grandmother died when my mother was a child and my grandfather had died a couple of years ago. When my grandfather died, my step-grandmother made it very clear that she was a *step*, and all ties were severed.

Pushing the sudden feeling of despair deep down, I focused on the task at hand. There wasn't time to wallow in sorrow or deal with the burning feeling in my chest as my heart mourned for her. But my body had its own ideas as my vision blurred from the tears that began to form. I screwed my eyes shut, forcing the tears back.

I leapt out of the window and landed squarely on my feet. It was something I'd done so many times that it was second nature. Sprinting to the back of the house, I followed the long driveway that was shouldered by woods. Large oaks, pine trees, and flowering trees that had wept their final buds shadowed me, keeping me hidden. But they made the surroundings dark and disconsolate as I cautiously walked along. Fall leaves crunched under my feet as I gingerly hiked through the shoulder of the vast forest. Eventually, the driveway had to empty out onto a road. But I had walked for nearly fifteen minutes and there didn't seem to be any signs of it coming to an end.

I listened for the sounds of passing cars or the bustle of human voices and interaction but there weren't any, just the mild unobtrusive sounds of nature. I took out my phone to dial 911 but I couldn't get a signal. My GPS couldn't detect my location. It was dusk, and there weren't many things I could think of that were worse than being lost in the woods following an interminable driveway at night with vampires stalking me.

Suddenly, I began to hear leaves crunching lightly under someone's feet. I listened intently; they were so soft, barely audible. I couldn't determine the direction they were coming from.

"*Mmm*, wolf's blood," stated a jarring female voice. Turning in the direction of the voice, I saw a tall slim woman with unnaturally orange spiked hair walk toward me. She made each step with smooth ease, projecting terror as she advanced. Charcoal eyes with just a hint of crimson watched me carefully as she circled me. An androgynous style enhanced her attractive angular features. Before she could take another step closer, I ran. My feet pounded hard against the terrain as terror drove me to run faster than I believed possible. I ran deeper into the trees, limbs brushing roughly against my face, slowing me down. The redolence of the trees made it hard to identify her location by scent.

"The blood of your wolf calls for me to have a sample." She appeared in front of me. I changed direction and she appeared in front of me again. With every direction I turned, I was met by the fanged menace.

"*Mmm*," she purred, inhaling deeply before moving to my

right side in the time it took me to blink. Her movements were quick, effortless, and terrifying as she whipped around me.

"Gabriella," said a throaty voice to the left of me. "You must tame your desires for now." The new vamp pulled back his lips, exposing fangs. My revulsion was hard to hide as I looked at this creature of the night—well, dusk, because we were hours from night. His teeth were filed down, leaving only fangs, making his appearance more monstrous. His angular frame was covered with a blanket of pale skin, and he was hairless, except for the veil of blond eyelashes. His bright red eyes ogled me as I stared back at him with morbid disgust.

Pushing past Gabriella, I dropped my bag and sprinted through the woods, darting past the trees, whipping over obstacles. I didn't hear footsteps, but that didn't mean anything since they seemed to glide on air as they walked. With movements as quick as a blinking eye, they could appear at any time.

I pounded quickly through the woods and thought I had managed to escape, but another vampire stepped in my path. He pushed his hand hard into my chest, sending me flying back several feet. I landed on my butt and gasped for the air he had knocked out of me.

"The party's just started, sweetie. Stay for a while," his coarse voice requested. He was quickly joined by the orange-headed vamp, who brushed her hand affectionately across his face and ended at his lips, earning a kiss.

His style was a contrasting complement to hers. Short, jet-black, messy spiked hair covered his head, two rings looped through his lips, and tattoos decorated the left side of his neck. His appearance and mannerism gave the clear impression that he enjoyed a certain level of pain, both as a participant and a dealer. He smiled, watching me as though he wanted me to take part in his games of pain and torture.

When they stepped closer, I kicked his leg. He crashed to the ground and I struck him. I was going for another thrash when

Gabriella grabbed me from behind by the throat. "Play nice, dear, or we won't, either," she threatened against my ear.

"It was just a love tap." He knelt in front of me, leaned in, and then ran his tongue along the side of my face. I cringed and tried to punch him, but Gabriella grabbed my hand and held it to the ground.

"I like you, too," he stated in a deep throaty whisper near my jaw. Cool lips brushed my skin.

He was positioned well enough so that with one kick, I could have him doubled over in pain from a groin assault. Before I could make my move, a loud cracking sound resonated. Gabriella shrieked, releasing her grip on me. The black-haired vampire pulled me close; his grip was tight as it looped around me, fastening my arms to my side. Flailing back and forth, I tried to pull away. He let out several painful hisses when I slammed my foot down on his.

"Control yourself. We can play later," he cooed in a husky voice. When I continued to struggle, he sank his teeth into my shoulder. Like a piercing knife, it seared through my muscles penetrating my flesh. I blinked back tears and struggled harder against him.

"Quiet now," he grumbled, pulling me closer. His body tensed; the long muscles of his neck protruded as a frown marred his face. Distracted by whatever was going on in front of him, he worked hard to make the muscles relax. Another loud crack, followed by a painful groan.

Crack! Winter stood over Gabriella as she lay on the ground, her foot placed on the vampire's torso. Crack! She had meticulously broken Gabriella's arms in multiple places. Moving with the swift grace of someone who had done this before, she slinked behind Gabriella, placing a knife firmly to her neck. Gabriella struggled to lift her arms, but it was a futile attempt. Winter had rendered them dysfunctional.

A cruel assurance covered her face as she smiled. "Chase, let her go or your Gabriella will be a distant memory of a love you used to have," Winter stated ominously.

He let out an angry sound before violently biting down into my shoulder again. My body clenched as I swallowed back a scream.

Winter countered by pressing the knife into Gabriella's neck. Thin red streaks of blood ran down it. "How long have you been together? Forty, fifty years? She knows all the weird things you like. From what I hear, they are quite sick, yet she still loves you. How long do you think it will be before you find someone like her again? How empty was your life before her? Own those memories, because, if you don't let her go, you will return to that life of loneliness," Winter challenged.

She looked at him with a cynical smirk as she waited for him to respond. Her mannerisms were cruel and expectant. She seemed to yearn for him to think just a second too long or ponder his love for Gabriella for more time than she deemed acceptable so she could finish the job. The obvious adoration of violence and torture covered her face. Flickers of delight bounced around in her eyes, making the terror she invoked surreal.

Chase's hold loosened, but not enough for me to break it. Gabriella's face twisted into an angry frustrated grimace as she looked at him. But with all the emotions displayed on her face, she never showed any form of doubt. It was as though she knew Chase would do anything for her and her fate was secure.

"Let Skylar go, Chase, and we will let you go unscathed to nurse Gabriella's wounds. You know she's just looking for a reason. Don't give her one," Ethan urged, walking toward him.

A young man stood behind Winter, his eyes fixed on the hairless vamp, who started to slowly advance toward them. Chase released me, throwing me to the ground. He ran toward Gabriella, and Winter moved aside, allowing him to sweep her into his arms. He hissed at Winter, exposing his fangs; the enraged look on his face promised unspeakable harm to her if he ever had the chance. He carried Gabriella off into the woods.

The hairless vamp charged Winter. As he lunged at her, he was met by the young man, who crashed into him midair, pulling him to the ground. The teenager quickly gained the upper hand, pushing the vampire hard to the ground. Pounding at the vampire repeatedly, he ended the brutal assault by pulling a stake from his back pants pocket and shoving it into the vampire's chest. The vampire gurgled out a horrid sound as the smell of necrotic tissue filled the air. I turned my head, but not fast enough to avoid seeing him take out a knife and behead the vampire. Nausea set in as the smell of death and blood filled the air. In the past twenty-four hours, I had experienced an overdose of violence and death, and I had had enough.

Ethan's steel-gray eyes remained glued on me. Each step he took made my heart rate increase to the point of erratic. The teenager and Winter stood on each side of him. Neither of them looked happy with me.

"Is anything broken?" Ethan's gruff voice asked.

"I'm fine."

"Good. Follow me and try to keep up," he commanded as he began to run. My shoulder ached but I couldn't show it. I followed them back to the house. The teenager stayed close, occasionally asking if I were okay and whether I needed to stop. Repeatedly, I assured him that I was fine, as I pushed to stay in pace with them step for step. The woods' unleveled terrain jostled my shoulder, making each step painful and the journey back seem longer.

Sebastian opened the front door before we reached it. The look on his face couldn't be classified as anger anymore. He had taken anger, dipped it in rage, and left it to marinate for hours. *No, the emotions on his face could make anger their bitch.*

He started to walk—or rather stalk—toward me. When I

recoiled, he took several deep even breaths, turned around, and with great effort, walked away.

"Anyone injured?" Dr. Baker asked, focused on Winter.

"Not really. You may need to check the problem," she stated as she jerked her head in my direction. "Chase used her shoulder as an appetizer."

He nodded. "Did everything go okay?"

Winter shrugged. "Chase really hates me now. He's probably plotting his revenge as we speak—undoubtedly something long, torturous, and bloody. I suspect if I tried to die too quickly, he would revive me just to prolong the torture. I win. I am clearly the one he hates the most in this pack." She proudly bared all her teeth in a grin.

"It's not a competition and definitely not one you should be involved in. Winter, what did you do?" It sounded like it was a question he had asked far too many times.

"I broke Gabby's arms in eight places." She looked away from his aggravated gaze.

"That was rather unnecessary," he stated with a reproachful glare.

"It wasn't my intention"—she gave him a genteel pout—"I had no other options." She turned toward him, giving him a look of limpid doe-eyed innocence, which he clearly didn't believe for a second. He cocked an eyebrow and shook his head slowly, obviously irritated.

She sighed so heavily, her lips rumbled from the force. "Okay, fine, they bug me! They are too weird even for vampires! *Ugh,* every time I see them I just want to break something on them. She dyed her hair this ridiculous burnt orange; she looks like a bruised carrot. He looks like a Goth Abercrombie & Fitch model." She flung her arms dismissively at the thought of them.

She sneered at me and did that weird eye thing once she caught me staring at her. I wasn't sure if it were the fact that she really hated Gabriella and Chase or she had a genuine love for violence, but I saw the pleasure she gained from torturing Gabriella. It was sadistic.

The teenager looked down at my wound under the torn fabric. "Chase is an ass," he stated angrily, a troubled grimace marking his unassuming appearance. I glanced at the young man with the olive green eyes and deep dimples. He held a look of innocence that would dare anyone to think that he was capable of the level of violence I'd witnessed. Short copper-colored wavy hair and flushed cheeks added to the cute, youthful facade. Standing well over six feet with a slim build, it was hard to think of him as anything more than the cute boy next door whose hair you wanted to ruffle. But the intimidating scowl on his face dared anyone to do anything of the sort without a death wish.

"May I?" Dr. Baker asked. I nodded. He removed enough of the shirt to examine the area and keep me covered. He looked at it for a long time, palpating along the bite mark lightly. "It's just a puncture wound, you'll heal just fine."

Maybe it will heal without any problems, but it hurts like hell. Minimally focused on my painful shoulder, I eyed Ethan as he paced heatedly in front of me. With each step, he seemed to become more infuriated. When he finally wore a sufficient hole in the floor, he turned to face me. His cobalt eyes had shifted to an intense gray, a warning sign that the wolf was in the driver's seat. If I thought I could have made it to the door, I would have tried to leave the room.

Stone-faced, he leaned into me. "What the hell was that? Weren't you supposed to stay in the damn house?" He was uncomfortably close to my face. His rage probably wouldn't be doused by any answer I could offer, so I remained silent, hoping he would just go away.

He inched closer, and the intense emotions that radiated off him made me uneasy. They physically affected me, making me feel queasy and anxious. I wanted him away from me. When he inched a smidge closer, I pushed him. He knocked my hand away.

Joan called his name in an even and calm tone but he ignored her.

"Why would you run when you knew the vampires were after you, especially at dusk? You cannot be this stupid," he growled, barely holding on to whatever control he had left.

"Ethan," Joan repeated in a much firmer tone. He whipped toward her, his face pulled tight into a frown, his eyes narrowed into thin lines.

"She chose to leave. It is an option I feel she should have been given in the first place. She's been through a great deal today. I don't think yelling at her like an uncivilized brute is going to make her feel safe in a home in which we are asking her to be our guest." Her face matched her voice, soft and kind, which just further enraged Ethan.

Ethan took several steps back and waved his hand toward me, inviting Joan to take over. He plowed out of the room.

"Skylar, I would like to ask that you trust us, but that would be useless. I don't know what I can do to earn that trust. I assure you that we are here to help. But another stunt like today and the ending may not be as favorable," she said as she guided me back upstairs to the room I had run away from.

"I shouldn't have left," I admitted, shamed by my behavior. I had made the typical stupid B-movie girl mistake, running away from assistance and getting myself into worse trouble. I didn't want to be that woman.

"No, you should not have run. Let's try this again. Skylar, I am extending an invitation for you to stay here as the Midwest Pack's guest and allow us to help you. Will you accept?" She was being very patient with me, but I could tell it was quite the task. The muscles around her lips tightened into a moue as she dealt with her own frustration.

I agreed without hesitation. Joan walked into the room in silence.

"Why is it so important to you that I am safe?" I asked before she could leave the room. I wished I could believe they were just good Samaritans, but they didn't strike me as the charitable type.

She sighed heavily, leaning against the wall. A pleasant smile covered her face but irritation was etched along the corners of her eyes and lips.

They really don't like questions.

"Regretfully, I can't give you much more information at this time. If this were merely a case of Demetrius or a member of his Seethe developing a blood-crush, it would be of little concern to us. We would not have intervened. However, the fact that Josh was notified of the vampire's interest in you warrants our involvement. You need reasons for our actions, and I assure you I understand. However, this is all the information I can give you. I hope this comforts your curious mind for the time being."

Nope, not feeling any comfort at all. Thoughts of Gabriella and Chase flashed in my head. A Seethe of people like them wanted me and no one was offering me answers. Extinguishing my curiosity was going to take more than a few soothing words from a kind stranger, as she told me that if it didn't affect their pack, they wouldn't otherwise care about my life. How do you find comfort in that?

Joan started out of the room, then backtracked. "You may join us for dinner if you would like."

"I'm not hungry." I lied. I was starving, but I would rather have Chase take another chunk out of my shoulder than dine with them. I would tolerate the hunger pains until they went away.

Her lips curled into a genial half-smile. "I'll have Steven bring you something."

. . .

Moments after Joan closed the door, the reality of the situation hit me. A compilation of emotions from fear to grief consumed me to the point where I felt suffocated. Tired enough to sleep, I closed my eyes, but the darkness only provided the backdrop for reenacting the events of the past twenty-four hours. Grabbing my stomach as it rumbled, I turned on my side and stared at the wall.

When three abrupt knocks rattled the door, I went to the bathroom to wash away all evidence of the few tears I'd allowed myself. The knocks continued and by the time I walked out of the bathroom, the teenager from earlier poked his head in before stepping in, carrying a covered plate. He set it down on the table next to me and handed me the messenger bag I had dropped earlier. He buzzed around, arranging the silverware, laying out the napkins, and filling my glass with water.

"Steven?" I presumed.

He looked up abruptly and then smiled, his cheeks lightly flushed. "Yes, I'm Steven. Sorry that was rude." He extended his hand to shake mine.

He shoved his hands in his pocket and took his time making eye contact with me again. "I hope you're hungry." He looked up briefly before focusing his attention back on the floor.

"Starving. The pillow started to look like a giant marshmallow."

He laughed and immediately his gaze lifted to meet mine, where it stayed. "You really should have eaten with us. The food would have been prepared the way you wish. It's a porterhouse, rare. Ethan prepared the food today, so it's probably very rare but it should be good. He cooks for our guests far better than he treats them." His cheeks sank into a dimpled smile.

I laughed. I liked Steven.

My mouth watered once I took the cover off the food and the enticing aroma hit my senses.

He looked oddly intrigued as he watched me eat. "Does

anyone ever call you Sky?" he asked as he took a seat in the chair across from the bed.

Oh great, he's planning on staying for a while. "Not if they want me to answer."

"I like Sky, it fits you. Can I call you that?" Dimpled enchanting smile and cherubic good looks probably allowed him to get away with calling people a number of things without consequence. All he had to do was punctuate it with that infectious grin, genial emerald eyes, and lightly veiled Southern lilt, and he could get away with anything.

"I prefer Skylar."

"As you wish, Sky-lar." He grinned and enunciated every syllable slowly.

I returned my attention to the food, doing my best to ignore his attentive gaze.

"You shouldn't stay up here the whole five days. You'll go crazy. It's a huge house. We have a game room, library, and a gym. You are welcome to use anything you like. Since you are going to be here, you might as well enjoy yourself."

It was interesting the way he made it seem like I had a choice in staying. If I left, a weird androgynous orange-headed vampire would try to attack me again. If I managed to survive, I would be face-to-face with two very angry werewolves. I wasn't sure which scenario was the least appealing. "I'll be fine."

"Joan won't allow you to stay up here the whole five days."

"You all sure have a lot of rules for your so-called guests to adhere to. Can't I just stay up here and be left alone until this Josh arrives?" I snapped, and immediately regretted it. It was pointless for me to take out my frustrations on the one person who definitely didn't deserve it. "I appreciate the offer but I'll be fine up here. It's a really nice room," I continued in a gentler tone. It would have been unnecessarily cruel to tell him that I didn't want to be around the were-animals.

"She doesn't want you to feel like you are being imprisoned."

"What is Joan, the housemother or something?" I asked half-jokingly.

He didn't even crack a smile. "No." He looked at me with impassive eyes. It was obvious he didn't plan on elaborating.

"Let Joan know that she shouldn't worry about me. I am okay."

"That won't stop her. It's just her way," he admitted with a half-smile.

I shrugged, too engrossed in my food to answer. He was right, either the food was very good or I was too hungry to care. It really didn't matter; my stomach was speaking to me, and the food was just what it needed.

"Are you the coyote who came to my house?" I asked between bites.

He nodded. A coyote was supposed to be the smaller version of the wolf. Steven's coyote hadn't gotten the memo. I vividly remember his massive form ripping a vampire to shreds, and I only knew it was a coyote because his nose was slightly longer than a wolf's.

"Are you the youngest member of this pack?" I took in the full effect of the nonthreatening teen who sat in front of me. Now showered, shaved, and groomed, his youthful appearance was more apparent.

"I'm the youngest of the primary-ranked members of the pack. I turn eighteen in three months."

"How do you become ranked?" I placed the empty plate on the table, sitting back on the bed and folding my legs under me to give him my undivided attention. The gentle teenager didn't seem as reticent as the others. *Perhaps I can gain more insight into the Midwest Pack.*

"It's based on dominance."

"So whoever's the meanest and the toughest wins." *That explains why Sebastian is the Alpha, and Ethan seems to be the second runner-up.*

"*Mean* doesn't have anything to do with it. It's a combination of things: mostly fighting ability, skill, and beast control. Were-hyenas are usually mean—really mean, in fact, but they are rarely ranked. Jackals and lynxes are tough but are not always the strongest."

"What's your rank?"

"I'm fifth and new to the position. I transferred from the Southern Pack about a year ago. I've been in this position for a little over six months."

"Why did you transfer?"

He shrugged an answer. *Good grief, they* really *don't like giving out information.*

"Where is the guy whose place you took?"

"The grave," he stated in a flat voice.

I snapped my mouth closed once I realized it was hanging open. Forcing the look of shock off my face, I searched for a good follow-up question. *What's a good follow-up to a response like that?*

"Old age?" I tried to pull off blasé and failed terribly. I wasn't prepared to react to a statement like that.

He shook his head slowly. His face, for a brief moment, lost that childish innocence as the predator within peeked through. "No. I killed him."

Please leave.

I blinked several times, and a placid look became my mask as it hid my horror.

He considered my reactions, studying me keenly. I wasn't sure if he was trying to shock me or determine how comfortable I was with the level of violence they seemed to encounter regularly. He chose his words carefully as he spoke. "He was killed during a challenge for his position. We are responsible for the safety of the pack. The strongest survive. When a challenge is made, the challenged can choose whether it's for position or death."

I assumed his voice was gentle and methodical for my benefit, to calm me. My heart raced; I was sitting in a room with a teenager who was just as dangerous as the others.

"He perceived my age as an insult. He could have declined the challenge and accepted lower rank or even transfer to another pack. We all understand and respect the importance of the strength of the pack. He was foolish to allow pride to influence his choice."

"And Winter? What is her rank?"

"She's third, and Ethan's Beta."

"Where's the fourth?"

"Gavin's not here."

"Where is he?"

"Not here," he repeated firmly. He seemed disconcerted by the mention of Gavin, but the tense look on his face dissuaded me from asking any further questions about him.

Steven stayed in the room for several hours. Even after our conversation turned to mundane drivel about television shows and books, he still stayed, seemingly interested.

"So you got the job as the babysitter to make sure I don't leave again," I finally stated, when he continued to hang around even after I started watching a show that was too estrogen-imbued even for me.

He smiled guiltily. "No, I am enjoying your company. I haven't met many female wolves. In this pack, most of them are much older than I am and aren't nearly as interesting as you are."

I looked at him suspiciously. He was probably lying through his teeth, but he was as cute as a button and could tell you that it was raining candy and look convincing enough to make you believe it. For that very reason, I believed I was sitting in the room with one of the most dangerous pack members in the house. With his charming ways and innocent features, you could never prepare yourself for the level of brutality he was capable of.

"If you get to know me, you'll find that I'm not that interesting. I play the flute and hate peanut butter. That is about as interesting as I get."

Smiling, he shrugged, and then he made a face. "The flute? Why? Were you assigned to be the school's nerd?"

I laughed. "It's a cool instrument. . . ."

"Yeah, it is if you want to make someone cry during a chick flick."

"When I play, it relaxes me. In the past, I've had problems preventing my animal from emerging when I get too upset. Playing the flute helps me stay in a calm state."

He nodded and gave me a sympathetic smile. "That happens a lot in the beginning, but it gets better. I never had too many problems, but Gav... some of the other were-animals have."

What is it with him and Gavin?

He grinned. "You are still interesting enough. It beats the hell out of sitting in my room watching television or hanging out with people I already know. I'm stuck here, too, until Josh returns. I might as well get to know the woman who has single-handedly sent both Ethan and Sebastian into fits of rage and still lives to tell the tale. Most don't." His eyes danced with amusement.

"Fits of rage? No, I sent them past rage. If Joan hadn't been there, Ethan was going to yell until his head exploded, or mine. I thought he was going to strangle me."

He shook his head. "He wouldn't have done that. We are not allowed to kill you, yet." He slid in the "yet" almost unnoticed. "Yeah, you really rub him the wrong way." He shook his head again and ran his fingers through his hair.

"In my defense, it seems like there are few things that don't rub Ethan and Sebastian the wrong way. They are a bit high-strung."

He grinned but looked uncomfortable with this conversation.

"I didn't mean to enrage them. I just wanted to go home." *Or anywhere other than here.*

"Whether you intended to or not, you really pissed them off. Try not to do that often, okay?" Although he was still smiling, his voice held a very serious undertone—a warning.

I nodded.

Steven stayed until my yawning, though unintentional, became contagious. He excused himself for the night.

I couldn't sleep that night. Instead, I decided to take my own personal tour of the house. It had come to a noticeable calm as I walked quietly in my fluffy purple print socks that matched my shirt and blended with my plum fleece pants. I rarely wore pajamas. In fact, I only owned four pairs, and they all paid homage to an obsession with my favorite chocolate treat wrapped in a hard shell: M&Ms. They were comfortable and utterly ridiculous—I loved them. I usually wore them the night before a full moon. It gave me something to smile about before I had to go to that place of darkness.

The flashlight on my phone lit the way as I tiptoed down the midnight hallway, down a different set of stairs, at the other end of the hallway. Joan had brought me back to the room this way but I wanted to explore some of the rooms we passed. The house was huge. Eventually, I came to the kitchen. Beautiful dark ceramic tiles covered the large open space. Stainless steel appliances, large double oven, and an island that was larger than our dining room filled the spacious room. To the left of the eat-in kitchen was a large dining area that comfortably seated twenty. How many people did they keep hostage—or as "guests"—at one time?

Most of the doors were locked. I pushed into a couple of them with force, hoping the locks would give. I realized a locked door meant stay the hell out, but curiosity about these people trumped common courtesy. The heavy doors wouldn't budge.

I don't know what would make me think they would. In a house where they spare no expense, I doubt locks would be where they decide to cut corners. Several of the rooms had a fingerprint lock, keypad lock, or both.

Finally, I stumbled onto an unlocked room, and I felt like I had hit the jackpot as I opened the double doors only to find a library. The smell of weathered paper, leather bindings, and subtle musk of were-animals filled the space. It was a drab white room with large built-in shelves. The only colors were the spines of the various books that populated the shelves. Most of the books had foreign titles and others were denoted just by symbols. I wasn't familiar with any of the books with English titles. At the far end of the room, tucked in the corner, was a small cabinet. I tugged at it, hoping it was unlocked. It wasn't.

After scanning the titles of several books I grabbed some of them, along with the binder I found on the computer desk, simply titled "VAMPIRES." I sat at the conference table in the middle of the room. The first book was filled with enchantments, curses, and spells, detailing their purpose and their effects on fae, elves, vampires, and were-animals. As I continued to read, my skin chilled. *Fae? Elves?* The idea of more beings I knew little of fueled my anxiety. I didn't like this world that I had been pulled into, with creatures that went bump in the night that I didn't even know existed—or how to stop.

This library wasn't to entertain but to inform, and it did just that. I tossed aside two books with symbols on them that I didn't understand—trying to figure them out was giving me a headache. I opened the "VAMPIRES" binder, ready to verse myself on the very things that were hunting me.

"This is a private library," said Ethan's familiar cold voice as he stood just inches from me. I jumped to my feet and took several steps back. I hadn't heard him come in. He was supposed to be helping me, one of the good guys—so to speak. But I didn't feel safe around him. When he was near, I went straight into flight mode.

He quickly reshelved the books. "The door was unlocked," I pointed out as I continued to distance myself from him. This was a task because his presence swallowed the small space we occupied between the books and the table.

"This is a private library," he repeated firmly.

"Then it should have been locked."

He glowered. "It's private just to you."

"Perhaps the next time you have guests, they should be informed of what's public and private domain."

His eyes roved over me, hitting every inch of my face, then my odd nightwear, and back to my face, where they lingered. The irritated expression turned down into a deep frown. Whatever it was about me that Sebastian and Ethan saw, they didn't particularly like it, and they weren't able to mask it.

When he continued to stare at me with his harsh penetrating gaze, I tried to return it with false bravado.

"What are you doing up?" he asked, closing the distance between us, towering over me.

"I couldn't sleep."

"There's a television in the room."

I shrugged. "There wasn't anything on."

"There are two hundred channels. Surely *you* could have found something to hold your interest." His lips kinked into a bemused grin.

Malicious, violent, smug, and *condescending. Is he working on points toward a jackass award?* "I prefer books over television."

"I will get you a *Cosmo* or something tomorrow," he stated derisively.

It's not that I didn't occasionally enjoy a *Cosmo* or any other fashion magazine; they were entertaining. But this smug bastard was being condescending and it was dripping off every word. "I prefer novels, and since I don't have my laptop or e-reader, I thought there would be something interesting in here."

"Fine. I'll bring you a couple of romance or YA novels off the best-seller list."

"I like legal thrillers."

He chuckled; it was a dark sound, tarnished with amused doubt. "Fine, Skylar, I will get you the books."

Ethan must have exhausted the allotted time his temperament allowed for him to be remotely cordial to people, because he was starting to look annoyed and disinterested. "You look tired. Maybe you should see if sleep will come now." He looked at the library door.

In other words, get the hell out of the library.

I smiled. "You're right." I grabbed the "VAMPIRE" binder, pressed it to my chest, and started for the door.

He snatched it out of my hands before I had taken any steps toward the door. He stopped before placing it back on the table, smiled, and then handed it back to me. "It'll be good night reading for you."

With his hand in the middle of my back, he guided me out, then locked the door behind us. He escorted me to the bedroom door to make sure I didn't make any more detours during my return. He dismissed me with a cool good-bye.

"Skylar," he called before I closed the door. "The next time you decide to sneak around the house, you should be a little quieter. You sound like a herd of stampeding elephants when you walk."

It was my turn to laugh. He had just *won* the jackass award.

. . .

I didn't sleep. Instead, I stayed up, brushing up on my knowledge of the things that were haunting me, or rather brushing up on the *most* horrid of the things that haunted me. This wasn't just a book of all the vampires, but a written account of the worst of their kind. Page by page, I read about vampires who were so horrific, vile, and cruel that a book was created for their acts to be documented. I tried to remember each name, burn it into memory. But by the time I had gotten to page fifty, all the names were a blur. Chase had made it among the *horribles* because he had a preference for staying to a bloodline. On any given day, he would feed off a family. Not just one or two, but families of five or more just for the sheer horror of it.

Then there was Sable, who slashed her victims into pieces, draining them into bottles for later consumption. She kept them alive until their body gave up their fight to endure more. Trevor liked children. Clover enjoyed feeding from pregnant women. Elera, during her first week as a vampire, killed over twenty-five people, unable to control her lust. Today, thirty years later, she still had that problem. Demetrius—Ugh*, where do I start?* He killed the last two Midwest Alphas and was responsible for creating over half of his Seethe by himself, which was over three hundred strong. He had enslaved people and kept them in barns like cattle, slaughtering them when he was hungry. He did this until the last Alpha stopped him. But his most heinous act was the creation of his Mistress, Michaela. She was the worst of his creations. Drawn to the psychopaths of the world, not only did she revere them but thought it was a good idea to give them super-strength and eternal life by making them vampires. Most of the more monstrous acts were done by her progeny.

As I stared at the book, I didn't know how to categorize them in my mind. Did I rank them according to how many they had killed or by the heinousness of the act? Now I was truly aware of how horrible the things were that haunted me. And I think that was Ethan's point.

My mind's overzealous desire to store all the atrocious information about the vampires kept me from going to sleep. It wasn't until 5:00 a.m. that I slipped into a nightmare-riddled slumber. At 9:00, I was awakened by knocking at the door. Scattered at the threshold were my laptop and e-reader along with a small bag full of fashion and celebrity magazines. I left the bag of magazines outside my door. I bludgeoned my nose to spite my face, but I couldn't give Ethan the satisfaction of knowing I indulged in such frivolity. But an hour later, I brought the bag in. I didn't care what he thought of me.

CHAPTER 3

"It's dinner time. Come," Joan stated, walking into my room after knocking and entering without waiting for an invitation. It was clear she wasn't going to accept another declination. I had been there for three days now and had declined joining them for breakfast, lunch, and dinner each time I was invited.

She took me by the elbow and led me into the dining room.

Ten people were at the table: Sebastian at the head, Ethan to his right, and Winter to his left. She was the only one who acknowledged my arrival. Well, she did that weird eye thing followed by a weirder tongue thing. A thin, forked serpent tongue darted out of her mouth and back so fast, it could have been easily missed. A deep growl came from Sebastian as he cut his eyes at her. She straightened, grimaced, and turned her focus from me.

Steven smiled at me and stood to pull a chair out for me.

I thanked him, grateful for his presence. He reminded me of Joan with his ability to make you feel welcomed in a less-than-hospitable environment. I sat down and he pulled out the chair for Joan to sit next to me.

"Thank you for joining us." Sebastian sounded polite but insincere.

I'm sure Joan had something to do with his kind regards to my presence at dinner.

"Thank you for inviting me," I responded with the same politeness and insincerity. I didn't want to be there. Everything about them was unsettling, especially how strikingly attractive yet tragically dangerous they were.

Sebastian was, in fact, just beautiful, and there was no way around that description. It pained me to admit it. I usually reserve such high compliments for those who exhibit such attributes both inwardly and outwardly. His personality was far from beautiful, yet describing him as handsome seemed inadequate. He sat there with an impassive smile that could quickly switch to a contemptuous scowl. His alluring features kept your interest far too long and begrudgingly, I have to admit it, personality aside, Sebastian was indeed beautiful.

Winter, with her uninviting stare and harsh ways, probably stopped traffic on occasions. Her complexion was flawless and sun-kissed. Long black hair framed her delicate round face while cold hazel eyes made looking at her a task. She looked of Middle Eastern or Egyptian descent. Her physique was statuesque and her movements were smooth, rhythmic, and sinuous like the animal she shared her body with.

I looked around the table at the various faces of the other were-animals, taking note of the appeal they exuded. Not all of them could be considered beautiful or striking, but they were, by far, more attractive than most people. Too attractive for one to believe they were part animal. I couldn't quite figure what made them so besotting. I kept my eyes on my plate. Looking at them was like watching predators on the animal channel. The prey far too often stood gazing at the predator, mesmerized by the fluidity of their walk, captivated by the intensity of their stare, disabled by fear, and too enthralled by the predator's dance to run, as they should. The end result: the unsuspecting prey was attacked and killed by the menacing predator. I sat at the dinner table just as captivated as any prey could be.

They attempted to make me feel welcome. But I couldn't ignore the quick glances, avid looks of curiosity, and lingering stares that didn't subtly state but silently scream: *What's so special about her? What is the link between her and the vampires? Why do they want her? What's wrong with her?*

Sebastian and Ethan were the only ones who kept their expressions vacuous, void of the queries that weighed down their pack.

"We are going for a run after dinner. Join us," Sebastian stated toward the end of the meal. I considered declining, but the expectant look he cast in my direction gave me the impression that it wouldn't be a good idea.

After dinner, everyone, with the exception of Winter, went to the back of the house. I stood next to Joan, waiting for instructions, but no one said anything. Instead, Sebastian began to remove his shirt, and the others followed. Within minutes, I was surrounded by naked male and female bodies.

Shocked by their reckless abandonment of modesty and discretion, I gawked at them. Joan leaned over. "They're a group of physically appealing people. Modest, they are not. They would drop their trousers on the highway during rush hour if it were legal." I would have been amused by her observation if I weren't so taken aback by what was happening.

They began to change into their animal forms. There were three other wolves besides Sebastian and Ethan, two coyotes, and something that looked like a dog, maybe a jackal. Another strange animal stood to my right with bleached pale willowy fur and deep jasper eyes. It was a dimorphism of wolf and dog and the most exotic of the bunch. Joan remained dressed and next to me until Ethan started to walk toward us.

She took his arrival as her cue to leave. I quickly took hold of her arm. "Where are you going?" I hissed in a low, anxious voice.

"I'm going to join Winter inside. I don't belong here. It is time for you to interact with others of your family."

"Family?"

"Wolves, dear. You've been a lone wolf far too long. Take this opportunity to bond with the wolf within and your family members," she suggested with a gentle smile, gently pulling from my firm hold.

"Steven's not a wolf and I am pretty sure they aren't, either." I pointed to the jackal and white-furred wolf dog—or whatever it was.

"Steven's a coyote, canis lantrum, a smaller member of the family. And that's Bryce, he's a jackal, canis aureus, part of your family, as well. He's new to the position, impulsive but nice. And the beautiful, white-furred animal over there is Hannah, an albino dingo, canis lupus dingo. She is rarest of us all and your distant relative. You are all canidae and family."

She pulled her hand away. "Go play with your family," she said sweetly.

Play? Maybe I had no idea what *running* or *playing* with my family was, but I was pretty sure I didn't want any part of it. Looking at the animals that stood around me didn't put me in the mind-set of playing at all, unless running for your life was some version of a game.

Ethan stood in front of me speaking while I busied myself averting my eyes from his nudity. Trying not to make a spectacle of myself, I forced eye contact with him. In his clothes, he looked fit, but naked, he was sculpted like a statue. Lean, defined ripples of muscles ran along his body. I was a wolf, too, but even when I worked out regularly, I could only be described as toned. There weren't ripples of muscles anywhere on my body. Ethan's physique was the result of wolf genes and hard gym work. He stood in front of me, confidently, lacking any signs of discomfort or reticence about his nudity, which was fine. I was uncomfortable enough for both of us.

"Change," he insisted.

I closed my eyes and concentrated, but I couldn't.

"It'll be easier if your clothes didn't restrict you. It usually hurts when you have to tear through them."

I don't care how natural or normal this is for them; standing in the backyard stark naked with people who are virtually strangers isn't going to happen. Not tonight or ever. I chewed my bottom lip nervously.

"You can go to the side of the house to change," he suggested, obviously annoyed by my modesty.

I quickly scurried to the other side of the house and undressed. Crouching at the side of the house, naked, I tried to force change. My face felt warm and yet my body shivered from the coolness of the night. I never intentionally changed and had no idea how to do it.

"Problem?" Ethan asked as he came around the corner.

Reflexively, my hands wrapped around my chest. Trembling, I nodded. When he took several steps toward me, I shied away. Rolling his eyes, he made an irritated grunting sound before he changed into his animal form. Just like that, he changed in the most effortless manner imaginable.

How did he do that?

The massive dark gray wolf trotted slowly toward me and nuzzled against my face. Without thinking, my fingers gently stroked his soft fur as he lowered his head, resting it on my shoulder. I changed. It wasn't painful like in the past. In fact, it was almost soothing as my body elongated and light gray fur began to take over my body. I stood on all fours for the first time after a deliberate change, and I had to admit—it wasn't horrible.

Ethan howled and an ostinato of howls responded from a distance, helping him find their location. The wolf song resonated through the air, and I felt compelled to join in. Ethan ran toward the sounds and I followed. For each step he made, I had to take two. Did I mention how massive his wolf was? When he had joined the rest of the pack, he stopped abruptly and howled again, making the most delightful harmonious sound.

The others joined in while I remained silent. As we ran through the woods, we stopped intermittently to playfully bite at and jump on each other. Steven pushed me to the ground and licked my face. His wet tongue slathered over it. It was absolutely disgusting, and I wasn't sure how to communicate that while in wolf form. When he did it again, I nudged him with my nose. He sneered, playfully growled, and tried to do it again. This time, I moved my face and growled, baring all my teeth. He finally got the message, pulling back his lips in a grin before running ahead. When they hunted a deer, I dropped back, allowing myself to enjoy the run. In the eight years since my change, I had never gained any form of pleasure from this part of me—until now. I felt elated. This was a pleasure that I never would have associated with being in wolf form.

I panted happily as we rushed through the woods, feeling the joy and freedom of giving in to my other half. It was definitely a new feeling for me.

After about two hours in the woods, we headed back toward the house. They began to change back to human form as they walked.

How the hell do they do that? Walk and change with the same ease as you change a shirt. I was still in wolf form when we got to the house. Sebastian walked past me. So did Ethan and then everyone else. No one seemed to notice or care that I was still in animal form.

Plopping down on the ground, I closed my eyes. *Concentrate.* I did everything I could to make myself relax. As odd as it seemed, I couldn't be more relaxed than I was at that moment. I was easing myself into sleep when I heard footsteps approaching. Ethan shook his head as he stood in front of me—naked. In wolf form, I didn't feel the immediate need to turn away. He growled something inaudible and touched the top of my head. Enveloped in warmth, pricks of electricity shot through me. My body started to revert to human form. It was the slow-motion version of the others but I was changing. He turned and went into the house.

I dashed around the house and dressed as I attempted to ward off my concerns. Ethan, and undoubtedly Sebastian, could force my change to human and wolf form. They had a significant amount of control over my wolf half, over me. How much was it? When in wolf form, could they command me to sit and I would be forced to respond? Could they override my volition and make me change when I didn't want to? I didn't want them to have that level of control over me, whether in human or wolf form. *How do I resist that primordial power?*

Engrossed by new worries over Sebastian and Ethan's recently discovered power, I nearly missed the trail of blood leading into the house. Winter leaned against the kitchen island, speaking softly with the two of them. I couldn't make out the low murmurs, which I assumed was an erudite tactic from living among were-animals with enhanced hearing. When I was about a yard from where they stood, she did that weird eye thing and frowned. She regarded me for a long time before she turned and walked away. Ethan and Sebastian followed.

"There's been an incident," Joan stated from behind.

Her voice was tight and hard. I turned to face her. "Someone attacked Winter?" I asked.

"There were several vamps on the property. They are getting quite bold," she continued through clenched teeth. This was the first time her animal half was exposed. Her eyes went predatory, changing to chestnut with a hint of a yellow feline ring. There was a snarl on her face. She looked ferocious—carnal and more threatening than I could imagine. It was easy to forget what she was. Her soft demeanor and nurturing persona made her seem so human—all human. But now, she was noticeably irritated and her stance, mannerisms, and even energy screamed predator—killer. I took a step back. I didn't fear her, but the instinct of self-preservation made me distance myself from the agitated animal.

"I thought vampires could only enter your home if they are invited."

"They can come onto anyone's property at will. This is the first time they've approached ours. Desperation has made them either bold or foolish," she growled out. Seeing her so angry and feral was uncomfortable. Responding to my uneasiness, she softened her tone. Within seconds, she was composed and adorned with her warm smile and kind eyes. She smiled in that disarming manner that entreated you to trust her, welcome her, and forget what she really was. But this time it didn't work.

"They are three vamps down now. I doubt they will be so bold again." I wasn't sure how reassuring that was. I couldn't decide what bothered me more: knowing that Winter, who hated me, could single-handedly take out three vampires, or that the vampires were getting desperate and bold.

~

After I showered, I lay back on the bed staring at the ceiling. The vampires were getting desperate. I had no idea what they were desperate about, but it involved me. Fear replaced my anxiety and was wreaking havoc with my respiratory system. I panicked. The short gasps weren't enough to supply my body oxygen. I lurched up into a seated position forcing my lungs to inflate. I took several long, deep breaths.

"You never learned to control your wolf. You let it control you." Startled, I followed the sound of the voice. Ethan emerged from the shadows. Noticeably agitated, he paced back and forth. His eyes were daggers, keenly focused on me. His tension pulsed through the room in waves, an overwhelming surge that stifled me.

He stopped and leaned against the dresser, awaiting a response. It didn't seem to warrant one. He was stating the obvious. Instead of answering him, I responded with a blank stare fixed on the door and waited for him to get the hint and leave.

"What, have you not gained control of your hearing, either?"

I looked down, avoiding his watchful leer.

"My hearing is just fine," I responded stiffly. "I've always been afraid of that part of me. It's a miserable inconvenience that I have to deal with each month during full moons and I chose not to deal with it any more than I had to." *Inconvenience? My period is an inconvenience. This is a hostile takeover of my life.* Every decision and every aspect of my life revolved around my wolf, especially since I experienced several unexpected changes brought on by loss of emotional control. Those often ended with my mother giving me several painful shots with a tranquilizer until I went down.

He pushed himself up from the dresser, walked over to me,

and leaned in closely as he inhaled, then frowned. His face was still just inches from my neck. If I were just a tad braver, I would have pushed him away. Keeping his eyes fixed on me, he took several steps back, studying me with avid interest. "You don't smell like a were-animal and the vampires enter your home without an invitation as though you were one of theirs." His eyes narrowed to slits. "Why is that?"

I couldn't begin to understand why he was interrogating me with questions that I couldn't possibly answer. Did he think I miraculously acquired information between the day I arrived and now? Refusing to give him the satisfaction of my frustration, I remained silent as cold eyes from a stone face glared back at me.

"I don't like it," he stated.

I lifted my chin with forced confidence. "You are welcome to go dislike it somewhere else."

"Not before I have answers. What exactly are you?"

"What?"

"What. Are. You."

"What answer do you need to make it easier for you to leave?"

The haughty look quickly disappeared. "If I staked you, would you start reversion?"

Steven had explained to me that vampires aren't killed by a stake like in every vampire flick imaginable. Once staked, a vampire putrefies and reverts physically to its dead state. The body slowly decays and hardens, becoming mummified. If they aren't decapitated during reversion and are allowed to feed, then they return to their natural state. Then you have a very angry and vengeful vampire to deal with.

"I am not sure. As a general social rule, people don't go around staking people. It's really frowned upon in mainstream society. But I suspect that it would be the same as with you—

pain and lots of blood. Sometimes I cry when I get hurt. So maybe I would cry a little, too," I smarted back.

When he laughed, it was a dark abrasive rumble. "Something about you is wrong. Off. I don't like it and I need to know what it is."

"If you need answers, I am not the right source."

He watched my hands as I nervously fidgeted with the silver charm bracelet around my wrist.

"You don't have an aversion to silver." He sounded surprised.

I wasn't going to play this inane game of "let's state the obvious" with him. I exhaled loudly, glancing at him periodically before directing my attention toward the door, urging him to leave.

"You're not a true were-animal?"

"Yet every full moon I turn into a wolf."

His gaze hardened and I felt like prey under a predator's leering stare. Would he attack? After a few minutes, he walked over to me and stood directly in front of me. His face just inches from mine. "What are you?"

I sighed, annoyed. "You tell me. It seems that everyone knows as much or maybe even more about me than I do. You are the one with the source who seems to have all the answers. We've played 'getting to know you' long enough. And I can assure you I am quite tired of it. It is time for you to leave," I stated firmly, walking to the door and opening it.

He marshaled a look of sheer defiance as he took a seat on the edge of the bed. I opened the door wider. He didn't move.

Leaning against the wall, I crossed my arms and waited. He kept a watchful glare on me for an excruciatingly long time. If his goal was to make me feel uncomfortable, he succeeded. He slowly came to his feet and paced the floor like a caged wild animal, watching me carefully as though I were a threat. I wished more than ever that he would just leave. His increasing agitation was making me nervous. If we were in the wild, I would be running for my life.

"Our information is limited on what you are. You lived your life ignoring the animal within. What else dwells in you that you chose to ignore? You don't expect me to believe you have been foolish enough to live this pseudo-human life with that woman you called mother, oblivious to all things."

I winced. *That woman I called mother*? Anger soon replaced my irritation. "That woman that I called mother was my mother by every definition of the word, despite the fact that she did not give birth to me," I snapped, stepping closer to him. "I am so sorry to disappoint you, but yes, I lived my life with no desire to know anything more about my origin other than the fact I am a werewolf. All I knew was both my parents were dead. I only wanted to live as a human or as human as this wretched wolf would allow me. I wanted nothing more than to do human things and ignore anything that made me anything but." I paused my rant to take a well-needed deep breath to calm down, but it didn't help. "Until I came here, I had only experienced my wolf during loss of emotional control. Every full moon, I was sedated and slept through it, locked in a cage. This is something I chose to do. And this is the way I chose to live."

He continued watching me attentively, unaffected by my angry outburst.

"If your job is to know, wouldn't your time be better spent trying to find out why the vampires have this newfound interest in me, instead of grilling me with questions I can't possibly answer? The sooner we know their intentions, the faster I can get out of this house. I believe that would make us both happy."

After several minutes of standing in silence and glaring at each other in the worst standoff, I conceded. "Should *I* leave?" I asked finally.

After intense protracted moments of silence and cold lingering glances at each other, he shook his head and left.

Once he was out of the room, a wave of anger washed over me. I sat back on the bed and attempted to control it, but it was about to consume me. My anger wasn't solely directed at Ethan. I was angry because my mother was dead and I couldn't save her. Life as I knew it had dramatically changed and I didn't have a clue what to do next.

My clash with Ethan had just made things far too real for me. I didn't know of any blood relatives who could help me deal with what I was going through. I had vampires coming after me for unknown reasons. And I didn't know how to control my wolf. That scared me most of all. *What will I do on the next full moon?*

Attempting to force the thoughts out of my head, I tried to control things. The twinge changed to a surge of those familiar pains I got right before I changed. *Dammit.* My fingers balled so tightly together that my nails pressed into my skin. I fought to control things the best way I could. Shutting my eyes tightly, I saw flashes of color before them. *Count backward from a hundred,* I commanded myself. This never worked in the past, but at this point, I was willing to try anything. *Now do it in Portuguese,* I told myself as I continued with my effort to find calm. But it was too far from my reach as I fought the flood of emotions that were building in me.

"You need to control yourself," declared Ethan's voice on the other side of the door. It had lost its harsh tone and was now a languid whisper. "You shouldn't change again today. It will fatigue you too much."

I know that. Who are you, Captain Obvious? Did he not realize I was doing what I could to stop it?

Ethan came in and sat next to me on the bed. I kept my eyes closed, fully aware that if I looked at him it would just compound the irritation. He was close enough that our arms touched, and I became very aware of his presence and the calm that his touch brought. He was doing something but I had no idea what. Ethan leaned into me, and a peaceful warmth engulfed me, sending me to a place of serenity where I wanted to stay.

I opened my eyes in time to see him walk out the door, and the blanket of calmness left with him. I was neither angry nor calm, returning instead to my place of abject emotions.

CHAPTER 4

The next day I stared out the window, basking in the bright sun as it gently warmed my face. I appreciated it for what it meant—no vampires. It was the first sunny day since I had been *invited* to stay with the were-animals. The other days were so dark and gloomy it seemed like dusk even at noon. Leaving the house would have invited another run-in with Gabriella and Chase. But today I was leaving the house to practice some well-needed escapism, no matter how impossible the task might be. Being confined here was so suffocating it was like constantly inhaling through a plastic bag. Until I came to the retreat, I never believed in cabin fever. *Seriously, how can someone get tired of being in their home?* But when it's someone else's home, it's more possible than you can imagine.

With my computer bag across my shoulder, I managed to navigate my way to find Sebastian's office. When Steven had given me a guided tour of the house, he brushed over the location of Sebastian's office as though he didn't want me to remember, but I made sure, if nothing else, I would remember that. I headed down the stairs, around the corner, passing the living room and the entrance to the urgent care, to a room several feet down the hall. I knocked on Sebastian's office door. When he didn't answer, I placed my ear next to it and listened for signs of movement or voices. I knocked again harder.

"What do you need?"

Startled by the baritone voice from behind me, I took several steps back. Sebastian didn't seem to walk but rather glide into his position with such stealth it was hard not to feel like he was only moments from attacking. He folded his arms across his chest as he settled against the wall. His brown eyes, as usual, regarded me as though watching paint drying would have been far more interesting. Curiously, he eyed my computer bag hooked over my shoulder, the scarf around my neck, my coral-colored sweater, dark jeans, and everything right down to my dark brown boots. Whoever packed my bags made sure I was prepared for whatever attire the weather called for. Today was an unseasonably warm fall day and I was about to enjoy it.

"Going somewhere?" he asked with a raised brow.

I still wasn't sure exactly where I was, but Steven, during one of our many conversations, disclosed that I was just thirty-eight miles from Chicago. This meant I wasn't too far from my home. It made staying there a little easier.

I nodded. "The city … I need to go to the city," I blurted out. "I don't have a car, and remarkably, the GPS on my phone can't seem to locate this place. A taxi is out of the question."

His lips pressed together, forming an unwelcoming line. "What do you need in the city?"

I need to get the hell out of here.

"I need to go to the city."

"What do you need? I will have someone pick it up for you."

I let out an exaggerated sigh. "I need to get out of here. I've been cooped up in this house for four days, and I can't stand it any longer. You claim I'm not being held captive—"

"You're not."

"Then I would like to leave for just a little while."

He stared at me for a long moment. It seemed like he was about to deny my request, when he glanced up behind me. A wisp of a smile slowly settled on his face. I didn't need to turn around. I heard her gentle gait and sensed the faint floral scent. Joan.

"Fine." He announced his forced surrender through tightly pulled lips, as though obliging my request pained him. I was willing to bet it was because he hated that Joan forced him to be amicable, when all he really wanted to do was keep me locked up.

"If it makes you feel better, I will stop by a church to get some holy water, and I am wearing a cross.".

He held the cross between his fingers. "Unless you plan on giving the cross to the vampire as a gift and providing the holy water as a refreshing beverage, then you are pretty much defenseless," he stated dryly. "They have an aversion to the cross, but it doesn't make them weak as legend would have you believe. If anything, it'll further irritate them, and they'll just take your arm with it as they snatch it from you."

I shuddered at the image. "Unless they're up for a daylight stroll, I will be okay."

"Ethan will take you."

Well, Sebastian, that would totally defeat the purpose of this day trip, which is to stay as far away from him as possible.

"Is Steven here?" I asked.

"Yes he is. Ethan will meet you out front." He walked past me into his office and closed the door.

Ethan met me out front in a dark SUV. He looked about as happy chaperoning me as I was about him taking me. It was quite apparent, even if I couldn't feel the palpable anger that surrounded him like a cocoon. The petty side of me found a little joy in that. *Ha! Ha!*

On the drive away from the house, I saw why the GPS couldn't pick up a signal and navigating from the house was so difficult. It was placed in the middle of no-man's-land, only enough land cleared of trees and vegetation to build the small compound. Calling it a house seemed so inefficient, and *estate* seemed too pristine. There were three exits, from the back, side, and front. It was close to a three-mile ride to get off the property. Then it dropped into a single-lane road that I'm sure wouldn't show up on my GPS, either. This was where you go to disappear, your existence camouflaged by nature and desolation.

I made a mental note that it was nearly half an hour before I was in civilized territory, where the map on my phone could determine where I was, where I felt that if I ran into someone, they wouldn't be hiding from the world.

He was quiet as he navigated through the city, darting in and out of the congested freeway traffic, pissing off people without remorse. After close to an hour of horrid Chicago traffic, we found ourselves driving through the crowded streets, bumping over roads destroyed by the menacing winter snowfalls. "Where do you need to go?" he asked, his voice rough, angry.

"Just park near 96th."

"*Where* do you need to go?"

I really shouldn't have been this petty but I couldn't help it. I just repeated my direction to a very angry Ethan, who looked like he was ready to make me his next victim.

We continued to drive down the street with Ethan shooting me baleful glares every so often. We lucked upon a prime spot just a couple of blocks from where I wanted to go.

I missed the city. It's not that I was a true city girl. Public transportation gave me the creeps. Traffic annoyed me as much as it did Ethan, although I would never let him know that. Paying ridiculous amounts of money to park, or driving around for thirty minutes just to find a parking space, made me understand road rage—or city rage. I despised buildings that were so preposterously tall that they nearly blocked the sun, which the Midwest rarely received. The obtrusive buildings made the areas seem bleak and gloomy. But the museums, art galleries, shopping, boutiques, and abundance of good restaurants made you ignore those other nuisances.

I got out of the car and started toward a coffeehouse just two blocks away.

He scoffed at me. "Are you serious? There's coffee at the house."

I didn't respond. It wasn't the same. It seemed like a lifetime since I sat in a coffeehouse sipping on chai tea while people watching. It was refreshing just to observe people being normal. It came so easily for them, and for me, it offered hours of entertainment. They had such simple lives without full moons, cages, and freakish capabilities. I needed a break from the new weirdness in my life.

Marissa's was comfortable, set up like a large eclectic room in a house. There were bookcases placed at each corner, filled with books that patrons donated for various reasons but mostly because the books sucked, and most people are conditioned not to throw them away. A variety of sofas, lounge chairs, and ottomans were scattered around the vast room. Several dining-style tables were peppered about. In the middle of the café sat a large, double wood-burning fireplace that leant the café its cozy atmosphere.

Not only did the café serve various coffee drinks, but it also had an appetizing menu, serving breakfast, lunch, and dinner dishes. That's how it remained so successful. People would come with their laptops or a friend and sit for hours in the cozy living room. Patrons would order everything from coffee drinks, alcoholic drinks, breakfast and lunch to dinner. It wasn't until your bill came that you were hit with the realization that you've been sitting in a restaurant for six hours ordering overpriced beverages and food and had the extravagant bill to show for it. I can't count the number of times I fell victim to this marketing tactic, but in the end, it seemed worth it.

I found a seat in a far corner on a loveseat and surfed the Web while I waited for Ethan to get the drinks. He walked slowly toward me giving a once-over to everyone and everything as he became familiar with the surroundings. My attention diverted from him to the two women sitting in the corner by the door who had been watching him since we walked in. One of them nudged the other and must have said something amusing about Ethan because her friend began to giggle like a schoolgirl as they watched him walk through the café.

I had to admit, he could get your attention. He was classically handsome with strong broad features, a defined jawline, aquiline nose, and cerulean eyes that would have been appealing if they weren't so rapacious and hard. The dark blue Henley shirt and khakis complemented his eyes and physique.

His good looks didn't go unnoticed by the barista who smiled at him enthusiastically when he walked up to the counter, showing all her teeth. I thought I even saw her bat her eyes a couple of times as she suggested several pastries.

He handed me my chai latte and a blueberry muffin. "I didn't want a muffin."

"The barista gave it to me," he stated, taking a seat next to me.

"I think she wants you to have her muffin, not me." I grinned as I handed it back to him.

He rolled his eyes. "What is she, sixteen?"

I glanced in her direction. She was at least in her early twenties and couldn't stop looking at him. Even the two women near the door still had their attention focused on him. Okay, he was more than just attractive, but everything from the tight clench of his jaw, the sneer of his lips, and his intense unwelcoming gaze screamed *jackass*. With that in mind, everything else seemed inconsequential.

While I checked my e-mail, Ethan sat back on the sofa with his legs crossed. He looked bored as he read a paper someone had left behind. There were several e-mails from my boss, Mrs. Alexander, regarding potential assignments. She must have been flooded with new requests for her services because she rarely contacted me about assignments. I often contacted her.

I worked as a health care auditor. Companies would hire us to perform a mock audit to ensure they would pass in the event of a federal one. It was a good job for me because it allowed a level of autonomy and flexibility to work around full moons and my full-moon hangovers. I was never in any given facility for more than six weeks. It was long enough to provide the human interaction I wanted and short enough to prevent developing relationships. Six weeks wasn't enough time for people to really give a damn about me. No one cared how my weekend went, what I did the night before, or why I didn't have any friends or lovers.

Mrs. Alexander was a nice and thoughtful person, but nosy to the point of annoyance. It wasn't her intention. Her company was built on her ability to snoop, interpret, and pry into documents for companies. Unfortunately, those qualities seemed to flood over into her personality. I kept that in mind as I carefully constructed the e-mail. If the letter seemed too serious, I would have to worry about constant contacts from her. On the other hand, if it seemed too trivial and gave the impression I didn't want to work, she would be offended—or worse, fire me. I kept it simple, telling her that due to a family emergency, I would be out of town for a few days. In a couple of days, I will tell her that I lost my mother. Right now, I couldn't do it because some part of me was pretending that it wasn't true.

After my considerable pleas, she allowed me to work as a contractor rather than a full-time employee. As full-time employees, we were required to come to the office to type reports and to assist other co-workers between assignments. The thought of spending hours a day with co-workers who were paid to investigate didn't appeal to me. Eventually, the questions would come and I would have to quit a job that I liked.

Initially, she adamantly refused, but she soon realized that I spent most of the day in my office hiding from her and the rest of the staff. During staff meetings, I gave my best impression of a wallflower, trying to become invisible in the sea of faces. Four months, six staff meetings and two intentionally missed employee birthday celebrations later, she called me to her office to negotiate a change to contract employee status. All my work could be done from home and she would notify me of meetings I needed to attend.

My working as a contractor was ideal for her, as well. I think she liked me well enough but I put her on edge. I wasn't sure what I did that was abnormal, but her vitals always seemed to quicken just a tad when I was around and the wave of uneasiness was hard to ignore. *What did I do? Did I move too quickly? Did I respond to something that I shouldn't have heard? Did my eyes go predatory wolf on the few occasions she irritated me?*

I finally closed my laptop, sat back, and sipped my second cup of chai tea. I savored every moment at a molasses-slow rate for Ethan's benefit as he sat next to me, sighing and making various sounds of boredom. When he began to tap on the table next to him, I cast a dark look in his direction, which he matched, inviting me to say something cross to him.

"You need to hurry up," he finally stated roughly. "I'm bored."

"Well, that's something you should take up with Sebastian. I'm *not* bored and that is why I wanted to come alone."

"That wasn't going to happen." He spoke to me in the same chastising manner you would use with a child after they asked to do something ridiculous.

I didn't bother giving him the satisfaction of a dirty look. "Then it seems like you need to just grin and bear it," I stated in a cloying voice.

He made a dark ominous sound that held a cloud of mischief. It made me look in his direction. Whatever look I held on my face amused him because he smiled. "Most people tend to want to stay on my good side. It would be good that you learn from their example."

Do most people tend to stay on your good side because you are a jerk they would rather not deal with? Instead of expressing my curiosity and subjecting myself to a day with an irritated wolf, I nodded once in acknowledgment. His impatience didn't make me finish my drink any faster, but my desire to antagonize him quickly disappeared.

We left the café and walked through the crowded streets of the city during the lunch hour rush. Ethan snarled and looked generally annoyed as people bumped into and scurried around him. I attempted to compensate for his crude behavior by greeting the strangers with a quick "hello" or "pardon us" as we darted between them. Ethan relentlessly swore and was an overall pain as he worked his way through the crowd. It was safe to assume that Ethan was not a people person. In fact, he seemed to have a general disdain for anything that wasn't a were-animal.

He stayed uncomfortably close to me. So close, it was invasive.

"Would you like to put a leash on me?" I finally snapped the next time he pulled me closer to him, once I gained a comfortable distance from him.

"Don't tempt me."

Rolling my eyes, I pulled my hand out of his grip.

"Where are we going?" he asked, irritated. Indiscriminately, I began to point to various stores along the strip. He looked down his nose but didn't say anything. His face was void of any expression, which was scarier than his many dark looks.

When I went into a candle store, he could barely contain his irritation. It wasn't easy for me either because of the strong fragrances that overwhelmed the small space, but I knew it was pure hell for Ethan, whose sense of smell was keener than mine. He liked making people feel uncomfortable. Now it was my turn. I was being petty beyond words, yet I couldn't muster any shame for it.

After the candle shop, we went to an arts and craft store, which held no interest for me, but it bothered him even more. I fiddled around, feigning interest in things that I otherwise would have ignored.

"You haven't bought anything. I thought you needed to get something," Ethan finally stated, clearly agitated for having to provide security detail on a useless trip.

"No, I said I needed to go to the city," I corrected indifferently. "I am going to check out some shops."

He snorted. "As long as we're done by four."

"Cinderella had to be in the house by the time the clock struck twelve."

"Cinderella wasn't being hunted by vampires that wake at dusk."

I continued to walk swiftly through the crowd, trying to distance myself from him, but he caught up with little effort. He clutched my arm with an iron grip. "Let's go there." He pointed to a steakhouse across the street.

"Are you ever *not* hungry?" I ate a great deal for a woman my size. However, after being in the house with the were-animals, I realized that compared to them, I had the appetite of someone suffering from anorexia.

"A hungry wolf is a mean wolf."

"Then you must have a tapeworm," I muttered under my breath as I followed him.

As soon as we walked through the door of the restaurant, we were greeted by a cute, curvy woman with girlish features that didn't fit her very grown-up appearance. Her blond hair was swept up into a twist. Overly glossed heart-shaped lips pulled into a wide smile. Large jasper eyes with eyelashes enhanced by dark mascara looked at Ethan with interest. She wore a uniform that clung to her, showing off her assets a little too well. Ethan took notice and returned her overly enthusiastic smile. He leaned into the podium and whispered his seating preference: in the back against the wall next to the windows. I assumed it was so he could neurotically watch everyone go in and out of the restaurant. She eagerly complied.

She escorted us to our seats and stayed for a while, playing the guessing game with Ethan as she tried to determine where she knew him from. As she blatantly disregarded my presence, I dismissed the urge to point out the lack of originality in her pickup line. After ten minutes of incorrect guesses, she finally determined that she recognized him from her gym.

Really? You've determined the attractive muscular guy goes to your gym. That's what you're going with? I sighed loudly. She looked over, rolled her eyes, and sauntered away to actually work.

"I'm sorry, would you like me to leave so you can continue this inane flirting?" I asked once she was no longer in earshot.

"No, I'm done, but thank you for the offer. I wish you could be this considerate most of the time. It would make being around you much easier."

I was a quick study and knew that verbal fencing with Ethan

would lead to nothing more than me becoming incredibly angry. Instead, I continued to stare at my menu in great detail.

When the waitress finally arrived, I had changed my order in my head four times. I decided on grilled chicken, mashed potatoes, and salad. Ethan ordered two New York strip steaks prepared blood-rare and a loaded baked potato.

"What's with you, chicken and salad?" he scoffed disgustedly once the waitress left.

"What do you mean?"

"You ordered chicken and salad, like a typical woman."

"I *am* a typical woman."

"No. You are not. You are a werewolf." His reproaching gaze lingered on my face.

"What would you have me do? Ask them to point me to the nearest pasture where I can find a grazing cow that I can attack and devour for lunch while you watch?"

"No, you can order real meat and have it prepared in a manner that's most appealing to your animal."

"I'm forced to be a wolf one night a month. I am a woman for the rest of the time," I responded defensively.

"The wolf is always there. The fact that you can hear the woman at the next table questioning her husband about his so-called business trip without trying to eavesdrop demonstrates that you are not just some woman. Or the fact that if necessary, you could take down most of the people in this room, even with your limited fighting skills, demonstrates that you're not just some woman. It's your wolf that makes those things possible. You may sit here and pretend to be just a typical pretty woman but you're a wolf all the time. You may have chosen the human part of you, but that won't stifle the wolf or make it go away, even if it is only allowed to take physical form during full moons," he asserted.

He was giving me his dominance stare again. I made a futile attempt to challenge him before looking down at my hand on the table. "And that's your wolf, as well," he said. "You may not be part of our pack but your wolf understands pack structure and knows its place."

I didn't want to admit it, but he was right. No matter how I ignored it or fought it—I was a werewolf and could never be wholly human.

"Once you truly accept the wolf, then you will see the beauty in it. Instead of running, learn to appreciate the enhanced abilities, strength, and senses."

What is he, the poster boy for were-animals? "When did you first change?"

"Eight."

"How did you deal with changing so young?"

"There wasn't anything to deal with. My father was a wolf and I couldn't wait until my wolf matured to change. I had the strength, speed, and senses early on, but it was the actual physical transformation that took so long."

I stared at him, surprised. Did he look at what we were as a gift? *Well, if this is a gift, what line do I need to stand in to make my return?*

"How do you change so fast?"

He shrugged. "You do anything often enough, it becomes easy. Become one with your better half and when you call, it will answer freely."

Better half? Who the hell is he kidding with that? Referring to my wolf as my better half was as ludicrous as wanting to change to it without the call of the moon.

I didn't think I would ever understand the way Ethan felt about his animal half, and he simply abhorred the way I felt about mine. Instead of arguing, we sat in uncomfortable silence as we waited for our food. Several times, I caught him looking at my eyes, not into them, but *at* them with that same peculiar look on his face.

"What are you looking at?" I finally asked.

He smiled. "You have nice eyes." I could feel my face burning a bright strawberry color. I looked away, becoming increasingly interested in whatever was going on outside as I mumbled a thanks.

When the food arrived and the waitress left, he stabbed his fork through my chicken and removed it from my plate and replaced it with one of his steaks.

The steak was delicious and prepared better than I could have imagined. Savoring each bite, I took my time eating each piece. Ethan smiled, sitting back in his chair as he watched me attentively. Once again, his attention focused on my eyes.

I've heard of breast men, leg men, and even butt men, but I've never heard of an eye man.

"It's rare I can bring a woman such pleasure with *just* food," he said with a smirk. His gaze shifted from my eyes to my ruddy cheeks.

As soon as we had taken our last bite of food, he placed cash on the table and rushed me out the door as though the sun were about to set within seconds.

This is my life now, fearing the sunset. I now had to find safety before the sun disappeared, ushering in the night and all the things that dwelled in it. At one time, I considered myself somewhat a creature of the night. I loved it, the calm and tranquility it offered. Now I was running from it.

Ethan stayed close to me, his arm at my waist as we threaded through the crowds. His gaze darted through the crowd. His hold on me tightened when the crowd thickened. He whispered directions to me as he guided me through the masses of people. It was the end of the workday and the city had become busier and more unsettling. The tall buildings blocked the sun, making the city look dark and oppressive. The sounds of rushing loafers, tennis shoes, and high heels against the asphalt were harsh and distracting.

The sordid combination of perfume, cologne, noise, chatter, and the negative energy from a long, hard day at work was overwhelming. I didn't mind the crowds. I hated the noise and smells. But it was the chatter that bothered me the most. Auditory discrimination was still difficult for me. Far too often, I found myself engrossed in several conversations without really trying. After several minutes of conversation-hopping, I was exhausted.

"This way." Ethan took firm hold of my elbow and directed me toward the alley behind a restaurant. It reeked from the garbage that filled the large bins that lined the narrow enclave. Debris that didn't manage to land in the containers blew across our pathway. The smell was nauseating. Leaning against the brick wall, he sank into the darkness. Someone walked toward us, but with the sun glaring behind him, I couldn't make out the face. Once closer, I realized I didn't recognize him, but he had a look of familiarity as though he knew me. As he inched closer to me, I greeted him with a placid smile.

Ethan appeared behind the stranger and with one sweeping move, he wrapped his hands around the man's upper body and twisted his neck, breaking it. The stranger let out a faint strangled cry before his eyes rolled back and blood seeped from his mouth.

Gaping in shocked silence, I stifled my cries. Ethan's eyes were a smoldering gray, and I knew who was in the pilot seat at this moment.

"What the hell did you do?" I choked out. I didn't give him a chance to answer before darting past him and running as fast as I could toward the street.

"Skylar, wait!"

I didn't bother turning around. There wasn't any explanation he could have given me that would have made this situation right. The man was human. There was a weakness to his struggle. There wasn't anything supernatural about him. He wasn't a vampire. *This is bad, really bad. What the hell have I gotten myself into?* My thoughts went into overdrive. *Why did I trust the were-animals? Have they really given me a reason to?* Nothing really made sense at this point. All I knew was that Ethan had just killed a human for no apparent reason and I needed to get away from him.

"Skylar!"

Ethan's footsteps pounded heavily across the pavement as he gained on me. My mind was bombarded by a dichotomy of thoughts that I couldn't sort out fast enough. *These people are murderers—period. All I need is to get to the street and catch a cab. I'll have to figure the rest out later.*

Running blindly to escape from Ethan, I collided with a man at the end of the alley. I fell and stammered out a quick apology. Before I could come to my feet, the stranger grabbed me and pulled me to him. He held me so tightly it was painful. I pushed his hands off my shoulders and flipped him over on his back. He grabbed my ankle and yanked hard, pulling me to the ground with him. He was human; breaking his hold was easy. But he was quick. Pulling something silver out of his pocket, he jabbed it in my direction. I couldn't quite see what it was until I gripped his hand and held it steady. A Taser. He struggled to connect it with my body. I kept rolling, moving and twisting from left to right to keep it from touching me. He may not have been as strong as I was, but human tenacity was a bitch. He worked hard trying to disable me with the Taser.

Quiet steps approached. Ethan grabbed the Taser out of the assailant's hand and lifted him off the ground with ease. His hand grasped the man's neck. The human struggled for what seemed like an eternity as Ethan squeezed the life from his body. The sharp pop of a gun firing resounded, and both Ethan and the assailant fell to the ground. My ears rang from the sound and blood from Ethan's wound splattered, covering both my face and shirt.

The new assailant ran toward us with his gun drawn. I moved closer to Ethan, the muscles of his neck pulled tight as he labored to breathe. He was close to changing. "It's going to be okay," I whispered, trying to sound soothing, but the panic tainted my voice.

The man steadied his gun, preparing to take another shot, this time at Ethan's head. I threw the Taser that had fallen next to my feet. It lodged hard against his face, sending him stumbling back. I lunged at him, helping him fall to the ground. He clawed at me as he tried to push me off him. Eventually I gained control and held him down, firmly thrashing him repeatedly with my fist. I pummeled into him with a violent rage, ignoring the distinct feeling of bones separating and pressing into my skin and reveling in the feel of fragmented bones and battered soft tissue underneath my hand. I hit and punched at him until he was limp, and I had sufficiently exorcised my anger and panic. I looked down at the bloody, disfigured man. He was dead.

Too shocked to feel any guilt, I stared at the results of my rage. My hands were bloodstained and bruised, and still I thirsted for more violence. It wasn't the animal part of me that killed this man. It was an act done by the part of me I considered human. The so-called humane part of me wanted to cause more violence and inflict more pain.

"Skylar." The sound of Ethan's voice pulled me out of my dazed state. I took another look at the stilled body and the results of the malevolence. I absorbed the violence, took in the horrific image, and wondered where the line between my animal and my humanity lay.

"It's okay," he whispered, leaning into me. His familiar calm washed over me. I leaned back against him trying to make the images of what I'd done disappear. Eventually, I gave up on that lost cause and followed him back to the car.

By the time we got to the car, Ethan was noticeably in pain. I drove as he settled back in the passenger side. He pulled out his phone. "I've been shot," he stated in a strained voice. "Of course it was silver. I wouldn't call you if it weren't."

Jeremy's voice came through clearly as he hurriedly tried to determine how far we were and the extent of the injuries. "Should I come there?"

"Skylar's driving, I should get there before there's too much damage." Each word pulled a painful grimace to his face. Sweat started to form along his brow and his color became ashen. He had already pulled off his shirt to assess the damage. I didn't have a severe aversion to silver so I never knew how traumatic it could be to a were-animal. Silver stopped the healing process, and the skin inflicted with the silver darkened, appearing to go through phases of necrosis.

I didn't know how much time we had. Ethan didn't look well and the traffic was horrible. We took a back road, which kept us out of stop-and-go traffic, but it added to our drive time.

"I think I can take the bullet out," I offered as we navigated through the back streets. My hands were quite steady, and in the past, I had exhibited the necessary dexterity to apply stitches to myself on several occasions.

It must have been really painful because he agreed without hesitation. We pulled over when we found an area less populated. I went to the trunk to see what they had. I figured they had to have an emergency kit or something. After all, these people had a hospital in their home. They did. I pulled out the emergency kit and a toolbox.

The bullet hadn't penetrated that deeply. I could feel the edge of it when I touched his chest. I used the alcohol, box cutter, and needle-nose pliers as best I could. Placing the box cutter firmly against the skin, I pressed it deep enough to separate the bullet from the tissue. I was so nervous, my hands slipped several times cutting him. He winced but never made a sound. Once I separated the bullet from the tissue well enough, I used pliers to dislodge it. When I finished, I cleaned and bandaged the wound.

After the bullet was removed, the tissue quickly repaired itself.

As I navigated my way through traffic, Ethan lay back against the seat, periodically glancing in my direction.

"Why did you run from me?" he finally asked in a calm voice. I glanced in his direction. His appearance was less distressed; his eyes no longer held the grayish hue.

"Scared … I was scared. I thought you had killed someone without cause," I continued in a small voice.

"You think I am capable of that?"

Yes. I think you're capable of that and so much more. "I didn't know what to think. Who were they?"

He inhaled deeply and I could feel his eyes bearing on me.

"They were part of the vampires' garden," he said flatly, his eyes still fixed on me. "They are humans who serve the Seethe in various ways but mostly as food supply. Some do it in hopes of being changed and others to satisfy their own perverted needs. Those who do it in hope of being changed become slaves, willing to do anything to please their Master, including abducting you."

He shifted in his seat and looked out the window. "You don't trust us."

I didn't know how to answer that question. "I've never had to trust anyone other than my mother. I don't think I know how to," I admitted. But it was only a partial truth. *No, I don't trust you and I doubt I ever will.*

I wanted to say something to put an end to this long uncomfortable silence. We drove the rest of the way in silence. Every so often, he looked in my direction, and I couldn't quite read his expression. After I pulled into the driveway, I quickly got out of the car and went to the passenger side to help him. He closed the distance between us as he stepped out of the car. His face was mild, almost gentle as he grasped strands of my hair. Rolling them absently over his fingers in a manner that seemed intimate, his gaze roved over my face carefully. "You need to trust us, or at the very least learn to fake it," he said in a cool voice. He held my gaze. His comment wasn't so much a suggestion as it was a well-worded threat.

Dr. Baker met us at the door, his face etched with concern. Holding the bullet between my fingers, I looked at it again and dropped it into his hand.

"Well done," he stated appreciatively as I walked past him. Since I was the reason for the injury, helping him didn't seem to warrant appreciation.

"How's the shoulder?" he asked Ethan before he walked past him.

"Still here."

"Meet me in my office. I still would like to look at it."

Ethan nodded, heading toward Sebastian's office, but he was out the door before Ethan could knock. His lips curved into a half-smile, giving the shoulder a once-over. "It's been a long time since you've felt the tinge of silver on your flesh."

"It's a pain one never forgets. I don't need a reminder of it anytime soon."

"Skylar, I see that your day trip was quite eventful. You now see that the vampires don't have to take a stroll in the daylight to get to you," Sebastian stated contemptuously. "There won't be any more trips for you until this is over. So don't ask again."

I started counting from a thousand, giving myself time to cool off before I ended up telling him what I thought about having to ask permission to leave the house. I missed several numbers in the process—too angry to concentrate. It's not that I didn't agree with him, because it was quite tiring getting attacked every time I left the house. *Would it have hurt him to ask me like an adult rather than command me as though I were a child?*

"Being attacked every time I go out of the house really makes for a bad day. And because of the ever-so-sweet way you asked, I think I can comply with that," I replied in a cloying tone.

His eyes narrowed into a glare before he directed his attention back to Ethan.

I started up the stairs but didn't miss him telling Ethan that Josh had returned. By the time I backtracked down, they had disappeared behind the office door. Since fighting with a controlling Alpha wasn't on my to-do list, I abandoned the idea of knocking on the office door.

By the time I had showered and eaten dinner, once again alone in the bedroom, I had grown impatient, waiting for them to let me speak to this Josh. I hadn't seen or heard anything from Ethan since we had pulled up to the house three hours earlier. Pacing the room wasn't helping, either. I wandered through the house, which had become suspiciously quiet since his arrival. Did Josh have the same effect on them that I had when I first came to the house? Did everyone just scatter? Blindly, I searched through the house, listening for an unfamiliar voice, tracking an unfamiliar scent, looking for that unfamiliar person. Each room I passed, I placed my ear to it, listening for anything—voices, screams, even a wicked cackle. I didn't care. I just wanted something.

My final stop was by the room Ethan stayed in, which turned out to be a bust. This Josh had to be somewhere in this house because I could sense something amiss. The problem was he could be anywhere in the maze of rooms and hallways of this absurdly large house.

Maybe it was a good thing I hadn't found him. He clearly wouldn't be alone. What would I say? *Hey, Josh, I was just stalking you. Can we talk?*

"Did you need something, Skylar?" Surprised, I looked in the direction of the sound. My ears easily identified him before I could see him.

"Ethan," I called out into the dark hallway.

"Are you lost?" He appeared in my line of sight.

"No, just looking around."

His eyes narrowed as he leaned against the wall. "What were you looking for, Skylar?"

"You. I was looking for you. I hadn't seen you since earlier and I wanted to make sure you were alright." I didn't care for lying to people, but I didn't want to tell him I was stalking Josh, either.

"I'm fine. You did well today. It is greatly appreciated."

I smiled. Before I could walk away, he stepped closer, forcing me against the wall. His palm rested on the upper part of my sternum keeping me firmly in place. He leaned in close, inhaling as he ran his nose along my jawline until his lips rested against my ear. I scowled.

He whispered but it came out as a growl. "You've lived so long in your human world that you have not developed the skills to successfully lie to a were-animal. Do you hear it—your heart rate. It's beating too fast, and your breathing's changed. It's irregular."

"Perhaps my heart is beating fast and my breathing is irregular because a scary werewolf has me cornered in a dark hallway." I hoped I sounded calmer than I felt.

He pressed closer into me. "I really hate to be lied to."

I challenge you to find a person who enjoys it.

"Tell me, what were you looking for?" he asked again.

"I want to talk to Josh." I tried to push myself up from the wall, but he pressed in harder, keeping me in place.

Too much time passed as he stood staring at me. "No. Not today."

"Yes. Today, and preferably now if you can make that happen." He let me push my way past him, but he held me a few moments as a reminder of who really was in control.

"No."

I was fuming by the time I turned to face him. He looked amused by my anger. If only he knew the many ways I was contemplating wiping that smug look off his face, it would have vanished quickly. "If he's here, why do I have to wait until tomorrow? Why can't we just get this over with tonight?"

"Because."

Are you kidding me? I never understood the answer "because I said so." I realized many people grew up in households like that, but my mother worked on logic. My household wasn't a dictatorship. There was a reason for everything, which I was always given. I needed a reason. "This is bullsh—"

"Skylar, you will speak to him when it is time. Throwing a tantrum isn't going to change things. Go to sleep."

Screw you! I may not have said it, but the hate-filled glare I cast in his direction said it far better than words could.

Harsh eyes shot back at me. The amused grin disappeared, replaced by a clenched jaw and scowl. "Go to the room or—"

Or what? Are you going to drag me there kicking and screaming? There was a tense, long silence between us. I was seething and he was infuriated.

Something changed. I think his anger tipped just a little too far because he looked like he was working hard to control it. It was obvious he wasn't used to many people defying him, and he wasn't handling it well now. My autonomic nervous system was yelling at me to run. Instinct urged me to get away from the irate wolf, but I refused to listen.

He sighed and spoke in a very calm voice. "Okay. You can speak with him tomorrow morning. Good night." He turned, and with a lot of effort, he walked away.

Did I just win? I thought I had, but as I walked back to the room, I didn't feel victorious. There wasn't an urge to do a chest bump or a fist pump. Ethan had agreed to let me speak with Josh tomorrow, which was what he wanted in the first place. It was a hollow victory. I may have only shortened the time to speak with Josh by a couple of hours or so.

I trudged back to the room only to find Steven sitting in front of the door with a textbook in his hand. He looked up and smiled. I still had a grimace on my face from my encounter with Ethan and couldn't force my face to relax into a smile to greet him.

"Hey Sky ... um, Skylar, how's it going?" he asked in a low drawl before he returned his attention to the book.

"Fine," I muttered.

He looked up again, "Sebastian or Ethan?" he asked with an amused smirk.

"What?"

"Which one did you have your little encounter with? Seems like each time you speak with one of them, you have that look on your face."

"Ethan." I stepped past him to go into the room.

Catching hold of my leg, he said, "You've been in this house four days. You've eaten with us twice. The rest of the time, you've been in this room hiding. You may have to be here a couple more days, so you might as well enjoy the amenities of the house. I can't let you continue to stay in your room like a prisoner. It's inhospitable. Joan will have my neck for it if it continues."

"No, thank you. The room's fine." I shook free of his hold.

"Come on Sky," he urged, rising to his feet. I didn't cringe at him calling me that as I usually did. It was probably because he said it with a slight Southern lilt. A Southern accent always seems to soften the harshest things. Add a pair of dimples, and I just couldn't correct him. Taking my hand, he led me down the hallway. We went down two flights of stairs and a corridor before entering the largest room in the house, the entertainment room. Equipped with a pool table, air hockey, several game consoles, foosball, darts, and a television so large it was as if we were in a movie theater.

"That's practical," I stated derisively, nodding my head toward the television.

"It's an indulgence. Makes sports more interesting and video games unbelievable," he stated enthusiastically.

He slowly turned, waving his hand toward the various things in the room like a game show host. "So what holds your interest?"

Nothing. Can I go now?

He pointed to the video games. I shook my head. Then he pointed to the pool table. I shook it more vigorously. When he pointed to the air hockey, I sighed and agreed. He wasn't going to give up until I decided on something. The dimpled coyote wasn't just being hospitable; he was here to keep me from stalking Josh again.

Fine, I will go along and play your stupid games.

We played five games, of which he won three. Once we finished, I stared at him, bored, wondering when he was going to stop holding me hostage and let me go back to the room. His face lit up as he went to a cabinet and pulled out a chess game. I smiled, which prompted him to set up the board.

"So was this your first kill?" he asked as he studied the board, waiting for me to make a move.

I nodded once.

"The first one is always the hardest. It gets easier," he assured me casually.

I looked up from the board. My eyes widened in horror as

they met his. "I killed someone. I don't want it to get easier. I want to feel bad about taking a life."

"Would you have preferred it be you or Ethan?"

"No," I breathed out.

"Skylar, things will probably get a lot worse before they get better. I don't want you to let things like that get in the way of you doing what is necessary to keep yourself safe."

"Things like murder?" I was astonished. I hadn't gotten to the point of trivializing life.

"Yes, things like murder." His face held a coldness that I wasn't sure he was capable of. For a brief moment, I got a glimpse of what others saw in him before they took their last breath, pure callousness over whether they lived or died. Then he smiled. With that one sweeping act, he quickly shattered the image of the callous killer. Once again, sitting in front of me, was the adorable coyote with the boyish charm.

"I don't want to see you get hurt, Skylar."

"I don't want to get hurt, either. I just need to stay safe without taking another life." I wished my voice didn't pick this time to crack.

He pressed his lips together, holding back whatever he wanted to say. He nodded his head slowly and directed his attention back to the chessboard.

We played several more games of chess, and I agreed to play a couple more games of air hockey, which I won. When I heard the front door close, I looked at Steven with a small knowing smile.

"He's gone. I guess you can stop running interference now."

He laughed. "I was just keeping you busy. You were roaming the house like you needed something to do."

"Why is this Josh guy being so well-protected?"

He was still smiling but it held a different quality to it—more reserved and astute. "It's the information that is being protected, not Josh. We've shared quite a bit of our pack's dynamics with you, and I urge you to practice some level of discretion. What you are allowed to know is censored."

"Even if the information is about me?"

He nodded. "You're an outsider. I am sorry, but that's the way it is. Believe me. Limited information is a good thing. You'll be safer that way." He lingered over the words as if they held special meaning.

He forced a smile. "Good night, Skylar."

"Night."

CHAPTER 5

The next morning, I was reluctant to answer the door, looking at it begrudgingly when it rattled. The sun shone brightly through the window and I looked over at the clock—it was three minutes after seven. Surprisingly, I had slept. I went to bed frustrated and woke up irritated, but at least I had slept. Exhaustion made it difficult not to. The knocking persisted. I rolled my eyes toward the door. "Come in," I mumbled into the covers.

Joan poked her head in and smiled. I sat up and returned the smile.

"Good morning."

"Morning," I responded with half-open eyes. I stretched, then excused myself to shower and brush my teeth. When I returned, she had two plates loaded with pancakes, bacon, fruit, and hash browns. She had already started eating.

"Sorry I started without you but I was starving. I went out for a quick run last night but I wasn't able to hunt. I am famished," she admitted between bites.

"You're not a wolf, are you?" I asked, cutting into my pancakes.

She chuckled at the thought as she shook her head. "Heavens no, I am a jaguar. That's why I didn't run with you all the other night. Felidae and canidae rarely run together. We usually go for speed as opposed to distance. Running with canidae usually just annoys us."

"How long have you been part of the pack?"

"Not very long—fifteen years."

If she had only been a member for fifteen years, what was she doing the other twenty- or thirty-odd years? "Is there an age requirement for joining?"

"No, but you need to be mature enough to understand and obey our laws. Although I believe they are quite reasonable, some were-animals find them difficult to follow. Violation of them has very serious consequences, so it is important that the person is mature enough to fully understand and appreciate them."

"Why did it take you so long to join?" I studied her. Joan didn't seem like the type that needed to live vicariously before settling for a life of rules and structure. There had to be something more that kept her from joining the pack earlier.

She smiled modestly. "I am feline—felidae. We are solitary creatures by nature. Pack life is often more difficult for us, unlike the canidae. They have very little difficulty accepting pack life—it's the nature of their animal. Of course there are always exceptions to all rules." She smiled at me warmly, giving me an understanding look.

"If it's so difficult, then why join?"

She had a look of introspection. "It's like being part of a family. There is a certain level of comfort that comes with being surrounded by your kind—like a family. And like most families, you have members you love and some you downright despise, but in the end, there is an inordinate bond. We are bonded by our animal and it can be"—she searched for the right word—"comforting."

"Is it difficult being part of a pack that seems to be so heavily populated with canidae?" I asked diplomatically. What I wanted to ask is how hard was it to be part of a pack that was heavily populated with wolves that needed to control everybody and everything.

"I am not part of this pack. I'm with the Southern Pack."

"Are you going to become part of this pack?" I wondered why she chose to be around the Midwest Pack if it weren't necessary.

She shook her head a little too enthusiastically. "No. Not at all. My pack would not allow me to petition for membership in this pack nor would Sebastian accept, even if I were interested."

She continued, responding to the curious look I gave her. "I'm the Beta of the Southern Pack. There's only room for one Beta member in each pack. Along with the primary and secondary ranked members, we take on the responsibility of dealing with the pack's safety. It unburdens the Alpha enough to deal with pack incidentals and politics. I assure you that it is a full-time job in itself. But ultimately, everything falls on the Alpha."

"Who's like … um, the Alphas' Alpha? It just seems like there should be someone who oversees everything, including the other Alphas."

She laughed. I liked to hear her laugh. It was such a musical sound, soothing. "We call him 'The Elite,' and it is Sebastian."

Of course, it had to be. That explained his personality and behavior. He held an air of entitlement that hundreds of were-species confirmed and supported. He never had his request or orders challenged. People just followed his demands, no question asked, and apparently, that is what he expected of all who came in contact with him.

"If you aren't petitioning, why are you here?"

"For you. I was sent for you. The Midwest Pack, although the strongest of the packs, sometimes has difficulty dealing with rather delicate situations." She blushed as though she misspoke. "Winter handles most sensitive situations. Contrary to what you have seen, she does have an amicable side. She has always had difficulty dealing with vampires and lone were-animals. Sebastian, being the leader that he is, requested that I be here when you were retrieved," she stated delicately.

As I studied Joan, I couldn't help but admire her subtlety and the sheer grasp she had of tact and diplomacy. I became oddly aware and unexpectedly leery as I considered how dangerous she had to be in order to be the Beta in her pack. Her appearance was quite deceptive. She was average in height with a slender figure and delicate curves you obtain with age. "Dangerous were-animal" didn't come to mind when you looked into her soft welcoming eyes and became charmed by her wide gentle smile. With that in mind, I realized that she, like Steven, might be one of the most dangerous people I had come in contact with since I had been in the house.

"It's a good thing that you are here. I don't think that Ethan or Sebastian like me, and I am pretty sure Winter hates me."

Joan put down her silverware. Her eyes lingered on my face for a brief moment. It was as though she were trying to decide whether she could be blunt or if she needed to handle me with care. Pursing her lips together, she picked up her silverware again. "I can assure you that they don't dislike you. Those in a pack often have a natural disdain for lone were-animals. Ethan and Sebastian are just abrasive. It's just their way, dear. They've been that way for years. Winter loves the pack and often has difficulty dealing with the responsibilities and dangers the pack assumes. She is still young in her position but old to the pack. It's very important to her." Her eyes showed understanding and sympathy as she spoke.

"I'm leaving tonight," she informed me after moments of silence. My heart dropped to my stomach. "I've been away from my pack far too long. I really need to go back. It's quite difficult to know what's going on with my pack seven hundred miles away," she said apologetically to the grim look on my face.

Joan didn't seem to censor herself when she spoke with me. I learned that the Midwest Pack had the most canidae, consisting mostly of wolves, coyotes, and dingos. They also had the largest big cat population: lions, jaguars, and tigers, along with the precious and rare were-snake. Putting "precious" and "Winter" in the same sentence seemed—wrong. It's not that she was the only were-snake in the world—she was just the only one who chose pack life. Most were-snakes and their ilk maintained human form and never gave into their animal, easily conforming to human life. I envied them.

Wolves, along with their relatives, were called by the moon. They were forced, like me, into their animal form during a full moon. Every one hundred and sixteen days or so, when Mercury rises, the felidae are called to answer in the same manner as the canidae are to the moon. Other were-animals like the ursidae and equidae are drawn to transits of Saturn. Cold-blooded were-animals were rare, and knowledge of their existence only occurred in the last fifty years or so. They responded to the lunar eclipse. And as rare as they were, so was their reaction to the eclipse. They were forced into their animal form and unable to return until completion of the eclipse.

"Why aren't you separated? Dogs in one pack and cats in another."

She patted my leg gently. "Don't call us cats and dogs," she warned with a smile. "It's an insult. We aren't animals in that same sense of those found in nature. We aren't bonded by our species but by the fact that we are were-animals. It doesn't matter who's the strongest wolf, jaguar, coyote, tiger, bear, or whatever animal form you take. It is all about who's the strongest—period. That is what makes us a resilient and commanding force."

. . .

I was able to control the urge to ask Joan to stay as she escorted me into a small room on the other side of the library. It was one of the locked rooms that I had passed that night during my self-guided tour of the house. I stood, anxiously awaiting Josh's arrival, surrounded by antique white walls in a room inundated by the scent of lavender. I inhaled again. Blood hadn't been spilled in this room. Two overstuffed, soft gray sofas were placed at each side of the room. Framed artwork of tranquil nature scenes—the sun setting, birds flying through a clear sky, a deer drinking from a river surrounded by mountains—decorated the walls. The light gray and silver panel curtains were open slightly, allowing rays from the sun to trickle in. The room seemed to have a calming effect, and I figured that was the point. It made me wonder why they wanted me to feel comfortable meeting this Josh.

Ethan entered the room, his face as usual displaying a hardened mask, making whatever was on his mind hard to read. Close behind him was a slightly younger man. His caramel-colored hair was a chaotic mess. He looked like he literally rolled out of bed, but with today's styles, it probably took him hours to perfect. A strong jawline and rugged good looks were accentuated by a five o'clock shadow. He gazed back at me with scenic ocean-blue eyes. Someone could easily drown in them, and with the level of confidence that graced his face, he knew it. I was sure he'd probably used it far too often to his advantage.

He wore a black graphic t-shirt, tattered jeans, and a small hoop earring in each ear. I counted at least six visible tattoos, which were poorly hidden by his t-shirt. A slight smirk covered his face as he strolled into the room, his thumbs hooked in the pockets of his jeans.

When he stopped directly in front of me, I gave him a passing look before looking at Ethan. I looked back at Josh, did another assessment, and then directed my attention back to Ethan.

This can't be the guy they're getting their information from. He wasn't what I expected at all. I expected someone older and more reserved with the ability to give off Yoda-like wisdom. Yoda he was not. In fact, he seemed like the type of person who would be the best source of information about the local bars, while maintaining his status as the beer-pong champ at the neighborhood's dive. Yet, here stood Sebastian's source. The very person for whom, on his word alone, Sebastian risked the life and safety of his pack to help me. My trust in the pack wavered.

He stepped closer to me, interrupting my thoughts. His lips changed from a wayward smile to a wide grin as though someone had said something amusing.

Oh crap, can he read my mind? I quickly switched my thoughts to the weather.

"The woman of my dreams," he stated smoothly, stepping even closer to me.

Woman of his dreams? Who is he kidding? Attractive I might be, and some men have found me appealing. I always considered my looks exotic, but "not quite beautiful." My adopted mother deduced that my mother was Portuguese or Brazilian but she wasn't sure of my ethnicity. I was a mishmash of very distinctive features that led to people always commenting on my exotic appearance. It was funny how exotic could mean really anything, but not necessarily pretty.

When I was younger, I sat at the mirror for hours staring into my olive-toned oval face, trying to pinpoint where my features went astray: dark green eyes, slight indistinctive nose, deep-set cheekbones, and supple full lips that made me wonder why women paid money to have such lips. My hair was a mahogany sea of waves that I forced into submission with relaxers and an arsenal of straightening aids. Between my wolf genes, sparse workouts, and daily five-mile jogs, my five-eight frame had found a comfortable place between shapely and athletic. *Attractive, I will give anyone that. But dream-worthy? I will just have to call it for what it is—bull.*

Josh stood so uncomfortably close that I had to take a couple of steps back. When I moved, he stepped even closer. "May I?" he asked as he touched my face before I could respond. His finger brushed along my temples before his right thumb gently brushed along the edge of my jaw.

"So you're the little lady who's been causing the big uproar," he remarked, amused.

"Are you getting anything?" Ethan finally asked impatiently, as Josh continued to fidget with my face for an unusually long time.

Josh rolled his eyes, sighed, and shook his head slowly. "How many times do I have to tell you that I don't get visions from touch? They come to me in my dreams. I was just taking this opportunity to play with the beauty from my dreams." He returned his attention back to me. He winked at me, and I took several big steps away from him.

Ethan huffed out something that I missed before heading out of the room.

Hey, don't leave me with this touchy freak.

Before Ethan could make it to the door, Josh demanded "Stay," as he moved his lips slowly, his eyes moving slightly down and to the right. The door slammed closed in front of Ethan.

Ethan looked more annoyed than impressed. "Oh look, cute magic tricks. I didn't realize the circus was in town."

"I probably can make a clown appear. Would you like that?" he asked in a light, amused voice.

"Well, if that's the best you can do, I think I will have to pass. Perhaps Skylar will find your performance amusing," Ethan griped back before he left, slamming the door behind him.

Josh chuckled as he directed his attention back to me. "Please excuse my brother. Although our parents went through great lengths to raise us well, he still behaves as though he had been raised by a pack of natural wolves." He grinned.

Brother? If the similarities went further than the good looks, I was not looking forward to talking to the pack's source.

Josh turned to face me, smiled, and took a seat on one of the oversized sofas. He patted the area next to him, motioning for me have a seat. Hesitating for a long while, I eventually sat at the far end. With an impish smile, he inched closer to me.

I looked up at him, scrutinizing his every move, trying to figure out what skills he possessed that warranted the pack's unwavering trust. "What are you?" I asked directly.

He continued to smile but never offered an answer.

"Are you psychic?"

He shook his head.

"Mage? Fae? Elf?" I remembered that when I looked up werewolves and vampires, they seemed to come up quite a bit, as well. Where there were werewolves, vampires were somewhere in the picture, and whenever there was chaos and magic, there seemed to be mages, fae, and elves present.

"No to all three. Do you really want to play the guessing game? We could be here all day, not that I would mind."

Tilting my head, I continued to study him. He was quite nice-looking, which made me think he was possibly something not so nice. "Are you some type of demon?" That would explain his magic and psychic ability.

"Do I look like a demon to you?" he asked with an amused grin.

"I don't know. Ethan doesn't look like a wolf, and the people who attacked us didn't look like vampires. I'm just fishing for ideas at this point." I was getting a little annoyed with the guessing game. "I don't believe demons exist."

"Really, the werewolf doesn't believe demons are real. I assure you they are quite real as well as their variant subspecies, but I am not one." He seemed to be enjoying this little game of questions. He was right. We could be here all day, which I didn't want.

"Honestly, until a couple of days ago, I couldn't imagine there were more than just a few werewolves in the world, let alone were-animals. And the mere fact that there are enough to create a pack is still inconceivable. So, at the risk of maintaining a certain level of naiveté in my life, I'm limiting the supernatural world to were-animals and vampires. But I am sure you are about to shatter that misconception. What are you?"

He stood, pulling me up and into him. His eyes paled along with his coloring, and for a brief moment, we were outside in the yard and then back in the house in the same spots. My hands clamped onto my head as I took a seat and waited for the room to stop spinning.

"Sorry. Just showing off. I'm a warlock."

"A guy witch?" I blurted incredulously, as the room eventually mellowed to a slow turn.

"Yeah, a guy witch," he repeated with a chuckle.

"Are you a were-animal, as well?"

He shook his head.

"But Ethan's your brother?"

He nodded. "He's my half-brother. His father was a werewolf. My father was just human. Our mother was a witch."

"You're the one who notified the Midwest Pack about me and the vampires. Are you going to tell me why they are suddenly interested in me?"

"Several months ago, a fae gave me a dream."

"Excuse me?"

"I was given a dream," he stated with a hint of a smile. I couldn't quite figure this Josh guy out. He was awfully forthcoming with information, but I wasn't sure how reliable it was. His face stayed fixed between a boyish grin and a smirk, making me wonder if he were having fun at my expense.

"In a gift bag or a box?"

He laughed but ended it abruptly. “Neither. Fae typically keep their distance from were-animals and vampires. They don’t particularly like them. The magic that allows vampires and were-animals to exist makes them wary. Through the years, the were-animals have managed to gain favor with some, but they still keep their distance, if at all possible. She approached me, concerned about your existence. ‘A lone wolf will stir the vampires and damage the pack,’ she informed me. She wouldn’t offer anything more than that. Eventually, I persuaded her to give me the dream, relieving her of the nightmares that haunted her to the point that she sought me out. I received them as they were relayed to her, in bits and pieces. It was enough information to cause alarm but not enough to provide adequate answers.”

His charming grin disappeared. “You started playing starring roles in my dreams where your fear-stricken face would pop up and all I could feel was your pain. When Demetrius made his grand appearance, it was then I knew things could only get worse from there. That is when I contacted Sebastian to watch you. Once Demetrius sent members of his Legion to your house, we actively intervened. I doubt we would have been successful in retrieving you if we had just showed up at your house and said ‘Hey, we have reason to believe that vampires are after you. Come stay with us until we find out why.’ I hear you were reluctant to agree to our help, even after the attack.”

“Can the fae help?”

He frowned. “She made it very clear that her hands are washed of this. I was told to count myself lucky that a debt wasn’t incurred.”

“Some gift—cryptic messages and puzzle-like images,” I muttered with an irritated sigh. “So the vampires want me, and somehow it will lead to hurting the pack.” *How could the vampires use me to hurt the pack?*

He took in several slow, controlled breaths, choosing his

words very carefully. "No, whatever it is, it will adversely affect the pack. That could entail numerous things."

"Like what?"

He leaned against the wall, withdrawing into himself. An uncomfortable silence filled the air. *There goes that damn censorship.*

Walking over to the window, I stared out into the thick woods behind the house as I subdued the rising fear in my stomach. He wasn't nearly as much help as I had wished.

"If this is all you have, then why did they keep you so protected? With the limited information you gave me, you could have put it on a Post-it and placed it on my door," I stated, flustered. I snapped my mouth closed before anything else rude came out. I turned to face the warlock, who still managed to maintain a pleasant smile, despite my impoliteness. I sighed heavily. "I apologize for being so rude. I've been in this house for five days waiting for you, and I don't have any more information regarding the vampires' interest in me. I'm frustrated."

"Any other time I would have had more information. I've spent the last month gathering the little that I do have. Whether out of fear or obligation, the vampires have many who are committed to protecting their interests. Getting the limited information that I do have was a chore, and I assure you, I can be quite persuasive when necessary." He smiled mischievously. I didn't doubt that one bit. With his relaxed demeanor, good looks, and welcoming smile, I was sure that when needed, he was quite charming and persuasive. The fact that he was Ethan's brother and closely linked to the Midwest Pack meant he was probably quite dangerous, as well. It didn't seem like a weak, genteel person would last long around here.

"Sebastian wasn't sure whether it was a good idea for me to meet you until I was better informed. From what I hear, you are not the most trusting person and prone to reckless behavior. He thought you would run again." He glanced up in my direction and raised a brow. "You don't plan on running again?"

"I have a feeling if I did, I wouldn't get far," I admitted.

"That's not a 'no.'"

"No." I hoped he couldn't detect a lie. Truthfully, if I thought I could run and stay hidden from the were-animals and the vamps, I probably would.

He stood next to me and stared until I looked in his direction. "Now that you are here, getting information will be much easier," he assured me. I wasn't sure why, but I trusted him. Perhaps it was because he was my last hope. The pack inexplicably trusted him, and I felt compelled to do so, as well.

Josh worked pretty fast. The next day we were on a plane headed south to meet with a source. We flew into the Savannah airport and drove eighty miles to our destination. I sat in the backseat of a rental car behind a coyote and next to a warlock, with a Beta wolf driving who had control issues that extended further than the pack's domain. The snarky, mean-spirited exchanges between the brothers kept me aptly entertained as I experienced the ugly side of siblinghood that they didn't show on television during prime-time hours. I'm sure they loved each other. After all, they were brothers. But whether they liked each other was in question. The two opposite personalities might complement each other in certain aspects, but on a road trip, it did nothing of the sort. By the end of the trip, I had had my fill of Josh complaining about Ethan's speeding and treatment of speed limits as a mere suggestion and Ethan threatening to leave Josh on the side of the road because he kept using magic to control the car's speed. We pulled up in front of a white ranch-style house surrounded by a wraparound porch. A slender man with cocoa-colored hair and large dark brown eyes walked toward the car, his lips curled into the most welcoming smile: genial, warm, exposing perfect white teeth. He was pleasant and the very epitome of Southern charm. As he sauntered down the driveway to meet us, he seemed relaxed until Ethan stepped out of the car. The smile vanished, the muscles along his neck and face became rigid cords as his lips pressed firmly together. Hesitating briefly, he ushered a fake smile and continued toward us.

"Ethan," he greeted in a neutral voice.

"Owen," Ethan responded in a cool, distilled voice.

Owen opened my door. "Welcome, Skylar. I'm Owen, the pack's host." He had a distinctive Southern drawl. His smile was contagious. I couldn't help but return it as he helped me out of the car. He quickly shook my hand before taking my bag. He acknowledged Josh and Steven with a quick nod and handshake and directed us into his home.

We followed him into the house. Ethan walked slowly behind us, assessing the surrounding area almost compulsively. It must be annoying to feel the need to neurotically study everything for threats, even when the probability of any was less than zero. We were in Joan's territory. She had set up the host, made all the arrangements, and yet Ethan walked through the modest ranch house looking for potential threats. He looked through the large bay windows to the back only to find a small vegetable garden, a solitary peach tree in the far-off distance, and acres and acres of unused land. He continued walking through, opening doors and checking windows as he performed a thorough security sweep. When he was finished, Owen tried—unconvincingly—not to look annoyed.

"I didn't realize there were going to be so many." Owen's gaze swept over each of us and landed on Ethan. "Perhaps you can wolf it tonight," he suggested to him.

Ethan chuckled, a dark, abrupt sound. "I don't think that would be a good idea. I hear you have some very motivated hunters here. But thanks for the suggestion."

Owen's lips pressed together into a thin line. "It's going to be crowded. There are a couple hotels about sixty-five miles away. I wouldn't be offended if you decided to stay elsewhere." The nice tone of his suggestion didn't match the looming glare he gave Ethan.

Ethan was about to respond with something that I'm sure was impolite, if not plain outright cruel, when Josh spoke up. "We'll make do. The accommodations here will be just fine," he interjected, dividing his attention between Owen and Ethan. His tone gently persuaded them to play nice. "Thank you for offering your home so that we can stay close to our destination."

Owen flashed a smile. "I am going to sleep in my office. Skylar, you will take my room, and there are two spare rooms. You guys sort out who gets the floor," he said, leading us to the rooms.

"I don't want to inconvenience you. You stay in your room. I will sleep on the sofa," I offered.

"I will have no such thing. That's not the way a Southerner treats his guest, especially a beautiful woman such as yourself."

I wondered how much of that slow rhythmic drawl was real. Ethan muttered a curse under his breath, and a gratified smile covered Owens's face. He showed them to the spare rooms first, then me to his room.

"Wow!" I breathed out in complete awe as I entered the room. My attention was captured by the mural of a lion walking out of the tall, thick grass. The realism of the picture was uncanny and strangely intriguing—captivating. Unlike the other rooms, which were painted a neutral khaki, this room was colored in deep greens and light browns, drawing you into the feeling of being in a savannah where the lion could openly roam.

"Were-lion, I presume." I twisted to look at him. He was staring at the wall as though he were seeing it for the first time as well.

"It's my best work," he admitted.

"It is absolutely beautiful." Stepping closer, I touched it. My fingers traced along the outline of the lion's eyes. "This isn't you in the painting."

He looked surprised. "No, it's a true animal. How did you know?"

I could feel his eyes on me as I looked at the mural.

"I just knew." I shrugged. The lion in the picture looked content as though he recently had mated or finished a kill. Owen's eyes didn't possess the same level of satisfaction. He was yearning for something. His eyes were distant and longing. His face puckered in dissatisfaction when he wasn't pretending to be happy.

"You're an artist?"

"An artist at heart and an accountant by trade," he admitted in a mellow voice. I should have known he held some auxiliary position in the pack. The way he greeted and interacted with Ethan indicated that they held the same pack position. Within the various packs, lower-ranked members showed some form of deference to the higher-ranking. They wouldn't make eye contact for more than a few seconds and they bowed their heads slightly upon greeting. It wasn't in the same manner one would greet a member of the royal family, but it wasn't far off. It was one of the more unpleasant things I noticed of pack life. The exceptions to that rule were those who held auxiliary positions, such as pack physician, financial consultant, attorney, and educator.

Ethan stood silently at the doorway. Josh, not too far behind.

Owen turned to face Ethan. "Is there something you need?" he asked in an icy tone.

"Interesting picture. You seem to have a lot of free time since you transferred from our pack," Ethan stated in a level voice.

"You'll be surprised how much you can accomplish when

you're not dealing with political BS and trivial pack responsibilities." He matched Ethan's tone with unassuming hostility.

Ethan dropped all pretenses of nicety. "Yes, it can be burdensome being the strongest pack in the country. It's not a responsibility that just anyone can handle."

That rattled Owen, and he was having a difficult time hiding it. His fists balled tight as he stepped toward Ethan.

Josh moved between them quickly. "It's been a long day for all of us. We should get some sleep. Ethan, you have to meet Joan's contact tomorrow and it's a pretty long drive. We have a ferry to catch. It's a good idea that we get some shut-eye. Now," he suggested in a firm, calm voice.

Josh's intervention gave Owen time to calm down and an obstacle that kept Ethan from getting to Owen. But the hostility between them was so thick it was palpable.

Ethan backed out of the room but stopped short. "Skylar, I'm right next door if you need anything."

Why the hell do I care? I was more likely to call Steven, Josh, or maybe even Owen before I called him.

"Okay." I wished they both would leave and do their primitive posturing elsewhere.

Owen snorted. "She's just as safe here as she would be in the retreat home in Illinois."

"I just wanted her to know I was close. After all, that is my job as the Beta," Ethan stated sharply before he walked out of the room.

Both Owen and I stared at Ethan's back as he left. I looked at Owen and was about to ask if he had challenged Ethan for his position and lost, but decided against it. If I were right, I was sure it wasn't something he wanted to discuss.

"Is there anything you need before you retire?" His Southern charm was turned on to extra-high.

I shook my head.

He smiled and said, "Have a good night." But he didn't move.

Instead, he stood gawking at me with a weird look on his face. It made me uncomfortable, and I didn't know how to politely ask him to leave *his* room.

"Sleep well," he finally whispered before he walked out of the room.

I took out the t-shirt and sweats that I had brought to sleep in when Owen knocked. Opening the door slowly, he poked his head in cautiously. "I hope this isn't too forward but I would like to photograph you. I paint from photos. I think you would be perfect for my next project."

The camera was in his hand, so declining wasn't really an option.

"I look terrible. I've been traveling for hours, my hair's a mess, and I haven't had a good night's sleep in days," I pleaded, hoping to discourage him.

"I don't want it for the aesthetics. . . . I could hire a model for that. There's something about you that I hope to capture. Please," he persisted.

I nodded once and stood in the most natural pose I could manage.

"Don't pose. Just stand there," he instructed as he adjusted the lens. "Now, say *death*."

I flinched, wondering if I'd heard him correctly. He smiled as he watched my reaction, taking several shots.

"Did I make you uneasy?" he asked as he continued to snap shots.

"No … no, I'm fine. It was just odd." *Odd is an understatement.*

"That word seems to bring out so much more in people: hate, sorrow, introspection, anger."

He continued snapping pictures and didn't seem like he was going to stop anytime soon. I took several sidesteps, moving out of his line of sight.

"I think you have enough pictures." I made an attempt to

sound both firm and polite. I wasn't sure if I quite pulled it off, but he stopped abruptly and gave me a forced smile.

"You have beautiful eyes." He raised the camera slightly and took another picture.

"Yes, they are," I heard Josh say as he leaned against the doorframe. I looked up, but Owen didn't move from his position or acknowledge Josh's presence. "We have to leave tomorrow at six," he informed me. Josh smiled when I gave him an appreciative look for offering a viable interruption to this weirdness.

I nodded. "I really should get some sleep," I stated politely to Owen, who still seemed to be oddly fascinated with me. It wasn't a physical attraction—I was sure of that. It was an odd form of curiosity that left me baffled. "Good night," I said firmly.

His lips tightened as he worked at a smile. "Night."

I closed the door firmly behind him, then leaned against it listening until I heard his footsteps down the hall.

Josh, Steven, and I boarded an empty ferry that would take us from the mainland to a small island nearby. It was fall in the Midwest and it was getting cold. Too bad no one let the people below the Mason-Dixon line know. I wore a small jacket over a thin shirt, something not thought of during late fall. I finally asked where we were going as we sailed across the murky river to the unknown small island. We inched farther from the beauty: large magnolia trees, blossoming flowers, and trees that bore the very best thing about Georgia—peaches.

"Sapelo Island," said Josh.

That didn't tell me much, especially since I was expecting us to stay on the mainland, preferably Atlanta. I wondered if sources ever lived in large cities or if we would always be traveling off somewhere to a land where man was either forgotten or barely acknowledged. "And who are we meeting?"

"A dream guide. When I have my visions, I can only see you, Demetrius, and the Seethe. So many pieces are missing, and if he's as good as rumored, he will help me put them together."

Josh seemed more than hopeful. There was a sense of desperation, as if this might be his final hope. He wore it so casually, displaying a level of confidence under pressure that made me a little envious.

The ferry docked at this little island, located on the far southern end of Georgia. It was a beautiful piece of land that at one time served as a plantation. Despite its distasteful history, it maintained its historic simplicity and charm with the help of the government and the locals. The island population consisted of less than a hundred. The ferry was more like a time machine, taking you back to an era of small towns, nature, and pre-industrialization. It was nature in its most simplistic and basic form.

Instead of a grocery store chain, they had a neighborhood market. There were two small churches adjacent to each other that previously were segregated but now were divided by denomination. A small gas station was within walking distance of the library, which was run by the locals on a volunteer basis. I didn't see a tower for cable, and both Josh and Steven seemed put off by the fact that they didn't have cell phone service.

We treaded through the marshland as bugs had dinner at our expense. We eventually came to a small blue house in the middle of the woods. Surrounded by trees and plants, there wasn't another house for miles.

Josh listened at the door for a moment, then knocked. He waited for several more minutes and knocked again when no one answered. Someone was home; I could hear movement. We walked around the house, and sitting on the porch was an elderly man. Deep creases from age and years of sun exposure ran along his creamy mocha forehead. He acknowledged our presence with a frown. A pair of mismatched eyes, one deep gray and the other cloudy topaz, did an excellent job of making us feel unwelcome.

When he stood up, his tall ragged appearance was intimidating—well, to me anyway. Steven and Josh seemed unaffected. "Thomas, I am Josh and these are my associates. I need your help," Josh stated directly.

Thomas looked at Josh intensely but made no effort to acknowledge Steven or me.

"I apologize for just showing up without calling. However, I had no way of contacting you. Based on your reputation, you are someone I need to talk to." Josh gave a small overtly friendly smile. His charms were wasted on Thomas, who continued to look perturbed by his presence.

Josh walked toward Thomas. Steven took my arm to stop my approach. Josh was less than a foot from Thomas when he was brought to his knees by some unknown force. Thomas's eyes glazed over as Josh struggled to breathe. His face paled, lips turned a horrid shade of blue. Then his eyes went blank. Thomas was doing this to Josh. My body tensed and adrenaline took over all logic. I headed for Josh, but Steven pulled me closer to him.

"Skylar, don't," he stated firmly near my ear.

"He's hurting him." I kept my eyes on Josh as he continued to struggle for breath.

"I know." He seemed unaffected by the situation.

"We have to help him!" Steven's grip tightened as I twisted my arm, trying to loosen from his grasp when he didn't make an effort to assist Josh.

"We can't," he said firmly. Josh struggled for breath. Then, in a swift movement, he was thrown back several feet, landing on his back. He was in reaching distance. When I tried to move toward him, Steven stilled me again. Josh's eyes were bloodshot, and deep blue vessels became apparent on his sickly pale skin.

I twisted against Steven, urging him to help. Instead, he focused on the area behind the house, intentionally ignoring the assault taking place in front of us. Thomas was hurting Josh and I had to stand there as an unwilling spectator. Suddenly, Josh waved his hand in front of him, and Thomas was thrown back against the house. A murky mist formed over his head and covered him.

"That's enough of that," Josh stated, standing up and gaining his composure before he walked over to Thomas, who was now in a trancelike state. Some color had returned to Josh's face and his eyes were back to normal. Once he was close to Thomas, he waved his hands again, bringing him back. Thomas shook for a few moments, ridding himself of the residual effects of the magic.

Thomas nodded his head to Josh, but I couldn't tell if it were concession or reverence. "How may I help you?" he asked in a deep rough voice.

"I need you as a guide," Josh informed him.

"Please, come in." He opened the door. I was reluctant to proceed. If that were a typical dream guide greeting, I wasn't sure we could take any more of his hospitality.

"I've had dreams and she's in them. She's in trouble but I can't see much more," Josh added as we walked into the house.

Thomas stepped closer and tried to touch me. I sidestepped and moved out of reach. He smirked and returned his attention to Josh.

"She can stay with the coyote. Her presence is strong. She doesn't need to be with us for the journey." Josh followed him out of the room.

"I don't mind coming with him," I offered. I didn't like the idea of Josh being alone with Thomas if he decided to treat him to another one of his welcomes, although I was confident he could handle himself if he did.

Josh turned around to look at me. "It'll be fine. He's done playing his little games."

I looked at him skeptically, wishing I had the ability to detect a lie.

He bit back a smile. "I give you my word."

I nodded once and reluctantly stayed put, feeling as if I had been unknowingly dropped into a foreign land where everyone expected me to know the norms and customs. Placed into a world where violence and hostile posturing were typical, almost expected, I didn't know how to adapt and wasn't sure I wanted to.

I paced the small room, which was illuminated only by the natural light from the small window in the center of the wall. The veneer bookshelves took up most of the wall space in the room. They were filled with books, mostly mystical and a few historical. Three small consoles were laid out throughout the room, covered with statues and figures. I wasn't sure what religion he subscribed to, but candles surrounded the figures along with a few ornate talismans. The pungent scent of incense filled the room. After pacing the floor for twenty minutes throughout every inch of the area, I took a seat on the sofa next to Steven, who looked bored out of his mind.

Steven eventually occupied himself by walking through the room, picking up, playing with, and occasionally sniffing some of the many talismans on the tables.

"You're going to turn yourself into a frog," I quipped when an odd-looking statue piqued his interest. He smiled, walked back, and sank into the narrow, worn sofa.

"You weren't born a were-coyote, were you?" I asked after we had sat on the sofa for nearly an hour in silence. Something about him was different: less instinctual, more learned behavior.

His lips pressed together, and his jaw became painfully taut.

When he finally looked at me, his face held the look of suppressed pain and grief. His mood turned morose.

"I am sorry. Sometimes I'm too damned nosy. Your past is none of my business." I was angry with myself for prying.

He made an attempt at a smile. Taking a deep breath, he spoke with a voice that was light and mournful. "My parents died in a car accident when I was a young child. My sister, eleven years older than me, took on the task of raising me. The insurance money took care of most of our basic financial needs, but she took on the role as mother so well. It was amazing how she went to college while working diligently to keep my life together as though my mother were still alive. I still went to summer camps, Boy Scouts, tae kwon do, and soccer. She cooked … real meals, not the crap out of a box, the same way our mother did."

He stopped briefly, taking a moment before exhaling a long ragged breath and continuing. "I was nine when my sister suddenly seemed on edge all the time. She believed someone was stalking her. We never saw anyone but she knew he was there and I believed her. Then one morning, she woke up with a bruise on her neck, which we later discovered was a vampire marking. He played with her like this for weeks." Grief lingered over his last words, and I felt his sorrow. He was quiet for a long moment as he composed himself. "She was being stalked by a vampire who had become captivated by her. He never made his presence known, except for the bite marks he left as gifts of his visit. He attacked her when he was finally overtaken by lust. I walked in on him during his attack and managed to kill him."

"You killed a vampire at nine?" I asked, shocked.

He nodded. "If he weren't so distracted with my sister, I might not have been able to, but I was terribly injured. It was Joan who found me and took me to the pack."

"But you're a coyote. If she turned you, why aren't you a jaguar?"

"She didn't turn me. Their third did. Jaguars, like most felines, prefer a solitary life. Many of them do not choose pack life. With everything I had been through, she thought I would choose to be alone, refusing to establish bonds with anyone. She wanted me to survive the change but also accept the pack as my new family. I was so badly injured that I would not have survived a wolf transition, so a coyote was the next best thing. Joan raised me, and I was part of the Southern Pack until I transferred to the Midwest Pack." He smiled as he thought of Joan and her convoluted plan to give him something he'd lost—a family.

I wanted to hug him, but I wasn't sure how he would respond. The pack seemed to have an odd thing about emotions. Instead, I rested my hand lightly on his leg. Eventually, his hand covered mine.

When Josh walked out of the room nearly three hours later, he looked uneasy. His bruising from his earlier altercation with Thomas had darkened, and he looked distant and deep in thought. "Your help will not be forgotten. Please feel free to call upon me if needed," he told Thomas before walking out of the house.

He left the house, obviously disappointed, while Steven and I rushed out behind him. Long, swift strides made his gait look more like a slow run.

"Was he able to help?" I asked, nearly running to keep pace with him.

He stopped brusquely and shook his head. "Not as much as I would have liked." He continued to walk toward the ferry.

I stopped abruptly, disappointed. We had come all this way and we were no better off.

"Skylar, we have far more information than before." He handed me a sketch.

"What is it?" I took the picture and examined it, turning it to look at it from different angles. It was a poorly drawn stone with a series of rings surrounding it.

"At this point, your guess would be as good as mine," he breathed out, frustrated. "Demetrius had it on in the dreams. It's newly acquired, and I am willing to bet it's the reason for his newfound interest in you. I just don't know what it is or what it's used for."

I stared at the picture, hoping it would jar my memory, but I had never seen anything similar to it. During the long walk back to the ferry, I stared at the picture, burning it into my memory. If needed, I could describe it and identify it with ease.

"What happened between you and Thomas? Why did he try to kill you and then help you?" I finally asked as we approached the sycamore-lined bank of the river near the ferry landing.

"He wasn't trying to kill me. It's a warlock thing."

"It's their silly pissing contest," Steven offered lightly behind us with a grin.

"Oh, you mean like the dominance stares. That's nothing but a pissing contest at the most primitive level." Josh gave him a glare.

Josh sat under a large sycamore and I sat in front of him, playing with the grass. "I guess you're the dominant warlock?" I asked, looking up from the grass that I had shredded into small confetti.

"I'm always the most dominant warlock." For something that should have given him bragging rights, he didn't sound very happy about it.

"Are you an Alpha warlock?"

He shook his head. "We don't have Alphas. It's based on magical levels, ranked from five to one. Level fives are the lowest level, which most don't consider worth mentioning. Their skills are no better than a cruise-ship magician's. Your level is often determined after training but most of us don't go through the testing. It's long, tedious, and rather unnecessary.

With witchcraft, you often know your level based on your skills and the magic you can perform. I'm a level one. With the exception of the Creed, the witches who govern us and are also responsible for training, I only know of ten other level ones."

He was looking out toward the water, his voice impassive as he spoke. I couldn't determine if he considered his abilities a gift or a burden. "Witches' gifts are passed upon death to their oldest child. Ethan should have inherited them, but because of the wolf magic, he couldn't. So I got it." He looked over and smiled, but he seemed so preoccupied with his thoughts that it came off as insincere, forced. "It's a lot of responsibility." A hand rustled in his hair as his thoughts drifted off somewhere. Perhaps he was imagining life without such responsibilities. He suddenly snapped out of whatever held his thought, his lips twisting into a smile that could bring a blush to most women's cheeks.

"If you are a stronger warlock, then why did Thomas attack you?" I asked, walking toward the ferry as it docked.

"It's a rather archaic practice by some older witches. When a favor is requested from a lower-level witch to a higher-level, it can be declined. If accepted, a very high debt is incurred. In this world, debts can be lethal. But a favor from a higher-level witch to a lower is rarely turned down. It is in their best interest to curry favor with them. He was just testing me to see who was stronger. He's a level two. I doubt he imagined I would be higher."

"They are quite a pair," Owen finally offered as I leaned against the pillar of his home, watching Josh and Ethan. They were too far away for me to hear what they were talking about, but Ethan looked engrossed and neither bothered to hide their frustration with the results of today's visit.

Owen had been behind me, quietly observing them as well. I

glanced over my shoulder to look at him. As I suspected, he was preoccupied with them—or rather, Ethan. Narrow penetrating eyes studied him. Owen stepped closer to me. "You'll be safe with them. Josh will work diligently not only to continue proving himself to the pack but also to impress his brother. Ethan's arrogance won't allow him to fail."

What's Owen, the narrator? I had become familiar with Ethan's and Josh's personalities and the dynamics of the house. I didn't need his play-by-play analysis. Besides, he seemed more interested in what was going on between them than I did. "What's your problem with Ethan?" I asked, turning to face him.

Stunned by my assessment, he smiled. I doubt it was possible to curve your lips into something less sincere. "My dear, I don't have any problems with Ethan. I hold him among the few that I admire." His very pronounced Southern drawl made his words sound wholesome and sweet. He was lying. I didn't have a basis for confirming it, but I just knew.

When Ethan walked toward us, the look on Owen's face didn't allude to anything that could remotely be perceived as admiration. It held disdain—utter, impenitent disdain. "We are leaving tonight," he informed me. Steven and Josh had driven away just minutes before.

"Where are they going?" Owen asked.

"He's going to meet with someone." He walked past us.

"Who?"

Ethan shrugged. "Don't know." His obvious disregard and blatant lying were anything but subtle.

"It's not typical for a Beta not to know what's going on in his pack," Owen's acrid voice stated.

"It's not typical for one who isn't one to care so much," Ethan lashed back in a tone so razor sharp, I felt the slashes.

Standing between the hostile were-animals, I absorbed the tension, wishing I knew the cause. As Ethan guided me toward the door, I could feel Owen's eyes stabbing him.

. . .

Josh and Steven returned nearly three hours later, and it was a good thing because there was so much testosterone flooding the house between Owen and Ethan, it was only a matter of time before they decided to do something about it.

I grilled Josh on the way back to the airport about what he found out. He seemed frustrated as I interrogated him. Finally, he admitted that his other source was unhelpful. But he said it with such ire that I knew they *chose* not to be helpful.

CHAPTER 6

Less than an hour after returning to the house from Georgia, I had showered, eaten, and was surfing the Web in an effort not to fixate on our trip, which I considered a useless endeavor. The only things that came of it were a picture of an object that none of us could identify, the knowledge that the people who disliked Ethan spanned farther than this side of the country, and the fact that warlocks' interactions entailed the same silly primitive posturing as that of were-animals.

Tired of feeling like I was wading in my shallow pool of knowledge, I decided to do something about it. I knew were-animals existed but because of their censoring, I knew little about them. The VAMPIRE logs made me well-versed on the psychopaths and degenerates of the group, but I knew very little of typical vampires—if there were such things.

There wasn't much information on the mainstream sites about vampires and were-animals, but there were plenty on the nuts-r-us sites, blogs, and forums dedicated to people with undiagnosed psychoses that led them to believe they were vampires. They would drink blood, participate in indiscreet sexual behavior, and favor the nightlife over daylight. They had screen names like “vampdaddy,” “vampgirl,” and “creature of the damned,” and their screen pictures were often Goth-influenced, with obvious prosthetic fangs. With each site, I found myself rolling my eyes and wishing they would meet a real vampire. That would surely cure their romanticizing of the creatures.

Other sites were dedicated to the idiots who claimed to be werewolves and attributed their asinine behavior to being “moon-called” as the animal within fought to escape. *Oh, brother!* There wasn’t any real information on were-animals. After hours of reading through tons of articles and blogs, I had gathered the same amount of information I would have from watching *Buffy the Vampire Slayer*, *Angel*, or *True Blood*.

Warlock and *mage* were often used interchangeably, but based on what Josh had told me, what I had, and what I had read, they were vastly different. Mages were limited to defensive magic and spells. Though some mages’ skills were better than others’, they didn’t seem to be as strong as witches and warlocks. Because of witches’ inherent gifts, they didn’t require the use of incantations or talismans to perform basic magic and were able to do both offensive and defensive magic and spells.

“I need help,” Josh admitted, knocking on the door as he entered. I snapped the laptop closed before he could see what I was looking at. I felt guilty as though I were spying on them. He grinned as if he knew what I was doing. Nothing in my research revealed that witches had the gift of telepathy; however, Josh was a lot more intuitive than anyone I ever met before. “What do you need?”

“An extra set of eyes.” He linked his fingers through mine and led me through the house to the library. Josh laid the picture between us as we sat at the conference table. “I can’t find out what it does because I have no idea what it is,” he admitted as the shadow of frustration shone through his typically relaxed demeanor.

Sprawled across the table were several books on witchcraft; the dark arts; and Greek, Nordic, Paleo-Balkan, and Etruscan mythology. The selection was joined by another stack of books with foreign titles that I had seen on my first day in the retreat.

"We are just looking for objects, symbols, and articles of power," he explained. "I just need to find the one I saw in my dreams."

The warlock with the disheveled hair, worn jeans, and graphic t-shirt looked out of place, surrounded by the odd books. He had changed his earrings from hoops to small studs. His appearance was something most men couldn't pull off. Wearing his confidence and charm as casually as his t-shirt, he made the reckless abandonment of the conservative style sexy. Josh was a refreshing escape in a place stifled by structure and rules.

He slid several books toward me. "Go through them and look for anything that resembles this sketch. Even if it barely looks like it, still let me see it."

At first, the task was tedious at best. I found myself drawn in by the stories. Brought into a world where were-animals, vampires, and warlocks existed, mythology didn't seem so far off. I considered the very origin of were-animals and vampires. Were the were-animals' existence the result of a curse bestowed upon the animal or human? Had they been forced to live in a limbo between human and animal in a state of horrid conflict? Or was it a gift from the gods to walk between the worlds of man and animal, enjoying the benefits of both? For me, it was nothing more than a curse with unfair retributions.

And vampires? Who and what deity did they anger to be forced to wander the earth in a lifeless body, only able to survive on the blood of the living? I am sure one could perceive it as a blessing for the immortality they maintained, eternal youth, speed, and extraordinary strength. I considered myself a monster, and yet I didn't rely on killing humans for my survival. How could they perceive themselves as anything better?

Several times Josh had to interrupt me to keep me on task as I glanced through the books. Usually, I am not so easily distracted, but the information was interesting, drawing me in. I found myself reading the stories, engrossed in the many tales of gods, were-animals, demons, vampires, and fae. Beguiled by the tales of lost powers, fallen gods, revered and feared demons, and all that in between.

"Interesting stuff, huh?" he finally stated, putting a book down and rubbing his eyes.

I nodded as I leafed through the pages. Josh left and returned with two large cups of coffee. I inhaled the robust smell of French roast, allowing it to overtake my senses before drinking.

"This is good."

"I wish I could take credit. Winter's a coffee and tea snob. I made the mistake of bringing store-brand coffee in the house. I think she considered poisoning me. You know she's venomous. That's how she maintains her position. Because she is an inferior species, most of the canidae and felidae have her at a physical advantage in animal form, but they won't challenge her. In animal form, they would have to be quick enough to avoid her strike. Enough of them have fallen victim to it that the lesson was quickly learned. That's why most challenges for her position have been in human form. Needless to say, she is just as dangerous in human form," he stated casually.

"She's venomous in human form, too?"

"No, but she is *just* as dangerous." He didn't have to tell me. I'd seen her in action and I was fully aware of how dangerous she was.

The break from staring at the books was much needed. My eyes were tired and starting to dry out. We had been at this for almost four hours and didn't have any pictures in the possible pile. Even Josh was showing signs of fatigue.

After another two hours of unsuccessful viewing, Josh placed the last book aside and leaned back in his chair. Deeply drawn into his thoughts, he began to chew on his lips absently. He stayed in that state for a long time before walking over to the corner of the room, unlocking the drawer at the bottom of a bookcase and pulling out three books. With a heavy sigh, he sat them on the table, looking as though he hoped we wouldn't find the sketch in them.

The books were very old. They felt different from the others as I brushed my hands across the bindings. Drawn to the weathered book at the bottom of the stack, I pulled it from the pile and slowly flipped through the pages. Fear stalled my movements abruptly as I heard the pages whisper to me. Shaking my head, I convinced myself I was just tired. But I couldn't deny that with each page I turned, there was a lure that became stronger. My fingers were forced to a page three-quarters of the way through it.

I closed my eyes. There wasn't a need to look at either the sketch on the table or the page in the book. I knew it was it. It pulled me to it, wanting to be found.

I turned the book toward Josh and pointed to the picture. He cursed under his breath, taking the book from me. I stared at the words on the spine. It wasn't in English. "What's the title?" I asked.

His face remained solemn and pensive. "It's in Latin."

"What's the title of the book?" I repeated firmly. He may not be familiar with Latin, although I found that highly unlikely, but he knew the titles of these books.

"Symbols of Death."

Of course.

When he shook his head and tossed the book aside on the table, I picked it up. It had various drawings and pictures of objects without any information regarding what they were. Scribed on each page was just a name of the object. It was a book created with the cruel and sole purpose of displaying the various things used to bring forth death, without offering the seeker any explanation. My fingers lingered, brushing over the picture. It didn't feel like death, not that I knew what death felt like, but it didn't feel the way I perceived death would feel. I sensed life—new life, which soon turned into something more alarming. A dark tug of energy crept up my arm, and for a moment, it held me. I gasped, jerking my hand back.

Too focused on his thoughts, Josh didn't see what happened. "Demetrius shouldn't have possession of anything from this book," he whispered dismally to himself.

He looked up from the floor and made an attempt at a smile as he considered the look of worry on my face. "Symbols of death aren't always used to bring forth death. They serve many other purposes."

Of course, and a gun can be used as a hammer, but how many people are using it as one? "I am sure the other purposes aren't good, either."

Slowly he shook his head. "We have to get it from Demetrius and return it."

"Return it to whom?" I asked.

"The book."

"The book?"

"Once the objects of this book are destroyed appropriately, they are returned to it," he stated as he took the book from me. He flipped through a few pages and turned the book toward me. The pages were a deep crimson, discolored as though the picture had bled into them. As I stared at it, I felt the eerie feeling that the thing in the sketch may have wanted to be found —but it didn't want to be destroyed.

~

The next day, Ethan, Josh, Steven, and I sat in the Jeep Wrangler headed to Layton, a suburban city outside of Chicago. Josh drove. Ethan kept a close eye on his brother, whose easygoing mood had been traded for something hard, intense, and troubled. He didn't tell me who we were going to see. In fact, since he'd sprung the *Symbols of Death* on me, he had remained scarce.

It was Steven who came to the room to tell me to be ready to leave in forty-five minutes. At first, I just considered them to be rude, keeping me in the dark so often. But they all subscribed to that "do as I say" rigmarole. When an order was made, you followed without many questions being asked. I wasn't used to that. You tell me to get ready and I want to know the "who, what, when, why, where, and how" of the matter.

When we arrived at a building, both Josh and Ethan seemed so weighted by their thoughts, it took them a moment before they opened the door. Josh led Ethan and me through the vacant office building while Steven stayed behind. The office of Nathan Green, PA, was dark, and the lobby empty, but the door leading to the offices was slightly ajar. The fact that he was closed for the day didn't stop Josh from heading back into the office area. Nathan, I presumed, didn't seem surprised to see Josh as he looked up from the papers on his desk. His craggy appearance hardened, piqued by the intrusion. Cold hyacinth eyes glanced in Josh's direction before honing in on me. At first, they held a look of inquisition, which quickly turned to revulsion, then abhorrence.

"Josh, is it?" he asked, his lips turning up in contempt as he glanced back at him. "I told you over the phone that I couldn't help you."

Josh crossed his arms, his sharp gaze meeting Nathan's intense glare. "I didn't believe you then and I don't believe you now."

Nathan pulled his attention from Josh, directing his focus on me, where it remained. Even when I turned toward Josh, I could still feel his eyes on me. "I found this in the *Symbols of Death*. It's the Gem of Levage. I need to know what it is used for. As a necromancer, you are quite versed in the objects used for ritualistic death and the other purposes they serve. What are its purposes and why is it important to Demetrius?"

He briefly looked at the picture. "I have no answers for you," he stated curtly as he rose to his feet. Slowly, he walked in my direction, chanting indistinct words. Taking several steps back, I tried to avert my gaze, but they remained fixed on his. Ethan stepped in front of me, but I could still feel Nathan's eyes searing through me.

"She shouldn't be here." I got the clear impression that he didn't mean that I just shouldn't be here in his office—but here in existence.

Josh put his hand in front of Nathan, keeping him from advancing any farther. "Tell me about the Gem," he urged in a stern voice that held a hint of threat.

"She shouldn't be here," Nathan repeated roughly as he glared at me with acrid intensity. His body tensed, eyes lowered as he started chanting inaudible words again.

"Stop it!" Josh demanded. "She is not one of yours to command."

"I sense the presence of the lifeless upon her, yet she doesn't respond to my call." He seemed perplexed.

"She cannot be called by you. I need to know what her relationship is to the Gem of Levage.".

"Do you have the Gem?" His eyes never left the place where I stood.

"No, I believe Demetrius has it."

Nathan's heart rate changed, fear brushed over him in a crescendo of waves. Ethan responded to it, closing the distance between them. "It will be in your best interest to start giving some answers," Ethan cautioned.

"Why haven't you taken her life? She should not be here!" he commanded sharply, his eyes still fixed on me. "You have been irresponsible for allowing her to live. Her sergence is wrong! It's all wrong. There's a void. She cannot be here!" Horrified by my mere existence, his anger spread like wildfire.

"Why shouldn't I be here?" I finally blurted. I took a step toward him, but Josh shot me a look that stopped me in my tracks. I should have been afraid, running from the building screaming. Nathan sentenced me to death, but I was full of questions. And Nathan was hell-bent against answering them. I needed to know what about me could evoke such a powerful response in a necromancer. Uneasiness formed a lump in my chest, making it hard to breathe. I tried to push down the feeling, but it wouldn't budge.

He responded by lunging at me with a knife. Ethan grabbed it from him and slammed him to the floor. Holding him firmly against the ground, he said, "You have only two options now: answer the damn question, or let me beat you inches from death, then answer the question. Either way, you will answer the fucking question." Ethan growled through clenched teeth, inches from his face. Ethan's demands were met with a vacuous stare as Nathan pressed his lips firmly together—silenced. We weren't getting any information out of this necromancer.

"Ethan, I see your skills of persuasion still leave much to be desired," stated a velvety soft female voice from behind us.

"Chris." Ethan greeted her bitterly without looking up. Standing behind us, a woman held a crossbow on Ethan and a gun on Josh. Dark brown hair tucked neatly behind her ear, drawing attention to her flawless, toasted-almond skin, heart-shaped face, and pleasing features. Lethal, umber eyes veiled by a long frame of lashes were directed solely on Ethan.

"Ethan, now *you* have two choices, sweetie. You can save yourself and your brother and let me have the little wolf, or you both can die in a very painful and bloody manner—after which I will ultimately get the little wolf. Knowing you, of course you are going to do the heroic thing and risk injury to yourself to save your brother and the little damsel in distress." She rolled her eyes, as sculpted arms held surprisingly still, keeping her weapons pointed at Ethan and Josh. "It's so textbook, Ethan, that it's rather boring. Let me warn you. I've made upgrades for you seemingly invincible were-types." She took several steps forward with an ease of movement I didn't think was possible in jeans that tight. Full lips curved into a smirk. She was quite impressed with herself.

"This cute little silver arrow is just long enough to travel to the spine, destroying all those wonderful vital organs in the process. When it makes contact with the tissue, it explodes into little silver shards, releasing neurotoxins that will wreak havoc on your nervous center while the silver prevents you from healing. Even Dr. Baker and his godlike talents won't be able to save you."

"That's counting that your skills with the crossbow have improved. But it couldn't get any worse," he responded caustically. He stayed kneeling over Nathan, but his attention was focused on Chris.

She smiled. "Oh, how I've missed you, love. I'm pretty sure I can shoot you from this distance without a problem This doesn't have to end ugly. Give me Skylar, and you and your brother get to leave with your lives. I will sweeten the deal by directing you to the guy who makes these handy little arrows—"

"We've already met," he interjected. "If you take a closer look at the arrow you'll find that it's not the original one you agreed to. I had him make a few little changes before I strongly encouraged him to seek another career path. He felt the need to leave the city."

She seemed relaxed as she took in the information but the clench of her jaw betrayed her true emotions. She shrugged. "Oh well, then I guess I will leave you to grieve the life of your brother." She gripped the gun tighter. She made a slight adjustment in her aim from Josh's chest to his head. Ethan stood, freeing Nathan from his position.

With Nathan unrestrained and Josh in imminent danger, I took a few steps sideways, placing myself directly between Josh and the gun. I was sure she wasn't willing to kill me. *Okay, I'm not a hundred percent sure, but my certainty is somewhere in the high ninetieth percentile.* But I was a hundred and ten percent sure that Nathan would kill me. In our current position, both Josh and Ethan could get to Nathan if he decided to attack me again.

"Oh, how cute. She values your brother's life. Isn't she the most adorable brave wolf." Condescension dripped off her words. "Honey, I just need you alive. It doesn't matter what condition I bring you in. I have no problem injuring you. Maybe if you were injured, you would be a little more compliant," she said in a cloying threat, her voice promising a world of pain that she would be only too happy to deliver.

"Kill her! You have to kill her!" Nathan demanded. "Demetrius cannot have her!" His voice quivered with rage. Once Nathan realized that she didn't have any intentions of doing that, his steps quickened toward me.

With one swift move, Chris turned the arrow toward Nathan, shooting him in the mouth as he opened it to speak. His head snapped back from the impact as blood splattered, covering Josh, Ethan, and the back of my shirt. I wasn't sure what the arrow was originally supposed to do, but once it made contact with the skull, it exploded, causing fragments of his skull to detach. Soft tissue disintegrated, melting from the remaining bone. Chris glared at Ethan. "You liar! That was supposed to be my gift to you."

He shrugged. "You can be a bitch at times, but you were never thorough. You always check just one. The one to your far left. So I left you one, to humor you. I never felt you were a threat to me and mine. Contrary to what you believe, you've never been a good shot with them. I am simply amazed that you were somewhat efficient this time."

What does amaze this guy? The shot was flawless and done with such ease and precision; she had proven herself to be as deadly as any were-animal. Would he be impressed if she had made the shot blindfolded? She matched the were-animal terror for terror, and he continued to antagonize her while the gun remained pointed at his brother's head.

His insults rolled off her. In fact, she seemed to enjoy it. Everything about these people was odd. "It was that bitchiness that made you fall in love with me," she retorted in a seductive purr.

Ethan didn't respond; instead, he crossed his arms and smiled. They stared at each other seeming stuck somewhere between loathing and simmering attraction.

I wasn't sure if they wanted to attack each other in a blaze of violence or give into their carnal lust and take each other right there in front of us. *You have to be kidding me with this!*

Josh let out an irritated sound. He was fuming as he walked toward her. I didn't know if I should follow him for cover. She had no reservations about murder and I feared for his life, although he didn't seem to possess the same level of concern. He looked at Nathan's mutilated body. Enraged, he turned toward Chris.

"Oh, Chris, just give it a break. You're a hot woman, despite the fact you've just threatened to kill me and my brother. You're a bitch, which probably means you are a great lay. I suspect that's the only reason you and my brother lasted as long as you did. I don't give a crap about you and my brother's relationship, including the ridiculous unresolved feelings you two seem to have. What I want to know is how does a hunter become a lackey for Demetrius?" He stood only inches from her gun. "It's rather beneath you, don't you think?" His face displayed his disgust if by any chance she'd missed it in his insult.

"Lackey," she scoffed. Moving inhumanly fast, she dropped the crossbow and grabbed me from behind. Her fingers pressed firmly into the side of my neck, obstructing my carotid artery, while she kept the gun aimed at Josh. Streaks of soft lights flashed across my eyes, clouds of fogginess formed in my head. Standing became a chore. She held me firmly as I staggered. She was fast, too fast to be only human—but she smelled human, and her presence seemed human. I thought I pulled at her hand, but I must have imagined it because her hand was still wrapped firmly around my neck.

"She'll be out soon. Just let me leave with her and I promise your brother will live," she informed Ethan. Ethan took several steps toward her and she prepared to take the shot.

"Come on Ethan, it's your brother." It was a hollow plea because I didn't think she cared whether or not she killed Josh. "You want me to believe that your commitment to the pack is greater than that to your only brother?"

Her hands were snatched from me and the gun knocked out of her hand. She was thrown to the floor. "Stay down," Steven commanded her as he caught me before I hit the floor. She had obstructed the blood flow for so long that I was on the verge of passing out. Blinking erratically, I tried to force myself to stay upright.

Chris jumped up and ran toward the door, breezing past Steven. He tried to grab her, but she blocked his arm, twisted it, and pushed him away. He stumbled back but managed to keep from falling to the floor, bringing me down with him. Ethan ran out the door after her.

By the time we got to the car, Ethan was angrily pacing in front of it. He rubbed his irritated inflamed nostrils. She must have used something to throw off her scent.

"Skylar, what the hell was that?" Josh snapped, turning from the driver's seat to look at me.

"What?"

"That dumbass stunt you pulled," Ethan interjected from the passenger seat. "It's bad enough we have to protect you from the vampires, a hunter, but now from your stupidity as well Must I give you lessons in safety and self-preservation?" I thought you would have the good sense to know better, but guess I was wrong. Let me help you with common sense: don't step in front of sharp objects, bullets, or anything in the firearm family because they can actually kill you! Or do you think of yourself as invincible?" he yelled, berating me as he shot me dirty looks from the front seat.

"Demetrius wants me alive. She wasn't going to kill me, but I wasn't so sure about Josh. While you were busy having verbal foreplay and making goo-goo eyes with your ex, I thought it would be a good idea not to let him get shot in the process. And since you feel so inclined to give me lessons in self-preservation, maybe I should give you some in appropriate choices. For instance, when your ex is threatening to kill your brother, it's not a good idea to provoke her. Just a little suggestion," I snapped back.

Ethan glared at me and I was glad we were separated by the seat.

Josh sighed. "The situation would have been handled."

"Before or after she used your face for target practice? I didn't realize you fancied being shot. I will remember that." I hated this world I was snatched into. It was a house of mirrors, where acts that others would have considered kind, or maybe even brave, were distorted into sources of irritation and reprimand.

Josh rolled his eyes, Ethan grumbled. Steven's lips meshed tightly together. His dimples deepened, suppressing a laugh. "Just don't do anything like that again," Ethan ordered. The tone of his voice made it apparent he wasn't in the mood for my rebuttals. I let out an exasperated sigh.

We drove back in silence while I spent the ride evading Ethan's reproaching glares. I was just about to tell him I got the message and he could stop with the looks when Josh said, "Chris has switched teams."

Ethan nodded his head slowly. "I guess. She's trading now. I smelled Demetrius all over her," he stated, disgusted. "She was always too fast to be just human, but now she's…" His voice trailed off as though the thought was too sickening to say out loud.

"She's a vampire?" I asked. She didn't look like a vampire, and walking in daylight definitely wasn't vampirey. She didn't even smell like a vampire. No, she definitely smelled human—human with expensive perfume.

Ethan's growl resonated through the car.

"She's performing blood exchanges with him. Through the exchange, she gains some of his abilities, like the supernatural speed exhibited today," Steven explained in a low whisper. I am sure Ethan knew what it was, but hearing the specifics was going to take him over the edge.

"She found a loophole, I guess. She always wanted the speed, strength, and advanced healing abilities of were-animals without the sun-vulnerability that the vamps have," Josh said, glancing over at Ethan, who had retreated to his angry place where it seemed like he was planning to stay for a while.

"Josh, don't," Ethan stated through clenched teeth.

"Chris was going to get what she wanted by any means. You should've just changed—"

"I said *don't*." Ethan gave him the same reproaching and threatening look I thought was just reserved for me.

Just when I was beginning to think I was special, I find out he's handing those looks out like lollipops.

Josh clamped his mouth shut as he struggled to keep his words to himself.

I stood in the sunroom, trying to block out the events of today. "She shouldn't be here" reverberated in my head as Nathan's attack tugged at me.

"Here. You look like you need this," Josh stated as he handed me a mixed drink of something fruity with a significant amount of vodka. He had one in his hand, too.

I didn't drink often, just an occasional glass of wine during the holidays. But I wasn't opposed to a drink or anything that would dull the pangs of my anxiety. I took a big sip from the glass and immediately started coughing. The strong liquor burned as it slid down, setting my chest on fire. No, I definitely wasn't a drinker. "Josh, what's wrong with my sergence and why shouldn't I be here?" I asked, once I had the coughing under control.

He was silent for a long time.

"Josh."

"Nathan is—*was* very talented. Most necromancers can read your sergence—your aura. Nathan was one of the most gifted. Many of them can't detect witches and mages, but he could."

"My sergence is wrong, so wrong that he wants to kill me?"

He took a long draw from his glass as his troubled eyes stifled me for a moment. "No—let's just say it's murky. No one has a sense of what you really are—it's troubling. You're a were-animal but you have a *terait*. In the corner of your right pupil, there's an orange quarter ring. Ethan noticed it the first day you arrived. I saw it yesterday. It's only seen in vampires and half-breeds when their bloodlust hadn't been fulfilled," he admitted with a heavy voice.

"Bloodlust? Should I have a bloodlust?"

"I'm sure you do. But I doubt it would overtake you as it

would a vampire or even a dhampir because your survival isn't based on its consumption. I'm sure a rare steak would satisfy your lust for an indefinite period of time." That explained why Ethan was always gawking at my eyes. He was just looking for the *terait*. I guess he wasn't an eye man.

I considered the way I liked my food prepared, rare to the point I was surprised it didn't move off my plate while I was eating it. I always thought it was a wolf thing—but now—no, that thought was too sickening to continue.

"So what does this mean?"

He bit down on the side of his lip as he considered my question. "By all accounts, you shouldn't exist. . . ."

"I'm not a vampire. I couldn't be cursed to be both—I just couldn't." My chest felt so tight that breathing was a task. I leaned against the post and took several big swallows from the vodka. It wasn't helping.

"Were-animals have natural immunity and can't be changed into vampires."

"Then can you explain this terait that seems to warrant me dying for?" I asked in a forced voice.

"I don't know," he admitted, shaking his head, his frustration apparent.

"Could I be like this if one of my birth parents were a vampire?"

Staring into his almost empty glass, he deliberated over my question. I doubted anything good could come from such extended consideration. "The probability is highly unlikely. Vampires maintain their ability to procreate about a week after being changed. Unless your mother was pregnant with you when she was changed, you couldn't be the offspring of a vampire. Becoming a vampire requires death of the human body and rebirth into the vampirism. It's a process that takes several days, and I doubt the most resilient child could survive it. To my knowledge, there aren't any known cases of a child surviving as a result of a vampire mother. All known dhampirs are the result of a new male vampire and a human mother. But if you were a dhampir, you would not be a were-animal."

He was still rubbing his forehead as though he were trying to work out a complicated equation in his head. "Were-animals and vampires/dhampirs have mated in the past, but there has never been anything documented nor even a plausible rumor that supports that an actual birth occurred. The conflicting processes kill the child."

"So I am an anomaly that shouldn't exist."

He gave me a small sympathetic smile. "You're an anomaly that does exist. Just like in the human world, anomalies exist all the time. Maybe not to this extent, but they do."

"Perhaps that is the reason Demetrius wants me: to either be part of his Seethe or to get rid of me because I am an anomaly?"

Josh chuckled. "I can assure you that they don't want you in their Seethe. They don't regard dhampirs. You are tainted with the blood of the were-animal. Centuries ago, they punished their own for fraternizing with were-animals, and a tryst of a sexual nature was penalized with death. That is not the case now, but they have extreme superiority complexes. They would never accept you as one of theirs. Demetrius prohibits association with dhampirs because he considers them 'deplorable half-breeds' and just as revolting as were-animals. It's rumored that Demetrius killed the child, the mothers, and the vampires for producing such half-breeds. It's rumored that he even killed his own and its mother. I assume the stories are true because new vampires are quite impulsive and reckless, yet exhibit extraordinary control when it comes to reproduction. Like were-animals, control usually comes with age and experience. I can only speculate *what* and *who* is responsible for compelling such control in young and inexperienced vampires."

He began to pace the area, anxiously biting on his nails. He didn't strike me as the type of person who could sit idle for long. "They tried to abduct you, not kill you, when they attacked. Under any other circumstance, you would have been under their radar and barely worth acknowledging. In my dreams, there is a distinct feeling of desire. They want you for something that will benefit them—that's the only reason they care that you exist. I need to figure out the link between you, Demetrius, and the Gem of Levage."

"And Chris? How worried should I be about her?"

"No worries. As long as you stay here, you're fine. She wouldn't attack you here."

"I shouldn't worry about Ethan's ex-lover? Then maybe I should worry about Ethan?"

He scowled, eyes flaring. "Don't ever underestimate my brother. He wouldn't let anything like an ex-lover keep him from doing his job well."

"Sorry. I wasn't trying ... I didn't mean to imply anything bad," I mumbled.

"It's cool. Be assured that the turbulent thing they once called a relationship won't keep either one of them from doing what they set out to do."

"What were they like together?" There wasn't any denying that there were some very intense emotions between them—somewhere between sheer longing and avid disdain.

Chortling, he found amusement in something he decided not to share. "The two of them together were like watching a forest fire and a tornado consume the same space. We watched their relationship crash and burn with morbid fascination. Their fights were so intense that you wondered who was going to snap first and kill the other person. And their make-ups were so passionate they could melt the paint off the wall." He looked away, his attention once again focused on his empty glass. When he looked, he seemed pensive. "They shouldn't have been together. I think for that very reason, they tried so hard to make it work. Neither one of them was willing to admit defeat as they should. But eventually, Chris saw it for what it really was and ended it."

He shrugged off the memories. "The love or whatever you would call what they had won't prevent them from doing what needs to be done. They were always odd that way." There was something in his voice, perhaps bewilderment over how they functioned as they did.

~

The next morning, I knocked softly on Sebastian's door, partly hoping that he wouldn't answer. "Yes, Skylar," his voice answered through the closed door. I stepped into the office. When he looked up briefly from his computer, he cast a look so cold and remote it felt like I hugged a glacier.

"How are things going?" I asked politely, shutting the door behind me.

He sighed a ragged breath. "I don't like small talk. Get to the point."

You don't like being polite, either.

"I realize things have been a little hectic around here, and the last time . . . "

"The point, Skylar." It was an odd paradigm that such soft brown eyes could pull off icy and unwelcoming with such ease. Mr. Congeniality waited impatiently. His intriguingly beautiful face became a pleasing distraction as I considered how to deal with the impolite wolf.

"I need to get something from my house."

"What?"

"It's personal."

He sat back in his chair, his lips tightening, the muscles twitching around his clenched jaw. "Then I'm sure it can wait." He returned his focus back to his computer.

I exhaled, exasperated, my patience a thread on the brink of breaking. Back at my house may be the very thing that could tell me why I was such an anomaly, why I was a werewolf with a terait whose sergence was so wrong a necromancer wanted me dead. "I can assure you that if it weren't necessary, I wouldn't be here. It is important."

He studied me. Deep, penetrating eyes roamed over me, ending where everyone else's did—the corner of my eye. That part of me that separated me from being *just* a were-animal and being an anomaly that apparently shouldn't exist. "Okay, I'll have someone take you."

"Can that someone be Steven?"

"No." He quickly returned his attention to his computer. When I stayed planted, he glanced up. "Did you need a good-bye or something?"

I turned on my heels to leave, wisely deciding to keep my sardonic response to myself.

"I am sure you know Nathan tried to kill me yesterday." I glanced over my shoulders.

He nodded slowly. "Necromancers are often prone to overreacting to anything that is different. I could understand his reaction if he had spent a couple of days around you. You seem to bring that tendency out in people." He gave me a smug grin.

Great, the Alpha made a joke. Isn't he clever? He had remained borderline rude and inhospitable since I'd been here. The one time he chose to hold a conversation with me, it's to say I am annoying. He was hilarious. When I didn't find the humor in his comment, his smile slowly transitioned into a smirk.

"Aren't you the least bit curious about what he saw?" I turned to face him. It was my turn to watch, to analyze. But he was indiscernible. His strong features and primal confidence remained stoic. Whether he was concerned or not, I couldn't tell. If he feared what I was, it remained a mystery.

"I trust Josh. He's not very concerned, so there is no need for me to be."

"Why do you protect my life when it would be so easy to end it?" I asked, surprising even myself with the statement.

He looked thoughtful, but I didn't get the impression he was considering my question. "*Easy* isn't the pack way. I would never take the life of a were-animal on the suggestion of a necromancer or anyone else other than my were-animals," he stated in a serious tone. "I am held to the laws of the pack as well. I have no cause to kill a lone were-animal that hasn't harmed the pack or violated any of our laws. We aren't murderers. You've never been extended a pack invitation. I am obligated to protect you. Just because it has been a rather daunting task doesn't negate our responsibility to do so. As long as you are not a threat to us, you are protected."

That sounded wonderful, even benevolent, if I ignored the fact that I was safe as long as he didn't see me as a threat to his pack. If things changed, then so would the value they placed on my life. "I appreciate all you have done, though at times it hasn't seemed that way," I admitted in a low voice.

His gaze wavered in my direction for a few moments. "Good-bye, Skylar."

An hour after speaking with Sebastian and being treated to his brand of hospitality and geniality, I sat next to his Beta, who must have attended the same finishing school. The vast space of the Range Rover was filled with the sound of music playing loudly. An angsty and deeply troubled male singer crooned his raspy voice over the sounds of guitars and drums. It was an inept attempt to fill the uncomfortable silence that existed constantly between Ethan and me. While I looked out the window, his fingers tapped rhythmically against the steering wheel. It wasn't to the beat of the music. The drumming of his fingers was in perfect sync with the erratic beating of my heart. He had succeeded. My discomfort around him had escalated to a physiological level.

Occasionally he glanced in my direction. The few times our gaze met, his attention went directly to the corner of my right eye. "If Nathan hadn't attacked you, would we be doing this?" he asked as we neared the house.

"I don't know."

"I asked you not to lie to me."

"No."

"What do you plan to gain from obtaining these *personal* items? The wheels are in motion. It won't change anything, Skylar."

"I know."

"Then why waste my time?"

We were in front of the house now. I briefly looked at him, and the longing hit me. I missed my mom, I missed my home and I missed my old life. "Ethan, I would never choose to waste your time. Any issues you have with being here should be taken up with Sebastian. I never asked for you to be my escort," I stated firmly as I got out of the car.

When I considered going back to the house, it never dawned on me how emotionally daunting it would be. Smelling my mother's scents, seeing the things, feeling her absence in the house was too difficult to handle. My hands were trembling by the time I placed the key in the lock. I could barely unlock the door.

Her scent was subdued by the smell of household cleanser. Someone had cleaned the house. The broken furniture had been removed, and the corner where my mother lay bleeding to death—not less than eight days ago—was now spotless.

"Who came back here?" I asked, looking around the room.

"Josh. He put up a ward that restricts vampires and others from entering your home without an invitation. There is a similar one on the retreat."

I had lived in the house all my life, and now I felt like a stranger in it. It seemed so long ago that I loved this home. It was where I wanted to be. When young adults were running from their childhood homes like the places were on fire, I was running to mine. For the first six months after graduation from college, I spent more time visiting my mom than I did at my place. Eventually, I gave up the charade and moved back home. I didn't think I could ever call this place home again.

I wrapped my arms around myself, wishing that were enough to make me feel safe here. "I have to go upstairs." I needed an escape from the room. He nodded, taking a seat on the couch.

I went to my mother's bedroom but loitered in the hallway for several minutes, dredging up the nerve to go into it. Her scent and presence lingered throughout, making it hard to breathe. I struggled to keep my bundled emotions from unraveling at that moment. I promised myself that I would come in, get what I needed, and leave. It was much harder than I expected. The sorrow pulsated through me. Before I could get a hold on it, I was sitting on the bed, sobbing uncontrollably.

Ethan stood at the door, staring at me. He looked uncomfortable, lifting his eyes briefly to meet mine before dropping his gaze back to the floor. Fidgeting with his pockets, it seemed as though he were looking for something to say, or rather, the right thing to say.

"I'm sorry. I thought this would be easier," I admitted between sniffles. He stared at me in silence, his face blank. He left and returned with a box of tissues. He handed it to me and assumed his position by the door, his focus on his feet, glancing up periodically. "May I have a few minutes?" I asked.

"Of course." He sounded relieved. He trotted down the stairs, then backtracked to the room. There was a subtle solace about him as he approached me. His hand rested on my leg as he knelt in front of me. "We should come back another time when you can handle this better," he suggested gently. "It's okay. I won't mind bringing you back later."

I shook my head, trying desperately at a smile. "I'm fine." His eyes narrowed at the lie. "I will be fine. I just need a few minutes." He nodded without hesitation and quickly backed out of the room.

It took about thirty minutes, but eventually, I was composed enough to do what I came to do. I pushed myself up from the bed and went over to the bookcase, searching for my mother's journals. I hoped they could answer why I had an odd ring around my right eye that liked to play peekaboo. But if nothing else, they could at least provide me with some answers to my birth and fill in the missing blanks of my childhood.

My mom kept meticulous journals about me. She had chronicled everything from what foods gave me nightmares to what months led to my worst changes. I never understood why, and some part of me felt like I was some huge research project to her because of it. But she was a researcher. She had a tendency to keep careful records on things that others would have ordinarily found to be a waste of time and energy. Once, during one of our few arguments, I made mention of it. I accused her of only wanting me around to observe me like a freak in a controlled environment. It was also one of the few times I made her angry: one, for referring to myself as a freak and two, for accusing her of wanting me for any other reason than the fact she loved me. I wasn't sure if she had stopped keeping the journals, but she never made it obvious that she had. Now, I hoped that she hadn't.

The journals were tucked away in a small footlocker in a corner of her walk-in closet. There were twenty-two books there and one in her nightstand, incomplete. Opening the fifteenth journal, I leafed through the pages, reading her barely legible string of loops and curves. The words "peppermint house" caught my attention, producing the suppressed memory of the one-time visit we made right after my initial change. The visit was a bust. The woman of the house took one look at me and stated, "The change has begun." She didn't elaborate other than to state that my new form had begun the process. *Duh, I was turning into a wolf every full moon. Yeah, the process had definitely begun.*

I remember my mother making jokes about how unhelpful the visit was. Now I wondered whether the women possessed more knowledge behind her words. Maybe we should have probed more, asked the right questions. I think we were too scared to ask the right questions, too afraid of what the answers might have been if we had. We never went back nor expressed the desire to do so.

I grabbed the first five journals and the fifteenth concerning the year of my change and put them in my bag.

Ethan sat idly on the sofa. Sensing my presence, he turned to face me. His often tense features seemed to soften. He looked genuinely concerned. "Everything okay?"

I nodded, walking toward the door. He followed close behind.

"I need to go to this address," I informed him in the car, handing him a piece of paper.

He frowned, looking down at the paper. "Why?"

"I think she can help me."

He looked down at the paper again and shook his head. "That's not a good idea."

I sighed. I didn't feel like going through this again. Every time I spoke with Ethan or Sebastian, I felt like I should have an opening statement, defense, and closing argument. "Ethan, I can't do this with you now," I wearily acknowledged.

"Then don't."

I rested my head against the headrest and sighed heavily. "I am not asking permission nor will I." It wasn't my intention to come off rude, but I was tired of being controlled. There was protection, and then there was blatant disregard for my autonomy.

"I won't let you do this," he stated in a dry, uncompromising tone. The harsh lines of his face returned. The Ethan who was concerned, understanding, and easily flustered by the show of emotions, had left the building, and the rigid, controlling, pithy Ethan had returned.

I counted the various arguments I could use, but the hard set of Ethan's jaw, lips woven so tightly it seemed painful, and the turgid muscle in his neck made it apparent that any rebuttals or arguments would be in vain. "Okay."

Surprise shadowed his appearance. The easy concession made him apprehensive.

We drove in silence. His penetrating gaze was split between me and the road. He stopped in the middle of a deserted street. "That was too easy."

I shrugged. "I just don't have it in me to debate with you now." Giving in to him just seemed like a wise choice but I hadn't given up on my quest to go to the house. I just would have to wait. Arguing with Ethan would have just left both of us frustrated, me more so than him.

He studied me for so long it became uncomfortable. He nodded and started driving. At the next light, he shook his head. "I don't trust that you will stay put," he admitted in a steeled voice as he picked up the paper, glanced at the address, and made a U-turn.

He was right not to trust me. My persistence had only been shelved temporarily. I had already decided that I was going to go to the address the next day. Leaving the house wasn't the smartest thing to do, but desperation and curiosity made me more brave than wise. I hoped that I could somehow coerce Steven into going with me. Of the were-animals, he seemed the most reasonable and palatable.

"Skylar, you've lived all this time not caring about what you were. Why is this now so important?"

He was right, and I was quite ashamed of it now. I knew nothing of my birth or how I came to live with my adopted mother. I ran from my past as though it were a hatchet-wielding psycho out to attack me. I was afraid of the truths it held. Every time my mother brought it up, I changed the subject—or worse—started a fight. I did whatever I could to evade talking. There was always that part of me that knew something was different, and if my beginning started off anomalous, then it would only cement my belief. As long as there wasn't proof, my past was what I made it. As far as I was concerned, the story of my life was that a nice, benevolent physician took me in after my birth mother died giving birth to me. No harm, no foul. Then I changed into a wolf. Big harm. Huge foul. And still I hid.

"I did. But that was before my mother was killed, vampires started stalking me, and necromancers started lobbying for my murder. If these things had never happened, I probably would have gone many more years not caring to learn any more about what I am. I was content with being oblivious. I'm not too proud to admit that maybe I made a big mistake in doing so. Maybe if I had made a point to know my past, then this whole mess wouldn't be happening to me now."

He opened his mouth to say something, but I held my hand up to stop him. "Perhaps this situation was unavoidable, but I still want to know what I am. Being around you all, I realize how very different I am. Why is my sergence wrong? And the terait? I'm not moon-called—I am moon-tortured. Nathan called me lifeless. I don't know why, but I really would like to find out." I tried to appeal to him. Some part of him had to understand.

"You are doing this based on the action and the words of a necromancer. Most necromancers are overreactive to the most minor anomalies," he stated incredulously.

Why wasn't the fact that a necromancer wanted me dead alarming to anyone else but me?

I sighed. "Ethan, you already admitted that something was different about me. If I'm not mistaken, you weren't too fond of it, either. I'm constantly reminded that I am different, not quite human, were, or other. I feel rejected by so many worlds. I want to know where I belong—I *need* to know."

There was a long jagged silence. "It won't change the current circumstances," he finally stated.

"You're probably right."

He parked across the street from the house. It still reminded me of a peppermint, but now it was dulled by inclement weather and age. I got out of the car and so did Ethan. I really wanted to go alone, but asking him to stay would have pushed the envelope further than he could take.

Walking to the door, I put on a brave front, hoping it would ease Ethan. He knocked on the door several times, but no one answered. Just as we turned to walk away, the door opened and a stocky older woman greeted us. Her long salt-and-pepper hair was braided and draped over her shoulder. Her opaque skin didn't show the physical signs of aging but her mannerisms indicated a level of wisdom brought on by living many years.

"You're back," she stated in a cool tone, apparently unsurprised by my visit.

"You remember me?" I challenged, finding it hard to believe that I left such an impression that she would remember me eight years later.

"Of course, I receive few visitors." She was lying and didn't really make an effort to hide it.

"Years ago you said that the change had started. What did you mean?"

She looked at me for a long time, then asked in a remote flat tone, "Eight years and now you seek answers? *Hmm?*" She forced a smile on her broad lips. "You want answers. Fine. But he can't stay." Her piercing gaze swept over to Ethan where it remained fixed. She studied him, and then frowned. Their eyes locked, unyielding and harsh. She didn't like Ethan, and based on the look he gave her, the feeling was mutual.

"Then she won't stay," he stated firmly. "Thank you for your time." Taking me by the elbow, he ushered me back to the car. When I stood at the Range Rover's door without opening it to get in, he exhaled heavily. "What?"

"I want to talk to her."

"You heard her. She won't talk to you with me there."

"Then you will have to stay here ..."

"No!"

"The woman's like a hundred. I'm sure I can protect myself."

"It doesn't mean she's not dangerous. Most vampires are several hundred years old."

"She's not a vampire."

He shook his head. "No."

"Ethan?"

"I said no. Now get in," he snapped, hoisting himself in and pushing the passenger door open.

Ignoring the opened door, I turned and started back toward the house. I didn't get far before he jumped out and grabbed my arm. "Must you always do the opposite of everything I ask?" he spat out angrily, turning me to face him. If I weren't so damned determined, the anger that washed off him definitely would have worked as a deterrent.

"Must you always be so dogmatic and unreasonable?" I lashed back. "We are here. What sense does it make to leave now? Just give me twenty minutes. That is all I'm asking. Please."

Unyielding, angry eyes glared at me. There were no signs of compromise on his face. Why did these things have to be so hard? "We both know I will return to see her. I don't think she's dangerous, but it would be a hell of a lot better with you available, if needed."

He raked his hands through his hair several times, tousling it. Cursing under his breath, he released his hold on me. "You are so frustrating!" he barked through clenched teeth. I was still staring at human blue eyes, so at least I wasn't infuriating.

"I know, but I am not trying to be. It's that horrible side effect of being me." I forced a smile. I inched toward the house. "If I'm not out in twenty minutes, or you hear anything suspicious with that freakish super-hearing of yours, you have my full support to charge in and do your Beta thing and rip apart anything in your way. I know you would like that."

I mouthed a thank you and watched as I slowly sent him into a panic attack—the kind only control freaks get when they are forced to give up a minuscule amount of power.

Walking backward, I kept my eyes on him until the corners of his lips turned up into a half-smile. I smiled back, mouthed another thank you and walked to the door.

The dull unkempt stairs had little cracks in the concrete leading up to a discolored and dingy welcome mat. I didn't have time to knock on the door before Gloria opened it with a smug expectant look on her face. The house may have looked like peppermint but it smelled like brimstone. Okay, I wasn't sure what brimstone smelled like, but it smelled like something odd and unworldly—with a hint of lemon Pledge.

"Come in, Skylar," she stated, removing the small glasses that sat on the tip of her nose. Taking slow cautious steps, I walked into the house. I tried not to inhale too deeply. I really hated the smell of the house. She directed me to the kitchen where I took a seat at the small cherry wood kitchen table. I looked around the small kitchen. Stainless steel pots and pans hung from an iron rack. Ceramic holders filled to capacity with utensils decorated the kitchen. Charming decorative potholders with a fruit theme were neatly spread about the kitchen. A matching fruit-decorated apron hung near the stove and matching curtains covered a small bay window that opened slightly, revealing a small vegetable garden. Except for the smell of the house, it was the type of kitchen a grandmother would have.

"Would you like some tea?" she asked, keeping a watchful eye on my every movement.

My hands fidgeted nervously. Eventually, I clasped them together, forcing the appearance of calm. "No," I responded in a nervous, low voice.

"How may I help you?" She brought her cup of tea to the table and sat across from me.

"You said I went through the change. Did you mean my change into my animal-half?"

"Are you a were-animal, dear?" She seemed interested, but something led me to believe that she already knew.

"Wolf."

"Really. So the evolution has begun."

"Will I change into something else?" I asked cautiously, fearful of the impending answer.

She thoughtfully sipped on her tea, but it was apparent she wasn't considering anything. She was just withholding information. "Do you really seek the answers of what you are?" Her eyes lowered, challenging me.

"Why wouldn't I want to know?"

"Ignorance can sometimes be a beautiful thing." She sipped from her teacup again, smiling.

"I've lacked knowledge too long. I need to know everything, including why my sergence is off."

She perked up. "So you've been read."

"Not intentionally."

"I ask you this with true sincerity. Do you really want to know what you are?" Leaning into the table, she watched my reaction carefully.

I inhaled deeply, taking in the horrid odor of brimstone and lemon. "I need to."

A smile of satisfaction marked her face. "Very well then. I will do this for you, and, in return, you will do me a favor."

It took a while for me to respond. I would owe her. My gut was telling me she wasn't a person you wanted to owe a favor. I reached for my purse. "No, I will pay you. How much?"

The small smile on her face remained. It was pleasant but didn't mask her avid curiosity. She wanted the information just as much as I did. "I will do this for you without cost or obligation."

She laid her hands palms up on the table. "Give me your hands."

I looked at them reluctantly. "What are you?" It was at that moment that I wondered what gifts she possessed that led my mother to seek her advice after my change.

"I'm a Tre'ase," she stated proudly.

I hated that I didn't know what it was because she seemed very proud of it. "What is a Tre'ase?"

"Give me your hands and you will find out."

I hesitated for a long moment. Could she hurt me with just a simple touch? I wanted answers, so I pushed my fear aside and placed my hands in hers. Her hands were cold, and as the minutes passed they tightened around mine, squeezing them to the point where it was uncomfortable. I stared in awe as she changed into a version of me as a child of ten. Two long braids hung down to my shoulders, my eyes a sharper green, my skin youthful and flushed.

"Danielle called you a freak on the playground because you always beat everyone at sports and playground games. You were faster, stronger, and more instinctive than them. Instead of embracing those attributes you chose to suppress them. You didn't want to be different. Why is that, Skylar?"

"What child wants to be different?"

"Most strive to be the best. You were the best, and yet you suppressed your talents to the point where you appeared to be less than average," she alleged in a disappointed voice.

"Because something deep in me already knew I was odd and that my abilities came from something unnatural," I admitted to her, so freely that it gave me pause. My feelings and thoughts spilled from me in such an unrestricted manner that it surprised me. "I hated that I didn't feel like a real girl."

"I wasn't a real girl?" asked my younger self.

"You weren't the way girls were supposed to be. You were too strong, your senses too astute, your ways too intense and your temperament too volatile for a girl your age. You weren't the way girls were supposed to be. You were an animal trapped in a little girl's body. Although the animal remained hidden, its ways were always present. Deep down I knew it was there." The girl smiled at me as she shifted into my wolf. The only thing that remained in human form was her hands as they held mine.

"I emerged, confirming that you were different. Did you believe you were the only one?" my wolf asked. Staring at it, I was astonished by its perfect replication of my wolf, right down to the color change from light gray to charcoal around my ears.

"You forever changed my life. I could never consider myself truly human anymore."

"Were you ever really human? Deep down, you had to know that humanity was never in your reach," stated the wolf as it changed into a human-shaped light.

I turned my head; the illumination nearly blinded me. The heat off it warmed my skin like the sun. I basked in it, strangely drawn to whatever it was. It felt oddly familiar to me. Once my eyes adjusted to the brightness, I focused on it.

"Humanity comes hard for you. If it were indeed what you are—then you wouldn't have to work so hard for it. Your animal is only a small part of you, and yet the human part of you is unnatural," said the iridescent light.

"It's the part of me that's most vulnerable."

"Because it's the part of you that is the least true to who you are." The light dimmed as it spoke.

"What part of me are you representing?" I turned my face away as the light grew brighter.

"Your evolution, Skylar."

"I'm going to become the sun?" I asked naively. *That seems highly unlikely.*

The light shone brighter as Gloria laughed. "I am the part of you that the necromancer saw. I'm your sergence, which is neither found in wolf, fae, elf, demon, or vampire."

"What does that mean? What am I?"

"You ask for the answer of what you are. This is all that I can provide. Your evolution depends on quite a few things."

"Like what?"

Her only answer was torturous silence. The cryptic answers I was getting these days were becoming tiresome. The illumination was glorious and nonthreatening. I couldn't understand why it would warrant a death sentence. It darkened for a second before changing into a vampire. Or rather what I would look like if I were a vampire.

My hair was curly and extremely long, draping limestone-colored skin so pale it was almost transparent. My eyes were a brilliant cross between vermillion and titian. I swallowed hard as the taste of blood filled my mouth. Its flavor didn't disgust me as it should. Instead it brought me pleasure—immense, irrefutable, and intense pleasure. The viscous fluid satisfied my palate in ways I never thought possible. I was experiencing bloodlust for the first time and it bothered me that I wasn't repulsed.

"How does it feel?"

"Unsettling," I admitted.

"Would you like to taste it again?" the vampire inquired softly.

I didn't respond for a long time. The vampire smiled expectantly, waiting for an answer. Reluctantly, I nodded my head once. I had to taste it again. The vampire smiled wider, exposing its teeth, which had turned crimson from the blood that dripped from them. The thick, savory fluid filled my mouth again, sliding down my throat, satisfying a longing that dwelled deep in me. Unable to fight it any longer, I gave into it. The smell, the taste, sent me into a euphoric state, its appeal too strong to deny.

"Can you embrace it, Skylar?" asked my vampire-self.

"No." I closed my eyes imprinting the feel and taste to memory.

"How does it feel to enjoy the taste of blood, to be roused by the smell, enticed by the aroma?"

Embracing the thought, I inhaled the alluring aroma of blood that filled the room. I didn't answer. It was unsettling how much I enjoyed the feeling. As I gave into the lust, I imagined myself a vampire. An existence where I craved blood, not just for my survival but because of the unquenchable lust. The type of existence that would cause me to murder without hesitation just to experience the alluring taste again. I knew me and my weaknesses. I would not be able to control myself or deny the lust. Easily, I could become the most horrid creature ever known. My weakness would become society's burden. The were-animals would inevitably kill me for my horrid actions, and I would deserve no better fate.

"I'm not a vampire," I stated softly. I hadn't answered her question, refusing to give her the satisfaction of the truth.

She nodded once, then morphed into a dark creature the color of charcoal. Its underlying skin was a thick leathery texture. Its eyes opened to expose an abyss of darkness instead of pupils. I was plagued by an amalgamation of emotions—mostly fear. They loomed over me, forcing me to feel each one with undiluted intensity. I felt them all, and then I saw it. True evil in its rawest form stared back at me. I trembled as its gaze bore into me. I clenched, fighting against its overpowering force. This form of evil wasn't just felt, touched, seen. It devoured you.

"Can you embrace this side of you? If you can't now, you will learn to because it dwells too deep to be ignored. Its power is so strong that you will succumb to it at some point." Its voice was a carbon copy of my own. A horrific sound escaped from the creature and something reached forward—a tail. It touched me. I jumped, clumsily snatching my hands away from it as I crashed to the floor bringing the table with me. My movements were awkward as I moved to my feet and lifted the table. Gloria, now in her original human form, smiled at me.

"What the hell was that!"

"Skylar, they are all parts of you."

I shook my head wildly. "That wasn't any part of me."

"I showed you nothing but truth. It was you who came to me desiring to know what you are. I gave you the answers," she stated firmly. "That's what's in you. Based on your life and the choices you make, that is your evolution." Her voice became soft and knowledgeable.

I searched for the right words, but I couldn't find any at that moment. That disgusting thing was not me and could never be. What choices would I make to turn me into that monster?

"Skylar, I think you should go. I hear your wolf coming, and he doesn't sound happy."

Good. I wanted to leave, and this gave me the perfect excuse for an exit. I backed out of the kitchen. "Thank you," I stammered, but it didn't sound genuine, probably because it wasn't.

"I will see you soon," she stated confidently.

I am pretty sure you won't.

I nearly crashed into Ethan, who was quickly approaching as I rushed out of the house. "Let's go," I coaxed, trying to pull him with me in my hurry to get away from the house. I wasn't sure what made me think he would be that easily redirected or that I could pull him with such ease. He didn't budge, forcing me forward into him. He took hold of my shoulder firmly as I trembled against him.

"What happened?" His voice, tight, as graphite eyes stared back at me. He looked as though he were ready to charge into the house.

"I fell out of a chair."

"You're lying. What happened?" he challenged with a frown.

"I fell out of a chair." I pulled away from him. He allowed me to slip from his grasp. He continued toward the house, while I moved in the direction of the car.

"Ethan, I simply fell out of the chair. Can we go, please?"

I continued toward the car, hoping he would follow me. He looked at the house and then at me, hesitating for a long moment. Eventually, he followed me back to the car.

The distress was hard to hide as I sat back in the seat. Still riled from leaving the scene without further investigating, Ethan was having a hard time keeping his attention on the road. I had been running from the truth for so long that I felt the need to own what Gloria showed me; if she was showing me truth, they were all part of me. But I couldn't. The ghastly demon thing that she showed me had me searching for a new place of denial.

"What happened?"

"Nothing."

His jaw tensed. "Don't lie to me. If you don't want me to know then just say so," he stated stiffly.

I let my head drop back against the headrest. "I don't want to talk about it."

"Did you find the answers you wanted?"

"I hope not," I responded with finality, hoping to put an end to this conversation.

CHAPTER 7

It had been two days since the debacle at the Tre'ase's house and I could go another lifetime without seeing myself as a vampire or that other horrid creature. Since Joan's departure, with the exception of Steven, I was ignored. Steven was gone. Not only was he the pack's angel-faced member, but he was the University of Illinois's mysterious and often absent engineering student. This week, he had several tests and couldn't miss classes.

I hadn't heard from or seen Josh since the incident with Nathan and was surprised to find him leaning against the doorframe of my room. He lingered at the door for a long moment, looking past me at the charming autumn view outside. The sun was setting. The wind gently blew the leaves of the trees into a whimsical dance. When his eyes met mine, they were heavy, solicitous. It made me suspicious—no, *scared*.

I slid the journals under the covers out of sight, waiting for him to ponder his thoughts long enough until he felt compelled to enter. Over the past two days, I wanted him to help me decipher some more confusing points I found in the journal regarding my birth. With the distressed look on his face and the worried haze over his eyes, now wasn't a good time.

"What's the matter?" I finally asked, realizing he needed a little nudge to get it out.

"I need your help," he admitted finally, walking into the room. Josh always seemed to saunter as though walking were too trite for him. But now his gait was lumbered by fatigue.

Staring at his tightly woven hands, he took a long breath. "I need you to come with me to meet with a source."

"Okay."

He looked surprised that I agreed so quickly with so little information. "If there were any other way, I assure you I would not have come to you." His tone was soothing. I doubt it was to comfort me. He seemed like he was in need of a comforting word or two.

"Josh, I will do whatever is needed in order to end this."

"It's risky isn't it?" I asked after a long silence. *Of course, you wouldn't be in this mood if it wasn't.*

"Magic will be involved. Very strong magic." For some unknown reason, my mind jumped to scenes of the Sorcerer's Apprentice from *Fantasia.* I envisioned shooting stars and dancing brooms, but based on his sullen voice and the look on his face, it wouldn't be anything of that sort. Still, the idea of dancing brooms and shooting stars brought a small smile to my face, and, these days, I took what I could get.

There was more to it; he looked uncomfortable, troubled.

"You don't like this source."

His lips curved slightly in a poor attempt at a smile. "I don't like vampires," he admitted.

We're going to see a vampire? I wasn't sure how optimistic I was about that. If he were betraying his Seethe to help us, could he be trusted? If he weren't part of the Seethe, how could he be of any help? It wasn't as if they were advertising their intentions to anyone who happened to inquire.

"Josh?" Ethan leaned against the frame of the door. Josh's face tensed even more as he looked over his shoulder toward him.

"What?" he asked through clenched teeth. Josh and Ethan made me wonder, had I a sibling, if the mere sight of them would antagonize me the way they did each other. But I guess if Ethan were that sibling, it would be possible.

Ethan jerked his head up, urging him out of the room.

Josh huffed out a breath. "Ethan, the decision has been made. Sebastian has agreed and she's agreed. Either you get on board or you can take your issues with it somewhere else."

"Out. Here. Now."

Josh bit down on his lips hard. He jumped up from the bed and plodded out of the room.

"What!" he demanded just outside my door. "This is getting so tiring. Do I need to ask your permission to use magic? Big brother, may I please use magic today? Pretty please? I'd be *ever* so grateful."

Ethan snarled in a low voice, "You're going into the lion's den and asking for his help. Are you insane?"

"Isn't that why you're coming?"

There was a long silence. "I don't like this.".

"Big surprise. What else is new?"

"I'm not in the mood for your smart-ass mouth."

"And I'm not in the mood for the overbearing big brother thing. What's the purpose of me being part of this if all you want me to do is sit down somewhere and perform minor magic tricks that a child could do? Sebastian offered me an alliance because I can do things you all can't. Let me do what I do best. Okay?"

Josh sighed heavily. "Ethan, I am not going to keep doing this with you. We will not have this discussion again."

"You *will* have this discussion as many times as I need you to."

"No. I won't. As far as I'm concerned, you can continue this argument alone. Go with us or stay behind and pout, I really don't give a shit." Josh's quick footsteps trotted down the stairs.

Ethan called him several times without getting a response. Heavy footsteps pounced across the hardwood floor as he went after Josh. The discussion was far from over, no matter how Josh willed it to be.

Three hours later, Josh walked behind as we went to the large SUV waiting for us. Winter was already in the driver's seat. Ethan leaned against the SUV, drilling Josh with a reproachful glare, which Josh tried his best to ignore. Josh had disappeared after his brief argument with Ethan, leaving Ethan to deal with his unexpressed anger, a skill he hadn't mastered.

I stopped short so quickly that Josh bumped into me. My eyes widened at the massive figure that stood in front of us. Although he stood on two legs and looked human enough, something about him just didn't seem quite so. The visitor was well over six feet eight inches tall, with black hair cut so short that he was nearly bald. Arms the size of small tree trunks were crossed over his chest. His gaze was penetratingly intense as he followed the others toward the car. His lumbering gait didn't match the fluid movement of the other were-animals. His steps were slow, reactive, and mechanical as though walking on two legs were unfamiliar to him.

"He's a bear, a transfer from northern Montana. A couple of years ago, he had some control issues and Sebastian helped him," Josh whispered in my ear. "If he were able to tolerate his human form, he could easily be an Alpha. He's smart, strong, and a born leader, but he is turned off by his humanity. He often stays in the woods in Canada, coming out as needed. Sebastian sent for him a couple of days ago."

If I saw Dakota on the street or in a deserted place, I

wouldn't be able to move fast enough to get away from him. I was glad he was on our side.

Forty minutes later, we were just outside the city walking toward a creepy mansion. Okay, it wasn't so much of a creepy mansion as it was a gray, two-story stucco house at the end of a darkened street. Still, it felt like we were walking up to the creepy house in every horror movie imaginable where you would ultimately meet your doom. The property was shadowy, large trees blocking much of the view; not even the moon could offer enough light to see the path in front of us. Beautifully manicured privacy hedges created a verdant tunnel, forcing us into single file as we traveled down an increasingly midnight path. I could feel my heart pounding through my jacket. And it didn't go unnoticed that this vampire lived very close to the overpopulated city, which I doubt was a coincidence.

The door was unlocked. The vampire didn't seem to have a problem with unwanted guests. Or was he expecting us? We entered the bleak Victorian home slowly. Our footsteps echoed against the marble floors. The home was a showroom—beautiful and cold. Intricately decorated silk-papered walls were adorned with classic art. The dark, cherry wood furniture was elegant, opulent, and antique. Each marking on the sofa look distinctly handcrafted. An exquisite pearl fainting couch was placed at the entrance of the living room. Grand, elaborate drapes framed the window and were pulled closed, darkening the room.

Josh took the lead, navigating through the house with ease. It was apparent this wasn't his first visit. He stopped briefly at the top of the basement stairs to turn on the small wall lamp that was insufficient for illuminating the stairway. We followed him down the cavernous passageway surrounded by concrete walls and steps. It was cold and stifling. The slight glimmer given off by the small light at the top of the stairs made negotiating the deep steps difficult. Josh used his phone to light the remainder of the way.

The end of the stairway was pitch-black. Josh's phone wasn't enough to light the large area. He pulled me closer to him as we moved farther into the basement.

We entered a large room; muted torchlights hung from the wall casting a marginal amount of light. A tall, slender man, wearing black slacks and a black button-down shirt, blended into the darkness as he waited for us on the other side of the room. He faced the wall, his long, lanky, pale arms tucked behind his back. A red tie held his long, dark hair neatly at the nape of his neck. He was poised elegantly and remained motionless as we approached.

"Josh," he breathed out, his back still to us.

"Caleb," Josh responded formally.

When he finally turned to address us, we were confronted with a vampire with crimson eyes and a face so pretty that it was wasted on a man. Ruby lips curled back into a smile, exposing bloodstained teeth. He licked his lips and looked in my direction. My attention shot to Josh, who was focused on the vampire.

"To what do I owe this pleasure?" He exposed his fangs proudly with each articulation. He walked toward us in a manner that was far too spectacular for a grown man who wasn't in a theatrical production. Each step and gesture he made was deliberate and flamboyant.

"A gift—for me? You shouldn't have," he whispered seductively as he moved quickly behind me. Holding my breath, I kept a steady gaze on Josh, who was surprisingly calm and controlled.

"You touch her, and you won't live long enough to savor the taste," Josh stated so casually you could have missed the threat.

Caleb threw back his head and laughed boisterously, once

again, a very dramatic and unnecessary gesture. Not that I was fond of vampires at this point, but I really didn't like him. He was just—too. Too pretty. Too seductive. Too dramatic. Too stereotypical vampire. Yuck!

Josh looked around the room slowly and cautiously. His eyes narrowed into a sharp line and his expression grew intense. "Reveal them," he commanded the flamboyant vampire.

Caleb smiled impishly. "It's okay. Show yourselves." With his command, we were surrounded by vampires as they stepped from the shadows. Winter's hand went to the hilt of her dagger, Ethan assumed a defensive stance, and Dakota growled angrily.

"I see you've been busy growing your family," Josh acknowledged. "The question is: Why are they here? Where's the trust?"

Caleb made a low amused sound. "You, I trust. I don't trust your ill-tempered brother. His reputation of having a short fuse and a violent response is where my trust ends. You brought him into my home and I want to make sure he behaves."

Ethan snorted. "And you think these newbie vamps can make me behave?"

"They'll make every effort to."

Ethan took several steps toward him and Josh put out his arm to stop him. "I need your help and have nothing to gain from violence against you."

Caleb stared at Josh for a long time scrutinizing him. "Very well." He waved his hand and the ten vampires disappeared again, although I doubt they went far.

"What can I do for my Josh?" he asked in a low, suggestive voice.

Josh frowned as he approached the vampire. "I need you to answer some questions."

"Well of course you do. You never come by just to say 'hello.' Why is that, Josh?"

Josh didn't answer. Instead, he gave the vampire a disapproving look. Caleb licked his finger then touched it to the air.

"*Umm*, your powers have strengthened since the last time we saw each other. Exciting!" I wasn't sure if he was indeed flirting with Josh or just trying to make him uncomfortable, but Josh remained calm and unmoved by it.

"Demetrius has the Gem of Levage and he seems to want Skylar. Why? What is the link between Skylar and the Gem?"

Caleb waved his hand dismissively. "The Gem of Levage is a myth."

"I assure you it's not. Demetrius has possession of it and plans to use it. I need to know its function and how Skylar is involved," he said, stepping closer to the vampire. Josh's mannerisms were slow and deliberate, indicating that he was in no mood for games.

"How would I know what dwells in the mind of Demetrius?" Caleb challenged.

"Because he is your creator, your father, if you will. Tell me. What's your father up to?"

Caleb's eyes became distant. He swayed slowly as though he heard music. Music that I assumed could only be heard in the head of crazy dramatic vampires.

"You know, I loved him dearly," he admitted softly. "Not the way you would a lover, father or friend, but the way you love a god. He was indeed my creator, making me something that surpassed all that I could hope for. We spent one hundred and five years together, feeding from whom we chose, taking what and who we wanted. Every desire we could imagine was fulfilled tenfold. It was a life that others only dreamed of. And then she came into it, Lilith. She was a controlling bitch who changed life as I knew it in the worst way. He created her but only lived to please her. She wasn't good for him—for us, or the family. She was slowly killing him, but he was too besotted by her to see it. When I killed her, he banished me from his family. He chose her over me! Hundreds he has created, trying to recreate what we had together. Now he has another, but no one will ever adore him the way I did," he stated ardently as he guided us— reluctantly—down memory lane.

Everything that could be creepy and inappropriate about this vampire was, including his unhealthy man-crush on his creator.

"Must I hear this tale every time we meet? I grew tired of it the first time," Josh stated, indifferent.

Caleb shook his head, cleansing himself of the memories. "I'm sorry that I bored you."

Josh shrugged. "I need to use you as a conduit."

"What do I get in return?"

"The same payment as usual."

Whatever "payment as usual" was had Caleb foaming at the mouth with desire. He agreed quickly. Josh rolled his eyes, visibly annoyed by the vampire. I later found out that Josh allowed him to feed from him as payment. The magic that Josh held produced a state of euphoria for vampires that surpassed any high they could get from drugs.

Josh walked over to me. "I need to use you as well, Skylar," he said in a low voice. He took my hand into his and gave it a reassuring squeeze. I trusted Josh, but it didn't stop my heart from pounding so loudly that I knew the others could hear it.

Josh took a knife and reached for the vampire's hand. Caleb shook his head in declination, took the knife from Josh, and sliced it across his own hand. Blood flowed freely from the opening. Josh took my hand gently. "It will only hurt for a moment," he promised. As he slid the knife across my hand, I couldn't stop the shriek that slipped out.

Josh cut his hand and took the vampire's hand and mine into his. Josh's chanted words started in a slow, easy cadence but soon flowed faster as his body jerked, becoming suspended in air. A pale, incandescent light surrounded him, producing warmth that enveloped the room. The room came to a harsh stillness. Without warning, Josh crashed to the floor and both the vampire and I flew back, hitting the ground, too. The gates of terror and despair opened, sending havoc throughout the room.

Covered in darkness, I forced my eyes to remain open, trying to catch sight of something familiar. My body grew rigid —paralyzed as an unknown force overtook me.

"Make it stop," I pled to Josh through the darkness. It continued to consume me as I struggled against its effect. My screams from both pain and fear pierced through the silence of the room. The vampire grabbed me in the midst of the darkness. "No!" I yelled out, pushing against the force that bound me. The vampire disappeared from sight but not before sinking his teeth into my wrist and drawing blood. The pains from his bite, combined with the existing aches, were unbearable. Something had taken my voice. I could no longer scream. I felt a new form of fear.

"Skylar," said Josh's voice in my head. It was soft and comforting as he attempted to calm me. But it didn't relieve the burning and tingling that engulfed me.

Josh leaned next to me, his hands brushed my face, his lips inches from my ear. He whispered, "*A-na rische*. Release."

The darkness was lifted, and I was able to see my surroundings, but the binding still held like a cocoon, restricting all movements.

Ethan, Winter, and Dakota were coming back to standing positions after being floored by the power that overtook the room. Josh stood and walked toward the vampire. Two fingers pointed toward Caleb as he used magic to hold him against the wall. The vampire struggled in vain to break free but remained immobile.

I was suffocating. I struggled to catch my breath and shake myself free of the binding. My pain-filled shrieks filled the room, making it shake uncontrollably, throwing everyone to the ground once again. Caleb was freed from his position. The only person who remained standing was Josh. He rushed over to me and touched my shoulder as he began chanting. The binding released, breathing became easier and the burning and tingling subsided. I collapsed, nauseous and aching from head to toe.

Ethan knelt in front of me, pushing sweat-drenched hair from my face. "Are you okay?" There wasn't anything broken and I was alive. But I was far from okay. I nodded slowly, trying to stabilize my ragged breathing enough to speak.

"You cannot leave without rendering payment!" the vampire yelled.

Josh turned and the rage that radiated from him made me queasy. Ethan's attention was pulled to Josh as though he felt it, too. I just wanted him to stop as it trampled over me, crushing me to the ground. Ethan lifted me, cradling me close into him. Another roaring storm from Josh's anger hit and I felt like something reached inside and twisted the fascia in my muscles. I cringed, digging my nails into Ethan, pulling into him.

"Josh," he called in a low controlled voice, trying to get his incensed brother's attention. He had to call him several times before he responded. His fury eventually diminished into a tolerable wave. Instead of feeling as if I were being ground into pieces, there were just sharp pricks against my skin. It was tolerable.

"Payment forfeited. You went after her. Count yourself fortunate that you are left with the sorry existence you call a life. You won't be so lucky in the future." The words spewed out of his mouth like venom.

Caleb stalked toward us, his fangs exposed as he lost himself to his emotions. The were-bear growled and for a brief moment, the house seemed to rock in unison with the sound. The vampire stopped in his tracks just before Dakota grabbed him and threw him back into the concrete wall.

We left the house, leaving Dakota behind.

Minutes later he returned, his eyes no longer exhibiting

anything remotely human. The hinges of the door screamed as he opened it forcibly. "As you wished, his life has been spared, though barely," he informed Josh.

Skylar, said Josh's voice in my head as I rested it back against the seat on the ride home. I tried to shake off the dull aches that rolled over me.

I didn't answer him. *Skylar,* he called again a little louder.

I groaned. His voice pulsed into my head and made it ache more. *Are you alright?*

No, I responded silently, too weak to let words form on my lips.

What's wrong?

I've gone mad, and now I'm hearing voices.

He chuckled; the loudness of it made me cringe. *It's just me. You haven't gone mad. Besides hearing my voice in your head, are you okay?*

That damn vampire bit me. I am really getting tired of vampires snacking on me. Other than that, I'm okay, I think. I shifted to find a position that was a little less painful. *Josh, what was that?*

That was magic, very powerful magic that got a little out of control. And for that, I apologize. His voice was strained and remorseful.

Did you get what you needed?

Yes.

Then you have nothing to apologize for. Things got a little more intense than anticipated.

That wasn't like Fantasia *at all. I was really looking forward to seeing a light show, shooting stars and possibly a dancing broom,* I admitted languidly.

He laughed.

What did you find out?

Let's discuss it later. I need to do further research to confirm the information. I trust Caleb within limits.

Is it bad?

Yes.

Is it impending-death bad? Or is it serious-injury bad?

He didn't answer.

Josh.

Both.

My body didn't bother to respond to the new information by showing fear. It had been in that state for so long, it had developed a tolerance to it.

Do the vampires want me dead?

Skylar, let me further research the situation. I don't want to alarm you unnecessarily. His voice was strained. He was hiding a hell of a lot.

Too late. I am already alarmed. Just give it to me straight.

I am not intentionally keeping you in the dark. It is important that I have all necessary information, not just for your sake but for that of the pack as well.

There was a long silence between us.

Will we be able to talk like this from now on?

No. It's a blood-bond connection I established with you in order to use you as a conduit. It's residual magic from earlier. I am about to release you from it now.

Why? I like it.

It's too draining on me to block you from all the thoughts and information in my head. When we are connected like this, I can read your thoughts, and if I am not careful, you can read mine.

Are the thoughts in your head so disturbing that they need to be hidden?

Nah, just magic and pack stuff. Just a lot of boring things that need to be censored.

I scoffed to myself. They *wanted* it censored—not needed.

I am sure the ability to communicate like this has benefits that surpass anything you'll want to censor, I challenged.

Yeah, but keep in mind I can read your thoughts, as well. You, my dear, for such a pretty, mild-mannered woman, have an utterly filthy mouth when you're angry and scared. You have quite an elaborate command of curse words. I forgive you for the dreadful names you called me. I agree. Caleb is unnecessarily melodramatic and far too pretty for a man. I am sure being wrapped in my brother's arms felt wonderful, but I doubt you could stay like that forever. Yes, he does have the tendency to make the ladies' hearts go pitter-patter and feel impossibly safe when they are around him. And you are right. It is quite unfortunate that he is a "raging jackass."

I had no idea how to respond to that.

Do you still like communicating like this? I find it quite entertaining myself; however, I am sure you will become annoyed at some point.

I am not enjoying it so much now, I admitted. He laughed.

Go to sleep, he suggested when my head hit against his shoulder as I dozed off for a few seconds. *Sweet dreams, dream girl.* A-na rische. *Unbind.*

Josh, are you still there? I waited a few minutes. *Guess not.* I repeated the words that he had spoken quietly.

"The bond was broken. You don't have the ability to reestablish it," he whispered in my ear.

I tried to rest on the drive home, listening to the soothing sounds of wind bristling through the window in an attempt to ignore the unspoken rage that was screaming, howling, and rapping through the quiet. Ethan was angry, shooting tension-filled glares in his brother's direction. Josh glanced up at the sharp lines along his brother's frowning face, and sighed as he relaxed back next to me. I didn't know whether his unease was from the aftermath of dealing with Caleb or the potential wrath he was going to have to deal with from an angered brother.

. . .

I had finally gotten to sleep after spending some time with Dr. Baker, a result of Ethan's overreaction to Caleb's bite. My pride was wounded more so than the throbbing puncture marks that he had given me. I should have punched him, kicked him in the groin, or even bit him back. It was easily treated with antibiotics and a bandage, but they both seemed concerned that a vampire drew blood, quite a bit. I wasn't your typical were-animal. I had a terait. For anyone else, it was a simple bite and a blood draw—nothing. In my case, it could possibly be something. But after careful observation, Dr. Baker's concerns were eased.

A quarter after midnight, I was jarred out of my sleep by the blaring sound of Ethan's angry voice. I rolled over and covered my head with a pillow, trying to drown out the sounds. But his incensed rants only got louder, ripping through the silence of the room. Finally, after several attempts to ignore the sounds, I got up and followed them down the stairs, across the great room to the small room just behind the library where I first met Josh.

Ethan was standing nose-to-nose with Josh, yelling at him at the top of his lungs. "What the hell was that?" You didn't have control of the situation. You told me you knew how to do conduits, and obviously, you didn't know what the hell you were doing! We could have been hurt tonight, and you could have been killed."

"Well, in theory I did know how to do it. It's not like I ever had the opportunity to practice." His tone was far too relaxed for someone who had an angry wolf screaming at him.

"You were reckless and put us all in danger. You asked me to trust you and let you do your job. Well, I did, and you screwed up! I should have been informed of all possible outcomes and potential risks."

The look on Josh's face changed as the sparks of his anger ignited. A similar form of anger emerged, matching his brother's. "Why did I have to tell you anything? You couldn't have done a damn thing about it! You are just upset because my magic is one of the few things in this house that you can't control. That is the only reason you have your panties in a bunch and that is just too goddamn bad. Go cry about it to someone who gives a crap. I did my fucking job! Are you doing yours? I wasn't aware that being a ranting ass was part of the Beta duties, but if it is, you are doing a hell of a job! We have information that we didn't have and otherwise would not have gotten, information that will help us. And if I weren't down here playing around with you, I could be doing my research and finishing my job."

Ethan's face tightened, his fist clenching into a ball as his nostrils flared. He grabbed Josh by the collar. "Don't push me, Josh. You won't like it when I push back," he snarled.

"Go ahead and push. I've just been itching to show you what'll happen when you do."

When Ethan didn't release him, Josh's eyes flashed. Using magic, he pushed Ethan away from him.

"I did what was necessary and got the job done. You think you could have gotten the same results storming into Caleb's home ranting, threatening, and beating him up? Sorry, but that tactic doesn't always work. Accept the fact that I achieved something you couldn't have. If your pride is a little battered, then that's your problem!"

"You smug, arrogant, son of a bitch!"

"Really. Smug? Arrogant? Surely, that is the pot calling out the kettle. Son of a bitch? That is no way to talk about our mother," Josh replied, his tone losing its edge. He relaxed significantly into his calm persona, after his tirade infuriated Ethan to the level he desired. His lips spread into a charming boyish grin that only ticked off his brother more.

Ethan screeched, giving into his anger. He pushed his brother with such force it sent him soaring back. Before Josh crashed into the wall, he waved his hand in front of him. A chair thrashed against Ethan hard enough to make him stumble. He flicked his hand, and Ethan skidded back farther across the room. Ethan quickly regained his footing and lunged at Josh, knocking him to the floor. Pressing his forearm into Josh's chest, he barked, "I'm not fucking impressed with any of the hack magic you managed to pull over these last couple of months. It's still amateurish at best."

"Let's see what I can do about changing your mind." He pushed Ethan off him, then held his brother immobile the same way he had with Caleb earlier. It lasted for quite some time until Ethan's eyes shuddered into an even deeper gray. He broke the hold and punched Josh squarely in the jaw. Pushing Josh into the door, he crashed into it hard, breaking past it and falling just a few feet short of where I stood. They were so blinded by their anger, they didn't notice me. Ethan charged toward Josh but collided with something … a force field? A thin film covered Josh like an egg, protecting him from any further assault from Ethan.

Amateur? Hack? Are you impressed with his magic now? I thought as I watched Ethan's rage magnify.

His face distorted into a frustrated grimace as he battered it with such force that it sent him flying in the opposite direction. Ethan charged at the field again with so much power it shattered and he collided with Josh. They held each other by their shirt collars. Ethan finally shoved them apart.

That was enough. "Stop it!" I yelled so loudly that my voice cracked from the strain. I moved farther into the room. "Ethan. Josh. Stop it! What the hell is wrong with you two?" As I inched closer, I wondered how I was going to break up a fight between an enraged wolf and a pissed-off warlock. Brothers who were behaving as though they were mortal enemies. Before I could move in and intervene, a deafening growl erupted, shaking the walls of the room.

Well, hello, Sebastian.

His grand entrance pulsated throughout the room and I'm sure the Greater Chicago area. Members of the pack flooded the room, responding to Sebastian's angered call. It was quite remarkable that no one reacted to the sound of the brothers going at each other like they were in an UFC title match. I guess this was just another day in the pack's safe house. Too caught up in their fight, they ignored Sebastian. As they charged at each other, Sebastian moved quickly between them. He pushed into their chests simultaneously, sending them crashing into opposite ends of the floor.

He made eye contact with Josh, who stared back hard before settling back on the floor. Ethan came to his feet. When his gaze briefly locked with Sebastian's—he remained still. The anger radiated off him as he struggled to extinguish it without success. Neither one of them made further eye contact with Sebastian. Instead, they glared at each other from across the room.

"Enough. Ethan, the conduit was risky but it was necessary and you are going to have to let it go. Inevitably, some of the things Josh does will present us with unavoidable risk. It's magic. It will always have its hazards. This is not new to you and it doesn't change because he is your brother. We have to trust him and grant him the necessary autonomy to allow him to do his job. He has never failed us. You are going to back off," he stated firmly. Ethan nodded once. It didn't douse his anger, which was so intense he had to turn his gaze from Josh.

Sebastian turned to face Josh. "And you. Stop being an ass. He's been your brother for twenty-four years, and you know how protective he is when it comes to you. Would it hurt you to give him a heads-up when you know things are going to get a little crazy? He deserves that much. You didn't give him proper disclosure, and you were wrong for that. He has every right to be pissed with you right now. When you know he's pissed with you, leave him the hell alone! Don't antagonize him. It's juvenile. This fighting between you two is no longer entertaining—it's just ridiculous and annoying. He's your brother, but my Beta, and you will respect him as such."

Josh's face tightened, a level of irritation and anger shadowing his appearance. "Are we done here?" he asked in a tight voice. When Sebastian nodded, he left, the doors opening and shutting behind him without him touching them. The front door slammed, and I heard his Wrangler speed off. Ethan stalked out of the room soon after.

I began to pick up the splintered furniture and broken accent pieces from the title match between Josh and Ethan. It took an hour to clean up before I returned exhausted to bed, yet sleep didn't come easily. I lay in the bed staring at the ceiling. Between the earlier magic exhibitions and the brawl between Ethan and Josh, my mind was in chaos. I stared into the darkness. A full moon was coming. I could feel it murmuring, tugging and poking at the wolf, letting it know that soon it would be forced to answer.

Giving up on any ideas of sleep, I pulled on a pair of sweats and headed down the stairs to the gym.

The basement gym was divided into three workout areas. One was set up like a typical gym with cardio equipment, weight machines, and free weights, far better than anything I could imagine in a home gym. The other room was rough and rugged: punching bag in one corner, a heavy bag in the other, and a large bench with metal barbells and free weights. It was perfect for the person who wanted a hardcore workout without the frills. The third room was used to spar. Unlike the others that smelled like sweat, it smelled like old blood, and though I didn't think pain had a smell, here, it seemed to have one. There was a large mat in the middle of the room surrounded by mirrors. In the corner, there was a glass-front cabinet stocked with numerous weapons used in martial arts, yet I didn't see any protective gear.

From the left, Ethan's familiar scent swept over me. Before good sense could prevail, I found myself walking into the second room. He was in the corner, shirtless with sweat running along the defined crevices of his body as he terrorized the heavy bag, no doubt wishing on some level it was his brother. His anger was like a fire sucking out all the oxygen in the room. I started backing away to make a quiet escape when he called me. "Come in," he urged, taking a break. I hesitated. I wasn't in the mood to be around the irritated wolf.

I considered ignoring him and heading upstairs. But instead, I walked farther into the gym. He started again with the heavy bag, pulverizing it with a series of kicks and punches. He eventually exhausted himself, breathing heavily. He leaned into the bag holding it in place.

"Speak," he commanded in a low drawl.

"What?"

"I can hear your heart racing and your breathing is slightly ragged. You have something to say. So say it."

First of all, does anyone else find your freaky super-hearing annoying?

He stood still for a while before he turned to look at me, awaiting my response.

My eyes stayed plastered on my fidgeting hands. "I think you were too hard on your brother," I muttered in a low voice, keeping my head down. When I looked up, he was wiping himself off with a towel, a couple of feet from me. I was an expert at denial but some things were just too blatant to ignore: strongly defined features, supple lips, intense mesmerizing graphite eyes with subtle hints of cobalt, and carnal power that was simultaneously appealing and repelling. His body looked as though he had been sculpted. Long sinewy muscles ran the length of his body. It was quite unfortunate that Ethan came wrapped in such a nice package.

"Was I?"

I nodded. "Yeah. I don't see what was so bad that would warrant you going off the way that you did." I forced myself to keep eye contact with him.

He stared at me for a long time. "He was rash and irresponsible."

"Josh is extremely powerful, isn't he?"

"He's been gifted with abilities that exceed most," he admitted reluctantly.

"You're quite modest. I've seen him in action. He's powerful —very powerful. What would you have him do? Sit back and not use his gifts to help when needed? You wouldn't tolerate that, so why expect that from him?"

A grave look came over him. He washed his hands over his face, frustrated. "You wouldn't understand."

"You don't trust him."

"Of course I trust him." He appeared offended by the accusation.

"Then you should start acting like it. Were there other options, safer options that he ignored? Or did he do what was necessary in this situation to get results?"

He exhaled a heavy breath, his face weighed down by his thoughts. "Being a warlock isn't like being a were-animal. No matter how inept you are as a were-animal, eventually you can control your animal. With magic, there are too many unknown variables that can change the outcome. It's the little variables that you don't think about that are the difference between life and death. I don't like it." Concern swept over his face briefly before the hardened mask returned.

"Everything has risk, including being a were-animal. He shouldn't have to deal with your anger every time things don't go as expected. It's not fair to him. I am willing to bet if things went wrong while you were in were-animal form, he would never react the way you did." I wasn't sure why I defended Josh. Perhaps it was because he gave me the impression that he was also pulled into this world and was just doing a much better job handling it than I was.

He was quiet for a long time, considering my statement and watching me carefully. "You surprise me sometimes," he admitted.

"Pleasantly, I hope." The hostility seemed to have melted away, and standing in front of me was someone approachable—well, as approachable as Ethan could be. There was something about him that always made me feel as though I were just a tendril from petting the wolf to being hunted by it.

He smiled, but his eyes were too intense to appear pleasant. "What was it like, being swept into magic like that?" There was an immensely curious look on his face, and I really wanted to tell him the truth. To tell him it was horrible, terrifying, enigmatic, and uncontrollable. I wanted to tell him how scary it was to be drawn into a rampaging tornado while you frantically searched for an anchor or anything that could somehow keep you grounded and planted to the world you knew. And the pain. I couldn't forget about the pain. So excruciating it felt like I was being filleted, my insides coiled then set aflame. I didn't want to lie to him, but if I gave him the truth, it would only make things worse for Josh.

He stepped closer, watching me closely with a gaze so probing I felt exposed—naked. Ethan stripped away all my barriers, exposing my secrets. He watched, listened, and then touched me. Long fingers trailed along my jaw. When he spoke, his voice was tranquil and low. "No need to tell your lie, or even the modified version of your truth. The answers are in the panic in your eyes, the rapid heartbeat of your anxiety." He stepped closer; his lips brushed my cheek as he spoke. "It's in the set of your jaw, clenching at the very idea of reliving that moment."

He took my arm into his hand, his thumb gently stroking along the pulse, his eyes fixed on me. "Your skin, it's cool"—he brought my wrist to his face and inhaled, his lips brushed across it—"and fear can be sensed by a predator no matter how faint."

I started to respond but he cut me off. "You *were* going to lie to me—"

"No, I wasn't," I rattled back. I hated lying to people and despised being accused of it when I really had no intentions of doing so.

The air was thick with an ominous silence. His lips curled into a faint amused smile. He brought my hand to his lips and lightly kissed the palm as he inhaled again. "Of course you would have. But why? Would it have been to protect Josh from his tyrant of a brother"—he chuckled lightly reminding me that my expressions often betrayed me—"or to ease my concerns about my audacious brother?"

He waited patiently for a response.

"Your parents must have had hell to pay when you found out the truth about Santa Claus and the Tooth Fairy."

He laughed. It was a rich, hearty, pleasing sound. It was then I realized I had never heard him laugh before. The laughter came to an abrupt stop. He looked over his shoulder at Josh standing behind him. Josh's focus moved from Ethan's left hand, which was still grasping mine, and then drifted to the other, which rested around my waist. It wasn't until we were under Josh's probing gaze that I was aware of how close Ethan was to me. His body molded to mine. It hadn't felt invasive, but now under Josh's watchful eye, it felt too intimate. He pressed his lips into my hand again before he released it and turned toward Josh.

Had Josh walked in unnoticed or did he just pop up, in the same manner he did when we first met? I might not be able to smell fear, but I was well-versed in sensing hostility and it came off Josh in a concentrated vapor. "You broke my protective field," Josh stated in a low somber voice.

Ethan shrugged lightly, "It was just a simple ward. Not very hard to break."

Josh's jaws clenched. His eyes glinted with ire. "Don't screw with me! That wasn't just a ward. It was a protective field, and there wasn't anything *simple* about it. A were-animal has never been able—"

"Josh." Ethan shot a look in my direction. His voice was soft, entreating as he spoke. "Your field was nothing more than a glorified ward. We break them all the time. Sebastian's broken them, Gavin's broken them, and even Hannah's broken one. It's just a broken ward. Let it go." Ethan stood just inches from him. Oddly, it was Ethan who was calm, working to defuse the situation.

Their gazes were locked in such intensity, I wondered if they were speaking to each other the way Josh and I did earlier. No, this was a different form of communication, the kind you can only have when you know a person in a way that only brothers could. It may have been silent but it was screaming in discord. More intense than what occurred between them earlier.

Josh tilted his head, considering the possibility. Frown lines crept above his brow as he retreated into his thoughts. He looked unconvinced. He shook his head slowly. "No. You're hiding things from me. How long—"

Ethan cut him off with a stern look, and then looked back in my direction.

Josh's glower remained on his brother as he spoke, his voice coarse and tense. "Good night, Skylar."

After he dismissed me, I left, walking at a snail-like crawl, hoping to catch some parts of the conversation. But they remained quiet. I could feel them, or rather, Ethan watching me as I ascended the stairs. It was doubtful they started the conversation until they heard the door leading to the basement close firmly behind me.

I went to my room after vetoing the idea of trying to sneak back downstairs to listen to Ethan and Josh's conversation. Fear of being around a pissed-off warlock and an irate wolf had little appeal to me at 2:46 in the morning. After tossing and turning for another half an hour, I had finally fallen asleep when I was awakened by someone calling my name. It was a deep whisper. The room was empty but a strong presence was felt. Something called me. It was unusually gentle, soft, alluring, but I could feel the urgency in its call. *Yes,* I answered. Relaxing into its pull, I allowed it to direct me through the house.

Its tug stopped as I entered the library, but the calling persisted. I knelt down in front of the bookcase, tugging at the bottom drawer. It was locked. Compelled, I ran my finger over the lock and heard a click, unlocking it. When I pulled out the *Symbols of Death,* it continued to speak to me in a low, demanding whisper, surrendering its secrets as it called my name.

At some point, this should have weirded me out, but it didn't. Why wouldn't it call me? It seemed so natural for it to do so.

Opening the page to the Gem of Levage, I whispered the title of the book in a low voice. It was as though knowing its name gave me power. Pulling it closer to me, I listened carefully to what it needed to say. But I was met with utter silence, a forced silence.

I'm listening, I urged the book, knowing at some point I was going to feel ridiculous. I waited for a few minutes for a response, but the silence persisted. I returned the book to the drawer and headed for the door. Pausing at the threshold, I had a distinct feeling that I had missed something important. It was that same sickening feeling you get right before you lock your keys in the car.

Walking back to the bookshelf, I took the book out again and held it. *What do you want from me?* Blood flashed through my mind. It wanted blood. Biting into my finger, I dripped blood over the picture.

Without warning or hesitation, it spoke loud and clear. A piercing pang shot through me. My body stiffened, I dropped to my knees, pulling in breath that didn't help ease the pain. I pulled the book closer to me, resting it firmly against my chest. My eyes were rigid. Closing them became impossible as the light slowly faded into complete darkness.

A deep red stone, enclosed by a series of bronze rings, dangled freely from the chain around Demetrius's neck. I'd never met him, yet identifying him was quite easy. His wavy hair, a midnight shimmer with hints of deep blue, stopped just short of his chin. Pale, flawless skin was aptly complimented by strong angular features and sharply defined jaw and cheeks. Black opal eyes with small ringlets of red looked upon me with great satisfaction. He could easily be considered handsome if he weren't the face of my death.

I shivered. Fear enveloped me as he walked toward me. I tried to reach out and touch the gem around his neck, but my movements were restricted by the constraints on my wrist. Bound against the wall, my arms were outstretched and my legs pinned close together. I was placed in this sacrilegious pose purposefully to make a mockery of the crucifixion. The air felt cold against my face, but my body remained a blazing fire, fueled by my fear.

Demetrius stood close, eyeing me from head to toe as though I were nothing more than a specimen under a microscope. He stroked the Gem of Levage affectionately. "Skylar." My name rolled off his tongue with a strong accent. He stepped closer, his lips brushing against my jaw as he spoke. "I thank you in advance for your gift."

His thin lips made dramatic precise movements as he spoke. They became the focus of my attention, promising a painful end. I could feel the dark presence of his Seethe, but they kept to the shadows. Their joy illuminated the room as Demetrius stroked my neck. I ached to move, but my bindings were excruciatingly tight, limiting even the least movement.

Demetrius turned to his Seethe. "On this night, my honored family, we shall fear the light no more. A wooden stake will be nothing more than an inadequate form of weaponry and we will never experience reversion ever again. Never again must we request admittance into anyone's home, but we become free to roam as we please. A cross will be nothing but a senseless object of religion. This will be the gift offered by our sweet Skylar. To Skylar." His voice, gentle, as he gave me insincere accolades. It was nothing more than a condensed eulogy.

"To Skylar," the Seethe responded in unison.

He was too close to my face. My panic and fear were making me feel ill.

"These things you will gift to us upon your death and for that I thank you," he stated in gratitude near my ear again. Without warning, he sank his teeth into my neck. I screamed.

"Shall we feed?"

Piercing pain engulfed me as sharp enamel penetrated my skin, drawing blood. I grew cold as the warm blood was taken from me. Bite after bite, my sounds of pain became nothing more than a whimper. Soon I was too numb to the feel of piercing stabs inflicted on the greater part of my body. When they finally stopped feeding, I could hear the sound of my slowing heartbeat. Words were spoken, but they seemed so far away that I couldn't decipher their meaning.

"The gift has been received," Demetrius said softly into my ear. My eyes widened in response to the overwhelming pain as he sank his teeth into me again. Drawing in deeply, he took away what little life remained. My heartbeat was barely an inaudible thump as the pangs of my torture stopped and my life slipped away. At that moment, everything became strangely bearable. I found that place between life and death, where I lingered. Then I was consumed by the emptiness of

crossing over to the other side. Death welcomed me freely—almost expectantly—it was strangely familiar to me.

Suddenly, I was lying on the library floor, blaring sounds of pain at the top of my lungs as the book clung to me. My body ached from the bites inflicted on it. My neck throbbed, recalling the sharp overwhelming pain of Demetrius's last kiss. I was cold as an ice block.

"Skylar," Josh called, but I couldn't respond. My eyes fixed on the ceiling, unable to move from the spot where I had witnessed and experienced my ritualistic death. Water—or perhaps it was tears—filled my eyes, stinging as it ran down my cheek. I couldn't blink, forced to relive the vision over and over like a living nightmare in three dimensions. The book penetrated my very being, sending gut-wrenching pain through me continuously as punishment for my request for answers.

"What's happening to her?" asked Sebastian's strained voice from behind me.

"I don't know. Skylar, look at me," Josh demanded as he attempted to turn my face toward him. I was locked in the position, unable to move no matter how I tried. Josh's hand covered mine touching the book. "*A-na rische*. Release."

He tugged at the book but it wouldn't budge.

"Shit!" He pulled at the book again with more force. "*A-na rische*. Unbind." He tugged at it again. The book heated to a lava temperature, searing my fingers. The smell of burning flesh filled the room.

"Why can't you stop this?" Ethan asked, frustrated, from a distant.

"She bound herself to the book. Somehow, she held on to the magic from earlier. I don't know how it's possible. I released her from it." Josh sounded panicked. He touched my face again, trying to get me to focus on him.

"Winter, I need you to charm her. She's holding the binding and needs to release herself from it."

Winter sat next to me. Leaning in, she whispered into my ear, "Skylar." Her voice was a harp-like musical sound that invited me to her. She moved in front of me, speaking words of trust and comfort as her hands covered mine. Her lips curled into an inviting smile as she spoke. Her voice held me captive, rendering me defenseless of free will as her familiar serpent eyes entranced me. I freely accepted the consolation she offered.

"Release yourself to me," she requested. Her finger placed firmly under my chin forced my eyes to keep in contact with hers. The very eyes that seemed peculiar and intimidating before were enchanting and beautiful at this moment. I couldn't resist her request. My will was expunged from my body. I gave in freely to her.

The *Symbols of Death* forced itself from my hold, landing in the middle of the room as flames ignited from the letters. The flames died out quickly as the book saved itself from destruction.

I was surrounded by a room full of were-animals who looked at me with morbid fascination and apprehension.

Josh inched toward me. "Skylar," he called in a composed level tone.

"Yeah." My throat felt like sandpaper and sounded close to it, as well.

He was frowning when he turned my head to look at my neck. I ran my finger along it and felt two bite marks. There were similar marks all over my arm, as well. I lifted my shirt and pant leg, more markings were on my stomach and legs where the vampires fed from me in my vision. Panic came on fast. Tears of fear and panic started to form. The more I tried to stop them, the more they fought to escape.

Sebastian walked over, knelt down, and examined the marks. He gave me a small, reassuring smile. "Skylar, it's okay. They're going away. Look." He showed me my forearm, which had been riddled with bite marks, now free of all markings.

He took my hand in his. "Get Jeremy," he instructed Steven, making great efforts to keep his voice quiet and calm. I didn't know how and why he wasn't freaking out, but his calmness settled the room.

"Everything's going to be just fine," he assured me as he sat next to me, resting his hand on my knees. My erratic breathing began to slow down to something resembling a normal breathing pattern. I didn't have it in me to speculate what abilities Sebastian possessed to do this.

The were-animals continued to stare at me strangely as though I had sprouted horns and grown a tail. Inconspicuously, I ran my fingers over my hair and down my back just to make sure I hadn't. Weird things were happening these days, and nothing seemed too implausible.

"You saw it, didn't you?" Josh asked in a strained voice.

I swallowed a response and bit down on my lips too hard, puncturing them and causing blood to seep into my mouth.

"What did she see?" Sebastian asked as he started to distance himself from me, since I seemed to be much calmer than before. I was calmer, but the images in my head hadn't subsided.

Josh sighed, filling the room with a heaviness that left everyone on edge. "Her death. She saw what they are planning to do with her." He was still frowning when he turned back to look at me. Placing his hand on my shoulder, his gaze held mine as he spoke to them. "I had to research the information further in hopes that what Caleb showed me was wrong. But"—he shook his head—"he showed me nothing but truth. The Gem of Levage is used to transfer power sources from one person to another, or in this case, from Skylar to Demetrius's Seethe. During the ritual, if there is a blood exchange by both people then they exchange abilities. This isn't anything very special for a vampire because it is one of their gifts and the very dynamics of the trade."

He looked at Sebastian, then Ethan, before continuing. I

wished we were outside because the strong emotions radiating off everyone made the air feel thick and suffocating. Leaning my head as far back as possible, I inhaled.

Josh took a seat in front of me. Distress covered his face as I listened to the tale of why I was going to die. "They want her abilities, and with the ritual, there only needs to be a one-way blood exchange. Once life is drained, with the use of the Gem, the donor abilities remain indefinitely. Their Seethe, which is well over two hundred strong, will possess immunity to light, will no longer go through reversion when staked, can enter any dwelling without an invitation, and will be unaffected by religious symbols. They will also gain her strength, making them significantly stronger and faster than you all." He stopped for a moment and looked at Sebastian, who was listening to him attentively. "This will be true of anyone they create thereafter, as well."

"But why her?" Ethan finally asked.

"Most humans, due to their fragile nature, can't sustain life long enough to complete the ritual. Apparently, this ritual has already been attempted by Demetrius using a mage, several humans, and a were-puma. They even tried a dhampir, obviously without success. Most dhampirs have human fragility and couldn't survive the ritual. They were just fishing for candidates until Skylar came to their attention." He looked at me, I assumed to see how I was doing. The panicked look that was now etched on my face should have let him know that I wasn't doing well at all.

"The mage was human, though he had magical ability. He was unable to survive. For reasons unknown to me, were-animals are immune to their magic. That's why they can't enthrall or change you all and the very reason they failed when they used the were-puma. Skylar is somehow connected to them. The terait is evidence of it." He pointed toward his left eye. "That is the reason they were able to enter her home without an invitation. I don't know how this occurred but it did. An anomaly at its worst. She heals as the were-animal does and would be able to survive to complete the ritual. It is not definitive whether or not the transference will work, but since Demetrius is going to such extreme measures to get her, he must believe it is highly likely."

Sebastian stiffened, seemingly taking the information worse than I did. He kept his focus on Josh, stealing short glances in my direction. Everyone else went through great pains to keep their focus anywhere else but on me. "Steven, take Skylar to Jeremy and let him check her out," he stated, taking me by the elbow and guiding me toward the door.

Who is he fooling with that? He wasn't that concerned about marks that were virtually gone. They no longer wanted me there. They needed to discuss things that they deemed sensitive pack information, and I was no longer welcome. I glanced over my shoulder as I followed Steven out of the room, and the tragically disturbed looks on everyone's faces made leaving the room easier.

Steven dropped me off at the office. I kept looking at him, wanting some type of assurance that things were okay. A look that said, *This was nothing. They had seen it all before.* But he looked concerned. It was the first time those lambent, olive green eyes looked so deeply troubled that it scared me.

I expected Dr. Baker to lock me in one of the recovery rooms with the padlocks that I had seen earlier. But instead, he examined me on a small table next to his desk in the corner of the large infirmary. He was assiduous as he went over the marks, examining them. Each touch was skilled and gentle as he handled my injured limbs. Was it because he was the pack doctor and had seen so much that there were very few things that rattled him, or was it because he had mastered stoicism to an art form? I wasn't sure.

He examined me for a long time, looking at things that had nothing to do with what occurred in the library. It didn't take me long to realize he was stalling me. From his office, I couldn't hear what was going on in the library. After Dr. Baker finished with me, he escorted me back to the room, taking the back way, ensuring that I didn't go past the library.

I waited until I heard Dr. Baker descending the stairs. I took the stairs on the opposite side of the hallway and headed back to the library. Standing just outside the door to the right, I was hidden only by the open door from the next room. The debate was so emotionally charged, they were unable to keep their voices down.

"So, if we retrieve the Gem, this will all go away?" Sebastian's edgy voice inquired.

"That's a great big if," Josh responded, frustrated. "I know Demetrius has it, but he has a protection spell on it. He's using dark magic, and I can't find it. I've tried several times today. Tomorrow, I'm going to talk to London. She is more skilled than I am in matters like this and may be able to remove the protection spell. Once we locate it, the rest is easy."

"Are you sure she will help? In the past, she always resisted assisting us," Sebastian said.

"That's before we helped her. She owes us, and I believe she will be relieved to no longer have that debt."

He sighed, crossing his arms over his chest as he was drawn into his thoughts.

Josh watched him intently. "Sebastian," he stated respectfully. "Storming in the vampires' home and threatening them until they give you the Gem won't work. A battle like that will end with a great number of dead vampires and were-animals, as well. We would be no better off."

"I am assuming that killing Demetrius won't help, either. Is it safe to assume anyone in his Seethe can perform the ritual?"

He must have confirmed because Sebastian made a frustrated sound.

"Then kill her," Winter suggested calmly. "She is the most imminent threat. At least that will give us time to find the Gem." Her voice was far too casual for someone who was suggesting the murder of another being.

"She's not the threat," Steven interjected.

"Stop it with that load of crap! You can't still believe she's not a threat," Winter rumbled angrily.

Apparently, this wasn't the first time Winter had suggested this option, but now with everything that had taken place, she had a more compelling argument.

"She isn't. Nothing she's done has threatened us," Sebastian stated firmly.

I walked from around the door that I used to hide me. If she wanted to see me dead, then she would have to say it to my face. As I stood at the threshold of the library door, it was Winter who noticed me first. I had lost my status as a person—now I was a *situation*. She held my gaze for a long time before she directed it back to Sebastian.

"Her very existence is a threat. She is not one of us, and we should stop protecting her as though she were," Winter stated sharply.

"Josh, what do you think?" Sebastian asked, his voice calm and level, a direct contrast to Winter's.

"She's capable of things within the magic realms that aren't typical of were-animals. But Winter can charm, which is atypical of were-animals' abilities, and she isn't a threat to us but, rather, an asset. I can't say Skylar isn't capable of being dangerous because I am not quite sure what she really is. However, she would never endanger us intentionally."

"I am not saying it would be intentional," countered Winter, "but she is dangerous for so many reasons, starting with why the vampires wish to have her. Is anyone else concerned that we really don't know what she is? You said yourself that the necromancer got a weird reading on her. Terait, were-animal, odd magical ability, there is something terribly wrong with her. Kill her and this all goes away."

"Until they find another sacrifice," Steven interjected. "Then what? Keep killing anyone who can be potentially used? Then what form of evil do we become? She needs protection, not death. What we need to do is locate the Gem and make sure the vamps never have the chance to use it."

"Yes, sounds so very simple. However, if it were that simple, then why don't we have the goddamn thing? Demetrius is going all out for this. His Legion—seriously, when has he ever used them? He's risking the safety of his Seethe to keep the Gem hidden with dark magic and accruing a huge debt in the process. He has the Gem and we have her. It's simple. Kill her, and things get a lot less complicated."

"Can you take the life of an innocent were-animal in cold blood, without cause?" Ethan asked calmly, but his voice held a twinge of unease, disappointment.

"For the safety of this pack, I'll do it without hesitation. If we keep this up, there will be a battle. Lives will be lost—our lives. And for what? Her? Ethan, if you find it too distasteful for your civility, then I will do it right now. . . ."

"Winter!" Sebastian snapped.

She exhaled a ragged breath. "She's not one of us," she declared in a desperate voice. Winter began to fidget, searching desperately for the right words to persuade them. "She is dangerous. We need to kill her. It will give us time to find the Gem and not have to worry about protecting her," she stated calmly. But it was a calmness that came from a place of resolve. Whether she convinced them or not, Winter had decided she was going to take my life.

"She's right," I stated with a heavy sigh, stepping into the room. I looked at Sebastian, who seemed to be the most approachable at this time. *Who would have thought?*

"I am not one of you, and I don't warrant this type of loyalty and sacrifice. It is a lot to ask. I am terrified of what I am capable of, so I can understand her concern. It would be easier to end my life, but I ask that you don't. I will leave."

I wanted to leave the house because the wavering trust I had for them had changed. It was only a matter of time before Winter convinced them that I wasn't worth saving. Trapped in the house with my potential murderers or being hunted and possibly captured by vampires to endure a ritual that would ultimately kill me left me between a boulder and a hard place.

"Leaving this house isn't enough. Your very existence is a danger. Death is the only option for you," Winter hissed so coldly it would have sent shivers through me if I weren't so numbed by fear.

Sebastian looked in Winter's direction but spoke to me. "Skylar, if I thought you were capable of protecting yourself, my pack would not have intervened. You will continue to stay here under pack protection until the Gem is retrieved. Your life is protected and all members of this pack will do what is needed," he stated firmly, directing the last part toward Winter. With much effort, her eyes returned to their deep hazel color.

"Then you are protected," she stated, her words mechanical and forced.

"Thank you." I glanced in Winter's direction. As much as I disliked her, I understood her position. This was her family, and I was putting them in danger. I had already lost my family. It was unfair that she could lose hers.

Winter stared at me. "Don't offer thanks to me. I do it because I am commanded to. If it were up to me, you would be dead right now," she admitted honestly, before heading out of the room.

Sebastian followed her toward the door and stopped her. "You take as much time as you need. She's under our protection, and if you kill her, I will enforce the law to the fullest extent. I don't want to, but I will." He leaned in, touching her gently in a fatherly gesture.

She looked at me again, then Sebastian. "If I kill her, the maximum punishment is exile from the pack."

"It is considered pack betrayal if a were-animal dies as a result of your direct disobedience to an order. The penalty is death," he corrected her.

Winter's face softened, her eyes gentle with a subtle defeat as they seemed to plead for leniency.

Sebastian took a deep breath, studying her intently. "Winter, if you kill her while I consider her protected, it is betrayal. I would recommend death and see that you die at my hands. If you blatantly disobey my orders, then you are no good to me or the pack because you can no longer be trusted. You've always followed my orders loosely and interpreted our rules in ways that were questionable at best. But it was never a clear violation of my authority."

She nodded once, looking hurt—really hurt. Subdued, she didn't seem like herself. If I hadn't been mistaken, her eyes seemed to glisten from unshed tears. With her head down, she left the house.

At the moment, I battled with the love-hate relationship I had with pack laws and obligations. I hated how stringent they were, and yet at this moment, they were the only thing saving me from Winter's wrath.

Ethan stood in the corner of the room. He had remained silent and expressionless, throughout the discussion. I fidgeted, wishing he would say something—anything. I didn't know where he stood on the matter and something about the way he looked back at me indicated that he didn't, either.

The murmurs downstairs continued long after I had

returned to the room. At times, the voices rose, fueled by passionate deliberations. I cracked the door but couldn't make out all the words because they moved the conversation to the kitchen and farther away from my room. I couldn't stop my heart from racing. The sounds of the house, which for a short period had brought me a level of comfort, now scared me.

Winter had given a compelling argument for my execution. Ethan seemed to be on the fence, and heated discussions were taking place only steps from the room I stayed in. None of these things did much to help me feel safe. Sebastian claimed my life was protected. But as quickly as he had given that protection, could he remove it? This torture was no better than what Demetrius had planned for me. It was enough to drive me insane as I sat quietly in a room, questioning my fate at the hands of the were-animals. I shuddered at the thought of how easily my life could be taken upon Sebastian's command. Did I still trust them that much?

CHAPTER 8

The discussions stopped about five that morning. I hadn't slept. Instead, I watched as the sun broke through the darkness. With only my wallet, a few weapons, and my keys, I opened the window and leapt out. I ran from the house as soon as my feet touched the ground. The sun shone brightly, which ensured that I wouldn't be attacked by vampires. I felt confident that I could handle the garden thugs if they showed up. However, functioning on the ten-minute naps I had taken between the sounds of the house left me less than sharp.

I hadn't formulated the best plan, but I was leaving anyway. I refused to sit around while everyone else decided my fate. If the vampires wanted me, they were going to have to search. I wouldn't make it simple by sitting in the pack's retreat. If the pack decided my life wasn't worth protecting, killing me would be as easy as a walk upstairs to perform the execution.

I had enough money saved in my personal account to stay hidden for a while. Going home to pack wasn't an option because that would be the first place they'd look. I planned on going straight to the airport. My passport was tucked in my wallet. It was always with me. It was a neurotic obsession because I partly expected a village of torch-wielding people at any moment to come to our home once my werewolf was discovered. Although it was a silly expectation, today I was glad my neurosis had driven me to such paranoid preparation.

I followed the path of the driveway but stayed deeper in the woods to stay hidden. I realized it wouldn't be long before they discovered I was gone. The powerful smell of oak accompanied by the enticing smell of pine was a pleasure to the olfactory senses, but it also dulled them. I needed *theirs* dulled to make it harder to track me.

As I hurried through the dense arboreal area, I made sure to follow the path of the driveway. The clicking of tongue against teeth brought me to an abrupt stop. *Damn.*

"Here, wolfie, wolfie," called Gabriella's grating voice. She appeared from behind the trees fully healed from Winter's assault and still sporting the atrocious orange-red hair. She looked weird—well, weirder—in daylight. Her pale skin was a grayish opaque color, taking away from her previous attractiveness. I shuddered, scared and confused because I wasn't aware that vampires could walk in the daylight. I had no idea what to make of this situation. She stayed close to the tree. I assumed she needed the shade. Taking steps back from her, I listened for Chase. If she were here, he wasn't far behind. She smiled, exposing bloodstained fangs.

What the hell is the vampires' deal? Why don't they feel the need to wash away evidence that they have fed?

She smiled as she quickly advanced toward me. Her movements were quick but not as quick as I remembered. I had her by the throat by the time she was within striking distance. Fear worked in my favor, my actions came swift and precise. I pushed her hard, and she landed with a thud against the tree she had come from. Turning quickly to my right, I plunged the stake into Chase. I didn't have a chance to direct my strike and thought I missed his heart until he let out a ragged gasp and fell to the ground. The foul smell of necrosis filled the air as the reversion processes started. Taking out my knife, I prepared to decapitate my first vampire.

Gabriella grabbed me roughly and tossed me to the ground. I swept her legs with mine and she crashed down next to me. Moving to my feet at what I thought was lightning speed, I still wasn't fast enough to beat her.

"I don't have time to play with you," she lashed out, dragging me toward Chase. She pulled the stake out of him and slammed me hard against the tree next to him.

"Stay." She pushed the stake through my right shoulder, impaling me to the tree. Taking the knife I dropped, she pierced it through my left hand. I screamed as tears blurred my vision.

Gabriella ran into the woods and came back quickly with a woman in her late twenties, dressed in running clothes. Her hands were bound with rope. She continued to struggle against Gabriella as she dragged her toward Chase. Her face was flushed from either screaming or crying, her eyes panicked with fear. She was covered in dirt. They must have grabbed her early this morning and kept her stashed in the woods. Gabriella loosened the bindings, and when the girl fought back, she hit her hard several times until she was unconscious. I moved forward from the tree, trying to loosen the knife or stake. Sharp wrenching pain overwhelmed me as I twisted and lurched in an attempt to dislodge at least one of them.

Chase took the girl's wrist into his mouth. Pulling his lips back he sank his teeth in and began to feed. I looked away; the sounds of him hungrily drawing blood from the poor woman made my stomach queasy. It took a long time—too long, as he drained the woman of her life.

Once finished, he stood up, looking good as new, the lifeless body lying at his feet. A rivulet of his recent feeding ran down his chin. Gabriella wiped it away with her thumb and then her tongue slithered out to lick it. "Welcome back," she said, pleased.

When he exposed his blood-covered teeth, terror swept over me. The horrible duo, reunited again. Ignoring the pain, I moved frantically from the tree, trying hard to release myself, disregarding whatever damage I was causing to the soft tissue.

"The big wolf is coming," Chase stated with a grimace, turning slowly as he scanned his surroundings. Gabriella smiled and started to walk toward me. He grabbed her hand. "We won't be able to take her now."

"No. We have to take her now," she urged, taking several steps toward me.

"The big wolf is here." His voice was strained, and his lips turned into a grim sneer as he tugged her toward him. Then they disappeared. Staring at the empty space where they once stood, I came to the painful realization that I knew very little of vampires' strengths, weaknesses, and gifts, which made them an even bigger danger to me. I laid my head against the tree. The wolf was definitely here. I could feel his anger smothering me. My throat began to close, fearing my encounter with the angry wolf.

Once he was in my line of sight, I prepared myself for an enraged rampage, but instead Ethan seemed unusually calm as he walked toward me. His face showed signs that he was working hard to achieve that level of control.

"Inhale," he instructed me, his face inches from mine. "Now exhale." As the air slowly escaped from me, he simultaneously pulled the stake and knife out. I wailed as gushes of blood spewed onto his shirt. I leaned against him, gasping for breath. His body was rigid as he held me against him until I could stand on my own. Once the pain had subsided to barely excruciating, Ethan stepped away from me. I doubled over, trying to catch my breath, fighting the bile that crept up. I was becoming too acquainted with pain and it was quite annoying.

"Look to see if there are others," he commanded Steven, a were-dingo, a were-wolf, and a were-panther, who were unfamiliar to me. They moved quickly, with the exception of the were-panther who snarled, then licked his lips. His short black fur shimmered in the light as he stalked toward me, responding willingly to the smell of blood and fear that inundated the air. Deep aggressive rumbles reverberated as his tongue darted out of his mouth, licking his lips. It took a step closer; Steven growled angrily, abandoning his undertaking and returning to stand next to me.

"Gavin, she's under our protection," Ethan stated firmly. The rumble came again deeper and more forceful. Ethan's stance changed as he raised a brow. Flashes of gray swept across his pupils. The panther stared at him for a moment then roared violently. Ethan took a step closer, crouched and growled, the most inhuman vicious sound I'd ever heard. Dropping his shoulder in recoil, the panther slowly backed away.

I leaned against the tree, wiggling my fingers, touching each finger to my thumb. I moved my shoulder up, to the side and back as shrill pain shot through me with each movement. Everything hurt like hell, but at least all my fingers still worked and there wasn't any apparent nerve damage. Ethan glanced in my direction several times but still hadn't spoken to me. I assumed he realized that if he did, he would succumb to rage and Joan wasn't here to intervene or coerce him into behaving civilized.

We walked back to the house, my wounds throbbing as we weaved our way across the unleveled terrain. Ethan's emotions were worn sufficiently on his face; the muscles of his neck and face strained as he fought to keep it together. Josh met us halfway in his Jeep and I sat next to him. Ethan sat in the back. I could feel his wrathful glare on me during the drive back.

Ethan jumped out of the car before it could come to a full stop, refusing to look in my direction or even speak to me. "Chase and Gabriella left a body on the property. All evidence of it needs to be removed. You need to do your thing," he stated, his voice becoming harsher with each word. When he finally turned to look at me, I wished he hadn't. A torrential wave of rage filled the space between us. I knew then that if Sebastian, at that moment, lifted his order of protection, it wouldn't be Winter I would have to worry about.

Josh must have sensed the anger and violence brewing in Ethan, as well, because he stepped between us and stayed there until Ethan disappeared into the house. Then he quickly took me to Dr. Baker's office.

Dr. Baker took one look at my shoulder and shook his head. "Silly, silly girl," he scolded as he palpated the area. Each time I winced, he grumbled an apology under his breath and pulled my arm back.

As he poked and prodded around the wounds, I flinched, periodically drawing my hand back, but he kept a firm grasp on it. "I'm sorry, but these types of wounds have a tendency to cause pain with touch. That's why we try not to get staked or stabbed." He was irritated with me. I had managed to anger a person who had patience and compassion like nobody I had seen, well, in this house, anyway.

Okay, I definitely see why some of them want to kill me.

He tore the remainder of my shirt off and let out a chain of irritated sounds. As he examined the shoulder, I didn't need to look at his face to know it was a mess. My fingers were still numb and the shoulder throbbed like hell.

"You won't be picking fights with vampires anytime soon, will you?" He took a syringe and medicine out of the cabinet.

"I don't think what happened between Gabriella and me today could remotely be considered a fight. If so, I think someone should explain to me what a fight is. I thought it involved two people trying to best one another in a physical confrontation. What occurred between Gabriella and me was a smackdown and I was the only one being smacked," I stated flatly.

He chuckled, then laughed. It stopped abruptly when Sebastian walked into the room, taking soft deliberate steps as he looked at Dr. Baker, then me.

When he stepped closer to me, his anger flooded the room, drowning me in his unspoken rage. I was too tired and hurt to display false bravado, so I kept my eyes glued to the floor, hoping he would leave soon.

"How does it feel?" he asked in a cold, flat voice.

"Hurts like hell."

"Good," he snarled.

I looked up and glared but cut it short to a mere glance when I saw the look on his face. His appearance promised an unfavorable response if I dared to even whisper the smart-ass comment that was forming in my head.

"She's not going to have efficient use of her left hand and right shoulder for a day or two. There's serious soft tissue damage," Dr. Baker stated, showing the sympathy that Sebastian was unable to give.

He let out a disgusted grunt. I could sense the storm brewing in the midst of the quiet rain as he inched uncomfortably close to me. Waves of anger flooded the room.

"You allowed yourself to be injured by your own weapons." His lips were pulled tightly together as he focused, trying to keep the wolf dormant. "I will tell you again. You are our responsibility." His increasing frustration sent me into a slow panic. I didn't know how to make this situation better. An apology or admission of stupidity would not calm the fury that was stirring within him.

His windstorm of emotions forced me to retreat. My eyes stayed plastered to the floor. I gasped when he roughly grabbed me by my face, lifting it until my eyes met his. Something I wished he hadn't done. Hearing his rage was worse than watching it erupt before me. "You realize the severity of what will take place if you are caught by the vampires? You've seen it and felt it almost firsthand. Mayhem will ensue and I could very well lose a large number of my pack trying to stop the shit!" His words came out angry and rough as they pushed through clenched teeth. "You do realize that your death will give them strength and power that will surpass ours, leaving them virtually unstoppable, giving them free rein to act in any reckless manner they choose. Unnecessary deaths will occur, and who will be there to stop them? We will try to stop the rampage, and possibly be successful, but will suffer great losses. I will lose people that I watched grow up all because you continue to act recklessly against us." His anger escalated to the point of no return.

I closed my eyes for a second and when I opened them, I looked over to Dr. Baker, who appeared uneasy. Sebastian stopped fighting the wolf that longed to surface. His eyes shifted to deep amber. In wolf form, they are striking against his dark brown coat with subtle hints of auburn. Now while he was in human form, I was too fear-stricken to notice.

"Do you want to die or are you really this fucking irresponsible with your life?" he ground out, his face inching even closer to mine. "If death is what you long for then I can make that happen right now." He grabbed me by the throat with one hand and raised me off the ground.

His arms remained steady as he effortlessly held me midair. I wiggled my feet, feeling for the floor that was far from my reach. He slowly added more pressure as I fought for breath. My eyes darted erratically around the room, looking for Dr. Baker, who had discreetly left the room. All that remained in the room was me, Sebastian, and his fury. He pressed even harder, and the bones in my neck started to creak and falter under the pressure. He was about to break my neck. If I gave into it for even a mere moment, I was sure it would be a clean break and a quick death.

I forced air into my throat, expanding it enough to allow me to breathe.

Is death what I want? I wished I could have given him a quick response, but I didn't know the answer. I was too scared to give a rational answer. Feeling fear at so many levels, reason had been pulled from my thoughts. The life I knew was gone, and I didn't know how to start another one. People wanted me dead, and I didn't know how to stop them. Those things alone were enough to make a person feel a little hopeless, desperate, and yes, maybe even suicidal. I wasn't sure if it were the pain that overwhelmed me or the helplessness that plagued me daily, but part of me welcomed a swift end to it all.

As I fought for air, desperation overwhelmed me and my only response was to shed tears that trickled down my face. The salty liquid splattered on Sebastian's fingers. He jerked back as though he had been touched by hot wax, dropping me to the ground. I stayed down. Bowing my head, I allowed the tears to flow unrestricted, hoping it would relieve some of the pressure that pushed hard against my chest. It was so uncomfortable that the passive act of my beating heart felt painful.

He lowered himself to the floor and knelt in front of me. "Look at me," he commanded. I took a deep breath and forced myself to look at him. He let out a sigh as he attempted to modulate the tone of his voice, still straining with anger, to sound gentle. "Skylar, you don't deserve to die because of what you are. It's not your fault. I am not holding you accountable for it nor should you. I want to protect you, but you are making it painfully hard … eyes up here." I brought my gaze back up once it had drifted back to the floor. He was a hard person to maintain eye contact with. "I don't understand you, and I don't wish to. Maybe you are depressed about your mother, or you're one of those emo-chicks with a strange obsession with death, or perhaps, you are just tragically stupid. Either way, I can't bring myself to give a damn. If death is what you want, then there is no need for my pack to waste any more time protecting you. I can no longer continue to waste resources that could be better spent finding the Gem of Levage. I will ask you once, and I expect an answer now. Do you want to die? If so, I will give it to you now, swift and painless," he assured me, his voice strangely calm and soothing.

Focusing his attention elsewhere, he gave me a moment to make a decision. The way his hand was positioned led me to believe that he expected me to say yes. Whatever choice I made didn't matter to him, and he wore the indifference casually on his face.

He was offering me a quick death, which was far better than what the vampires would give me, but I wasn't ready to die. I shook my head and fought back the tears. This was my life and it scared me. Just two weeks ago I was trying to figure out where to go for vacation and whether or not to try bangs. This was so different from my old life and I didn't know how to adapt.

"I'm afraid," I finally admitted.

"There isn't anything wrong with fear unless you allow it to control your actions. I want you to survive this. You are protected and that order extends to you, as well. You will do whatever is necessary to keep yourself safe from harm. Don't run away again, because if you do . . ." He allowed the threat to trail off. He didn't have to finish, I knew the ending.

I nodded my head.

When Dr. Baker returned, I was seated at his treatment table and had wiped all evidence of my tears from my face. He applied stitches to my shoulder and wrapped my hand. It took a while to get to the room because the least movement caused excruciating pain. I had been tired before but now I was just beyond exhausted. My emotions had run so hot and cold today that it left me in an empty well of despair. I would probably sleep well. It might be filled with nightmares, but at least I would sleep.

It took me a long time to shower. You never realize how much movement is involved in removing your clothes until the least effort produces searing pain. Eventually, I undressed and sat at the bottom of the shower, watching all the grime and pink water run down the drain. My hair received the same treatment. I glopped in shampoo, worked it in as best I could, and stayed under the water until it no longer looked gray from the dirt.

I didn't have the pain threshold to put on clothes. Instead, I wrapped a towel around me and headed for the bed. It didn't matter that it was early morning; I wanted to sleep until this day was no longer a living nightmare.

After finding a comfortable position that brought my pain level down to a tolerable ache, I sensed that Ethan had walked into the room. He didn't knock. I wished he had done something that would have given me a warning to prepare for him. There was still a brute harshness to his features, a sign that he was still holding on to his anger from earlier. "Sit up," he commanded in a dry voice.

I didn't move; instead, I watched. He wasn't trying to intimidate me. Well, I didn't think he was. Ethan stalked rather than walked, and his movements were so precise, lithe, and coiled that it always seemed like he was seconds from striking. I didn't want to be around when he finally did.

"Now." His voice wasn't harsh. Instead, he seemed bored. Was he bored with being angry with me? Or was he no longer entertained by contemplating the many ways he wanted to annihilate me?

I rolled into a sitting position, bringing the covers with me. "If you've come to reprimand me, I can assure you I've been appropriately chastised and frightened by Sebastian. If you came to threaten to kill me, Sebastian beat you to it, as well. And if you came to yell at me, can you please wait until tomorrow? My ears are still ringing from my encounter with Sebastian," I stated in a tired voice.

As he knelt in front of me, I prepared for virulence. Instead, he cupped my face gently, inspecting the bruising on my neck. Lightly, his fingers brushed along the marks. If I didn't know better, I could easily mistake his look for empathy.

"You shouldn't have run again."

Do they get mileage points or something for stating the obvious?

"It was stupid," I admitted.

His lips tightened, then he exhaled a deep breath. "It was dangerous." He sat back on his heels, his gaze falling somewhere behind me. I think if he had looked at me, the anger would have rushed back to him like a wildfire.

"I don't know what is more insulting: your belief we have no honor and would go back on our word to protect you, or your fear that we are so craven that we would attempt to kill you while you sat unknowingly in our home. We are animals, it would be against our natural sensibility to hunt a captured prey," he stated softly.

Yay, if they decide to kill me, they will at least give me a running start or at the very least wait until I make it home.

"My running was by no means a reflection of my thoughts of your honor or integrity as a pack or a hunter. There is validity to Winter's argument, and I can honestly see how you all could agree with her. The pack is your family, and I expect you to take necessary precautions to keep them safe," I responded in a low rasp. My throat was raw from too many bouts of screaming over the past two days. "If the roles were reversed, I couldn't say that your lives would be safe at my hand. If any of you had been an imminent threat to my mother, it would be nothing less than dishonest to say I wouldn't have taken your lives to protect her."

"The same would be true with us. If your presence in our

lives were to put us in imminent danger, I couldn't say that your life would hold much value to us, either. Our pack is in no danger at the vampires' hands. This is not the first time we've had less than favorable dealings with the vamps, and I assure you that it won't be the last."

"Winter thinks I am a danger to the pack."

"She is, along with the rest of us, concerned with your *unique* characteristics. But at this time, you aren't a direct risk to us. If things were to change, then we would revisit the situation. But for now you are safe."

"In other words, if I were a direct risk to the pack, then I would have cause to fear for my life."

He nodded without hesitation, then moved closer. His hands rested at my side, against the skin on my lower back, where the sheet had left me exposed. Warm, firm fingers pressed into my skin. His touch, delicate and tender, was belied by his words. "You would be treated like any other threat. But you are under our protection and that is something we do not take lightly."

Well, say what you will about them—they're a direct and brutally honest bunch.

"It is a good thing that you didn't kill Chase. The vampires lust often but love infrequently. Chase and Gabrielle are *lynked*, similar to being mated. He created her, and they have been together for, I believe, fifty-three years, never straying and never parted. They vowed their existence to each other. If you kill one, you must kill the other or suffer the wrath of the survivor. Whatever you saw in your vision would be nothing in comparison to the torture you would have endured at Gabriella's hand if you had killed him. She wouldn't care about any consequences because he is her existence and she is his. Once a hunter tried to make a name for herself, caught Chase, tortured him, and left him for dead. Horror tales evolved around the torment she endured once Gabriella found her."

For once, my incompetence worked to my advantage. "I

thought vampires had an aversion to light. How were they able to walk in the light like that?"

"Borrowed source. The older ones can walk in light if they consume enough to sustain them. Usually it takes about three lives to give them twenty minutes of light. There are only a few vampires who can travel, but they aren't gifted in that manner. This means they must be feeding from an elf and accumulating a large debt to do so. Elves do not help without getting much in return. I am curious to find out the specifics regarding that debt. The vampires have accumulated a great deal of debt on your behalf. You are important to them."

"Yeah, I get the point. Chase and Gabriella have made it painfully obvious," I responded derisively.

"Even more reason for you to start making wise choices. Skylar, please understand if you keep pushing us, we won't have any other option—" He left without finishing the sentence, but I knew how it ended: *We will have no other option but to kill you.*

It was just a mere fourteen hours from the time Gabriella had stabbed me in the shoulder and hand with my own weapons and Sebastian strangled me. I was staring at the television mindlessly. Flashes of light bounced in front of me from the television, and I stared at it with little interest. I had no idea what I was watching. It may have been an infomercial.

After Ethan left, I lay in bed for five hours but slept for about two of them. Now I was using the television to get my mind off the throbbing pain in my hand and shoulder, but it didn't help. Dr. Baker wouldn't give me anything for the pain and I had begged him at least four times so far. He refused, stating that because our bodies metabolized it so quickly it would be ineffective.

Steven knocked on the door but didn't wait for a response

before entering. “Brought food.” He carried in a tray of food. He eyed the bandages on my hand and shoulder, pulled out a knife and cut everything up into easy-to-handle, bite-size pieces.

“Thanks.” I hadn’t eaten since my run-in with Gabriella. My stomach seemed so full of anxiety and distress that eating was the furthest thing from my mind.

“You are very welcome, troublemaker,” he stated with a grin. “Boy, you really rubbed Sebastian the wrong way, and yet you are still here.”

“Barely.” I showed him my memento from my talk with Sebastian.

“It’s not that bad compared to most. The bruising is minor. He must like you.”

“If this is a *like* mark then I don’t want to see how he responds when he hates you.”

“He’s direct.”

“That’s a polite way to put it.”

While I ate, Steven paced the room, making idle small talk. I watched him suspiciously. “I’m not going to run again,” I stated, realizing he was on security detail.

He smiled as he walked over to the window, pulled out a key, and locked it. “Of course you won’t.”

“Are you going to lock the doors, too?” I asked sarcastically.

“No, you seem to have a thing for windows and there is no need to tempt you. By the way, I am your roommate while you stay here. I hope you don’t snore.” He grinned.

“You are not sleeping in here.”

“There’s a very angry man downstairs who would disagree with that.”

“I’m not going to run again. I promise.”

“And I believe you. Unfortunately, Sebastian doesn’t, and it is my understanding that if you leave again, he’s going to …” He brought his finger from one side of his neck to the other, making a garbled cutting noise. “Sebastian doesn’t trust you.

But Joan likes you—a lot—and has adamantly appealed for your life, and Sebastian respects her opinion. Technically, when you ran this time, he was well within his rights to kill you without dishonor or violation of pack law. I'm the compromise because if you run again, he will kill you on principle alone, and nothing Joan does or says will stop him. I promised Joan I would do whatever was necessary to keep you alive."

I stared at Steven's grave face. "Would he kill me?" I asked seriously. When angered, I had no doubt he would do so. But now, since everyone had calmed down, was he capable of doing such an act on principle alone?

He nodded once. "Sky, contrary to how he acts, he likes you but he stands by his principles and pack laws. At some point, Sebastian will lose his patience with you. Believe me, you have pushed his mercy to the limits. Be considerate of that with your future acts." He was staring at me, urging his warning with all sincerity.

Steven stayed while I finished off my dinner. We were playing chess when he was summoned by Sebastian. I assumed Sebastian had a change of heart and decided to trust me, although it wasn't quite deserved.

Once he left, I lay back and closed my eyes to welcome a much needed sleep. The pain in my shoulder and hand felt tolerable, and fatigue had taken over to such an extent that keeping my eyes open was a chore. When Steven walked into the room, my eyes could barely open to look at him. "You are freaking kidding me! Go away!"

"That is no way to greet your roommate."

"This is ridiculous!" I spat out, frustrated.

"Then you should take a stand. March downstairs and tell Sebastian that you won't tolerate this type of treatment. Give him a piece of your mind, using all your self-righteous anger. Go ahead. I'll wait." He gave me a sly smile as he took a seat in the corner.

"You're on the floor."

"Of course." He turned his back to me and began to undress.

I rolled my eyes and dropped back onto the bed. The rustling sound of him removing his clothes caught my attention. I turned to find him standing totally naked without an ounce of shame. Although there wasn't a thing about his body that would warrant shame, a little modesty wouldn't hurt. It was doubtful that there were many teenagers who would want to hide a physique like his. The wispy way he looked in clothing was deceptive. Steven was tall, lean, and athletically built, with long striated muscles covering the greater part of his body. I was sure he'd had his share of mothers and daughters looking at him with prurient intent.

I plopped back on the bed, covering my face with the covers before he could catch me looking.

"Good night." He changed into his animal form. Padding over to me, he licked my fingers. It was absolutely disgusting. It was his pleasantry while in coyote form, but I still didn't care for it. I went to the bathroom to wash my hands. When I returned, the coyote was asleep against the door. *Why lock the door when you can just put a big-ass coyote in front of it?* I wasn't going anywhere, even if I wanted to.

The next morning, I awoke to Steven growling at the door to get out. The sun shone brightly through the blinds. It was nearly twelve. I slept longer than I had since I had been in the house. He growled a response as I let him out of the room. I am sure he had better things to do than guard me. The pain from yesterday's encounter with Chase and Gabriella was substantially better, but it still made showering challenging. I moved slowly and gently under the running water, examining the mementos from yesterday's attack. The wounds on my shoulder and hand were healing well. I hoped there wouldn't be scarring. The bruising on my neck was barely noticeable. But now there was a new, raised, rough mark, resembling the Gem of Levage, on the right side of my lower back.

Dressing quickly, I went to the library, searching for Josh. Anytime he was in the house, the library was where he could usually be found. Surprisingly, he wasn't there.

"He left early this morning," informed Ethan from behind me. "He believes Caleb had something to do with what happened to you last night. He was quite infuriated by his betrayal. I hope Caleb lives through the meeting." His words sounded so insincere it was doubtful he cared.

He watched me with interest once I turned around. His hair was wet and he smelled like soap and Winter. Ethan, even when relaxed, always made you feel like you were under the watchful eye of a predator. His soft blue eyes with the gray undertones sharpened when his wolf was awakened. They were not as vibrant as his brother's, but managed to be just as alluring. "How are you feeling?" he asked casually, taking a step closer to me.

"As well as can be expected. How's Winter?"

He smiled, looking playful while doing so. I wasn't sure what amused him more: the fact that I could smell Winter on him or that I acknowledged it.

"She does her job so well I often forget how young she is. She can be quite emotional when provoked. She doesn't like you."

Really! What could possibly have given that away? Was it her rampage the other day as she advocated for my murder? I think it's safe to assume that when people lobby for your murder while expressing how truly wrong you are, you aren't one of their favorites.

"I had to talk to her last night. On rare occasions, I seem to be the only one capable of reasoning with her. She feels things quite deeply, whether it's love or hate."

So Ethan was the voice of reason between the two of them. *That's not a ringing endorsement of a person with good temperament.*

"I've been marked," I blurted.

He looked confused. I turned around and showed him my back. He knelt down, his fingers pressing into my skin as he examined the new marking. His thumb carefully ran across it, his fingers fanning out across my stomach. He took out his phone and pressed a button. The voicemail picked up. "Josh, come to the house when you're done, I need you to look at something." His fingers pressed into my abdomen as his thumb ran rhythmically along the marking. I took in a deep breath, trying to ignore how good his touch felt on my skin.

CHAPTER 9

When Josh walked into the bedroom, his eyes were dull and worn from fatigue and lack of sleep. He smiled, but it didn't hold the same charm as it usually did. Things were starting to wear on him, and he wore the telltale signs like a badge.

"Skylar," Ethan cued me from behind him. When I lifted my shirt, Josh glanced. "She is bound to the Gem. It will go away once the Gem is destroyed It's not a good idea to bind yourself to such things, Skylar," Josh cautioned.

"It wasn't my intention …" I eyed the floor. "It called me," I finally admitted after a moment of silence. I still remained cautious with information I relayed to them, aware that one were-animal considered me a threat to the pack. I didn't want the others to begin to side with her.

"You held on to magic," Josh stated, intrigued. His brow rose as he brought his hand thoughtfully to his chin.

"I guess." I shrugged. Ethan looked at Josh, trying to read the attentive look on his face.

"Binding yourself to things is something were-animals can't do. It falls in the realm of magic—quite advanced magic. It's the reason I can use others as conduits. The only explanation for what happened is that you held on to the magic you were exposed to at Caleb's house. When Caleb bit you, it was enough of a blood exchange for you to attain a bond with him and me. That is why you experienced what you did the night before last. You were still bound to him by blood and magic, but he couldn't call you. If I had been aware of your magical abilities, I would have done a different unbinding spell," he informed me as he paced the floor. "It was his intention to draw enough blood to call to you last night, forcing you to respond to him. Once you did, he would have given you to Demetrius with hopes of returning to the family. In the past, he has been a reliable source, but his betrayal has made him a liability." He was angry —so angry that I wondered if, indeed, Caleb had lived through Josh's last visit.

He took a deep breath and began to mouth something, and then he touched my arm. I drew back when a weird sensation shot through me.

"Touch Ethan," he instructed me.

I hesitated and then reached slowly toward his arm.

"Ethan?" Josh inquired whether he felt anything. Ethan shook his head.

Josh studied me for a moment, then he looked at Ethan. "I just wish I knew what you were. When I met you, I didn't sense magic. Now there is a weak presence." I saw the bewilderment and frustration on his face.

"You need to find out," Ethan stated firmly before he left. Glancing at Josh, I could only imagine the pressure he must feel, given such as a daunting task.

"Do you think Winter was right? Could I be something really bad?"

He was silent for a long time. Too long for anything that was going to come from him to be good. "Why did you ask that?"

"Because when I went to see the Tre'ase—"

"When did you go see a Tre'ase?" he interrupted hastily.

"About five days ago with Ethan. He didn't tell you?"

"No. But I doubt he realized he should have." His voice was strained, and small. Frustrated lines formed along his brow. "What happened?" he asked with spurious calmness. He was bothered. His face betrayed his attempt to conceal it as the corners of his mouth coiled into a frown.

I told him the details of my visit, right down to the creepy demon that startled me.

"Did you make a bargain with her?" he asked impatiently.

"I don't think so." I hesitated as I recalled the events of that day.

"Thinking isn't good enough. I need you to be certain."

I thought about the whole incident, frame by frame. I shook my head. "No, I didn't make a bargain with her. But she seems to think I will come back."

"Skylar, you must never go back to her. Ever. A Tre'ase is a demon that feeds you the truth sprinkled with tidbits of deceit. They offer the promises of a better future and the removal of undesirable attributes. It's all a trick to remove your gifts. And with everything you lose, you still end up being indebted to them. Believe me, you never want to be indebted to them."

I nodded. "But was she wrong?" I pushed the issue.

"She wasn't wrong, but she gave you a skewed version of the truth," he admitted.

I groaned but it sounded more like a distressed whimper. "Everyone seems to be able to tell how really wrong I am, except the people I trust to help me."

"I wish that were my gift but it isn't. In the supernatural, where magic exists in many forms, certain anomalies are expected and accepted." He looked down at his hand. "I am reluctant to take you to someone who may be able to tell us more, especially right now. The word is out that the vampires have an interest in you. There are people who I can go to, but most of them can only be trusted within limits. I would be placing you at risk unnecessarily."

He was staring at the wall, his face taking on a grave appearance. "There are many in this world who can't be trusted. If you do have desired gifts, some will try to take them—often by force, deceit, and death. I'm not sure how many alliances the vampires have formed. It may be a good idea to restrict interaction until the Gem is in our possession."

Josh was always straight with me. I committed to doing the same and trusting him with everything. I took the journals out of my messenger bags and handed them to him.

"I hope these will help. Most of the journals are a simple read, but the beginning is a bit confusing. Maybe you can sort it out. "

He skimmed over the first page, and then stared at me for a moment. It was as though he were hesitant to find out anything more about me, but soon returned his attention back to the journals.

Slowly I walked the floor as he took on the task of reading the chronicles of how I came to be. Flipping back and forth between pages, his frown lines appeared, disappeared, and reappeared as he read.

He stayed on the same page for a long time before looking up at me insightfully. "Sit down, Skylar."

"I'll stand." I leaned against the wall and watched as the new information cast an unsettling look on his face.

"Sit," he stated in a tone that didn't leave much room for objections. He pushed the chair next to the bed toward me. "It's a good idea that you do."

Unable to drop my gaze from his, I blindly found my way to the chair and plopped down in it.

"What do you know of your birth?"

"Apparently, Elena came upon a vampire after he brutally killed my father and was attempting to do the same to my mother. But my mother died anyway, forcing Elena to perform an emergency C-section to deliver me," I stated mechanically. I had read that part so many times I could recite it verbatim. Of the journals, the first pages of how I came to live with my adopted mother were the sparsest. She must have still been in shock when she wrote it.

He sighed. His hands washed over his face. Apprehension piqued but he quickly put it to rest. I had missed something. "Have you ever heard of a spirit shade?" he asked in a tight voice. I shook my head. "Some believe this story to be a myth while others consider it a cautionary tale. Emma was a very powerful witch distraught over her daughter, Maya, who died at two years old. Driven by sorrow and desperation, she struck a fool's deal with a Tre'ase. She bargained for the return of her daughter's life in exchange for all her gifts." Josh shook his head as he continued. "In exchange for her daughter's life, she gave the Tre'ase her gifts of morphism and foresight, which you've had the opportunity to enjoy." He chuckled a deviant sound. But he was far from amused. He seemed piqued. "The Tre'ase returned her life but not the body to store it in. Like I said, they are quite the tricksters. Now Maya wanders through this existence, looking for people who are willing to allow her to shadow their lives as her host. Forbidden to force her way in, she must be allowed entry. That's the sorrow of her life. If no one allows her in, then she exists but cannot live. Quite a sad tale it is for her to be allowed to exist but unable to touch, to feel, to truly experience life unless through a willing host."

"The Tre'ase that I met was the same one Emma went to?"

He shook his head. "Witches', elves', fae's, and demons' gifts are transferred through lineage but also can be gifted to others upon death. Many chose not to do so, holding the same belief of humans who refuse to donate organs, fearing it will change their status in the afterlife. The Tre'ase you dealt with could very well be the same; however, it is possible it's the offspring. Nevertheless, they are just as untrustworthy," he offered.

I had no idea why he was telling me this. Taking in the confused look on my face, he frowned and continued. "That night the vampire wasn't trying to kill your mother. He was trying to turn her and you in the process. He forced her to feed from him, starting the conversion into vampirism," he stated in a tight voice. "Elena interrupted the feeding, which would have completed your creation and sealed your fate as a vampire from birth, an undead baby."

"I thought creating a vampire child was forbidden," I forced out, trying to ward off the nausea that was coming on fast.

"It is. And if things ended as he planned, once your existence became known, your creator, you, and your mother would have been killed. A child born into vampirism will never fend for themselves and remain eternally dependent on their creator, essentially an eternal burden. It is cruel to create something that can never thrive on its own. Creatures even as immoral as the vampires can appreciate the cruelty in that."

"Elena saved me by killing him before the process could be completed."

His face crinkled. I missed something again. Something quite important. "No. Your birth mother killed him." He turned the journal toward me. "Read it."

"'…and this life I shall take.'"

He waited for me to respond, but I wasn't sure what he was waiting for. "Your mother performed a death curse to spare your life. It's an amateurish spell and the penalty for performing it is your life. You can see why it's something done as a last resort. By killing him, she thought she would save your life."

There was protracted and uncomfortable silence before he continued. "But she was wrong. You didn't survive that night, either," he added in a low grave voice.

I stared back at him, a slow panic rising in the pit of my stomach. "I survived." *Duh, I am standing in front of you.*

He shook his head. "No. You didn't. You are an innate were-animal and the conversion to vampirism had started. No one survives that."

My teeth started to hurt from being clenched so hard. I heard everything he said, but processing it took a while. Partially because I went into flight mode and, for me, that was to evade. My mind didn't want to grasp what he was saying, although I knew very well what that meant. "I ... How ...? What?"

He began to read, "The woman whispered part in English and part in Portuguese, 'This life you shall have. This life I shall take.' The fanged creature exhaled, hardening before he crumbled into dust."

"Your mother was Maya's host and allowed her invitation into you on your behalf before she died."

We stared at each other for a long time. He was searching, attempting to interpret the blank look on my face. I couldn't talk because I was too busy telling myself to breathe. "What am I?" I finally asked in a dry voice.

"Your mother was either a gifted human or a witch. I'm not sure which. You are just a werewolf with gifts." He looked troubled, as though he didn't know how to deal with me any longer. I jumped to my feet and began to aimlessly walk around the room.

"No!" The word ground out in such a harsh distressed sound that I didn't recognize it as my own. Josh looked at me, confusion and apprehension marking his appearance as his eyes followed me and I continued to pace back and forth.

"What?"

"No!" Again, the voice sounded unfamiliar to me. "In one sweeping moment, you don't change my life like that. You don't get to sit there and calmly tell me that I am an abomination— an abnormality—that has no place in the human world or this one. You can't just brush it off as me being 'just a werewolf with *gifts*.' I am a werewolf with a terait that needs to have blood for it to disappear. I am a werewolf that serves as a host for a demonic spirit. I am a werewolf that can hold magic. I am not *just* a werewolf!" It started off softly, but in the end, I was standing in the middle of the room yelling at him.

He took a long time to respond as though he were looking for the right words to make things better. But what were the right words to tell someone that they were an abnormality that this world had never seen?

"She's not a demonic spirit," he eventually responded in a low, calm voice, the same voice I suspect you would use for someone who was perilously close to jumping from a twenty-story building. "She is neither evil nor good, taking on the characteristics of whoever hosts her life. She is at the mercy of your behavior."

I sat down. My hands covered my face. They felt cold and clammy. *Of course, they're cold and clammy because technically I'm dead.* "I don't care what she is! I want her gone."

"I suspect the only reason you exist is because you are her host. If she is forced out, your existence might not continue." His voice was soft, sympathetic.

Josh began rambling about something, but I couldn't listen anymore. Forced to find a comfort zone, I tried to allow my mind to escape to a place less shocking. But I couldn't find that place. "Stop talking! Please." Taking in a large breath, I held it—a little too long because I became light-headed.

"Skylar? Are you okay?" he asked, concerned.

I finally stopped pacing and stared out the window.

He asked me again. "No. I haven't been okay for a long time," I admitted, feeling my control slipping. *Should I be okay with this?* I shook my head slowly. "I don't want this, any of it."

"Okay. But I can't change what happened at your birth. At

the risk of sounding harsh, you are going to have to deal with things because they aren't going to go away."

I didn't have it in me to do so at the moment. He gave me a look of such sympathy and concern that it made me recoil.

A few minutes passed. I continued to stare, zoning out. The part of me that regulated my feelings stopped working. Every emotion one could feel washed over me and became too hard to sort out. "Ethan, I need you in here," Josh's extremely calm voice requested into his phone. I doubt he wanted to be stuck in a room with a freaked-out wolf.

"What the hell happened?" Ethan asked in a low, tense voice as he entered the room, responding to my dazed state.

"Nothing," he snapped defensively, stepping closer to Ethan. "She's just having a little trouble dealing with some new information," he whispered.

I wanted to be anywhere but there. I needed respite. Dropping to my knees, I prepared for the change to wolf, which I inevitably failed to stop. It came so quickly that I doubt I could have stopped it, even if I wanted to. I stayed in wolf form for only minutes before I changed back to human form. The transition between human and wolf continued five more excruciating times. In the end, I sat on the ground, trying to catch my breath, exhausted from the series of rapid changes. Giving into the exhaustion, I collapsed and fell asleep on the floor.

When I opened my eyes, there were four other pairs staring back at me: Josh, Ethan, the albino dingo, Hannah, and Steven. I sat up, securing the comforter around me that someone had covered me with. I looked at the clock. I had only slept for thirty minutes, which explained why I still felt tired.

"Are you okay?" Josh asked in a tight voice, keeping an unusual distance from me.

I nodded.

"Are you sure?"

"Why?" I asked in a tired voice. *Of course I'm not okay. Why can't you just accept my lie?*

"Your eyes are an ugly white color." It must have looked really odd because he was unable to hide his repulsion. "And there's a field of protection around you. I've brought it down three times, but you keep putting it up each time we approach you. Can you release it?"

"Of course I can. I'm on it," I responded sardonically.

He smiled "Okay. I got it. *A-na rische mendu.*"

I assumed it had fallen because Josh inched closer to me.

"And my eyes?"

"Back to emerald and gorgeous," he responded with a trademark charismatic smile. There was something more behind his smile—apprehension. I blinked several times to see if they felt different. Uneasiness remained on Hannah's face as she backed out of the room. She shook her head and left. *I guess she's late for the "Skylar should be killed" meeting with Winter. I'm sure they're having one hourly by now.*

Ethan stared at me from the door.

"Josh, what was that?" He was trying to sound calm, but he was upset and doing a poor job of hiding it.

"She was still holding on to magic. She just lost control, but she should be fine." Josh looked like a child who had done something that could have gotten him into trouble.

"She can do the same type of magic you can?" Steven asked Josh, but he kept his eyes on me, displaying the same look of uneasiness as the others. I was freaking everyone out today. *I should get a gold star or something.*

"Yes, as long she holds on to my magic. But she doesn't know how to control it."

"How long is she going to be like this?" Ethan inquired hostilely. "The last thing we need is her using powerful magic she can't control."

Josh closed his eyes and began to move his lips slowly before he placed his hand in front of me just inches from my body. He flicked his finger and I yelped in pain.

"Stop it!"

"I can't find any other magic sources here. I think she used it all." But he didn't seem confident with his answer.

Ethan's face still held the traces of agitation as he looked at his brother. He nodded.

"I'm going to borrow these," Josh informed me as he grabbed the journals and left. Steven stayed a little longer to make sure I was okay. After I assured him several times, he reluctantly left, leaving me behind with Ethan, who was leaning against the doorframe, frowning.

"I need to get dressed."

"Then get dressed." He was oblivious to my need for privacy. When I stayed crouched on the cold floor, hugging the comforter around me, he made an annoyed grunt before turning around to give me some privacy. I hastily grabbed a pair of jeans, t-shirt, and underwear and got dressed.

"How did you live as you did?" he asked with his back still to me.

"I'm not sure what you are asking." I stood up, pulling up my jeans and buttoning them.

"Living in the unknown and being content with it. I operate best when I know all there is to know about things. If I was in your position, there would not be a source I wouldn't go to find out about myself." He turned to face me with a look of genuine confusion.

That's because you are a narcissistic control freak, I thought, and was really close to expressing it, but he wasn't being malicious so there was no need for me to be snippy with him. As odd as I found the were-animals, it dawned on me that I was probably just as odd and terribly complex to them. "You won't understand because you don't seem to understand fear."

"I understand fear just fine, just not as a recipient," he stated plainly. I doubt he really ever felt fear. I don't think the pack allowed it or at least allowed you to actually own up to it. They seemed to possess two distinct emotions—stoicism and rage—and slight variations of the two.

"Then you won't understand me or any explanation I try to give you."

"Try me." He took a seat in the corner and waited. Ethan was curious, but not for the typical reasons most people were. I was a job and his job consisted of knowing the ins and outs of the situations at hand. I was an anomaly—he felt obligated to know as much about me as possible. Despite the reason, I was ready to use him as an outlet. My chest felt like lead from holding it all in and I needed a release.

Taking a seat on the edge of the bed, I directed my gaze to a spot on the floor. "Early on, I knew Elena wasn't my mother, even before she told me. I didn't need her to tell me. There was something different—wrong with me. I thought I was protecting her by not discussing it but deep down I knew I was protecting me." I looked up briefly.

Ethan was watching me carefully. He reminded me of Josh at that moment, hungry for information and seeking answers to the many questions surfacing in his mind. "But why not confront the fear?"

"Because of the night terrors. At six, I had nightmares of creatures much like the were-animals, but angrier and more frightening than you all could ever be, which is saying a lot because you all are very scary." I glanced up at him. His lips twisted into a half-smile. "They attacked me in my dreams and I could make them disappear, but I didn't know how I did it. I would just imagine them gone, and poof, they went away. They never injured me but just terrorized me for months. It wasn't until one clawed me and I awoke with this mark, that I realized it wasn't just night terrors." I tugged my shirt to the side to show him a mark on the top of my shoulder. It was a small rise that barely resembled a claw mark. To most, it looked like nothing more than an oddly shaped birthmark. "I killed him—well, in the dreams I did, but after that, I never had them again. When I told Elena, she cried. That was something I had never seen her do before. I made her cry. Can you imagine what that did to me? I was a freak that had odd dreams, weird abilities, and she didn't know how to help me. I did that to her and I never wanted to do it again. After that, I made it my goal to be as normal as possible, at least until my change into my wolf. Now, knowing what I do of my birth, I guess she was frightened for me and not of me."

I had never told this story to anyone, and there was a combination of feelings stirring inside of me. I felt unburdened and uneasy. It was relieving to finally tell someone who wouldn't consider me a nutcase. Unfortunately, the person I was telling it to was the very person who admitted that if I were ever a risk to the pack, he would murder me without giving it a second thought.

Ethan hadn't moved or said anything since I started talking. Absorbing the information, he leaned back farther in the chair, looking at a spot on the wall.

"So when you changed, you thought you had become one of the monsters that terrorized you as a child?" he asked with a frown.

I responded with a forced smile. "I didn't want to be that creature. I just wanted something about me to be normal. Changing into an animal once a month was far from normal."

He pushed himself up from the chair, walked over and sat next to me. My body tensed. He pulled back the shirt to look at the scar. "Do you feel like a monster now?" he asked, running his finger along the mark.

I didn't respond. We saw our wolf-half differently. There was no need to insult his belief by telling him that if you weren't wholly human, there weren't many things you could be considered. Even with the new information, changing into a wolf once a month didn't make me feel less different or anything short of something that was too wrong to exist.

"At one time, we were all monsters, creatures of the night that were nothing more than living nightmares. The vampires, were-animals, witches, and demons commanded the night in bloodshed and terror. We all have evolved throughout the centuries—some more than others. Evolution had to occur, some by force, others through adaptation, and many through their connection with their humanity. Those weren't your night terrors. They were Maya's memories. The memories of those times in which she lived in people whose lives were nothing more than a nightmare in living form," Ethan stated in a level voice. "She seems to exorcise the horrors of the lives she lived when you sleep. That explains why your nights are so restless. I often hear you in your sleep, but I always assumed it had to do with what was going on now."

"I never had problems sleeping until now."

His lips twisted amused. "I'm sure that's true from your viewpoint, but what do the people say who sleep on the other side of your bed or in the house with you?"

My mother noted restless nights in her journals, but who didn't have an occasional nightmare? His comment about company in my bed wasn't worth dignifying with an answer, so I ignored it.

Ethan didn't leave immediately as I expected him to. Instead he lingered, staying close to the window, looking out of it. I think he was admiring the view of the woods. The house was surrounded by it, but Steven seemed to do the same thing. So I assumed I must have had the best view.

"Why didn't you tell your brother we went to see the Tre'ase?" I asked. Even if he didn't know what it was or about its reprobate nature, seeing my reaction after I met it surely would have been good reason to discuss it with Josh.

"I forgot," he stated, his attention still focused out the window. His breathing—normal, heart rate—normal, the timbre of his voice—unchanged. They were all the signs that he was telling the truth. But he was lying.

"Have you been there before?"

He turned toward me, his face placid and eyes deep and intense. "No." There was something about Ethan she didn't like. I doubt she was that judicious to determine she disliked him from the few minutes he'd spent in her home. Either she knew something about him or that wasn't the first time they had met.

"Are you lying?"

"You shouldn't go back to the Tre'ase. It wouldn't be safe."

Well, that's a moot point because the only way I'm going back there is unwillingly. And I'm going to put up a fight with anyone who dares to take me near there again. "You didn't answer my question. Are you lying?"

"If I were, answering that would defeat the purpose of doing so." He walked out the door.

"The magic you're able to do, did she tell you about it?" I blurted before he could get out of the room. He'd broken Josh's protective field, and it really had left him angry and bewildered. It wasn't arrogance that fueled those feelings, it was the fact Ethan was able to do so, and Josh didn't know how. There was only one explanation for that.

He turned, keeping the same vacuous look on his face. Not one emotion betrayed him. "Breaking a ward is hardly witch magic. Were-animals break them all the time. It would be beneficial if you learned to do so, as well, or you will find yourself denied entry into many places you may want to be." He left before I could interrogate him anymore.

CHAPTER 10

Josh sat in the library, his legs propped up on the desk, thoroughly engrossed in the journals as though he were reading a novel by his favorite author. He didn't bother to look up when I walked in. "Your mother was quite the chronicler," he stated as he continued to flip through the journal.

I smiled; it was the only mask I could manage at that moment. I committed to no longer wallowing in the panic and grief that the newfound information had forced on me. Being mad at Josh about it was just ridiculous. So I did the next best thing. I accepted it. But it was turning out to be a harder task than expected. I could barely breathe as I asked, "You find out any more interesting things about me?"

He shook his head, and I exhaled a sigh of relief. He placed the book on the table. "You hold magic as though you were a container. Once you use it up, it's gone. You have to reestablish a connection in order to use magic again. Anytime you form a blood connection with anyone, you are able to store their magic and duplicate their abilities. There aren't many who can do that."

I thought he would have been repulsed by it, but he seemed intrigued, elated.

"Then I should able to do the same things you do—like the protective field, but this time intentionally?"

His eyes brightened as he nodded his head. "Want to try one?" he asked enthusiastically.

I nodded once in assent, and his grin grew wider. It was at that moment I realized he was a magic addict, drawn to it without recourse. It may have been his burden initially, but now he found immense joy in it. I wondered if I were being a fool, falling victim to its allure.

"You will be using me as a conduit, which means you will be bound to me," he informed me, coming to his feet.

"Will the same thing happen to me as before at Caleb's?" I asked cautiously. That was an experience I would rather not duplicate.

"Yes, but it won't be as intense." He grinned. "We will be bound, connected. I can hear your thoughts, so keep it PG and no more name-calling. And any impure thoughts you may have about Ethan's strong muscular arms around you should be kept under wraps."

"All comments were made under extreme duress. I was out of my head at the time."

"Okay, let's pretend that I believe that."

Pulling the knife out of the sheath at my ankle, I handed it to him. His brow rose, I guess wondering why I walked around with a knife strapped to me. I didn't know why, either, but if it made me feel safe, I was going to do it. Cutting his hand then mine, he clasped my hand in his and chanted several words. The lucent silhouette of the protective guard surrounded us. Then it dropped. "Your turn," he said.

"How do I do it?"

"There's no spell for this. Defensive magic is at my command. Will it and it will manifest."

Clearing my mind, I focused. I willed. Nothing. I tried it again. Still nothing. "I can't do it."

"Skylar, feel what I am doing," he instructed. He placed the protective field over us again. I felt the wave of power that drew into us. He released my hand from his grasp. "Now you do it."

Closing my eyes, I tried again to imitate what I thought he had done. Calling the magic to my command, I opened my eyes to a thin shimmering gold field surrounding us—similar to that of Josh's. "Cool," I whispered. I could feel the energy pulsate through me as I became one with magic.

Josh studied it, then he pushed his hand straight through. "It would be even cooler if it weren't just a glamour. It works fine as an illusion, but if someone's trying to hurt you, then you are screwed. Make it stronger."

I closed my eyes and called the magic to me again. I didn't feel anything change but that's not to say it didn't. I reached out and poked my hand through the glamour. It hadn't worked.

"Skylar, protect yourself."

I nodded, but I had no idea how. "I'll try," I stated unenthusiastically. Josh made it look so easy, but it wasn't.

He nodded slowly as he distanced himself from me. "Protect yourself, Skylar." The drinking glass that sat on the table near us flew toward me. I dropped to my knees to dodge it. Then a book came in my direction and barely missed hitting me. It wasn't until the table slid across the floor toward me and I had to physically stop it, that I became irritated. "Josh, stop it!" I yelled.

"No," he stated firmly. "Skylar, protect yourself."

He waved his hand, pushing me back against the wall where he held me firmly. His face lost its typical friendly disposition to the point he was scaring me. His lips moved and I felt a sense of warmth creeping up my arm, and I was pulled forcibly to the ground, causing alarming pain.

"You are hurting me!" I shrieked through clenched teeth.

"Then make it stop," he challenged.

"I can't," I responded desperately.

"You're not trying."

"I don't know what to do!"

"It's in you. Command the magic to do what you will. You want me to stop, then make it stop."

I tried again, commanding the wave of magic in me to do my bidding, but nothing more happened other than the useless glamour that covered me. I was frustrated and in pain. "I can't do this," I admitted in an exasperated breath.

When he didn't stop, anger bristled and all I wanted to do was hurt him. I could feel my face becoming flushed. "Just leave me the hell alone!" I yelled at the top of my lungs.

With a quick wave of his hand, he made it all stop, and I slid to the ground. I rested my head against the wall catching my breath. "You're a jerk," I hissed, wiping my hands over my face.

"Sorry, that was very wrong of me. It has been my experience that most perform better with a noxious stimulus and high stress situation. Are you okay?"

"I'm not mostly." We had established that enough times that it wasn't even debatable. His eyes held a level of remorse that made staying mad at him a challenge. If I had been in better spirits, I would have happily taken it on and forgiven him once hell froze over. "I don't want to do this anymore. It was silly to ask."

"It will get easier. I apologize if I scared you, but don't let my stupid behavior prevent you from exploring your potential."

"I can't do this right now. We just need to hold off for a while."

"Of course."

He stood up and offered a hand to help me up. When I took it, his eyes rolled back and his breathing quickened. "Skylar, let go of me."

My hands remained fastened to his, unable to release it. "Skylar, let go!" he commanded in a tight voice.

"I'm trying. What am I doing? Tell me how to stop it!"

Unable to respond, his eyes darkened the way they had at Caleb's. My hands sweltered with heat, then we were both thrown back, hitting opposite ends of the room with force, a force so hard it knocked most of the books off the shelves.

"We need to help you control the way magic affects you"—he stated a few ragged breaths—"I guess I got what I wanted—you protected yourself."

"Sorry."

"Nothing to apologize for. You're right. We should stop experimenting until I have a better understanding of your abilities with magic," he admitted as he stood up.

"I agree," stated Ethan dryly from the doorway. "What good is it to save her from the vampires, only to let her kill herself with magic?" Disapprovingly, he looked at us, shaking his head, then glared at Josh before he left.

"I think you're in trouble again," I whispered.

"With Ethan? I dare you to find a time that I am not in trouble with him. Ethan's not a fan of magic. Too uncontrollable for his liking."

We sat there in silence. My fingers absentmindedly found their way to the imprint of the Gem. I stroked it, becoming familiar with it as though it were new.

"The protective field—it can be broken by were-animals, like when Ethan broke yours?"

Josh's gaze shifted away from mine. "Were-animals can break wards. They do it all the time." It was the same manufactured statement that Ethan had fed him a couple of days ago and me yesterday. I considered pushing the subject, but I had a feeling I was going to get the same spiel he just gave, or simple variants of it.

"And vampires? Can they break them, too?"

"Wards cannot be broken by the young ones, but it's always the older ones you must worry about. If you encounter one over a century old, know they didn't get that old without having special skills and a few tricks."

How do I protect myself when there is a disclaimer with most things, putting a wrinkle in the fabric of the rules?

Josh and I had started to put the books on the shelves. Well, he started, since every time I shelved a book, he removed it and reshelved it somewhere else. This was Josh's domain, and if anyone decided to encroach on it, he was going to make it difficult. I am sure he and no one else knew the system he was using. It didn't have a pattern or even a rational placement. "Shouldn't I be able to find the Gem because of what happened the other day?" I asked as he took another one of my shelved books off the bookcase.

Josh looked at me with a blank stare. He wasn't considering it. I knew that face all too well. I had shocked him. He nodded slowly, biting into his nail. Being around the were-animals didn't improve his look of impassiveness. He had a telltale look when things made him extremely nervous. And his telltale was screaming at me.

"If you knew how to control the magic, you could call it to you, but in turn, it could do the same. If its power surpassed yours, then when it called, you would answer and would be unable to fight it. You might very well find yourself knocking at the vampires' door ready to give yourself to them. It's too dangerous to try."

"No, I don't want to do anything like that. If I am bound to the book, then am I not indirectly bound to the Gem?"

Apprehensively, he nodded again, trying to figure out where my line of questioning was going.

"Suppose I went to the Seethe's home." I looked at Josh, whose frown lines deepened. "If the Gem were in the vampires' home, I would be drawn to its location in the same manner I was drawn to the book, right?"

Josh wasn't speaking. Instead, his jaws were wrenched so tightly together that I could see the muscles of his neck become turgid. I was sending him into a medical crisis at the very thought.

"Well?" I pushed.

He took a long time to respond as he considered the question. "Yes, in theory, but they have a protective spell on it that may prevent you from finding it. . . ."

"And that's the riskiest tactic I've ever heard. There is no way Sebastian would agree with that," Steven interjected, walking into the library. Josh looked a little startled, but I wasn't. My roommate's scent had become very familiar to me, so I knew he was near.

"I'm all for risk-taking, but suicide missions aren't my forte," Steven continued. "Let's say we take you there, and you don't sense it. Do you think we would get out of there with you? We might as well put a big red bow around you and place you at their doorstep."

"They rest during daylight. We can go then," I suggested.

"Yeah, they rest during the day. They aren't comatose or oblivious to their surroundings. Their sense of smell is just as good as ours, if not better. Sorry, but your scent is very distinctive. They would know the very moment you entered the house." He took a seat at the table.

"It's not a bad idea, just too risky. Daytime would be the worst time to go. From what I have observed, they are the most active at the end of the week. They hunt longer and use that time to satisfy their other desires, as well. The best time to go would be at night Friday or Saturday," Steven suggested.

He sat quietly for a moment, periodically looking over at Josh, who seemed to be fighting off a bout of cardiac arrest. Josh's hand covered his face. "Let's discuss it with Sebastian and

Ethan and get their thoughts before we consider this any further."

Steven nodded, holding a similar look of anxiety that he wore more subtly than Josh. I wondered which one I would send into a panic attack before I left. When I came up with the idea to go to the vampires' home to look for the Gem of Levage, it seemed like a good idea. After careful consideration and debate, it seemed like a good idea to Steven and Josh, who then took the suggestion to Sebastian and Ethan. And after more and louder discussion and debate, it seemed like a good idea, and they agreed. Now, sitting in the SUV, driving down the street toward the Seethe's home, it seemed like pure insanity.

Like Caleb's home, it was located closer to the city than the pack's retreat. It was just minutes into the land of suburbia. We turned down a street populated with large two- and three-story opulent European-style homes. We stopped in front of a buff-colored, palatial, Mediterranean-style brick house. Unlike Caleb's home, the vampires didn't seem to care about privacy. The lawn was sedulously manicured with small shrubberies, outlining the path to the house. One look at the lawn, house, and small garden in front of the house, and you would expect a traditional family behind the doors—not a bloodsucking family of the undead.

We got out of the car while Josh and Gavin stayed behind. As I walked toward the house, my heart was beating fast and erratically with each step. The shadow of night covered us, allowing us to move undetected to the home. This block didn't seem to take part in anti-crime strategies like streetlights as other blocks did. Except for a few porch lights and one streetlight on each end of the unusually long block, it was virtually dark. I doubt it was coincidental. Nor did I think it was coincidental that the door was unlocked, inviting visitors who would undoubtedly never leave.

Ethan opened the door and entered first. I was surprised. As with Caleb's home, it was beautifully decorated. I expected the typical tacky gothic décor I had seen on the Web or the dark creepy vampire lair in the campy horror flicks. The urban chic décor, complete with dark contemporary straight-lined furniture, went far beyond my expectations. The home even had a fully furnished kitchen with stainless steel appliances. I had no idea why. Perhaps their garden members needed to eat, and maybe at times, the vampires themselves had a hankering for a sandwich.

Standing in the foyer of the house, I closed my eyes and concentrated, anticipating that same pull that led me to the *Symbols of Death* would soon take over. When I didn't feel anything, I stepped in farther. The scents of the house were distinctive, just like the were-animals' retreat. I expected the house wouldn't have a scent because they weren't alive, but it did, indeed. It was an odd smell, a cross between fresh linen and blood. I crept up the stairs with Ethan walking obnoxiously close.

I pushed a slightly ajar door farther open, entering the dark room with light-filtering blinds that smothered even the slightest hint of light from the moon. I expected a coffin or something coffin-like, but instead, there was a sumptuous king-size bed decorated with richly colored pillows and a duvet. The room was meticulously neat, preposterously spacious, and everything I didn't expect.

I continued through the house. A distinctive scent caught my attention, and I followed it to the far end of the hall to a bedroom that I was sure belonged to Demetrius. Everything about it seemed to exude him and the presence I felt during my vision. The walls were painted in rich cinnamon with light accents. Decorated with tasteful artifacts, mahogany-textured furniture, and unique wall art, the room had an exotic feel. Demetrius's scent, I assumed, overwhelmed the room, but Chris's scent was heavily enmeshed throughout, as well. Obviously, Ethan sensed it, too, because his breathing stopped for a short period, and his face twisted in revulsion before he backed out of it. I stayed behind, trying to get a feel of it. If the Gem were anywhere, it had to be here.

When it wasn't easily found, frustration took over my search. I began rummaging through the drawers, looking under the bed and through the closets. With each failed attempt, I closed the doors harder. Eventually my pursuit became nothing more than me opening and slamming drawers and doors.

"Skylar, we are not here for that," Ethan stated coolly as he stood at the door.

Sensing my frustration, he placed a hand lightly on my shoulder, "Demetrius is smart. I doubt he hid it in his underwear drawer. Just do what we came to do, okay?"

I walked out of the room and went into the other six rooms, sensing nothing. *Oh, come on,* I thought desperately. I closed my eyes, waiting for that enigmatic pull that would lead me to the very thing that would end this madness. As I walked through the living room, kitchen, and dining room, I searched through any nearby drawers and closets, when Ethan wasn't looking. I was committed to the idea that I wasn't leaving without the Gem of Levage in my possession. I couldn't.

I started toward the stairs to search the basement when Ethan's ears pricked: he turned his head slightly. "We need to leave," he whispered. I hesitated, desperately wanting to continue the search.

"Now," he urged, pulling me toward the front door.

"Unexpected guests," stated an expressionless man with a northeastern dialect, leaning against the wall. His lips curved slightly into a forced smile. When he turned toward me, his smile vanished. His peculiar, verdigris green eyes shone so brightly it was like staring into fluorescent lights. They stared back at me intently.

He pushed himself up from the wall, his face void of all human expression. He kept a keen focus in my direction. He wasn't breathing, but I could hear a faint heartbeat. *What the hell is he doing with a heartbeat?* When his lips turned up again at another attempt at a smile, he exposed his fangs. *Okay, he's definitely a vampire—I think. Well, he's definitely not human—I think.* He wasn't quite human, but didn't seem to be a true vampire, either. A creature stuck in a place of in-between. I had no idea what he was, but unless he had the Gem in his possession, I didn't much care.

Standing poised, he held the confidence of one who knew that he could defeat his opponent if necessary. His gaze shifted back and forth between me and Ethan before staying fixed on me. "It's her. The one that our Master desires," he stated in a low whisper. With his flat affect, indiscernible heartbeat, and absent breath sounds, I couldn't tell how he felt about *her*.

Steven moved quickly behind him, grabbing the in-between in a chokehold.

"Steven, release him," Ethan requested calmly, keeping his eyes on the questionable vampire.

"Take Skylar to the Tahoe. I will be there in a moment. I need to talk to..." He raised his eyebrow, waiting for a name. `

"They call me Quella Perduta, Quell for short" He forced an Italian accent with the pronunciation of his name as he rubbed his hand across his neck. Intrigued and bewildered, I couldn't bring myself to stop looking at his oddly-colored eyes.

"They call you 'the lost one.' I dare not ask why," Ethan responded smoothly.

A mischievous smile crept onto Quell's face. "Good, because I dare not answer." His voice was just as smooth as Ethan's. Quella Perduta looked like a porcelain doll. His features were so perfect that you couldn't help but stare, while you played "look for the flaw" in your head. His short, wavy, deep brown hair complimented his strong jawline and striking good looks. He should have been appealing, but instead, he just looked—odd. His unnaturally astounding beauty made him more disturbing than alluring. Perfection was his flaw.

"What were you called before?"

"It doesn't matter because he no longer exists. Since my creation, I have been Quella Perduta." His expression was bleak. He made an attempt at a smile again, but it seemed like more effort than he was capable of. "I may indeed be considered the lost one, but they value my existence tremendously. My Mistress and Master will be quite saddened if it were taken. I guarantee revenge will be sought." His face was a plain mask, showing little movement and no emotions as he spoke. The thing that stood before us was just a shadow of a person—a heartbeat without a life. Was it strange that I felt sorry for him? He didn't seem to belong in this world any more than I did.

"You should have no fear of that. I dare not attack you in your home without cause. You refrain from violence against me and I will do the same," Ethan stated diplomatically.

"Very well, then how may I be of service to you?"

"I need you to relay a message to your Master." He looked over to Steven and nodded his head in the direction of the truck. "I will find my way back to the house."

Steven led me out the door. Once the door closed behind us, I ran toward the back of the house with Steven close behind me. When I reached for the door, he pulled me away. "What are you doing?" he hissed in a low voice.

"I need to go to the basement," I stated anxiously.

"No. We need to leave," he responded decisively through clenched teeth as he tugged at me.

"Steven, if it's there, then this all ends tonight. Please."

He pulled air in deeply through his teeth, making an annoying hissing sound as he weighed in on the idea. Looking around, he inhaled the area thoroughly, assessing for other vampires.

"Okay," he reluctantly conceded. I walked down into the dark room. Absorbing the energy in the room, it felt familiar to me. Perhaps it was because it was the location of my future murder—if the vampires had their way. I took a couple of steps, bumping into something hard. I ran my hands across it as my eyes adjusted to the darkness. It was a coffin. A plain, wooden coffin with three locks attached to it.

"It's for punishing their own. They drive them to madness locked in it, depriving them of all stimulation, food, and interaction. Then they kill them by taking them apart, piece by piece. They are horrible creatures with few rules. If, by chance, you violate them, the punishment is quite severe," he whispered in my ear. He handed me a small flashlight. I roamed it over the obstacle. I leaned my ear toward the coffin. I heard movement. Someone was in there. How horrible was this creature in the coffin that even vampires deemed it bad enough to punish?

I knelt down, trying to get a sense of the Gem. But there was nothing. *Would they hide it in here with the punished?* I considered breaking the locks to open it, but Steven shot me an angry look that quickly deterred me.

Several ritualistic drawings and runes were on the walls of the relatively empty basement. They were prepared for my arrival. I rubbed my hand over the drawing, slowly walking through the area. Still I felt nothing. *Damn. This is where I would be murdered.* The exact chains were attached to the wall. My heart started to beat fast against my chest. I didn't want to give up. A certain level of relief came over me as we started this adventure, hoping that after tonight it would all be over. Frantically, I searched throughout the basement once again looking in, over, and under everything.

Frustrated and discouraged, I walked over to the wall with the runes. Pricking my finger with my teeth, I went to touch it hoping that I could establish some type of bond that would lead me to the Gem.

Steven growled as he wrenched me roughly from the wall. "What the hell are you doing? We are not trying any of that weird shit here. You have no clue how it works and how to control it. Come on, we are out of here." He pulled me toward the door.

"Steven, we may never have another chance. Please. If this works, then it all ends tonight."

"And if it doesn't and you bind yourself to magic you have no control over, then we are screwed! It wasn't even forty-eight hours ago that you bound yourself to that thing. Did you forget the feeling that soon? Where is your head?"

I was so desperate for this to end that I was behaving recklessly. The taste of defeat was acerbic against my tongue. We were so close yet so far away, and I just couldn't walk away empty-handed without doing everything possible to find the Gem. There was that line, however thin, between reckless and tenacious. I wasn't sure where it crossed, but I wanted to get as close as I could so that even if I failed, I'd know I did what I could.

I considered ignoring Steven and spilling blood over the runes. But if I made things worse, once again opened the gates of hell and fell into an abyss that I couldn't get out of, then I would have crossed the line. I would have been reckless and put others in harm's way because of it. I couldn't do that.

"Sorry," I whispered, following him as he led me to the door. When we finally got to the car, Steven's face had softened some, but I was still looking at icy green eyes as he glared at me.

He let out a frustrated sigh. "I know you were just trying to help, but stop playing with magic for now. You don't know what you're doing, and playing these binding tricks is only going to get you in trouble."

"Well, tell magic to stop playing with me," I mumbled under my breath.

As we sat in the backseat, Josh listened to our back and forth, and gathered the gist of what had occurred. He looked at me, unable to mask his frustration with me or the situation. I couldn't tell which. "It's here. I feel the presence of dark magic." He breathed out. We sat in silence in front of the house. As strong as Josh had proven to be, he was limited when it came to dark magic. Josh looked at the house once more before he started the car. "It was too big of a risk. We shouldn't have come here," he finally acknowledged. I didn't like the tenor of his voice. It held fear, and the withdrawn look on his face didn't do much to improve things.

I sat in the living room, my legs bouncing nervously against the sofa as I gnawed at my nails. Watching the door, I waited impatiently for Ethan to return from the vampires' house. As a vaguely familiar scent approached me, I tensed. I heard a hard step pattern descending the stairs. I stood up at his approach and found myself face-to-face with Gavin.

His lips curled slightly to form something that should have been a smile if it hadn't held such an air of disdain. Dark, piercing, almond-shaped eyes with a distinct shimmer of malice stared back at me. His midnight-black hair was pulled back with a tie, while stragglers from the binding hung down to his neck brushing against his deep tawny-colored skin, hollow cheeks, and broad features. He was slim, built perfect for agility and stealth, comparable to a swimmer. He stepped closer, invading my personal space, siphoning out the air and replacing it with his indignation and strife. The look on his face displayed his contempt and his overwhelming desire to wrap his hands around my neck and squeeze. I imagined him watching me struggle minute by minute, second by second, as he pressed the last breath out of me.

"I guess I should apologize for the other day," he stated coolly.

"Why? Are you sorry?" There wasn't anything about his disposition that expressed remorse. I was no fool. He was using this opportunity to own up to his actions. He was proud of himself and was here for the sole purpose of gloating. He wanted me to know that he was the panther that wanted me dead in the woods.

He didn't answer. Instead, he focused on that little corner of my eye that seemed to draw everyone's attention. Daily I checked for it—it was gone, but the results of its existence remained my sin and burden to bear. I was different, an anomaly, something that most people didn't want to exist, and those who did only wanted me for a short time, until I served the Gem's purpose.

"Terait, strange magical abilities, a sergence that clearly shows that you are not one of us. What have you done to Sebastian that he protects you when your life should have been taken?" His gaze chilled me. It was a rhetorical question, but there was intrigue coloring his words. "You are just an abomination of oddities, and yet we continue to let you live when, by all accounts, we shouldn't."

How surprising, a were-animal wants me dead. This was becoming so repetitive that I barely felt threatened anymore. I was tired of being threatened, tired of people wanting me dead without any qualms about voicing it.

Gavin was a transfer from the East Coast, Brooklyn to be exact. Steven said that being the strongest pack in the country had its advantages, but one disadvantage was that other packs dumped their "problem children" with them as a last resort. I wondered why he was transferred. Was he transferred because he was too much for his pack to handle? Was it common practice for him to take on the roles of judge, jury, and executioner? As he glared at me, he'd completed two of the three roles and was waiting out the final.

"*You* are vermin, something that should be exterminated. I should be the face of your death."

I stepped closer to him.

A person can only hear how terrible they are, how wrong their existence is, how much others want them dead so often before you just want to scream, fight, and yell. You want to tell them, show them, and make them see that you should be here, and you damn well planned on staying. "But you won't be. You may feel it in every bone in your body, sense the desire so deep that it hurts. But it will continue to be a hunger that you can't satisfy. Go ahead and wish I was dead, hope for it with everything you have, but as long as Sebastian says I am protected, you won't do a damn thing about it."

The mention of Sebastian was enough to make him straighten and control his ensuing wrath. It was my only trump card, or rather, my wild card. That's what he was—a wild card. A trump card overrode all. A wild card was fleeting, changing at the dealer's discretion. Sebastian had chosen to protect my life, and anyone who disobeyed would pay with their life. That is how he felt now. If he ever changed his mind, removed his protection, I was screwed.

With that, I started up the stairs before my fear betrayed me, leaving me exposed in front of a predator who wanted me dead.

"You won't be protected forever," he cautioned.

Without turning around I responded, "Perhaps, but until then, killing me will be nothing more than just your arousal fantasy."

Ethan returned soon after my run-in with Gavin, but he had been in the office with Steven, Sebastian, Gavin, Josh, and

Winter. She had returned minutes before Ethan. Her attitude toward me hadn't changed as she greeted me with an ill-intentioned glare. They stayed in the office for a long time. Most of the words remained indistinguishable so I eventually gave up listening at the door and retreated to the kitchen, which I was sure would be his next stop.

"Yes, Skylar?" Ethan asked in a rough unapproachable tone as he entered the kitchen. I didn't speak, waiting until I could see his face to determine my approach. His voice was anything but welcoming and so was the look on his face. The marking of a long day, unease, and exasperation turned his face into a mish-mash of unpleasantness. He went straight to the fridge and started pulling out food.

"Go ahead. I can wait till after you've eaten," I said as I sat down at the table.

After he had warmed up leftovers of tenderloins with a side of chicken, he sat at the table. I looked at his plate and shook my head. I didn't think he'd ever eaten a vegetable. "I know you identify with the wolf, but your human half needs vegetables."

He looked at me smugly, walked to the refrigerator, broke off a small stalk of broccoli, took a bite and swallowed it, barely chewing it. "Satisfied?"

I shrugged. "It's your health."

He attacked his food the same way I'd seen him do to the poor unsuspecting fawn the first night I went on a run with them. Once his plate was empty and the only traces that food ever existed were the bones, he pushed it forward and waited impatiently for me to speak.

"What happened with Quell?"

"We are trying to negotiate with Demetrius."

"Negotiate? For what?"

"We asked for the Gem, and in return, we would overlook certain indiscretions that we haven't in the past."

"Indiscretions?" I was unable to hide the disgust in my voice.

"What type of indiscretions? Did you agree to let them kill a certain number of people while you turned a blind eye? Do they get to kill expectant mothers now or maybe children? Can they now turn children and kill whomever without any recourse? Or will you provide carry-in for them once a month?" I asked, outraged.

The look on his face confirmed that I may not have been exact but I wasn't far off. Disgust left a dank taste in my mouth.

"Skylar, you need to calm down." he ordered.

"No, I won't calm down! What the hell did you do?" I came to my feet.

He stood, too, and approached me. "This isn't a good situation. It is a necessary evil. It is a much better alternative than them actually gaining possession of you and all boundaries that restrict them being lifted. I assure you, they won't stop until you are theirs." He stalked toward me, backing me to the wall. His hands rested on each side of me, blocking me from moving. I couldn't look at him. Sliding down to the floor, I pulled my knees up to my chest.

"I know this is a bad situation," I admitted. This situation was an absolute mess. The amount of guilt I felt was too much to handle at this moment.

He sighed, but it came out more like a suppressed growl. "The cards are dealt and we have to play with what we have. You can't wish them away nor will tears wash the situation away."

I looked up at him, showing him a face free of tears. He was truly a piece of work, a real douche extraordinaire. "I'm sorry that loss of life is so frivolous to you. We can't all be as callous as you seem to be," I snapped.

"If I were as emotional as you are, I could never perform my job. Sitting on the floor overwrought with emotion is a luxury this pack cannot afford. We have to make very hard decisions. Decisions I wish came with a better resolution, but we must weigh them all and go with the one that is easiest to live with."

I knew this. I was just too angry to allow reason to have a place in my rant.

"Sucks to be you right now, huh?" I finally let out, meeting his gaze. His face was so solemn and withdrawn. I think he felt the same way.

Leaning against the counter, he seemed to have drifted off somewhere. "I would love to go into their home and just wipe the place clean, rid us of all the bloodsuckers. But that would guarantee a war that would leave far too many casualties," he admitted, shaking his head. I thought I would sooner ice skate on the rivers of hell before I would ever feel sorry for Sebastian and Ethan, but at this moment, a wave of compassion was directed solely at them. *Go figure.*

Like everyone else in the house, I waited for Demetrius's response. I heard the front door of the house open and her scent traveled throughout the house like a vapor. Standing on the landing at the top of the stairs, I watched Ethan and Sebastian greet Chris with sneers that might as well have been a welcoming hug the way she warmly smiled to greet them. She knew how to make an entrance.

Leaving Quella Perduta standing at the door, she took slow precise steps as the heels of her boots clicked against the hardwood floor. The fitted white button-down and jeans left little to the imagination. For a person who oozed sex appeal, she made great efforts to make sure no one missed it. The in-between remained at the door, uninvited into the home.

She smiled demurely. "He's harmless," she stated, directing her attention to Sebastian, "ask your Beta."

"Maybe so, but a vampire will never be invited into our

home. It is our misfortune that you don't require one," Sebastian stated abrasively.

She continued to smile, his insult rolling over her like a gentle tide. Steven went to close the door on the in-between, but Chris stopped him, holding the door half open.

"Demetrius received your message," she stated as she stepped closer to Ethan. "He wasn't too thrilled about your little visit to their home. I think his exact words were, 'That damn wolf entered my home and left his stench in the house,'" she stated, amused.

"If I can stand his, he surely can stand mine."

"That is not the point. You all know better. How dare you! I don't believe you to be this stupid, so I assume the little doe-eyed wolf with all the gumption was behind this plan. She's too new to this world and doesn't know—"

"Chris, I made Demetrius a proposition. What was his decision?"

"And it was quite a proposition, but regretfully he declined. In fact, Quell, what were his exact words?"

Quell took a step forward just short of the threshold as he acknowledged both Sebastian and Ethan. His face was still void of all emotions as he spoke softly and gently. "I apologize. My Master never responded but his declination was implied."

"He laughed, sweetheart. Your offer never even got a response. It's over. The fact you all are sneaking into their home and making bargains shows that you know this as well."

"I assure you it is not over. Attempting to provide a civil resolution to a rather distasteful situation was our intention. If failure is what Demetrius desires, then it is what he will receive," Sebastian confidently responded.

"Certainly you don't value the little wolf's life so much that you will risk the safety of your pack?" she asked, incredulous.

He sneered, taking several steps toward Chris. He was quite intimidating, yet he had little effect on her. She smiled at his approach. "Her life has very little to do with this. It is the life of the many that we are concerned about. What would the body count be if the vampires were allowed the freedom that the powers of this world saw fit to deny them?" he challenged.

"When the were-animals' restrictions were removed, not less than a century ago, the vampires' should've been, too. At one time, the were-animals were tied to the Moon, Mercury, and Saturn, like children. Now your kind is no longer a slave to that which calls them. Instead, you all are allowed to take animal form at will. This is something that more than a century ago was unthought of. Back then, when the animal was unleashed, it was a vicious murderous creature unable to control its primal impulses. Were-animals were nothing more than death that traveled on four legs. Now you feel that you are superior to the vampires because you all somehow evolved to a lesser evil. *Pshaw!* You all are no better than the vampires. Dwelling just below the surface still remains that wild, ferocious animal—no matter how hard you try to assume domestication. Why do you think lone were-animals still exist? Because some of your kind still long for the primitive ways—to be the very embodiment of death. They are what you used to be in its purest form—raw, uninhibited, merciless—true predators."

Anger and contempt eclipsed a shadow over Sebastian's face. "I am by no means domesticated or presume to be. We are predators and that will never change. We have evolved over the years, making our existence easier. However, restrictions still exist. We still have to answer to that which once restricted us like the vampires to the night and you to whatever demonic force that holds your interest. We still have something that we answer to. Centuries ago, we formed packs when our kind chose to not kill for entertainment and to stop being the things that nightmares were made of. Our restrictions were modified because of the penance we paid. Perhaps the vampires should learn from our example. I don't know why these restrictions exist, are modified, or even removed. Nevertheless, they are our restrictions—our rules. Demetrius doesn't get to spurn them because they are hard and he lacks self-control to deal with them," he responded with a curtness that matched Chris's.

"Please trust that Demetrius will practice discretion and self-control with the new freedoms. He just wants his people to enjoy the same privileges that are given to others."

"Really? You expect us to believe that Demetrius and his Seethe know anything of control? That's your compelling argument? Far too often, Demetrius has been known to kill his donors. After being a vampire for over a hundred and sixty years, he still manages to lose control when feeding. His control is quite limited, and it is wise that you remember this and be careful as you trade with him—or maybe not. Maybe we would be better off if he did lose control."

Slight irritation peeked through her charismatic demeanor. "I don't really care what you believe. Your pack members will die if you continue with this. I know you like to think that you are more powerful than the vampires. In the past, they were content, allowing you to hold this belief because you were too insignificant to challenge. But now he grows tired of the pack's intrusions. You have been warned. I advise you to take this seriously and not be as foolish as your Beta," she stated brazenly.

"What do you get out of this, Chris?" Ethan asked, tilting his head slightly as he scrutinized her reaction. He was frowning as he stepped closer to her. "You really seem to be determined to make this happen. What are you getting out of it?"

"It's a job. I take my jobs quite seriously."

"You've always been good at your job, a quality I greatly admire about you. But you are not speaking as a hunter doing an exceptional job." His face reflected new knowledge. A small knowing smile formed on his lips. "He's agreed to turn you, hasn't he? He turns you right before the ritual and you get to have what you've always wanted with no penalties. It's a win-

win situation for you. I guess then you can stop being his blood whore." He attempted to sound cool and aloof and not angry, but he couldn't. She pushed his buttons in ways he was unable to hide. She reeked of Demetrius. I could smell it all the way upstairs, so I knew he could, too. It bothered him, and he was having a difficult time masking it. I wasn't sure what bothered him more: her implied betrayal against the pack, or the fact that she was in bed figuratively and possibly literally with Demetrius.

Ethan glared at Chris, his fists clenched tightly at his side.

Too caught up in the drama that was taking place downstairs, I was surprised by the soft footsteps as they approached. An unfamiliar were-animal stalked toward me with a determined angry gait. Backing away, I started to scream. He lunged at me. Grabbing me, his hand covered my mouth while he pulled me toward the room. Frantically, I reached for the knife that I kept bound to my ankle. I tried to break his hold just enough to allow me to move. Finally it did. A sharp sound radiated through the room as his hold gave. Another hand replaced his around my mouth pressing firmly against my face.

"Shh. It's me," Steven whispered in my ear.

I nodded. When he released me, I turned to look at the were-animal whose head was twisted in an odd angle. He was dead. Steven's eyes looked angry and feral as he picked up the body and carried it into another room.

"Stay up here," he urged as he started down the stairs. I was shaking too uncontrollably to answer. He stopped midstride and walked back to me. Lowering me to the ground, he placed his arms around my shoulder and sat with me until the shaking stopped. "It's really okay. You have to calm down. You were safe the whole time. We knew they were here," he whispered.

My head bobbed up and down repeatedly, but I hadn't heard him because my mind was too preoccupied. They got to me in the house. I couldn't dismiss the fear. I grabbed his hand and held it so tightly in mine, I was sure I would hear bones break. He stayed by my side until I found something that resembled calm before pulling away. "Just stay here. I promise no one can get to you while we are here."

Inhaling deeply, I found my words hidden somewhere under my fear. "Okay," I stated. Pulling the knife from the sheath at my ankle, I gripped it tightly. "But if someone does…"

The corners of his mouth curled into a faint smile. "If anyone does, go for the throat. You can't lose that way," he stated before he headed for the steps. I inched toward the steps to watch him as he descended.

"It's done," Steven stated in a rough voice as he came to the bottom of the stairs. Gavin and Josh entered the room from other directions of the house. Gavin's shirt was stained with blood, his face hard and his eyes smoldering as he attempted to calm the raging animal within. They nodded at Ethan.

Ethan directed his attention to Chris. "You had five people with you, hiding outside: a mage, two lone were-animals, and two members of the gardens. The were-animals are dead; pack law would not allow us to spare their lives. The members of the garden are dead, as well. You can give Demetrius and his Mistress my condolences. The mage's life was spared, but he will not be returning with you," he informed her casually.

Chris looked unaffected. She shrugged indifferently, "Casualties of war. Something you too will soon experience," she stated confidently. Her bravado and composure under hostile situations were attributes I reluctantly admired. But she was heartless, and even if she weren't an advocate for my murder, I doubt I would like her.

It was a brutish standoff as they stared at each other, neither showing desire for resolution. Ethan took several steps closer to Chris and she smiled invitingly. They gazed at each other with such intensity it ignited the room. One hand gently stroked the back of her neck, while the other pushed away strands of hair from her face.

Leaning forward, he gently kissed her on the cheek. Then their lips connected in a passion-filled kiss, a kiss that lasted only a few seconds, but the intensity behind it sent it into another time zone. He rested his cheek against hers and inhaled as they stood in front of an audience behaving as though the room consisted of only them. I watched their exchange, strangely captivated, drawn in by the eroticism and intrigue of their chemistry. I was ashamed of my voyeurism, yet I couldn't seem to turn away. One could not describe or even comprehend what bound them, but whatever it was, it was intense—strangely alluring. For that moment, you understood why they were once a couple when good sense should have forced them to separate. Whether or not they loved each other was unknown, but the passion between them was undeniable.

His lips brushed against her ear as he spoke, "You are usually quite wise in your decision making, but this time you've chosen the wrong side. Leave tonight. You can no longer be part of this. You are welcome to return when this is over. I've warned you far more times than you deserved because of the love we once had for one another. Now you can only repay my consideration with your life. Tomorrow I go for a hunt and you are the prey. If you are found, then your life is mine to take," he declared in such a soft, subtle tone that one would have thought he was reciting poetry to her rather than threatening to kill her.

She stumbled away from him, losing much of her grace in her movement. I wasn't sure if it was the threat or the sincerity in his eyes that did it, but she was obviously shaken. Taking in slow, steady breaths, she straightened in an attempt to gain some composure. Ethan's demeanor and stance held no threat. Maybe that was what scared her the most. His composure meant that he wasn't being driven by emotion, but by pure intent. There wasn't any doubt to those observing that if he found Chris, as distasteful as it might be, he was going to kill her. She was brave. I doubt anyone would question that. It wasn't her intelligence that was in question at this moment. Would her desire for superhuman abilities trump good old-fashioned common sense?

She looked at him with a look that was tender and alluring, in an effort to appeal to something they once held. Unmoved, he gazed at her with dark, cold, penetrating eyes. "Casualties of war," he stated coldly.

She backed out the door, or rather, staggered, and I could hear the panicked skips in her heartbeat. No matter what she did to suppress it, undoubtedly there was fear. Quell followed behind her, never displaying any changes in his mannerism, despite the show.

The next day, true to his word, Ethan left the house and was gone for hours. When he returned, he smelled of the various scents of the outdoors and many other things—but not Chris. I didn't smell blood or death on him, so I assumed Chris had left, and I was sure that Demetrius wasn't very happy about that.

CHAPTER 11

When I stirred, Steven directed his attention from the window just long enough to pick up the beautifully wrapped box laying against the wall to hand to me. He immediately went back to the window, focusing on whatever held his attention before.

The card simply displayed my name in lovely script letters. My fingers glided over Owen's signature in the bottom corner of the portrait that I pulled out of the box. I stared at the woman in it that was supposed to be me. The eyes were a deep moss, somnolent, lost in a place between ineptness and naiveté. All color and vibrancy were absent from the woman in the picture. The lifeless depiction that reflected back at me looked tenuous, ineffectual and fragile. *Is this what Owen saw when he looked at me? Is this what others see?* I frowned at the picture.

"Do you like it?" Steven asked.

"It's nice," I lied before putting it back into the box and sliding it under the bed.

I hated it.

But I would never tell anyone. I still couldn't figure out why Ethan hated Owen; he was kind. Maybe that was why. Periodically, he called to check on me to see how the Midwest Pack was treating me and to reassure me that I was safe with them. But now I realized he wanted me to stay put because he didn't think my safety should be left to my own devices.

"You sleep better these days," Steven acknowledged as he stood at the window, mesmerized by whatever was out there. Showered and dressed in loose-fitting jeans and a white t-shirt that did little to complement his fair skin, he looked like a child, standing by the window, fascinated by the first snowfall of winter, longing to go play in it.

"I guess Maya finds it comforting to have a ferocious coyote near," I stated with a half-smile, getting out of the bed. He was so distracted by the view outside that he barely turned to respond with his typical grin. Now that he consistently slept in my room, his presence was comforting. At night, we stayed up talking until neither one of us could keep our eyes open. Sometime during the night, he managed to change into coyote form.

Standing next to him, I followed his gaze toward the woodland, admiring the view. It was easy to get lost in the acres of greenery, trees, and foliage. The trees gently swayed with the morning breeze, a gentle dance that soothed as you watched.

After I showered and dressed, I returned to find Steven standing where I left him: staring out the window, mesmerized. "There's a full moon tonight." He closed his eyes, listening responsively to its whisper. "Can you hear its call?"

Do I hear its call? Of course I do. It usually started days before until it forced me to answer. Steven yearned for it in a way that I couldn't relate to.

"I'm sorry you can't appreciate it the way we do," he stated softly as his attention remained out the window. Admittedly, mine was, too, as I imagined a life of being moon-called rather than tortured. Sliding to the floor next to him, I leaned my back against the wall and watched him. He was so drawn to it that it was intriguing to see his appreciation for something for which I held such contempt. Soft captivated eyes focused on and revered the very thing that forced us almost monthly to give into our animal form.

"Have you always felt this way about the moon-calling?" I asked.

He knelt down, his gaze meeting mine with a thought-provoked smile. "My affection for Joan had to grow and I love her more than I thought I would be capable of, but my feeling for the moon was immediate," he admitted. "When it calls, it's the one time when you transform into your animal and allow yourself to give in fully to the primal urge of your beast."

"You enjoy this? Giving into it, being driven by urges and needs that aren't your own?"

"But they *are* our urges. Deny them, and when it is unleashed, the results are horrific. Embrace it, and the animal is tamed by you."

"I hate the feeling that I am not in control of my body and actions. The first and only time I changed in an uncontrolled environment, I woke up next to a deer that I savagely attacked. My control lost to a point it disturbed me. I gave in to primal urges that I knew were not my own."

He moved, positioning himself in front of me, his appearance hauntingly gentle. "You lack control because you choose to live as though your animal-half and human-half are two different entities. You will never gain that control when you live that way. I don't know how to show you how to do this. It's a matter of acceptance on your part."

He sat back on his heels. "There are many of us who have control issues, but it's not the animal that's the problem—it's the person. Just like you find typical humans with rage issues, there are were-animals within them, as well. It's not the animal that is losing control—it's the person inside, allowing it to take that control. It is their desire to be led only by primal urges. I've never known that lack of control. I think it has a lot to do with being a changed rather than innate were-animal. I've found that innate were-animals seem to have to work harder at control. They have a greater affinity toward the animal, allowing it to have more control than necessary," he informed me, his hand briefly touching mine.

"So when you ripped into that vampire, you were in control the whole time?" I inquired doubtfully.

The smile on his face exuded so much innocence that I provided my own answer. He had to have lost control at least a little. No one would be capable of that level of carnage without being driven by something inhuman.

"I'm a killer, Skylar."

His acknowledgment felt like a sucker punch to the gut. "You are not a killer." Because of unavoidable circumstances, he had killed. I had done the same, but I refused to consider myself a killer. What self-respecting person would want to?

"I kill when necessary, and I make no apologies for it."

There was a long uncomfortable silence between us, and I tried to figure out how I felt about the self-proclaimed killer who slept in my room every night, the coyote who I witnessed kill without remorse and whose smile and warm demeanor made me want to ignore it all.

He gave me a determined look as he responded to my discomfort. "Are you afraid?" he challenged.

Considering his question, I took a long time to think about it. "No. Not of you," I admitted in a small voice. Maybe it wasn't the wisest thing, but I couldn't help it. "I can't be afraid of you. These days, you are one of the few people who comfort me."

He nodded once. "Skylar, I am a predator and so are you. I just give into mine, while you hide from yours. We are all capable of some horrible things. I've done some horrible things that I would do again, if necessary. I need you to never forget that—"

"I get it. You've made that perfectly clear. You're a remorseless killer," I stated sharply.

"Skylar, the sooner you recognize this, the better off you will be. You will be faced with people who are like me. Don't assume they are harmless. Know that as easily as I killed that vampire and that lone were-animal, I have killed others with little regard. They will be capable of the same. I tell you this for your safety," he said earnestly.

My voice dropped to a saddened whisper. "I get it, you're a predator and a killer, and I should never forget this." I was disillusioned and angered.

He stared at me with full concentration as he held my gaze. "You shouldn't."

There was another long tense silence between us that made things too uncomfortable for my liking. "Should I be afraid of you?"

The long silence was quite discouraging, "If it is in my control, I will never do anything to hurt you." .

That wasn't the ringing confirmation I was looking for, but that was what he could offer. Being part of a pack, some decisions were not his own. They were demands he had to follow. "Why is that?"

He shrugged and then smiled. "I like you. You are"—he searched for the right words—"odd. And you have the self-preservation skills of a bunny. But you are kind and untainted by this world. I feel you could use a friend."

"I really could," I acknowledged to the teenager with the olive green eyes, who somehow possessed the gift of showing gentleness and malevolence simultaneously.

He gave me a quick pat on the knee. He tried to stand but I took hold of his arm. I didn't want him to go. He lowered himself back to the floor and leaned back against the wall next to me. We stayed there in silence as I tried to find the same comfort that the call of the moon brought him.

~

Sebastian was the first to change into wolf form. Ethan followed, then approximately thirty other canidae pack members. The full moon called in the deep of the night. They willingly answered, and for the first time in my life, so did I.

The night was colored by a crescendo of melodious howls that resonated throughout the thick woodlands as we ran through the vast area with unbridled freedom. The large oak trees waved in the breeze, the grass hummed under our feet, and ebullience radiated throughout the space.

Is this what it should have felt like answering the moon? What have I denied myself all those years hiding and subduing this side of me?

I had surrendered to the joy and reveled in the pleasure of something I had denied myself far too long, when the deep musical howls stopped abruptly. The padding of joyous paws against the grassy terrain became hard bounds against the earth. The euphonious sounds were replaced by Sebastian's angry growl. The pack reversed and started sprinting back to the retreat. I couldn't see what was going on, but when a surge of anger and hostility washed over me, I knew it couldn't be good. I pulled back toward the trees, aware that my dark gray coat did not blend well with them and would not keep me hidden. But as the others surrounded me, it made it difficult to pick me out. They emerged, their faces pale and their eyes various shades of crimson and black onyx. Baring their fangs, they held their weapons of choice: crossbows, swords, and guns.

We were being attacked. Sebastian charged first, taking out two vamps before hitting the ground. He caught one quickly by the throat; the other fell victim to his claws. He stalked deeper into the woods, responding to the sounds of rustling trees exposing the location of more vamps. Ethan killed several vampires as well, shredding them into pieces, before he crashed to the ground panting, his body convulsing, as he reverted into human form. I heard invocations coming from the left of the woods. As the commands came faster, pushing magic stronger than anything I felt with Josh, the other were-animals, including me, crashed to the ground, jerking violently as we were forced back into human form.

My gaze followed the sound. Hidden within the coppice were four witches, fingers entwined as they continued chanting, forcing us back into human form.

Ethan saw them just as I did and started running toward them, but before he could reach them, they disappeared, leaving the were-animals weaponless and more vulnerable to the vampire attack. Ethan was right; the vampires had gone through great lengths to get to me, including becoming indebted to witches strong enough to perform a reversion spell.

In the midst of the commotion, as the others continued with their transition to human form, Winter ran toward us at speeds that made the vampire motion seem slow. She held a sword and severed the head of one vampire in mid-flip. Her sword moved rhythmically with her, like a dance partner with whom she held the lead. She took out the legs of another as she landed before him, beheading him. Her movements were so graceful and riveting it could easily have been described as art if it weren't so violent. Between the wrist guard and her sword, she had taken out four vampires and was working on a fifth. A group of vampires began to part like the Red Sea. Through the midst of the vampires walked the man from my nightmares—Demetrius. He was more terrifying in person. He held a sword as he walked toward Winter.

Her face that once held immense confidence went blank. The closer he got, the more terrified she looked. He proceeded slowly, prolonging the terror as a sadistic smile covered his face. When he was close to her, he swung, and she barely blocked it from striking her. She went from being an aggressive fighter to defensive prey. She stumbled and fumbled her way through the fight, losing the poetry in motion that distinguished her skills. When the last strike sent her sword flying across the forest, she protected herself with the wrist guard. The sword caught her on the shoulder. She screamed, the pain kicking in her survival instincts. Dropping down, she kicked his legs from under him. He fell but recovered quickly before she could attack. He grabbed her, and then tossed her back several feet with minimal effort as though he were handling a child's doll.

He was advancing toward her when Steven, still in coyote form, lunged at him. Jamming the sword upward in a semi-circle motion, Demetrius pierced Steven's torso and slid the blade through his abdomen as though it were going through butter. Steven plummeted to the ground, crying out in agony. It was a sound so torturously painful I could go another lifetime without hearing it. He lay on the ground panting hard as he changed back into human form, exposing the full gruesome details of his wound. Demetrius walked over, pushed the sword farther through his stomach and twisted. Steven's face trembled, his body shuddering but he didn't cry out, refusing to give Demetrius the satisfaction of his pain. With a smug look on his face, Demetrius pulled it out and started toward Winter.

The smell of Steven's blood and distant whimpers of pain flooded the air. Josh suddenly appeared with swords, crossbows, and other weapons for the defenseless were-animals. He tossed a sword to Sebastian, who grabbed it in midair. Brutal anger settled on Sebastian's face as he stalked toward Demetrius. He also picked up the sword that Winter had lost earlier. He twirled both in unison, demonstrating his exceptional swordsmanship. I wasn't sure if he did it as a warm-up or an attempt to intimidate Demetrius. If it were the latter, the effect was lost on him. The vampire held a look of complete satisfaction as though he were now presented with a worthy opponent.

They fought intensely but not a single stroke made contact

with either of them. The sword fight seemed to last forever as they moved quickly and strategically attacked each other in ways that would have ended the life of an inferior fighter.

As I watched, I inched farther and farther away from the cloak of night toward Steven. I needed to help him.

"Skylar!" called Winter frantically from across the woods, running toward me. I didn't turn to look at whatever she was warning me about. I just started running toward her. But it was too late. A firm grasp took hold of my arm. Spinning on my heels, I struck at the vampire's face, but she blocked it with little effort as she grabbed my other arm. I tried to wrench it away from her but couldn't break her hold. Gavin moved toward us but wasn't able to get close enough before she pulled me to her, securing my arms against my body. "It's over," she whispered.

Then we vanished.

In minutes, we were standing in the basement of the Seethe's home. Vertigo hit and my head spun, a horrible reaction to my magical voyage. Just as the room came to a manageable still, the dark-haired vampire pushed me to the ground. As she circled me, I spun on my butt to keep an eye on her. The door was only a couple of feet away, but I doubt I could make it there before she stopped me. Standing, I forced a display of courage under the watchful leer of a predator.

She smiled, stepping toward me until she was just inches away. "Welcome, Skylar." She used such a pleasant tone one could easily believe she meant it.

"And you are?"

Her lips turned up into an angelic smile. "Michaela."

Great, the Seethe's Mistress. Any hopes I had of fighting my way out dwindled. I didn't know a lot about the vampire's Mistress, but I was sure she didn't get the position and maintain it by being sweet, understanding, and benevolent. I inched toward the door. "You won't make it," she calmly warned. "I won't kill you, but I will make you wish I did," she continued in a mellifluous tone.

I stopped moving.

"That's a good girl."

"I haven't been a girl for a long time," I surreptitiously looked around the basement for the Gem. It had to be close, since they planned to perform the ritual soon.

"You haven't been in this world long enough to be considered much more," she stated, amused.

I guess when you're a hundred-plus years, a little less than a quarter of a century is still considered one's youth.

Her head tilted slightly as she stared at me for an uncomfortably long time. "The others will be here soon, and you will be dead not long after. I wish I could say it will be quick and painless, but it will be neither." Her tone was soft with a subtle nuance of kindness, but the little gleam of joy and excitement that danced in her eyes betrayed her.

Staring at the wall, she seemed to have zoned out briefly, but not long enough for me to get to the door. "You will be an exciting gift for us. We have waited so long for someone like you, and if it weren't for your creator Emmanuel's disobedience, this would not be possible."

Emmanuel—the monster had a name. "What was his purpose for creating me?" I asked.

Her eyes rolled dismissively, and I thought she wouldn't answer my question. But she obliged me. Why not? It was the final request from the walking dead. A request equivalent to a last meal as one is led to their execution. "Once they've satisfied all their desires and fantasies, many of our kind become restless. They long for the things they feel they missed in their pitiful misspent human life. That foolish man longed for a family. Your mother quickly gained his attention because she was the very image of some woman he had a fondness for during his dreaded human life. So close to giving birth, he was convinced that in one sweeping act he could create a companion and a baby to fill his perceived empty existence. He deserved an ending far worse than he received. If it had been up to me, I would have bound him, set him on fire, and watched him burn for entertainment. His crime was stupidity at its worst, but his foolishness led to your existence, so I guess it wasn't all for naught," she absently continued.

Michaela turned her head slightly, inspecting me the way one would an expensive item before the purchase. "It's been too long since I've enjoyed a sunset, and children." Her deep jade eyes gave in easily to her longings. "The sweet, pure taste of children's blood is like no other. As the years have gone by, parents have become more and more cautious with their little ones. Finding a child playing till dusk is so hard. I rarely have the opportunity to enjoy their decadent taste before the blood becomes tainted with age, but you are going to change that. Soon, very soon, I will be able to visit the playgrounds again."

"It is forbidden for you all to turn children," I reminded her with a grimace. The very thought sent chills down my spine, and it was torturous to hide my disgust.

"It is against our laws to change a child, as well as expecting mothers, and it is harshly punished, but we can feed as we please. Skylar, I have existed in this world far too long to give in to my urges and kill my food. I am quite careful with the little ones, for they are indeed a treat," she stated lightly as her face brightened for a brief moment. The basement was empty, but I wished there were something to bludgeon her with. The very thought of her feeding from children angered me to the point of violence.

"Shush, enough of that talk. You are going to work me into a state and I will have no one to satisfy it." She inhaled the air near me again. "Gabriella said your scent was beguiling but she often gives in to the dramatics, so frequently I ignore her. For once I must agree with her." She was touching me, and I really didn't like it.

"Don't touch me." I slapped her hand away from me. When she grabbed for me again, I stepped out of her reach.

Her lips curled into a smile. "You fight now, but soon you will welcome my touch because it will signify the end of your suffering. You will desire that very much. I believe if I had the chance to know you better, you would offer endless amusement. I wish I could keep you as my pet." She stroked my hair in the same manner you would a dog. I jerked my head away. She grabbed my face and kissed me hard on the lips. There wasn't any sensuality to it—no attraction. It was an unwanted sexual advance just for the hell of it. Because she thought she could.

That was the final straw. I was leaving the house. I shoved her hard, and she flew back, crashing onto the floor. I ran for the door, giving thanks for small favors when it was unlocked. I bolted out of the house, my fist balled tightly at my side as I pounded across the yard anticipating her to show up at any time, which she did, before I could gain any significant distance from the house.

"I should learn not to play with my food," she stated angrily as she grabbed a fistful of my hair and pulled me back toward the house. Digging my heels into the ground, I hit blindly at her but only a small percentage of my blows made contact. Hell-bent against going back to the basement, I grabbed her by the arm and tossed her to the ground. Coming to her feet hurriedly, she threw me back and I landed hard against a tree. She slapped me, and the bones in my face groaned as pain scorched through me. If I hadn't realized it before, I knew now—the vampires didn't need to be stronger. She outmatched me, though I was an inch or two taller than her and significantly denser than her waiflike frame.

She clenched a handful of my hair and pulled me toward the house but stopped abruptly, hissing at the empty space behind her. Josh appeared in front of her, holding out a cross. When he pressed it against her chest, she shrieked and knocked it to the ground. He whipped a knife across her neck. She grabbed at the wound frantically. It wasn't deep enough to kill although I wished it were. I wanted to finish what he started. The thought of her feeding from children made me feel a level of hate toward her that would not soon dissipate.

"Close your eyes," he instructed, reaching for me. I closed my eyes, and when I opened them again, we were back at the retreat. The dizziness hit harder than before as I sank into the wall. The room continued to spin out of control and closing my eyes didn't help. I definitely preferred the old-fashioned way of traveling.

Josh inhaled deeply, leaned against the wall, and slid to the floor, where he rested his head.

"Wow," I breathed, still leaning into the wall for support.

"Not the best way to travel," he admitted. He closed his eyes, exhausted from such an extreme use of magic. He was probably depleted. Between clothing and arming the pack during the ambush, fighting crazy vampire Mistresses, and mystical travels, he had thoroughly stretched his magical muscles.

When I took a step toward him, a protective field went up and quickly fell. "Sorry, bad habit. It's like my security blanket." He smiled. He looked worn as he rested his face in his hands.

The door opened and Ethan walked in, covered in blood, carrying Steven. When he saw us, his face relaxed as he continued toward the infirmary. Sebastian, Gavin, and Winter were expressionless as they followed close behind him. I moved from the wall and fell in step behind them. I couldn't understand how he could look at Steven's wounded body and hold it together. I was just moments from losing it. Dr. Baker stopped me at the door, his face twisted with sorrow, his eyes darkened by grief. It was as though he didn't believe Steven was going to make it.

"She can stay," Sebastian stated as he looked at Steven.

When I was close enough to see the totality of his injuries, I gasped. The muscles of his face and neck were strained as he struggled to breathe. Ragged shallow sounds emanated from him. I was unable to hold them any longer, several tears slid down my face. Gavin rolled his eyes, disgusted. Perhaps I should have been embarrassed by my display of emotions, but I couldn't find it in me. If anyone in this house deserved my tears, it was Steven.

My hand rested on his chest just above his wound. I bit down on my lips and tried to blink back the rest of my tears, a sob forming a ball in my throat. Sebastian stepped in closer to Steven and looked down, his face void of any feelings. I didn't know how he was able to watch and remain stoic as Steven's life slipped away. Placing his hand over mine, he moved it directly over Steven's wounds. Steven's chest rose slowly and less frequently as though he were taking in his last breaths. No matter what I did, I couldn't stop them—my tears began to fall freely.

I stood over Steven, bawling as Sebastian's hand became blisteringly hot over mine. A potent force shot through me, combined with my heart tie to Steven, and was amplified by the energy from my heart. My heart burned. I tried to pull my hand away but he held it in place. I leaned against him to keep from toppling over. Ethan, Gavin, and Winter doubled over onto the ground. An onslaught of pain rolled through me as Steven opened his eyes. His lips parted and he inhaled deeply. The wound started to close, his breathing decreased to a more normal rate, and the grimace on his face lost its intensity.

Sebastian stepped back from Steven, looking drained. Slash marks that were identical to Steven's covered his stomach. Breathing hard rasping breaths, Sebastian's eyes switched quickly between his human and animal forms. Eventually he gave into it. An exhausted wolf collapsed to the ground—

motionless, taking shallow intermittent breaths. I lowered myself next to him. As he lay there stilled for the moment, I was mindful that all eyes had turned to me. I ignored the urge to touch him or offer some form of comfort. Surprisingly, Winter knelt down next to me, rubbing her hands soothingly along his massive animal. The uninviting look she shot me had me coming to my feet quickly and leaving the room with the others not too far behind.

I leaned against the wall outside the room and breathed a sigh of relief. Steven was alive.

Hours later, I braced myself while Sebastian and his fury erupted throughout the house shaking it like a quake. Ethan and Winter cringed each time the volcano erupted, spewing curses and threats directed at Demetrius and his Seethe. The others seemed unaffected, but it was Ethan and Winter who were controlling the emotions. When he first started on his rampage, the various were-animals started to show through. Some of them even went into mid-change but were quickly changed back by Ethan. It was draining on them and their faces showed the signs of exhaustion. The last thing they needed was a house full of enraged were-animals.

"They violated the rules. . . ." he growled. "You never attack during the call of the moon." Sebastian was a man who valued principles, rules, and laws. The fact that the vampires blatantly disregarded them filled him with contempt and anger. Sebastian was enraged and we were suffering for it. He ended his rant by throwing a sofa across the room. I jumped, startled by the sheer demonstration of aggression, but no one else did. They must have grown accustomed to such dramatic displays of anger. It was one hell of a tantrum.

. . .

After Sebastian's extreme outburst, I showered and grabbed some food, which I ate in the room. The further I distanced myself from Sebastian and Ethan's rage, the better I felt. Dr. Baker was still working on Steven, so I hadn't been able to see him again.

The television was watching me as it had been for the past hour. I turned it off and went to the library. I found the VAMPIRE logs and looked for Emmanuel. Emmanuel, the person Michaela referred to as my creator. *Creator*—I hated that word. It implied that I was sired, and the very thought made me cringe. The implication that I was put in the same category as a vampire was unsettling.

Scanning for information, I noticed that some of the pages had been recently updated, I assumed by Josh. Chris's relationship with Demetrius was noted because he wasn't known to trade with a human before. Josh had also placed a symbol by Chris's name but I wasn't sure what it meant. I assumed that it was because vampires were only known to trade with fae, witches, and even demons to temporarily have use of their gifts. It was never a benefit to them to trade with a human, so such an act was noteworthy. Or it could be because it was Ethan's ex-lover.

Emmanuel did indeed make it into the VAMPIRE logs. He was created by Michaela, who apparently found him amusing as well. Fascinated by the turmoil and havoc he caused as a human, she naturally was drawn to him, believing he would make a great addition to their family. *Why not gift a raging psychopath with eternal life and super-strength? That's rational thinking.* With an extensive history of violence, alleged rapes, and assaults as a human, he easily incorporated his poor life choices into his new life as a vampire. Like his creator, he had a sick perversion for feeding from children and pregnant women. He became a menace in the otherworld. Josh had made a notation of his role in my mother's death, and he also referred to him as my creator.

Putting aside the disgust, I was impressed that Josh had already figured out that it was Emmanuel who killed my mother. I was created by a vampire who was considered a psychopath even by vampire standards. Things just kept getting better. When Dr. Baker entered the room, I placed the binder on the bookshelf, grateful for the distraction. "Steven would like to see you." His voice was soft and weary, showing all the signs of a long, hard night.

I followed him back to the office. He had placed Steven in one of the recovery rooms. In the small space, the smell of blood and antiseptic lingered. Steven lay on the hospital bed with Steri-Strips across the wound on his abdomen and chest. For anyone else, an injury like that would have taken a massive number of stitches, but as a were-coyote, he was patched up with a few Steri-Strips, a good pack doctor, and a very powerful Alpha.

"Hey," he greeted me lethargically. His skin was still pale and his voice a hoarse whisper. When he attempted to smile, his lips barely curled.

"Hey, yourself. How are you?" I pulled a chair up next to the bed.

"I'm good." His voice was strained. "The real question here is how are you?"

"I'm not the one with a gut wound."

"Yeah, but you had to have cracked a couple of ribs with all the sobbing and crying you were doing earlier," he stated flippantly, this time successfully achieving a half-grin.

"Excuse me." The words barely came out through my clenched teeth as I glared at him.

After seeing my response, he straightened. "It was a joke—bad joke. Sorry. I'm just not used to such … um … you know—" He stopped abruptly, having difficulty finding the right words. "Overly human displays of emotions. It's been a long time since I've seen tears from a were-animal. It's just not our way."

"If being unsympathetic and heartless is what you strive to be, then you can have it. I can't watch someone nearly die and pretend like nothing happened," I snapped as I stood up. "Steven, I thought you were going to die! I'm not sure how a were-animal should react in that situation, but I can't watch someone almost die because of me and not become emotionally affected by it." It was then that I realized I didn't fit in anywhere. I wasn't whole enough to be human, animal enough to be a were-animal, vamp enough to be a vampire.

I exhaled. "I don't belong in this world and I doubt I ever will. The deaths and violence are too much for me. The smell of blood makes me ill, the violence leaves a bad taste in my mouth, and near-death experiences give me ongoing nightmares. Make fun of it if you like, but it's not going to change the way I am. And if you think it's okay to be like that, then you are an ass," I stated bitterly before I stormed out of the room.

"Skylar, come back," he called out after me.

I paused, but decided to continue to my cell that was cloaked as a beautifully decorated room. I was too tired and frustrated to deal with an argument and I couldn't yell at him anymore.

"Please," he added with a tense sigh.

Wavering briefly before turning around, I walked back to the room. I leaned against the doorframe, my arms folded firmly across my chest. A large part of me didn't want to leave him, but I couldn't be around him if he was going to be a jerk. He had just knocked everyone further down the list while he held strong at first place.

"I appreciate your concern. I really do. Being part of a pack for half of my life, I've grown accustomed to our way. All other things seem unfamiliar and odd to me. I can appreciate that you worry about me. It was inconsiderate of me to belittle your actions and trivialize your feelings, and for that, I am sorry." He gave me a reserved but sincere smile.

Wow, Joan has trained you well. Equipped as he was with her talents of diplomacy and grace, armed with a youthful angelic appearance and boyish charm, I found it impossible not to forgive him for any of his wrongdoings. He could very well get away with anything and probably had.

Returning to my chair next to him, I said, "You know, you should bottle that and sell it at the farmer's market. You can call it 'sugar-coated compost.'"

He laughed, and immediately winced, grabbing his stomach. "Still hurts."

"Well, it happened just a couple of hours ago. A gut wound like that, even for you super-furries, is going to take time to heal."

"I know. I've never been injured this badly before," he admitted in a low voice, putting a lot of effort into disguising his fear about his near-death experience. "Farmer's market, huh? That's what every were-animal wants to hear. I sound really hardcore, a menace for all to fear." His joking led him to hold his stomach.

I laughed. "I assure you—you are quite scary. Speaking of scary, I met Michaela today."

His mouth twisted. "Well, you're here, so I assume the meeting didn't go well for her."

"Did you know she likes to feed from children?"

He nodded with a partial frown.

"She found me amusing and wished she could keep me as a pet."

"That's not unusual. Gabriella and Chase are similarly amused with Winter and had the misfortune of expressing it on several occasions. They even asked if she would consider joining them in their bed." He scowled. "That was a bad day for them. One of his tattoos is covering a scar she gave him as a result of that lewd proposal."

Well, that explains why she hates the terrible duo so much. "Aside from the fact she wants to murder me so she can go around feeding from children, she seems like a big bowl of crazy."

He chuckled. "Demetrius likes his women to be eccentric, with a certain level of passion."

"You realize *eccentric* and *crazy* aren't synonymous."

"For them, it seems like a very fine line. From what I hear, she is actually more palatable compared to his former Mistress. She was touched in the head and tap-danced on the line between sanity and crazy every inch of the way. Apparently, she was quite the menace."

That very thought was sickening. *His last Mistress was worse than Michaela? How in the hell could that be possible?* Michaela enjoyed feeding from children and was responsible for a significant number of the vampires found in the VAMPIRE logs. She saw perverted and potentially psychopathic behavior as an opportunity to populate their Seethe. I leaned forward and lay my head on the bed next to his leg. "If I never see another vampire in my life, it will be too soon." I let out an exasperated sigh.

Patting me on the head, he said, "You're not a very good wolf. The challenge should be exhilarating."

"What about me ever gave you the impression I was a good werewolf? I am probably the worst ever created," I whispered into the side of the bed.

He chuckled. "Worst … that's a stretch. You're just not a very good wolf yet, but I assure you, I've met worse." His eyes were starting to droop. He was getting tired, and so was I.

"Sleep," I insisted. He didn't require much urging. Once his eyes closed, he drifted off into a deep sleep.

I fell asleep in the chair leaning forward on his bed, moments after he had. He still slept in coyote form in my room and I had become accustomed to being near him. His deep, raspy breathing had become rather soothing.

When Dr. Baker woke me up and suggested I go to my room,

I declined. He looked at Steven, who had fallen asleep with a couple of strands of my hair interlaced through his fingers. Then his gaze shifted to my hand, which was placed haphazardly on his legs. He gave me a disapproving look. "His wounds need to heal, so it's best if he doesn't overexert himself," he commented, stepping toward the door. "You two will have to behave the next couple of days," he added sternly.

I stared after him incredulously. *Was he serious with that? Ew! Is any display of concern automatically an assumption of a sexual relationship in this house?* If I weren't half-asleep, I would have responded with something clever, but in this state, it would have just come out bitchy. I changed from my position, moving farther from Steven, feeling dirtied by Dr. Baker's insinuation.

CHAPTER 12

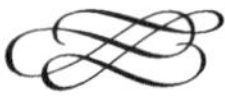

"I need help," I admitted to Winter's back.

She grunted. "You need help. What else is new?"

I ignored the insult. I didn't need her friendship, just her help. "Show me how to fight," I blurted. She continued to hit and kick the punching bag as though she hadn't heard me. With the same aggressive gracefulness she held during the ambush, she spun to kick the bag, and faced me with an unwelcoming sneer.

Steven seemed to have healed just fine, but Dr. Baker still had him on bed rest, which just brought out his antagonistic tendencies. After he attempted to leave the room several times, Dr. Baker threatened him with sedation or the cage. He eventually stayed put. So my first choice wasn't available. Winter was a better choice, though not necessarily the wisest. Winter, a serpent and a lesser species, maintained her position as third among those who possessed strength superior to hers. Whatever skills she had that gave her that edge, I wanted. The next time I encountered a vampire, I hoped they regretted the experience.

There was a look of utter contempt. Then she smirked and

asked, "You trust me to do this?" She slunk around me quickly in a taunting manner, inevitably making me regret my request.

"Yes." I watched her carefully, but I wasn't confident with my choice, and she sensed it.

She made a harsh, abrupt sound, which I'm sure was supposed to be a laugh. She began to walk away. I waited for her to tell me to go to hell in the only way she knew how—cruelly.

"I need to learn how to protect myself," I uttered loudly before she reached the door.

She noticeably tensed before she stopped at the door. "I am a snake. I am faster and more agile. That is my advantage," she stated conversationally as she went into a series of flips that landed her directly in front of me. Her palm pushed into my chest so hard that I forcibly exhaled as I hit the ground.

Standing over me, her eyes changed between human and snake in a disturbing sequence. "You are a wolf: strong, instinctive and aggressive. That is your advantage." She extended her hand to assist me up. Once I was up, she flipped me to the ground using a hip toss. She circled me, taking slow, measured, predacious steps. I had a hard time convincing myself that she wouldn't kill me.

Her voice lowered into a harsh hiss. "You are so much trouble. Protecting you is an unnecessary chore. We have died for you, faced injury for you, and still Sebastian tries to protect you. You don't deserve our help." She hovered over me, her face inches from mine.

"You have the opportunity to make it easier. Do something about it instead of standing over me blaring hateful words."

She scurried behind me, her arm fixed around my neck and her legs wrapped around my torso. "Are you afraid?" she inquired harshly next to my ear.

I was too stubborn to admit that I was.

"I could kill you right now. Simply choke the life from you and end it all right now. Do you think Sebastian would care? I could give him any trite excuse, and he would accept it without question. He doesn't want you here anymore than I do, but he is committed to our laws more than I am. I doubt he would even be angry with me."

My breathing became erratic as my heart pounded. I tugged at her arm but it didn't budge.

"Sebastian would punish me harshly to keep up appearances, but he wouldn't kill me over you," she crooned self-assuredly.

The pressure around my neck increased, making it difficult to pay attention to her rambling. I tugged at her hands but it was pointless. She had me at a positional advantage. The salty beads of sweat tasted bitter as I twisted and turned, trying to free myself from her hold.

"Are you afraid that this could be the end?" she asked. My struggle intensified. All I wanted to do was release myself from her and get the hell away. "The more you struggle, the firmer the hold becomes and the harder it will be to breathe. If you die from this, then it will be your own fault. I remain blameless. Now answer me. Are you afraid?"

I hesitated before slowly nodding my head.

"Good." As quickly as she had achieved the position, she abandoned it. "Fear always works as a good motivator. And if you are pissed off with me, that'll help, too. Come, let's make you a decent fighter," she said in her horrifying Jekyll and Hyde reversal of personality. She smiled as she offered her hand to help me up. I looked at it as though it were poisonous to the touch. Ignoring it, I pushed myself up. *Psychotic bitch.*

Winter was trained in several types of martial arts: bando thaing, which contributed to her knife and sword skills; aikido; and jujitsu, the holds of which she said would help disable larger opponents. She kickboxed, which was her favorite because of its total "brutality." And, of course, she was trained in the more traditional martial arts of karate and tae kwon do.

While others were on the playground developing social

skills that allowed them to interact well with others, Winter was in a gym, kicking someone's ass. Now, dealing with her as an adult, it was quite apparent she should have been on the playground learning social skills.

Winter made no secret that she was only helping me because my protection should be my responsibility alone. She approached training me in the manner she seemed to approach most things—intensely, aggressively, and with intent. Her only request was that when we sparred, I'd treat it as though I were fighting for my life. Unfortunately, for the eight hours a day we practiced, I felt like I was. Fighting with all I had still didn't seem like enough. My kicks weren't quick enough, my strikes clumsy, my holds just firm hugs, and my punches, laughable. "Your only goal is to bring me down. No love taps—save your girl-crush for a better time!" Her shrill voice haunted me even in my sleep.

Practicing daily served as a good distraction for both of us. The vampires seemed to have abandoned any ideas of more attacks or they were taking time to prepare for another more elaborate one. Josh hadn't returned since the attack and I was starting to worry. I had read everything in the library that was relevant to me and couldn't look at another page.

"Why are you on the ground? Get up! You are not adapting. You know my moves. Use your instincts. Within minutes, if not seconds, you need to adapt. Anticipate what they are going to do. I am just asking you to take the few things I have shown you and apply them. How hard is that? You can't be this pitiful!" she finally said on the sixth day of us working together. As I lay on the ground, I reluctantly met her deep penetrating glare.

Disgusted, she frowned, turning her attention toward the door. "Perhaps you are," she ground out. Then she walked out.

I waited for fifteen minutes for her to return, but she never did. That day I practiced for three hours alone and beat the hell out of my make-believe opponent who didn't happen to be a meticulously trained snake that moved like lightning and hit like a sledgehammer.

On the ninth day, I lay on my back with the familiar taste of blood in my mouth, metallic and bitter. I had been in this position so much that I had learned to accept it.

"Get up," she commanded, standing over me. I was slow to respond, having a hard time trying to find the motivation to continue. Winter was still dominating me with what she considered basic techniques that even "a child could defend themselves from."

I contemplated giving up. Beginner's luck had run out days before and the intensity of our sparring increased. I hadn't adapted and there wasn't anything instinctual about my responses. It's not as though she dealt with me cautiously in the beginning, but now she treated me like I was a skilled fighter without any excuses for my defeat. The problem was—I wasn't.

My body ached and I hoped my skin would eventually change from the deep raspberry and blue that covered most of my upper body.

"Get your ass up now!" Winter commanded angrily.

I didn't move, my body refusing to be subjected to further abuse. I needed some time to embrace the defeat.

"Fine. I'm done here." She began walking away.

"Wait," I urged, hobbling to my feet.

When she turned to face me, I was met with hostile eyes. Charging at me, she pushed me to the ground. She locked both my arms and legs, rendering me immobile. Leaning into me, she sneered. "How does it feel to know that you are this helpless? You're nothing more than a victim ... prey, unable to protect yourself from the things that hunt you. Embrace it. Own the powerlessness, because it's yours to bear. It's what you are—a perpetual victim. You make me sick," she hissed, inches from my face.

She released me. As she stood over me, her loathing rushed over her in a wave. Shaking her head slowly, she spoke in a rough voice. "It's not hard. The only thing you have to do is stop me from kicking your ass. Protect yourself. You've shown the ability to perform the techniques with textbook precision, yet you suck at integrating it to defend yourself. I can't work with this. You are a pitiful excuse for a were-animal. A greater species? *Hmm,* I think not." She headed toward the door.

If things were as they should be, I would be at home with a significant other or friends enjoying a simple human life. Full moons would be nothing more than a lunar phase, and Winter would be gracing the pages of numerous fashion magazines as nothing more than another overpaid and underfed model. If things were as they should be. But they weren't. Instead, she was here, a constant reminder that I was defenseless in this world. I was part of the greater species that had proven to be anything but great.

No, things weren't as they should be, and the reality of it hit me hard. It was a cold, rude awakening, slapping me in the face. It angered me.

"Go ahead and leave, you sadistic, narcissistic bitch!" I snapped, coming to my feet. She stopped abruptly and turned, seemingly less surprised by my outburst than I was. "Nine days you have trained me, which should have been eleven, but you were so disappointed that I didn't meet your unreasonable expectations that you stood me up two days in a row. Daily you have beaten the hell out of me and not once did I give up, though I assure you I wanted to. You have been unnecessarily cruel and exceedingly brutal. I have done everything I could to meet that challenge. I never asked you to treat me with any form of mercy. At some point, you could have pretended to possess some shard of human decency and not gain so much pleasure in bringing me pain. I am not your enemy, but you treat me as such. I asked for your help and you made me wish I hadn't, every moment. I think I have earned some level of patience from you. If you want to give up, fine. Do it. But know that it is not my failure, it's yours."

She was now standing inches from me with an indiscernible look on her face. I was so enraged that the fear of her retaliation was the furthest thing from my mind. "I am tired, my body aches, and as disappointed as you may be with me, I assure you it cannot be any more than I am with myself. You think I don't want to kick your ass? Believe me, I do. You deserve it." I was fuming at this point, grinding out each word through clenched teeth.

She challenged me in a brusque voice as she took a step closer to me. "Then do it." We stood nose to nose.

I took a step back and jabbed, which she blocked with little effort, but missed the second blow that hit hard against her face. A spin kick landed hard against her side and she stumbled. When I attempted a sweep, she blocked it, countering with a strike that sent me tumbling to the floor for what seemed like the hundredth time that day. She leaned in. "Know that if you can't do better than this, I will be the only one walking out of this gym today. I will break you, like I did Gabriella, into little pieces."

I lay there, once again defeated and hurting. My desire to jump up and give her the beating she deserved didn't trump the utter feeling of abject failure.

"That was a wonderful speech you gave. Almost epic. Too bad it's not like in the movies where you make this dramatic speech that leads the underdog to victory. Here you need to actually have skills to win. You are not the first person I've trained, just the slowest to adapt. Sorry, but it isn't my failure. It is all yours. Get. Up. Now."

I looked at the door, seriously considering what my chances

were of making it before Winter stopped me in the most painful manner possible. Perhaps she was right. I was always going to be prey. Predatory behavior was innate to them. Why was this so hard for me? I was stronger than her, and at some point, I should have dominated her at least once. I gently touched my bruised swollen face.

"Fine," she stated in a calm voice. "Don't get up." She hit me in the face, and then again and again. By the third time, everything was numb and I barely felt her fist smashing into my face. When she went to hit me again, I blocked and countered with a sharp strike into her nose. She looked surprised as she faltered back and covered it. She pulled back blood, smiled, and wiped it away. A look swept over her face. . . . *Respect?* But it was gone so quickly, it could have easily been missed, and even misinterpreted.

I came to my feet and attacked her with everything I had. It ended with her locked in a hold. I had no idea where to go from there. It was intended to dislocate the joint but I wasn't able to get the hold entirely correct, leaving two advantage points. If I saw them, I knew she had to, as well. The only thing holding her in that position was force and my desire not to be pummeled by her again.

When she broke the hold, we came to our feet almost simultaneously. "See? How hard was that? You brought it. That is all I was asking." I was a better defensive fighter. While I waited for her to attack, I admired my handiwork. Winter had bloodstains from the nosebleed, a black eye, and some minor bruising on her arms and face. I am sure I looked a lot worse.

"Are you ready to give up?" she asked.

I shook my head.

"Good. But we are done for now. Go see Jeremy. He'll give you something that will have those bruises healed in no time. He's like a mad scientist with all types of questionable concoctions. Don't question the stuff. Just take it."

Once I was sure she was gone, I collapsed back onto the mat.

I showered instead of going to see Dr. Baker. Someone knocked on the door as I examined the extent of my bruises. I looked as though I had gone through the windshield of a car or worse. My whole body was a giant bruise.

When I opened the door, Ethan was leaning against it. "How bad does it hurt?" he asked with a frown as he walked in. I cringed as he gently touched the bruises on my face. No matter how gentle the touch, they hurt.

"I've never been hit by a car but I'm willing to bet it feels a lot like this." I forced a smile onto my swollen lips.

"Put this on your face," Steven suggested, holding up a cold pack as he walked into the room. He stopped for a moment to take in my appearance. He made a soft whistling sound as he held the cold pack against my lips.

"You should see the other guy," I muttered through freezing lips.

"I have seen the other guy, and unless Winter is suffering from internal injuries, then she fared well. Have you gone to see Dr. Baker?" Steven said with a smirk.

"Not yet."

"Make sure you do. I can't begin to imagine what you are going to look like in the morning." Steven frowned, looking away from my battered appearance. "No matter how good you are, you will never beat Winter. She has to win at all costs and cheats when she begins to lose." Steven was loud enough to be heard outside the room. He must have known she was close.

"I do not!" Winter retorted from down the hall.

When she walked into the room, she had a small jar in her hand. Now that she was showered and dressed, it didn't look like we were involved in the same fight. Ethan's lips twisted up into a crooked smile. "Winter, you do cheat," he taunted. "You changed to animal form the last time we sparred, and that, my dear, is cheating."

"Really. I'm a snake, how is that cheating?" she responded with a playful smirk.

"It wouldn't be cheating if you went into midform and were just a cute little four-inch snake, but when you change to true form and I'm fighting a five-foot venomous snake, then that is cheating. And don't forget the fact that you poisoned me."

She smiled coyly. "It's still not cheating if the person you're fighting is over five feet."

"You poisoned me!"

"I was there. I don't need the recap. It happened six months ago. It's time to let it go. Besides, you were paralyzed for like, what ... five minutes? No need to whine about it." She huffed as she handed him the jar and started to walk out of the room. She reversed back toward us. "I'll meet you in the gym at noon. You need to convince me it wasn't a fluke."

Once Steven left, Ethan opened the jar and turned his nose at the pungent odor. "Are you sure you want this stuff on you?"

"Does it work?"

He shrugged. "I've never been bruised to the point I needed it. And if I were, I doubt I would care."

"Look at me. I am willing to try anything." I took another whiff of the cream and frowned.

I pulled away when he started to lift my shirt. "I can do it." I took the jar from his hand.

He snatched it back. "What about the bruises on your back?" He nudged me around and I pulled up my shirt. "Do you feel better now that you have been Winter's whipping girl for the past week or so?"

"How many fights have you had in your life?"

"I have no idea."

"Technically, I haven't had any. I have been pounced on by Gabriella and Michaela, and I killed a human because of my unfair advantage. I've been brought into a world that I eagerly await to leave, but until then, I don't like being the victim. When trouble finds me, should I wait around for my knights in furry armor to swoop in and save me?" I took the ointment from him and began applying it to my face.

"I swoop?"

"Yeah, but it involves a lot of growling, snarling, and making your trademark angry face. And I must not forget the eyes, the scariest thing of all." I tried to grin, but my face hurt too much to make more of an effort.

He took a seat and I wondered what about me gave him the impression I wanted company. Staring at me for a long moment, he eventually averted his eyes. "You look terrible."

"Apparently that's the general consensus." I took a quick look in the mirror. I slathered the cream on so thick that it looked pasty on my skin. I took several aspirins out and swallowed them without water.

"You know what drives Winter to be as good as she is?" he asked.

Pure unadulterated bitchiness and a little bit of crazy.

"She's a lesser species and a very attractive woman. She thinks that everyone underestimates her because of it. It really pisses her off."

"Well, do you?" I asked earnestly.

"I've known Winter for a very long time. I knew what she was capable of then, and I have seen what she is capable of now. Only a fool would underestimate her. There are very few fools in this pack, but quite a few exist in the world. Those who do underestimate her, do so at their peril," he stated.

"What drives you to be the way you are?"

He raised a brow. "Do I interest you?"

"Among other things, I find the were-animals quite interesting. Yes, it interests me that you maintain your position among a group where being the most dominant matters. What drives you to do this?"

"I am not challenged often because I make it known that the challenge for my position is to the death. Most are not willing to wager their life that they will beat me."

I smiled, although I didn't find anything amusing about this new discovery. "Like in a game of poker where you raise the ante enough to force the challenger to fold."

"That analogy implies that I am not playing with a winning hand, and that I buy myself out of the situation with the threat of potential death. I am in my position because I earned it, not because I bluffed my way into it," he stated firmly. "If the penalty was just an ass-kicking, then I would be challenged constantly. Every young member who has something to prove would challenge me. Frankly, I would get bored. There isn't much pleasure in fighting someone whose skills are markedly inferior to yours."

"Winter seems to find immense pleasure in fighting me," I pointed out.

"She thinks you are weak." He assessed me for a moment and then said, "I do believe she's changed her mind about you." Something about the way he said it made me think he had, too.

Hmm, and all it took was me calling her a bitch and punching her in the nose.

"Do you think Winter will ever challenge you?" I asked.

He considered my question for a while and then frowned. "Maybe, but it wouldn't change how I deal with challenges."

Perhaps he was responding to the look on my face; he continued in a gentle voice, "I would never jeopardize this pack. If I was no longer fit to be Beta, I would step down. If Winter or Steven ever challenged me, then they see weakness that compromises the pack. If they see it, so will others outside of this pack. If stepping down is best thing to do, I will."

With that he left, but I had a feeling that he would rather die defending his position than stepping down.

No longer bruised and battered, I continued to train with Winter. And she continued to live up to her badge of honor as queen bitch. Either I had become significantly better over the past days or she did make an effort not to leave me looking as though I were a victim of an automobile crash. I liked to believe that her level of disdain was dwindling. But the marked look of contempt and pleasure every time I crashed to the ground was a rude reality check that I would never find favor with her.

CHAPTER 13

Josh rested on the sofa. Dark shadows formed around his eyes. His five o'clock shadow had grown to a light beard. He still pulled off that chaotic sexiness without a quiver. It looked as though he hadn't rested much in the two weeks he was gone. He sat up and smiled when he heard me walk in the room.

"Long nights?" I asked.

He nodded slowly as he leaned back against the sofa. Closing his eyes, he rested his arm over them to block out the light.

"It's been done," he stated in a sluggish voice, responding to Ethan's approaching footsteps. "London believed she disenchanted it, but there is really no way of knowing, except to see the Gem in action. She wanted me to let you know that this clears her of all debts and we are never to ask her for assistance again. It was pretty bad. She's a tough girl and a great teacher. Far more knowledgeable than even the level ones I know. Next time something needs to be disenchanted, then I will do it." He moved his arm to look at Ethan whose face shifted to a scowl at the very idea of it.

"I called Claudia. She's expecting us at two o'clock," Ethan informed Josh, who straightened up on the sofa at the mention of this woman.

"You are always one step ahead of me." Josh smiled. "Skylar, you're coming with us."

Yay, field trip. I didn't need another one. Each time I went on one, someone either tried to scare me, kill me, or take a bite out of me.

At one that afternoon, standing next to Josh, I fidgeted with my sweater while I waited for Ethan outside the retreat. It was an unseasonably warm fall day. On days like this, I would ordinarily go for a hike or even a leisurely jog through the nearest trail, appreciating the gentle tones of bronze, orange, and deep red as the leaves fluttered to the ground when a strong breeze hit. It seemed like a lifetime since I enjoyed such things and perhaps another lifetime before I could do it again.

Ethan pulled up in a monstrosity of a vehicle, a dark green Hummer. They stopped making them years ago, yet he somehow acquired one. Every time I had seen one in the past, I'd always wondered what type of person needed such a vehicle in the city. Now I had my answer.

"Nice ride. I bet you it's great on gas and a reasonable choice for navigating through the jungles of the interstate and war-torn suburban neighborhoods," I said, climbing into the passenger side.

He cast a look of aggravation in my direction. We drove in silence most of the time while Josh lay down in the back. Ethan periodically looked back at him, obviously concerned. Josh wasn't looking well these days. When he opened his eyes and caught Ethan looking, he gave him a sideways grin. "Just like college. All night partying and class in the morning."

"Yeah, but I was ashamed of your behavior then. Not so much now," he said returning Josh's grin.

Would it hurt him to just tell his brother he was proud of him? He should have been because Josh was working his magical ass off and not one time did he complain.

Fifty minutes later, we stopped in front of a large brick building just off the city's main street. We walked into a palatial art gallery. Track lights illuminated the exquisite modern and abstract art that covered the textured white walls. The floors, a bittersweet color made of crackled cement, added to the eclectic decorum. Unique sofas and uniquely styled benches were placed throughout the gallery. I wasn't sure if they were for lounging or part of the celebrated art.

The gallery showcased some of the beloved and most sought-after artists that Chicago had to offer. The inimitable flare of creativity pulsed through the large room. I could stay here the rest of the day surrounded by the artists' interpretations of beauty and creativity if only to appreciate the sculptures placed throughout the vast gallery.

I had finally caught up with them when I found myself drawn to an intriguing picture. It was a portrait of two boys. The smaller of the two lay on the bed; his eyes were closed. His pale brown hair in disarray, his face relaxed into a tranquil canvas as he slumbered. The older knelt close to him. Flickers of gold in his ash-brown hair complemented his deep blue eyes that seemed too intense and tempered for someone of his age. His posturing was warm and protective as he crouched closely to the sleeping boy. The picture was untitled and the artist unknown. I stared at it until Josh's hand slipped behind my back and urged me forward.

Stepping farther into the gallery, we were greeted with an earnest smile from a slender woman in her midfifties. Her delicate, dusk brown waves were pulled back into a bun. She was the epitome of regality and sophistication in her dark blue business suit completed with a pair of dark blue satin gloves that contrasted beautifully against her alabaster skin. It was the most peculiar style, yet on her, it didn't seem out of place.

"Ethan, Josh," she greeted sweetly as her eyes lit up. Her voice had a hint of an accent but I couldn't quite place it.

British? Australian?

"It's South African, dear," she responded, smiling. Her voice was pleasant as she kept her focus on Ethan and Josh.

"It's such a pleasure to see you two.". She leaned in and kissed the air on each side of their cheeks. Placing her hands in theirs and holding them firmly, she said, "It's been far too long. How have you been?"

"Please accept my apology. I've been very busy," Ethan said regretfully. Josh chimed in as well, offering his apologies. As they humbled themselves in her presence, displaying undeniable reverence, I wondered who she was to evoke such behavior. Josh was generally cordial and polite with everyone, but Ethan made it painfully apparent that he wasn't a "people person."

"We will make a better effort in the future," Josh promised.

"No worries. I see why you've been so busy. She's absolutely lovely. Whose is she?" She directed her attention to me.

You have to be kidding me! "Whose is she?" I stared at her, waiting for the inevitable punch line that never came.

"She is lovely," Ethan responded as his eyes met mine briefly, "but she is neither of ours. She is the pack's responsibility, and we need your help."

The smile quickly vanished from Claudia's face as she looked at Ethan, then Josh. He nodded his head once. Her head bowed as if she had been given disturbing news. She looked uneasy as she walked toward me. She slowly removed her gloves. With a faint smile on her face, she took my hand into hers.

"Relax, dear," she urged as her eyes held mine before they phased into a distant gaze. Time stood still as her reaction evolved from emotionless, to complete sorrow, terror, and eventually settled on something in between. She dropped my hand suddenly. The level of grief that wafted from her made me shudder. Her hand gently touched my cheek before a tear ran down her face. "I'm sorry, dear."

"Good-bye, Ethan," she stated coolly. She turned to face Josh. "You need to take care of this—all of it. Do what is necessary. Hard choices need to be made and they need to be done rather quickly," she commanded insistently. Josh looked like he was recovering from someone punching him in the stomach.

"What should I do?" he entreated, despondently.

She stepped closer to him, touching her ungloved hand to his cheek. "Josh, you know what needs to be done, you've always known. You will do what is necessary because you always have." She had a faint smile.

His shoulders sagged. A sullen look overtook his features as troubled eyes held her gaze. His fingers interlocked with mine as he walked toward the door, trying to guide me with him. He tugged a little harder when I called after Claudia to get her attention. She ignored me, walking swiftly toward the back room. When Ethan started after her, she turned, holding out her hand to halt him.

"You come to visit me as much as you please, but don't you ever do this to me again without warning," she snapped.

"I'm sorry." He lowered his head, remorseful, stepping back slowly from her.

"No need for apologies. Just don't do it again. I expect better from you, Ethan. Next time such rudeness won't be forgiven."

"I'm sorry," he muttered again.

Who the hell was that woman?

We sat in silence for the majority of the trip back to the house. Josh looked as though he was submerged in cement and feeling the weight of it as it overtook him. An appearance that usually held self-confidence looked unnerved and uncertain. The look on Claudia's face played over and over in my mind. I closed my eyes tightly, forcing her expression aside. A person doesn't see that kind of emergence of sorrow, horror, and fear without it leaving them feeling a little unsettled.

Ethan's face remained fixed in a distracted state as he stared out the windshield. When he turned to face me, he looked troubled. I wondered what was going through his distressed mind.

"Who and what the hell was that?" I finally asked, breaking the silence.

"Our godmother. She has the gift of foresight. We rarely come to her for assistance because it is too hard on her. We don't know if she is an *empath,* but she feels things too deeply not to be," Josh responded in a dry voice. And I doubted that they would ever ask.

"They are going to kill me. Nothing we do is going to stop that," I choked out. Whatever she saw in my future couldn't have been good. That hadn't been a tear of joy, and neither one of them had a look of potential victory. Almost instantly, I could feel the pain of fanged enamel pressing into my flesh, draining me of life.

Josh couldn't hold eye contact with me. He turned and looked out the window as I waited for his denial. A spirited response of how things were going to be just fine. But his only response was painful silence.

"Josh?" He took a long moment before he looked in my direction. When he did, I wished he hadn't. Strained, worried eyes stared back at me. "I'm going to die, Right?"

He nodded once. "Yes."

Yes. I was going to die. Again.

Josh stood at the threshold of the room. Uneasiness radiated from him. The brave front that he once exhibited throughout this ordeal was shattered. Frustration, fatigue, and discouragement now painted a worried frown on his face.

It had been three days since we had seen Claudia, and during that time, he remained scarce. He only came to the house occasionally to look things up and would leave before I could ever talk to him.

"Claudia spooked you," he acknowledged, sitting in a chair across from me. He carefully watched me as he fidgeted with his hand.

"Everything that has happened lately has spooked me. She was just the grand finale," I admitted. As he walked in, his gaze darted nervously throughout the room.

"Skylar, things are getting bad. We've already been attacked. Two were-animals are dead and Steven nearly died. What happened two weeks ago was just a taste of the many things to come. Honestly, I am surprised it has taken them this long to act. They will only get more aggressive and violent until they feel their point is sufficiently made. I've tried everything and I can't find that damn Gem. I'm running out of ideas here and I've exhausted all possible sources," he vented, frustrated.

"Your effect on magic has made things more complicated. If we fail, and they perform the transference, they will be stronger and have access to magic that may render them invincible and a true threat. I have no idea of the extent of your magical ability and the power you will give them. I don't know how to prepare for things."

He started rambling. Some of the things made sense, but most of it didn't. Eventually he would get to the point, so I just waited it out. He was pacing the floor when he came to an abrupt stop.

"Given the situation, I think you've handled things pretty well."

With limited options, I handled things the best I could, making some painstaking mistakes—pun intended. What were my alternatives?

"What are you prepared to do if we can't gain possession of the Gem?" he asked in a strained voice.

What options do I have? Can I call Demetrius and ask him nicely not to kill me and I would be ever so grateful? He didn't strike me as the type to give in to pleas for mercy.

He bit down on his lips as he continued to ponder things. Finally, he exhaled, conceding to whatever debate was taking place in his head. He walked toward me and handed me a vial of thick purple liquid. "It's Trincet, known as 'pleasant death.' You take it, and in less than a minute you are dead."

It seemed to shimmer invitingly when the light hit it. "Is there such a thing as a *pleasant death*?"

He shrugged. "Depends on your view of death or the alternatives."

He waited, looking past me, his attention on the wall behind me as I reflected on the situation. "Don't make the decision out of idle heroics or the romanticism of self-sacrifice. You have nothing to gain from that."

"I have no desire to do, either. I guess if I am going to die anyway, I would rather be in control of how it happens. If the results are the same, why leave things worse off? Sixty seconds, huh?"

"Give or take a few."

I closed my eyes and waited out the sixty seconds. It seemed like such a long time at that moment. When I opened them, Josh was staring at me with empty dull eyes. I had finally broken him.

"You would take your own life?" he inquired in a low, surprised voice.

Why not? I had tried before and knew I was capable of doing it again. I wished the thought of imminent death brought me more fear, but it didn't. The idea of dying torturously with the vampires feeding from me scared me, but not death by poisoning.

"Your death will only stop them temporarily, until they can find another suitable person. Lives will continue to be lost. They won't stop until their goal is achieved. Their passions aren't that easily extinguished."

"I know."

He stared at me for a while, searching for answers. "You don't fear death," he acknowledged, amazed.

I shrugged. It didn't terrify me the way it should, especially since my mother's untimely death. In fact, my life was the very epitome of death. My biological mom died giving birth to me, and my father died minutes before. I died at birth and now hosted the spirit of a witch's formerly dead child. Death didn't scare me. It was the brutality that I associated with it. A painful death was unsettling. No one went quietly into the night and just closed their eyes, drifting into an eternal sleep, the way it was done in the movies. I wouldn't be opposed to a peaceful rest if my life ended in a beautiful sleep.

"You puzzle me. I don't know if you are selfless or just suicidal."

Suicidal—I didn't like the word—it seemed selfish and self-indulgent. *Killer*—it was stronger. I was willing to kill Skylar Olivia Brooks.

Since our first meeting, Josh was undeniably comfortable and friendly, behaving as though he'd known me a lifetime. Now he looked at me as though I were a stranger whose acquaintance he wasn't sure he wanted to make.

I felt self-conscious and guilty, like somehow I betrayed him. "I am not suicidal. Just because I don't fear death doesn't mean I want to die. I've just mastered the skill of elementary math. One life is less than the many lives that will be lost if things continue in this manner. Believe me, if there were other options, death would not be my first choice. The vampires aren't going to just wake up one day and say 'Gee, the were-animals are making this too hard—let's give up.' And I've seen what they are like with the restriction. I don't want to imagine what they would be like amped up on werewolf strength and new magic."

My gaze drifted to the floor; I couldn't stand him looking at me in that manner. "I see the situation for what it is. I doubt I would have lived this long without you all intervening. You all have done so much to fulfill an obligation that shouldn't have been yours in the first place. You've fought harder than I expected and sacrificed more than I deserved. All that can be done, has been. Eventually, the were-animals will grow tired of protecting my life or the vampires will eventually succeed. Either way, I end up dead. I have had so little control of things in the past month that it feels a little empowering to possess a little—even if it is just over my death."

Things were bad. I would gladly choose a painless death over what I experienced in the library any day. Admittedly, I wasn't as brave as I thought. If a stiff upper lip and a gallant fight were all that were needed for this to come to a fairy-tale end, then the battle would have been won long ago.

He nodded, slowly taking in my words before kneeling in front of me. "Skylar, use the Trincet as the last possible option. It's a choice when our failure is apparent and absolute. When all things have been exhausted and your death at the vampire's hand is imminent."

Avoiding his gaze, I didn't agree. "When failure is apparent." *What does that mean? When all the people who agreed to protect me are dead or so badly injured that they are no longer a threat? Does he really think I would agree to that?*

I shook my head. *When I feel the risk is greater than the reward, then that will be the time.*

He stood and took several steps away from me. "Agree."

"No." I placed a firm grip on the vial. I held it so tightly that my nails dug into my skin, leaving deep red indentations in my palms.

We stared at each other, resolute and lost for words. He sighed. "Give me a couple of days.".

I nodded in agreement. Although I wasn't afraid to die, I wasn't in a hurry to do so, either.

CHAPTER 14

I don't want to die.

There had to be something I could do. Could Demetrius be reasoned with? What could be exchanged or offered that would be worth him giving up total freedom? The ritual, could it be done without me having to die? Even so, the end result would be vampires unrestricted and stronger than most people who could otherwise regulate them. I dropped my head into my hands, inhaling the dank smell of failure and fear. The house had been quiet, too quiet. Sebastian, Ethan, Josh, Winter, Steven, and Gavin were in the office where they had been for hours. Each time I went past the office, there always seemed to be more silence than conversation.

"No! There is no way in hell I am going to let you do that!" There was more concern than fury in Ethan's escalated voice.

I came down the stairs just in time to see Sebastian's office door swing open and Ethan storm out, with Josh trailing not far behind as he followed him out of the house. Keeping out of their line of sight, I stayed close to the house watching them. But they were so preoccupied, I doubt they would have noticed me.

They stood nearly a foot from each other, and I expected

another brawl, something aggressive, tumultuous and violent, but instead, Josh stood motionless, watching his brother, his face shadowed by conflict, longing, and doubt.

When he stepped closer, Ethan's jaw clenched tighter. "I don't care what you have to say. I am not going to let you do this," he stated firmly.

Josh's eyes lowered, his thin veil of lashes failing hide his troubled eyes.

Ethan looked withdrawn, his gaze lifting periodically to meet Josh's. Then he turned his back to him focusing on the verdure. "You owe her nothing," he said softly.

"I don't. But I owe you. I owe this pack. You know Demetrius won't stop. If it's not her, then it will be someone else. He hates you and despises Sebastian. When he succeeds, it won't be long before he comes after you. What happens if the person he uses is stronger than Skylar and imbues him with strengths and gifts that exceed anything she offers? Then what?'

Ethan turned to face his brother as his hands washed over his face. When he swallowed, it looked painful, as though it was glass that went down. "Don't do this to protect me. I can take care of myself."

"If things get so bad that you can't ...?" Josh asked in a low, sullen voice as his gaze dropped from Ethan's. His face was distant and morose. When he looked up, his face said it all. *If something happens to you, then what will I do*? "You wanted me to become 'blood ally,' because this pack is a force most won't oppose, to ensure my safety."

Ethan exhaled a long ragged breath. "This is dangerous. You've never tried anything at this level before and there is nothing I can do to help you if it fails." He looked defeated by the harsh truth.

"The favors that we curry, the alliances we have formed, the power we enjoy are all the results of our successes. If we don't stop this, our failure will be apparent, our weaknesses exposed.

The fae trust us, and the elves have given us their unyielding respect because of what we have achieved. This one failure will ruin it—will ruin us, and you know it."

He did. And it was displayed aptly on his face. Yet it seemed to mean nothing if his brother's safety was the cost. Josh sighed. "You are going to have to let me do this."

Whatever Josh was about to do must be dangerous because he made no qualms that he could care less what Ethan thought about him using magic, and voiced it a time or two. They looked at each other for a long moment as if they were trying to freeze that moment in time. Ethan walked toward his brother and pressed his forehead against his. He inhaled a long ragged breath. "Okay."

Pulling away abruptly, he headed toward the woods, leaving a trail of clothes as he changed into his wolf, disappearing into the mass of trees.

Josh watched him disappear between the dark florets of trees and greenery. When he turned toward the house, his gaze briefly met mine. Weary and nervous eyes held them for just a millisecond. As he walked closer, I could sense that whatever he was about to do scared him. His heart rate was a series of rapid beats. It was then that I realized emotions had a smell, and intense fear reeked like sewage. I followed him into the house, and when I couldn't stand it any longer, I grabbed his arm.

Sebastian and Dr. Baker waited for him at the other side of the room. Sebastian's face was the picture of stoicism, impassiveness. Dr. Baker didn't possess that skill. Tension lines formed around his eyes and lips as concern marked his appearance.

As a blood oath ally of the pack, Josh was just as committed to them as any other member. Josh was standing on a precipice being forced by his sense of obligation to take steps far too close to the edge. I felt the need to save him before he plummeted too far. I kept a firm grasp on his wrist. "Are you going to tell me what's going on?"

"Nothing big, just magic," he lied breezily. I kept my hold on him, my fingers pressing into him, probably painfully, cuffing him to me.

Josh pulled away. "Don't," he commanded before walking briskly toward the infirmary.

I fell in step with him. "I'm going with you."

Josh stopped short and pierced me with a stern look. "No."

"I can help if you need it," I persisted.

He looked frustrated as he ran his hand through his hair. It was already so disheveled and messy it didn't really change his look. It was the same look he had the day I met him, except then he was confident and relaxed. Now, he was concerned and tense.

Frowning, he started to walk away again. "You will just be in the way."

"In the way of what? You've exposed me to magic before, very strong and dangerous magic. Why not now? I'm not afraid. I'll be there to help if you need it."

"Skylar, we don't have time for this," Dr. Baker finally interjected from behind me.

"Fine. Then we shouldn't waste any more of it on an argument you won't win. I'm going with you. Enough said." I started walking behind Josh.

"Skylar, stop it. You can't help with this." Josh was exasperated. Nervousness and fear overshadowed his face, and it was absolutely heartbreaking to look at him.

Before I could respond, Sebastian grabbed me from behind, bundling me into a bear hug and dragging me away.

"Let me go!" As I fought against him, the grip tightened, making it painfully hard to breathe as he took me down a flight of stairs. I yelled a slew of threats, colored by enough swear words that in any other situation, I would have washed my own mouth out with soap. I heard the squeal of a door opening just before he tossed me onto the floor of the cage.

"Sebastian, let me out. Now!" I demanded, rattling the cage. He barely looked in my direction. My anger was inconsequential.

"I'll let you out when you manage to gain some remnant of control, young wolf, because right now your behavior is unacceptable," he said with a voice so calm and level it was infuriating.

"Oh screw you! I can't believe you are going to let Josh—"

"Calm down and shut your mouth." His voice was extremely composed, but his eyes were ablaze, his fury barely under control as he stepped closer to the cage. I snapped my mouth closed. I wasn't calm by any stretch, but I had a feeling that if I didn't get my anger under control, if I lived to next week, I was probably going to still be in the cage.

I walked over to the corner and sat, pulling my knees to my chest and closing my eyes. The gentle sounds of his breathing as he stood in front of the cage served as a reasonable distraction. "If you tell Josh to wait, he will," I stated softly. Beyond my understanding, they followed his commands blindly. If he asked them to quack like a duck while standing on one leg, I doubt there would be many who would refuse.

He shook his head. "But I won't." He started up the stairs.

"What if I told you I could fix this?" I walked to the bars, gripping them firmly. I pressed my face against the cool metal, and it felt good against my flushed skin.

He looked sorely disinterested when he turned around. "I would say you are as delusional as you are impulsive."

I clenched down hard on my teeth trying to choose my words carefully, although, all I wanted to do was yell at him. "But I can fix things." I thought of the Trincet discreetly hidden in my computer bag.

Staring back at me were dark brown eyes that seemed harsh

rather than inquisitive. I was telling him I could fix things, and he looked about as interested as he would be in watching a kitten play with yarn. It was enraging.

"Even if the Trincet were still in the room and I allowed you to use it, your death wouldn't serve any other purpose but to relieve you of your guilt. The number of losses would be greater because Demetrius would start a new search, destroying anything in his path until he found your replacement."

I dropped my eyes to the ground. "I can't believe you are willing to sacrifice Josh for this. You protected my life adamantly with very little reason; doesn't he deserve the same? You can't let him risk his life for this. In the long run, your pack will suffer greatly. Are you prepared to live with that? I'm not."

He came back down the stairs and stood in front of me, staring at me with cold eyes. "We all bear burdens that at the time we feel we won't be able to handle. You live long enough, you learn to deal with many things."

The guilt was becoming an unbearable weight, and I was collapsing under it. I wiped away a stream of tears that ran down my cheeks and cursed them when they wouldn't stop.

He stared at me with discountenance. "The world you have lived in has been so small and sheltered that you can't grasp the significance of things. This is bigger than you. Even if you weren't involved, we would have done whatever necessary to stop Demetrius from completing the ritual. You take the time in here to get over yourself."

He was up the stairs with such smooth graceful strides, it was hard to believe that just moments ago he was standing in front of the cage, chastising me.

I had been in the cage for about three hours when Winter came down the stairs, a smirk on her face. "Maybe this is where you should have started off." She went on to amuse herself by listing what she considered the many stupid things I'd done over the past weeks that should have landed me in here. She stopped suddenly. Her ears pricked, listening keenly to the sounds upstairs.

"Damn," she stated under her breath through gritted teeth. She quickly punched in the code to the cage and opened it. Halfway up the stairs, she yelled down to me, "Don't close the door. When you have a disgruntled, volatile were-animal on your hands, the last thing you want to have to do is fumble codes."

I quickly followed Winter up the stairs, where a short blonde who was too curvy to be were-anything stood at the door. The scorn etched on her round supple face made her would-be soft features hard as she followed Dr. Baker into the infirmary, holding her bag closer to her. Winter stared at her until she disappeared behind the double door. Then she closed her eyes and bit down on her lips hard.

"What's wrong?"

She cursed. "Pala's here. This can't be good." She looked uneasy as she continued to look at the empty space where Pala once stood. "He's going to bring Ethos into this," she whispered. Her face was stringent with concern.

"What does this mean?"

Too focused on her thoughts, she didn't seem to hear me. "Winter." She shook her head, directing her attention to me.

"Ethos is very powerful and the very essence of dark magic. Some say he is a warlock, others a demon. No one really knows. He's the strongest source of dark magic, which is not of the world we live in. Well, not in the sense that you would think. There are people who practice its art and are allowed to borrow it. In return, they are in servitude to him. Pala is a servant of Ethos. Josh is going to use her as a conduit, binding himself to her in order to use dark magic to find the Gem. She will be in control the whole time. Anyone who is in servitude to Ethos should never be given control of your body and mind." She spoke swiftly, her attention focused on the double doors dividing us from whatever Pala and Josh were doing. I sucked in a breath, recalling what took place when I was used as a conduit with Caleb.

"Why would he do something like that?"

"This wasn't his initial plan. Obviously plan A failed, so he moved on to plan B." She rubbed her hands over her face and sighed. "We are not prepared for plan B."

If plan A leaves that fear-stricken look on Winter's face, then how bad is plan B?

She started to pace, her words barely audible. "He must not have had any other options. Obviously, the locating spell he used in the Chasm failed. He wouldn't call upon Pala unless it did." She continued pacing the floor, working through things as she tried to find a reason why Pala was here.

"Chasm?" I asked, interrupting her frantic pacing. So engrossed in her thoughts, she either didn't care or forgot I was standing there.

She looked at me impatiently and took several controlled breaths. "Between natural and dark magic is the Chasm. The Chasm is the last place where witches who practice natural magic can go as a source of answers or to perform magic, which is neutral. It's not necessarily a safe place to be, but often, when you are trying to find the source of dark magic, it works. Most locating spells are done in the Chasm, but the stronger the dark magic you are trying to find, the less helpful it is. The magic hiding it must be too strong, so he is going to use her to locate it. She's so strong, she should be able to locate anything."

When she heard a noise from the room, she stopped her pacing and raced around the corner to the other side of the house until she found Ethan. "Pala's—"

He rushed around the corner toward the room before she could finish the sentence. I followed behind, breaking into a run to keep up with them. We plowed through the door to find Josh lying on the floor, thrashing violently. Pala sat next to him, her hand gripping his tightly. Her eyes were closed, but the sound of three were-animals rushing through the door momentarily distracted her. She opened them, exposing pupils that were absent of all pigmentation, cold and piercing. She shrieked, making a loud, reedy sound that brought us to our knees. We covered our ears simultaneously at the force that swept through the room with chilling power. The only person who seemed unaffected was Sebastian, who had just entered the room. Suddenly, the room came to a halting calm. Josh lay motionless, his eyes paling. He was alive. I could hear his shallow, ragged breaths. And his body was intact but he wasn't wholly there.

"Release him," Ethan commanded Pala through clenched teeth, his eyes so gray there wasn't a hint of humanity to be found.

"I am not finished," she responded in a sharp, dark tone inconsistent with her doll-like appearance. He lunged at her, but Sebastian intercepted, pushing him forcibly and sending him back several feet. Ethan crouched and snarled at Sebastian, baring the edges of his teeth. Sebastian's eyes narrowed into an aggressive glare before he returned the posturing. Within seconds, the level of rage that filled the room was all-consuming as the flames of hostility ignited.

Sebastian seemed to have been in a calmer state until a rolling aggressive growl from Ethan consumed the room. The sound continued to resonate moments later, leaving a ringing in my ears. It didn't take long for Sebastian's soft brown eyes to sharpen into amber and home in on Ethan. They were now wolves in human form, ready to give in to their carnal nature.

They were snarling at each other. I wasn't sure what a challenge entailed, but I thought I was about to witness the beginning of one. Sebastian took a step forward. His face—the hardened grimace of an animal ready to attack and prepared to kill. Winter panicked when Ethan took a step forward.

She moved slowly and timidly, reaching out for Sebastian. "Sebastian, please. It's his brother," she said in a small, soothing voice. "He's just trying to protect him. I know you understand that. He's not challenging you. You know he would never do this to you. Not like this."

The grimace remained on his face, eyes still fixed in a hard glare on Ethan. There didn't seem to be any signs of this coming to a nonviolent end. Logic had left the room minutes before and the only thing that remained was unmitigated primal rage. I wasn't sure how to defuse this bomb, and Winter looked like she was struggling, too.

"Sebastian," she continued, so softly that her words came out as a faint whisper. She tried to gain his focus. Reaching up, she used two fingers to guide his focus toward her, but he wasn't easily distracted as he maintained a predator's glare on Ethan—angry and intense. She took several steps over placing herself directly in front of him. "Sebastian, please look at me. It's not a challenge."

Placing her hand on his cheek, she directed his face toward hers, to meet her gaze. "It's not a challenge," she whispered. At that moment, she seemed unnaturally gentle, like Joan. Her mannerisms lost their typical abrasiveness that seemed to be the very essence of her personality. This may have been the most docile I had ever seen her. Winter stood between Ethan and Sebastian, and if they decided to proceed in a fight, she would probably be trampled. But this seemed to be the best way to handle the situation. If she attempted to stop them with similar aggression, the end result would be unnecessarily volatile.

Winter didn't do submissive, nice, humble, or even pleasant. However, she knew that in assuming submissive, neither Ethan nor Sebastian would hurt her. For the first time, I could see why Joan held Winter in such high regard. This realization was an epiphany: Winter was third for more reasons than her fighting ability. She did what was necessary, despite how uncomfortable or hard it was. *Crap, disliking her is getting harder.*

She continued to speak in a low, gentle voice. Her movements slow, calm, and overtly meek. "It's his brother and our blood-bonded ally. His aggression is misdirected. You know he would never do such a thing if his brother wasn't involved. Sebastian, it's not a challenge," she assured, keeping eye contact with him.

The aggressive sounds began to decrease to a noticeable calm. His posturing relaxed slightly. She looked at me, directed her gaze toward Ethan and then the door, hinting for me to get Ethan out of there.

No, thank you. If I left with him, that would leave me alone to endure the full power of Ethan's rage. I remembered vividly what it felt like to be in Sebastian's presence after the vampires' attack. But I knew I had to. With emotions so turbulent, all it would take would be the wrong thing said or done and we could be back to where we started.

Sebastian straightened and stepped away from Winter. "Ethan, we need Pala alive for now. It would be better if you stepped out. Seeing him this way may be too hard to handle. I will protect his life as though it was my own," he stated in a surprisingly calm manner, although his eyes still maintained the deep tones of his wolf.

Ethan took in a ragged breath before his face relaxed. He nodded and left the room with me close behind.

After I closed the door behind us, he kept his focus on it. Within minutes, he reached for it and I grabbed his hand. Graphite eyes and an aggressive sneer dared me to stop him as he made another attempt for the door. I pushed him away.

"Move," he barked. I was just as frustrated with the situation as he was, I wanted to snap right back at him.

When he didn't stop, I pushed him back again. "No. Not until you calm down," I stated firmly. I couldn't stop him if he used force. We both knew it. He didn't know that I wasn't above playing dirty pool and kneeing him where it counted. He'd be pissed, but he would recover, and it would be a lot less violent and rapacious than what he and Sebastian would do to each other.

There was harsh glacial silence between us. He stood so close, I felt crowded standing in front of the door. I inched closer to the door, forcing more space between us. Stepping back, he paced the floor with wild inhibited force as he tried to suppress his anger, rage, and frustration. I exhaled softly. "I understand—" but before I could finish, he was just inches from my face.

"What *exactly* do you understand?" I didn't want to look at him, but it was hard not to, with him so uncomfortably close. The emotions pulsing off him were so turbulent, they were hard to ignore—he was hard to ignore.

Frustrated as well, I wanted to snap back at him. But what purpose would it serve to poke the bear—or rather, the irate wolf? "I understand what it's like to feel you are responsible for endangering others who feel obligated to protect you. I understand how infuriating it can be to wish you were the one dealing with Pala instead of standing idly by watching Josh take risk that should be your own. I understand what it feels like to be so angry that all you want to do is curse, fight, and kill, but know that it won't make things any better. I understand more than you care to know," I said softly.

His angry scowl melted but the intensity of his emotions didn't falter. He leaned in, resting his face in the crook of my neck. Warm breath nicked at my skin. Moist lips pressed against my pulse. He moved closer. I could feel the intensity of his heart and the rapidness of his breaths.

"I am sorry," I whispered. "I know it doesn't mean anything

to you, but I wish I hadn't come into your lives and created such problems."

"It's not your fault." His lips brushed lightly against my face as he spoke. He repeated it so softly it was barely audible. I think it was to remind himself. His lips were a feather touch against mine. When he pulled away, I wasn't quite sure if I'd been kissed.

Then he kissed me again. Firm lips pressed against mine, sinuous and attentive. But it quickly changed to something intense, ravenous, sensuous, and intoxicating. I could feel his anger, rage, and frustration as he expunged them into the kiss. Grasping fistfuls of my hair, he pulled me closer to him. I felt every emotion flood into me, leaving me breathless.

I was submerged by lust and sensuality that I'd never experienced, yet simultaneously felt trampled and shattered. If I were a wall, he had just put his fist through it. I pulled away and slipped past him. Standing several feet from him, I dealt with the diametric of emotions he made me feel: sated and empty, paramour and prey. We stared at each other for a long time. The silence wasn't intense, awkward, sensual, or even comfortable. It was diaphanous. As though every emotion felt, exchanged, and absorbed had shattered, leaving only faded remnants of their existence. "I need to see how things are going with Josh," I stated, ending the odd silence.

He nodded, stepping back from the door, giving me space.

I wasn't in the room long before I felt his presence near me. Sebastian sensed it as well. He turned and their eyes locked. I held my breath in anticipation of what would become of this moment. Ethan brought his hand to his chest and extended it in nonverbal apology.

Sebastian shook his head as if to say an apology was not necessary. "If the roles were reversed, I would look to you to save me from myself." Winter had missed the whole exchange as she closely watched Pala. Her look of scrutiny turned to clear suspicion as she looked at Pala and Josh, who was now starting to look sickly. "Something's wrong!" she shouted as she lunged at Pala.

"He's strong. I couldn't resist having him for myself," she admitted, making little effort to hide her pleasure. Pala held Josh's hand firmly even after Winter grabbed her. Pala's free hand took hold of Winter's wrist. The room dimmed, and Winter's face became a series of grimaces and suppressions of pain before she was thrown back, crashing into the door. A dark smile covered Pala's face, finding pleasure in the pain—in Winter's pain.

As she continued smiling, darkness emanated from her in waves, stifling the air. All Josh needed was to use the magic, and I had the ability to hold magic. I grabbed the knife that lay a few feet from her and whipped it across my hand. Blood welled in the palm of my hand just before I grabbed Pala's and held it tightly in mine. I recited the same words that Josh had when he was bound to me at Caleb's and a few days later when we practiced the protective fields. As soon as the last word fell from my lips, the surge of magic ripped through. It was nothing like Josh's magic. It was rough and bleak, chilling me to the core. Pala bucked under me, screaming out as I tugged at her magic, pulling it toward me.

Torrents of darkness flooded me, submerging me, binding me to this tenebrous world of dark magic. Pala refused to be divested of her power and fought for it ruthlessly. She tugged with violent jerks, but it was in vain. The magic migrated toward me then latched on as though it were where it belonged—as though it were part of me.

Unwilling to give into defeat, in her final act of vigilance, she called to her master. The name *Ethos* slipped from her mouth with immense reverence.

True darkness arrived, bringing its host, its master. Molten heat and obscurity surrounded me, announcing his arrival. I knew that face. It was one I would never forget. At Gloria's home, I'd been presented with a diminutive version. Now I felt him—potent, dark, and evil. Its power and presence could never be ignored because it was darkness in its purest and rawest form.

He didn't pull. He drew it toward him effortlessly. I pulled back. He drew harder and I wrenched back with everything I had because Josh needed this and I refused to fail.

I gave one more powerful pull that left me nearly drained. I won.

But I hadn't won. He had conceded. Staring at me with delighted curiosity, his portentous gaze held mine. I had piqued his interest, gotten his attention and made my presence known. This wouldn't be the last time we'd meet.

With a pithy smile, he relinquished a burst of his magic. Flooded in darkness, I was submerged into its swamp. Suffocating, I tried to claw my way to safety, anchor myself to something familiar where I could breathe and find comfort away from the darkness. I thought, *This is how I am going to die,* when someone grabbed my hand. Josh. The comfort of his magic, neutral, cool, and placid, enveloped me. He whispered an incantation and I was dragged away from that place of comfort right back into darkness, back into infinite midnight, but it was different now. The obscurity was illuminated by embers of light that flickered around us.

Our bodies were somewhere safe in the retreat. Our minds were forced into darkness as we looked for the elusive Gem of Levage. We roamed around in the bowels of darkness as cold air whipped about. Gusts of wind pushed us, urging us away.

I wasn't sure what I expected but it wasn't this. There weren't rooms, closets, or even small spaces that enclosed the hidden items. As we traveled through the abysmal space, the closer we came to an area, various objects revealed themselves. Slowly their surroundings were disclosed, giving you a clue where they could be found in our world.

In front of me was a lockbox. As I neared it, a stone was revealed. It wasn't the Gem of Levage, yet I got the feeling it was just as dangerous. I started to grab it. "No," Josh's voice ordered sternly, "just the Gem of Levage." Was this a one-shot deal? Once we found our desired object, were we forced out?

I took several steps away from it and continued my search.

Thick mist filled the space, further separating me from Josh. The air roughly hit against us, shuffling us about. We weren't wanted on this side of the realm. We weren't supposed to be here, and it was doing everything possible to let us know this.

When I turned to my left, a closet opened, revealing an illuminated orb. Next to it was framed art, unique sculptures, and delicately designed vases. The orb was in a gallery not very different from the one Josh took me to. But I didn't reach for the item this time. Instead, I stared at the art, imprinting all the unique things to memory for future reference if I ever needed to find this gallery and the object in question.

Turning in full circle, I took several steps and encountered a man—or something very manlike. Bronze skin, liquid gold eyes, thin lips curved slightly into an inviting smile. He stood, his sleek thin frame motionless, but he was alive. I took a few steps closer, trying to see what landscape would be exposed, revealing his location. But nothing was revealed. Slowly I walked around him and he followed, turning to keep a watchful eye on me. He wasn't what I would consider beautiful; he was strangely awe-striking, enchanting. "You're very warm," he stated softly. Inching closer to me, he reached out to touch me, and I was yanked back hard before he could place a finger on me.

"Don't let him touch you—ever. And once outside this realm, if you see him or anything like him—you don't touch him or let him touch you. You don't go near him. The only thing you do is run like hell," Josh snapped.

I needed to get out of there. We were in a house of devastation, dark and evil. Josh was calm during the search but since the encounter with the bronze man, he wanted out fast. His search was more erratic, moving through the abysmal space at such a speed, he was giving me a headache.

As I searched, I found swords, talismans, gems, and charms. I am sure they all could be found in the *Symbols of Death* or worse. I wanted to take them and destroy them for no other reason than they existed when they shouldn't. But every time I considered it, Josh was there discouraging me. We had been in this place too long. It seemed like hours. Perhaps it had been days. Finally, when I thought we would never find it here, Josh's excited voice blasted through the dank space—he had found it.

"Get us out of here! Unbind us now," he urged, and I could feel the panic in him. I whispered the words Josh had before to unbind me but nothing happened. I did it again. Nothing. Josh could feel my anxiety, and when I said the words again, he said them with me. Within seconds, we were pushed—no, we were violently expelled—expunged from there.

Although we were free of that place, I was still holding on to dark magic. I was no longer connected to Josh, and it came back with a vengeance. I couldn't breathe. This magic was nothing like his. It consumed you, drowning you in its power, in its effort to take over. You didn't control dark magic. It controlled you, subdued you, and only allowed you to live in order for you to serve its purposes. I screamed but it went unheard as though I hadn't opened my mouth. My words were swallowed by its power.

Instead of pulling it toward me, like I had done before, I pushed. Lying on the floor, my heart raced at an erratic rate. I tried to force the magic out of me. If this didn't kill me, the heart attack would. Glass crashed and broke over me, wood splintered, things swirled across my face, metal smashed into my body. The magic clung to me, refusing to be cast out.

Josh, help me. I tried to bring up a protective field to shelter me from the things that were uncontrollably whipping against and crashing into me. Then warm fingers linked with mine, a firm body lay over me. The five o'clock shadow felt rough and bristled over my skin as he pressed his face against me. Darkness faded. Midnight melted into pewter, then faded slowly into something not quite white but translucent. Everything settled to a calm.

I opened my eyes to find Josh's face, relaxed with sinfully playful eyes, staring at me, the weight of his body pinning me against the floor. He stayed there for several minutes watching me, intrigue and curiosity covering his face. I was so sick of getting that look. I let my head drop to the side, absorbing the feeling of being away from the darkness and in a familiar place, comfortable, soothing.

Josh didn't move. His body pressed firmly against me. "Um ... I think you can get off me now." He grinned, moving just a smidge, giving me barely enough room to slide from under him.

I was alive. I was here. I wasn't darkness, death, or obliteration. Just when I was about to do my happy dance, fully accompanied by jazz hands, I got a view of the infirmary.

I had survived but the room hadn't: six of the hospital beds were upside down, the medicine cabinet was smashed to pieces, the room dividers were crumpled and lay against the wall. One of the double doors had survived but the other was hanging off the hinges. Anything that was glass had shattered to pieces. Broken plaster continued to crumble and fall from the wall where someone or something had crashed into it.

"I did this?"

Josh nodded slowly.

Of course I did. That's why Ethan, Sebastian, Winter, Dr.

Baker, and Steven were standing across the room looking as though they had just watched the devil give birth to twins.

I had cuts on my arms, my shirt was torn, and I was drenched in sweat. I gave the room another quick glance, said something about needing a shower, and promised Dr. Baker I would clean up. I made a mad dash out of the room I had just annihilated, while they gave me the *What-the-hell-was-that?* look.

I showered twice, trying to rid myself of the scent of dark magic. Its aura, though subtle, was present, clinging to me, and I couldn't stand it. Even the overly floral body wash didn't drive that dank, crisp feeling away. The more I thought about what I subjected myself to, the more panicked I became. I lay on the bed, staring at the ceiling, forcing a serenity that I so desperately needed.

"You continue to astound me," Josh admitted as he walked into the room.

"Maybe you should raise your standards—you are far too easily impressed." I kept my eyes on the ceiling.

"And you don't give yourself enough credit. If it weren't for your quick thinking, I would have met a less-than-desirable fate. You saved my life."

"I don't like dark magic," I confessed, sitting up.

Josh's eyes were dancing somewhere between interest, confusion, and apprehension. "You don't have to tell me. We were there for your handiwork." He grinned and knelt in front of me, his expression one of avid interest. "I can't control dark magic, so you converted it, allowing me to control it and prevent you from injuring anybody during your rampage. I don't know anyone who can do that."

"I can tell by the grin on your face that you think this is a good thing?"

"It's a *very* good thing. I can't begin to imagine the possibilities!"

"Where was the Gem?" I asked abruptly. Josh needed to be

redirected off this magic trail. It intrigued him more than I could possibly understand, and the very mention of something new and exciting made him easily forget the task at hand. For nearly three weeks, we'd been looking for this elusive Gem, and it was effortlessly placed on the back burner when his attention became focused on my odd effect on magic.

He blinked, remembering the purpose for everything. He chuckled. "It was in the Seethe's home."

I shook my head briskly. "No, it couldn't be. I looked throughout the house in every place it could possibly be hidden."

"It was hidden using a glamour."

"But you could see it?"

He nodded. "Do you remember seeing a bible on Demetrius's nightstand?"

I remembered seeing it and thinking how odd it was that Demetrius owned a bible because he was as soulless as the devil himself. I hadn't missed the irony of the situation.

"Demetrius has a rather disturbing sense of humor and a very strong contempt for symbols of religion."

I'd walked past the Gem and even stared at it with weird curiosity, never once seeing it for what it was. At that moment, I agreed with Ethan. I hated magic, too. It was too perfidious for my liking. The thought that this could have ended weeks ago didn't sit well with me.

We were quiet once again. I wasn't sure what he was thinking, but I thought about the night's events. "Why did Pala attack your magic that way? It's not like she could use it," I asked.

"Most of it she wouldn't be able to use, but there is a small part of dark and natural magic that are *respicts.* It is magic that has no boundaries and can be done by both holders of dark and natural magic. If she had taken any of my magic, it would have just enhanced the *respict* magic and killed me. The only way an exchange of magic can be made permanent is that the donor must die. Pala's pretty strong. We don't want her stronger. She wants more power than Ethos will allow her to have."

Josh looked at me with the same eyes I vaguely remembered from our first meeting. They hadn't looked like that in so long; I had forgotten how welcoming and gentle they were. "Skylar, you are able to do some really cool things with magic. I think we should explore your effects on it more."

"No thanks." I directed my attention elsewhere. I didn't want to give any hints or misinterpreted messages that I had any interest in what he was suggesting.

He jerked as though I had slapped him, and if he continued suggesting such foolishness, I just might have to. "No. Why? Aren't you the least bit curious about what you are capable of?"

"No. Not really. If the Tre'ase showed me an inkling of the truth—even if there were some deceit, I have a connection with Ethos and some very dark things. I don't want any part of it. Did you ever stop to think that the reason I can affect dark magic is because I am strangely connected to it? No. I don't want to explore it. I don't want to unlock any potential gates to that world and find out I am something horrible—evil.".

"She showed you a version of the truth."

"Really? Josh, I was the one there. I experienced it. I don't want to be your science project or some type of magician's apprentice." It came out harsher than intended, but I needed to get my point across. I was scared. I didn't voice it, but he had to sense it and chose to ignore it. He was excited and I was terrified.

He stood up, staring at me intently, his hand brushing over my shoulder lightly. The dark magic was gone—I think, but its remnants remained, an aftergloom. I felt it and I was sure Josh felt it, too. It was easy to see that magic liked magic. It was drawn to it, found pleasure in it, and was ensorcelled by it.

He leaned down, his face so close to mine that his lips brushed against me. Soft hands cupped under my jaw, cradling my face. Although I didn't want to ever go near it again, I don't think Josh felt the same way. He seemed to be drawn to it. His curiosity and intense intrigue couldn't be overlooked. He was attracted to it, for no other reason that it was intense, enticing and strong.

When he spoke, I could feel his breath a warm breeze against my lips. "Okay. But I think one day you will want to explore it, and when you do, know that I am here to help you."

"What part of her 'no' did you not understand, Josh? Don't pressure her into dealing with things that she really should avoid," Ethan's stern voice urged as he walked into the room. His gaze fell to Josh's hands where it remained until he'd dropped them from my face, and it followed Josh until he had backed away toward the door. Ethan's gaze moved in my direction, then cruised over to his brother and found its way back to me. "Thank you for saving Josh's life."

"No one in this pack should ever thank me for anything. I am still alive because of you all."

"We did not intervene to protect you," he stated honestly. "If you were just a person that Demetrius desired, we would have never intervened. I wish I were ashamed, but it is our truth. Your death would have given them power that we could not allow them to have. That is the only reason we protected you."

"I know. Despite the reason, it was my life that you protected. For that, I feel deeply obligated." If they hadn't intervened, I surely would not have lasted this long against the vampires.

"An obligation is a debt, Skylar."

I shrugged. "I am indebted to your pack."

"Choose your words carefully," he warned.

I tried to decipher the meaning behind them. His face was blank and indiscernible. Josh's appearance was similar. I had missed something. Any other time, I would have made a greater effort to figure it out, but I was too tired to try. "Should I not appreciate what you all have done? I would have died a torturous death if it weren't for your pack. Is it wrong that I feel that I owe the pack a great deal?" I was unable to hide my confusion.

He closed his eyes, shaking his head slowly. When he opened them, he gave me the same look you give the town's imbecile. Sighing, he said in a reserved, professional voice, "On behalf of the pack, I accept your debt. Understand that at some point, you will be asked to repay it." He stood to leave.

What the hell just happened? I could see Josh shaking his head slowly out of the corner of my eye. He looked at me one last time before giving me a wry, forced smile, and then he left the room.

My eyes trailed Josh as he exited. At that moment, my brain decided to boot up and start functioning properly. Then I realized what I had done. "Is being indebted to the Midwest Pack a stupid thing?"

Ethan's lips pressed tightly together. "Being indebted to anyone is never wise. But there could be far worse things. I advise you to, in the future, choose your words carefully and be cautious about whom you accumulate debts with."

"Can I retract?"

"No. Your debt has been accepted," he stated with a complacent grin before he left.

Oddly, the newly acquired debt didn't bother me. I felt truly obligated to Midwest Pack. I lay back on the bed, finally allowing myself to feel a certain level of relief that I hadn't felt in so long. We knew where the Gem was and the all-consuming sense of victory filled the house.

CHAPTER 15

I started pacing the moment they left the house that night. After a very angry exchange between Sebastian, Ethan, and me, it was agreed that I stay behind. Or rather, I was forced to stay in the house by the two highest-ranking control freaks. Sebastian made it very clear: "Skylar, it's a simple extraction if things go as planned. However, if they don't, you in the vampires' home with the Gem is a bad combination. One we choose to avoid."

I couldn't argue with his logic. Yet I wanted to be there when it all ended—no, I needed to be there. The desperation must have been sensed because our exchange ended with them leaving Dakota, the bear with less-than-human-like behavior, behind to make sure I complied.

First, I sat on the bed doing my best impression of a kid who hadn't gotten her way, pouting like a brat. Then I started to worry about their safety when several hours had passed and they hadn't returned. I was sure a fight occurred, and my heart skipped at the thought of their impending danger. The carpet would soon be worn thin, as I paced it neurotically.

Light footsteps in the hallway caught my attention. I listened closely. They weren't Dakota's. Despite being a were-animal, when in human form, he was clumsy and awkward. The steps were cautious and lithe as they ascended the stairs. The scent was familiar, but not quite memorable. I stood behind the door listening as they came closer. "Skylar," whispered the Southern drawl from behind the closed door. It was Owen. When he opened the door, I stayed behind it, hidden.

"Skylar, we must go! You aren't safe here. Demetrius is sending someone for you. They found the pack in their home."

"What happened to Sebastian—?"

"They're dead," he interjected quickly. He grabbed my arm and we started running down the hall.

They're all dead? Something just didn't seem right. It's not that I believed they were invincible, but for the strongest members of the pack to be taken out so quickly? It didn't sit well with me. They had the element of surprise. I couldn't conceive that the vamps could overtake all of them so soon. I came to a halt right before we reached the stairs.

"Owen, why are you here?" I asked suspiciously, backing away from him.

He lunged at me, his heavy body knocking me to the floor. "I was sent here to retrieve you. Now be a good wolf and come with me," he growled as he started to stand.

I helped him up by flipping him over my body. Then I kicked him in the ribs while he was on all fours, sending him onto his back. When he attempted to get up, I jabbed my elbow into the bridge of his nose. Using my elbow as leverage, he pushed me away. I countered with a spin kick, connecting the side of my foot with his face. He fell, but didn't stay down long. Enraged, he grabbed me by the face with viselike force and pushed me back, sending me into the wall, hitting it with a thud.

Sliding on my back, I inched away from him. But he moved with catlike stealth, perching over me. "Before I was the Southern Pack's accountant, I was the Midwest's Beta." His eyes changed to a light brown with ringlets of deep yellow, making them appear feline. "Your little bodyguard will not be able to help you. He's indisposed at the moment. It's just you and me, kid. Do you really want to play this rough?" he snarled out angrily.

I continued sliding away from him. "Don't make me hurt you," he threatened. He yanked me up by my arms. When I pulled away, he grabbed me by the shirt and pushed me against the wall.

Leaning into me, he inhaled. "You have Ethan's scent all over you. Has he had you yet? It doesn't take him long to have his way with most females he comes in contact with." His lips kinked into a display of avid disgust. He was incensed. So angry, he was trembling.

"Who was she?" This had nothing to do with Ethan's indiscriminant sexual behavior. There was a *she* involved. You don't see that level of contempt without it being personal.

He glared at me, his grip tightening, pressing harder into my throat. "Know that you meant nothing to him. They never do! You were just a simple conquest. Just because he can!" he snapped. He was slamming my back against the wall with each word. Each push harder, rougher, less controlled. A volcano on the brink of erupting. I didn't want to be there when lava spilled, destroying everything in its path.

Hard lines formed around his increasingly ruddy face. "Chris was mine! He only wanted her because she was mine! He had to be Beta because the position was *mine!*" He was panting hard, his eyes frenetic, his face twisted into a nefarious scorn.

Oh, this is what were-crazy looks like.

When he jammed me into the wall again, I kneed him in the stomach. He went down to his knees, hard.

I started to run but he recovered, grabbing my leg and yanking me toward him. My calf burned under his viselike hold. I smashed the heel of my hand into his nose. It halted him for a moment but didn't break his nose as I had hoped. But it was enough of a distraction to allow me to escape. I couldn't take him in a fight. I ran. I leapt over the rails onto the first floor, landing awkwardly. I either twisted or broke something in my right foot. I wasn't sure which, but the jagged pain that shot through me was definitely a sign of an injury. Owen's footsteps pounded angrily behind me as I ran to the basement. I dashed into the cage, pulling the large metal bars closed behind me. Locked in, I couldn't get out—but he couldn't get in, either.

"You're not as helpless as I was led to believe." I'd grown to hate that pronounced Southern drawl. He slinked down the stairs slowly, keeping his eyes on me the entire time.

"And you're a bigger ass than I could ever imagine," I snapped between breaths.

He pounced around the cage rattling it. The first time he did it, I jumped. Standing in the middle of the cage, I watched as crazy, anger, and malcontent fused together, creating the enraged person standing in front of me. It was the only thing separating me from my brush with his insanity.

When he rattled the cage again, I didn't move. He could be as mad as his lanky frame would allow, but he wasn't getting in the cage. A look of satisfaction danced across his face. He started punching numbers into the keypad. "Remember, I used to be part of this pack. They were probably too stupid to change the code when I left." The access light must not have changed colors because he pressed in more numbers, and the look of triumph vanished from his face.

"Guess they aren't stupid."

"Shut up!"

"What? No more good ol' Southern hospitality? Where's it hiding? In the same place with your integrity and pride?"

He roared.

"Impressive. Now can you try to sound like a lion?" Antagonizing him was stupid, but I noticed that when he was distracted or angry he didn't function well. If I kept him distracted enough he wouldn't be able to try to figure out the code.

His fingers worked frantically, punching in a series of numbers as he rambled on. The access code must not have lit up because he slammed his fist into it.

"That's not going to open it," I pointed out.

Returning his attention to the keypad, he punched in more numbers. "I am going to kill Josh first and make Ethan watch. Then I will squeeze the life out of Chris right before I kill him, giving him just enough time to mourn their deaths," he hissed.

I chortled. "You can kill Chris if you want, but it won't bother Ethan. He threatened to do so not less than three weeks ago. He threatened her after he kissed her passionately in front of everyone. They're very hot together. I wonder what they were like when they actually loved each other." He stopped abruptly and stared at me, disgusted. Ethan not only took Chris from him—his words not mine—but cared so little for her that he would kill her. "And his brother? He'd prefer death than to living without him. Killing him after murdering his brother would be an act of kindness, not vengeance. Didn't really think this through, did you?"

Now he was just punching numbers into the keypad without thinking. Nearly trembling with anger he spoke in a calloused tone. "He's a self-absorbed bastard, but everyone ignores it because he's Sebastian's golden boy, his future successor. Everyone's so enamored by his charm and wit they won't see him for what he really is."

"What is he, a simple-minded were-animal who betrayed his pack to help Demetrius? Is he a dishonorable man who abandoned his obligation to his pack because of jealousy and revenge? Oh, my bad, that's *you*."

His eyes were blazing with fury. Swift hands darted through the bars to grab me. I moved just in time to get out of his reach.

He rattled the cage, his fist beating against it brutally as he made sonorous roars that resounded through the room. I cringed until the sound came to an abrupt end. "Yes, the cage can be unlocked by rattling it real hard and yelling at it. Keep doing that. I'm sure that'll work."

Gaining control of his anger, he stared at me with a long haunting gaze. But his appearance had lost all remnants of humanity. It was raw, animalistic, stripped down to his purest primal form. "I would have killed you. If I had been the Alpha, and *you* were this big of a risk to my pack, I would have killed you as you slept here in our bed."

"Your ability to kill someone in cold blood, who has entrusted you with their life, is impressive only in your warped mind. Ethan didn't take your position. He relieved you of a job you didn't deserve," I shot back.

Who would have thought that type of iniquity lurked behind the sweet Southern drawl? I shook my head. "You know what Demetrius plans to do with me, and you are okay with that? They'll be stronger than the were-animals. Are you prepared to be responsible for that?" I was revolted.

"Who do you think gave him the Gem? I couldn't use it, but I made sure I would benefit from it."

Somewhere in the crowded space between his anger and craziness, he found peace because he had calmed down as he studied the keypad.

"I suppose you think you will control the Midwest Pack when Sebastian and Ethan are gone." Looking up briefly, his gaze roved over me, but he ignored my question.

He smiled. It was dark and ominous. I tried not to show fear as his fingers worked anxiously, punching in numbers.

"Demetrius may kill everyone who will challenge your power, not for you but just for the hell of it. Then he'll kill you just because you'll be a nuisance. All of this will be for nothing," I reminded him.

The gold ringlets of his eyes were sharp and intense as they focused on me. His gaze was lingering as he studied me. Inch by inch his eyes roved over me. His voice was soft, cynical, and eerily calm. "We all have weaknesses. Michaela is his. She's passionate, gregarious, and intrepid. She has a thirst like no other. A thirst that has led her to commit murders that she shouldn't have, murders that, if ever exposed, will cause a war between them, the elves, and fae. With my help, he's covered them. If he betrays me, everything comes to light. Don't worry, my little wolf. I am protected."

The crazy, frantic, belligerent Owen was far less scary than the calm psychopath he had turned into. He returned his attention to the keypad, staring at it, deep in thought. Now, I really couldn't let him in here. "Betrayal of your pack, abetting murders, alliances with vampires—the trifecta. Are you proud?"

As though he had taken a sedative, he couldn't be riled. I needed him upset, unfocused, hysterical—in that state of mind he was ineffective.

There was a long discouraging silence. I knew he could hear the panic in my heartbeat and my paced breathing.

"No matter who intervened, you would have been found. You haven't lived as unnoticed as you believe. You wear the daily struggle of your existence on your face—a tortured soul. It could very well be art if it weren't so tragic." He stopped fiddling with the keypad and stared at me. "You lay trapped between the world of the lifeless—which you cannot share in. The wolf—which you don't want any part of. The unknown—which you fear. And humanity—which doesn't want you," he admitted serenely. "Now that the pack has gone through such extremes to keep you alive, you think you deserve to exist. You don't. If not the vampires, it would be someone else. Your life is an abomination. Don't ever think you deserve to live."

I refused to let this psychopath with a grudge, solely based on a woman and his hurt pride, get to me. I refused. But saying it was harder than actually doing it. On so many levels, he was right. Dark magic clung to me as though it sensed a kindred spirit, I had a terait that linked me to the vampires, and I was a were-animal that hosted a spirit shade. My death was my birth. "I am no more of an abomination than you. I didn't have a choice in what I am. You did."

There was a look of resolve on his face—acceptance of what he was—what he had become, and he didn't care. Quietly he punched in the code and snatched open the cage door. Before he could step in, I charged at him, trying to knock him down as I left the cage. Instead, he crashed to the ground, pulling me down with him. We struggled and eventually he held the advantage. After pulling me from the cage, he hovered. Rage distorted his face. The predator in him lurked, ready to inflict violence and pain.

"I hope your death is painful," he snapped, catching his breath as he licked the blood from his lips. His lips were busted, nail marks covered a great deal of his face and neck, and bruising was starting to shadow along his left eye. Infuriated, he hung over me, clasping my arms across my body and clenching my legs together with his.

An aggressive feline rumble radiated within the large room. Owen stiffened. His hold on me loosened. In an open space, my ears might not have continued to ring from the sound as it did at the moment. He stood up and looked in the direction of the sound. The jaguar slowly padded toward us. When it was close enough, the full power of its presence was felt. It growled, baring its teeth and periodically licking its lips.

When I stood, my ankle gave and I collapsed to the floor. I crawled over to the wall and sank into the corner, hoping to go unnoticed. I didn't know this animal and wasn't sure if it was a good thing that it was here.

"Did you think I wouldn't find out? I gave you time, hoping you would choose loyalty to your pack over your hatred for

Ethan. You've held this vendetta against Ethan for too long and now I must end it." Joan's voice emanated from the feline's mouth. If I weren't so damned terrified, I would have been impressed by her unique ability to speak while in her animal form. I inhaled a ragged breath. There was nothing about the creature that stood before us that held the same warmth and kindness that I had come to know and adore in Joan.

"You don't like pack life, either. You just accept it. You detest the rules and unwillingly follow their ways. We are cut from the same cloth. It is a life we chose, but by no means enjoy. Help me, and I promise the life that you want can be ours. We can change the pack to function the way we see fit. Joan, you want this. I know you do," he assured her, attempting to persuade her. Somehow, that honey-sweet Southern drawl had returned.

"We are not the same. I may not always like the rules, but I respect them and understand why we have them. I stand by pack honor and commitment in ways you will never understand. Your deceit and disloyalty is nothing less than appalling. The debt for your betrayal must be paid with your life. I am here to claim payment," she stated as she soared toward him.

Owen started to change, but before he finished his transformation, the jaguar's claws ripped into him, tearing his upper torso from the mid-changed lion's body. She tore into the remains, viciously hurling pieces of him throughout the room. When her wrath was finished, her eyes still contained the fire of anger that she tried to extinguish. She tracked back and forth closely in front of me as deep rumbles escaped from her. I kept my eyes on her, avoiding the gruesome display of severed flesh that surrounded me. The aggressive sounds were eventually reduced to gentle rumbles as she calmed herself. Finally, she languidly stretched at my feet gently while licking her paws.

. . .

I hadn't moved from my spot when Sebastian walked down the stairs, followed by Ethan, Winter, and Steven. Sebastian surveyed the area and then looked down at Joan, who let out a stifled roar. Sebastian nodded, I wasn't sure to what, but he seemed to get its meaning.

Joan returned to her human form and Steven rushed past Sebastian, taking off his t-shirt and handing it to her. Her human eyes showed no signs of the viciousness her animal displayed. As she looked over the area, it was, in fact, sorrow that covered her face.

"Pack betrayal," she finally stated hoarsely. "It was an error on my part to convince my Alpha to take him in." She sounded regretful.

"There is no shame in trying to save a pack member's life when possible," Sebastian stated.

Joan shook her head, looked at the results of her actions again, and left the room. Pack life was hard for her. I sensed her pain and sorrow. If she were a solitary creature, her only obligation would be to herself. And at this moment, I didn't doubt that she longed for that life.

Steven followed her up the stairs. "Mom," I heard him whisper. She turned, smiling at him. She rested her hand on his cheek. His returning smile exposed those mesmerizing dimples.

Her face relaxed some as she hugged him. She accepted violence as part of their lives, but she didn't have the same adoration for it as the others had.

After Steven and Joan left, I looked around for Josh. I inhaled the air and couldn't pick up his scent. I heard Josh's voice as he emerged next to me. I jumped, bumping into him and almost falling to the ground. I nearly growled at him. I had been on edge all day, and the last thing I needed was him popping up without notice. "Not cool, Josh!"

He grinned. "Peace offering." He held the Gem of Levage in front of me. I took it gingerly. It seemed so much smaller than I imagined it. The very thing that changed my life as I knew it fit neatly in my hand. A palm-sized menace that might not have destroyed my life, but changed it beyond repair.

"How do we destroy it?" I asked Josh, my eyes still fixed on the Gem.

"A simple spell I can do in my sleep."

But the Gem of Levage had no intention of being destroyed. It drew me in, strengthening the bond that we shared. The imprint on my back began to sting. I clenched my teeth and took in a deep breath suppressing the pain. *Protect me,* it demanded. I felt the need to do so at all costs.

Josh reached for it. I closed it into my hand and pulled it close to my chest.

"Skylar, give it back to me," he ordered in a low voice.

"No! You can't destroy it!" I yelled, inching toward the stairs.

His hands opened as his eyes changed into an abyss of darkness commanding the Gem to him. I could feel the pull of his magic, willing it toward him. My fingers clenched around it. "No!" I felt the Gem's power take over me. A cataclysm of power shook the house, bringing Sebastian, Winter, and Ethan to their knees.

"Skylar, you cannot protect it. It needs to be returned. As long as it exists, you will always be in danger. Others will be in danger." Josh attempted to reason with me.

But it needed to exist because it had not served its purpose. It desired to cause chaos and needed to do so at all costs. It had no intention of being destroyed and was forcing me to protect it. He stepped closer and I pushed him, knocking him into the cage. He came to his feet quickly, waving his hand in front of him, throwing me back with such force, I barely missed hitting the wall.

The Gem adhered to me, refusing to leave, forcing its

protection, appealing for its existence. "It doesn't want to be destroyed. We need to keep it." Josh, of all people, had to understand that certain magic had to exist. It had to be here in this world. It had a purpose that needed to be fulfilled.

"No." His lips moved quickly, reciting incantations in an attempt to release me from my binding to the Gem. Words, foreign to me, were expelled from my mouth as though they were my own, countering his demands. The bond continued to strengthen, filling me with power, controlling me, forcing me to meet Josh's challenge.

Protect me. I felt the need to do so. To defend its existence as though it were my life. Ignoring the throbbing pain of my ankle and foot, I started up the stairs. Ethan grabbed me and pulled me from the third stair onto the ground, holding me firmly against it. Josh walked toward me, his lips moving more feverishly. Extending his hand, he reached out for the Gem. His commands were strong. My fingers trembled around the Gem, but it wouldn't let my fingers extend to release my hold. Instead, it pushed Josh back. My lips moved just as quickly, invoking spells to counter his demands.

Standing over me, he extended his hand, reaching out for the Gem. His face, a gentle plea that I was forced to ignore. "Skylar, please," Josh urged.

"No."

Josh's lips, which were moving quickly performing spell after spell, came to a deescalating stop. He looked at Ethan, remorse shadowing his face. He nodded once toward Ethan. In one swift move, Ethan pulled out a knife and plunged it into my chest, keeping a firm hold around my neck to halt my breathing. The pain was shrill at first, then slowly, it receded as I accepted what was happening to me.

I couldn't look at it. Instead, my focus stayed on Ethan. The regret that briefly eclipsed his face had faded into obscurity. Void of emotions, cobalt eyes retreated to slate gray as he looked back to me. I held the gaze of the man who did exactly what he said he would do. He protected me. He protected me as long as I wasn't a threat to his pack, and when I was—he killed me.

Death—I thought I would fight it. Ward it away from me as I had done before. But as it inched over my body and took hold of me, I found it to be comforting, like a warm blanket that covered you as it coaxed you into darkness. Yet, I still felt sorrow for the life lost—my life. I couldn't stop the tear that managed to escape. Ethan's thumb swept across my face wiping it away. It was then that he dropped his gaze from mine to the knife in my chest.

The knife held strong magic. I could feel it overtaking me, preventing the osinine from working to heal.

Protect me, demanded the Gem of Levage. I couldn't. I was too busy trying to survive. Although my mind and spirit had freely given over to death, my body refused to go without a fight. My heart struggled for each beat it took. The odd thing about dying is once you start to do it, the heart doesn't beat at an erratic inaudible thump as you would imagine. Instead, it gargles and battles, twisting in your chest as it struggles to hold on to what it knows—life. Soon it gives in to the unwinnable fight. It's the breathing that continues for a few seconds after the heart has lost its battle.

The Gem released me from my obligation. I conceded to the darkness. Death.

I never thought about what it actually felt like as you slipped into it. There weren't any lights to walk toward—just darkness. Unaware of heaven and hell, or the place that people like me would go, I took ownership of the darkness. I welcomed Death —it was familiar to me.

CHAPTER 16

Shrouded in blackness, I heard a soft voice call my name. It wasn't Josh's, although I expected to hear him. It was a feminine voice. Remaining quiet, I embraced the state of limbo. Between life and death was an odd place to be. But my life was a tragedy. I was reluctant to accept death, so I remained in this state, unable to concede to either. "Skylar, you can't stay here," stated a soothing voice in my head.

"I guess introductions aren't needed," I responded, my current state making my comment harsher than intended. There was an abrupt silence. "Maya, I presume."

She remained quiet. It was an uneasy silence.

"I hear Josh calling for you to remove me from this body," she stated in a gentle tone.

"And you want me to stop him?"

"No. My journey in this world has been long, although not often happy. Eleven hosts I've endured, and only one brought me anywhere close to what I considered a life. For that I am grateful." Her voice was a soft fluid sound, offering me comfort. In this current state, I found little.

"You are curious about your mother, now more than ever.

My memories of her life are yours to explore. Will you allow me to do this for you?"

Did she expect me to say no? She was giving me something, that even in my dreams, I could never expect to experience.

Maya came to my mother when she was eighteen, shortly after she became aware of her magical gifts. "Drawn to her magic, I wanted her as my host. She wasn't very strong, but she possessed gifts I wanted to experience. She declined my request several times. I tried to persuade her with the promise of enhanced magic as a result of hosting me. She wanted nothing to do with me. To her, I was nothing more than a spirit of evil, attempting to make a fool's bargain with her. I told her my story. Then I assured her I don't bring evil to those who host me. It already dwells in them. How could I blame her?

"Most request my presence in their life. She was the first that I asked. Months had passed and she never called to me. I had given up all hope. Then she finally did. Sorrowed by the story of my lost life, she considered me 'deserving of a chance at life.' The idea of enhanced power had no appeal to her, but the ability to help me did. I knew then she would give me something others had failed to give—a life worth living."

"You picked hosts based on their ability to provide you with power?" I asked cautiously. Now I was skeptical of how pure she actually was. Why such a thirst for magic and power? If a fulfilling life was what she sought, why not seek the life of a human who could offer her a worthier and less complicated existence?

She took time to answer the question, but I wasn't sure if it were to offer me truth or a convincing lie. "I am drawn to power. It is the nature of my being, but it is not a necessity. The thirst to live in a body with immense power is a flaw I remedied long ago. I learned early on that those with the most power are often too corrupt, providing the most unfulfilling and disappointing life imaginable. Unfortunately for me, most of my hosts have been chosen out of pure desperation. I hate the form in which I was cursed to live. An existence of not being able to touch, feel, and sense things as a whole being is far worse than any nightmare one could imagine. There isn't a method to how I chose the lives I shared. Regretfully, far too often, my choices were flawed. It's only upon their death I am granted leave. I was forced to experience the lives of monsters who only existed to torture, hurt, and cause sorrow to others. It was a vile and disturbing existence for me." I thought I felt her shudder at the memories. What had she been through? I wanted to ask her, but I doubted she would answer.

"What gifts did my mother possess that drew you to her?"

"The ability to compel. It was an amazing gift that she chose not to use. The idea of controlling people's desires made her feel like she was robbing them of their autonomy—their life. Never before had I experienced such a devout consciousness from a person."

"Have all your hosts been human?" I asked, unable to believe that the horror and iniquity she described could be carried out by only humans.

"I can be hosted by those who are wholly human and humanlike."

"Humanlike?"

"Were-animals."

You're not winning points here, calling me humanlike.

"Will you allow me to continue guiding you through your mother's life?" she asked patiently.

"Yes." I was aware when someone was trying to redirect me. It was quite the chore determining which was more important: exploring my mother's life or gaining more insight into the life of the being who had lived in me all my life.

Maya took me through the journey of my mother's life. Like a movie, I watched threads of her existence. I had the opportunity to see my grandparents and discovered that I had three aunts and one uncle: Aunts Caitlyn, Beth, and Madalena, and Uncle William. Glimpses of notable moments in my mother's life allowed me to watch her interact with my aunts and uncle. The relationship between them seemed strained, but I didn't know why. Maya edited, but I guess she had to. I didn't have twelve years to experience it all. But each moment was so surreal. Even when I was shown a brief flash of my grandfather's funeral, I felt immense sorrow for my mother.

She guided me through my parents meeting, dating, and eventually falling in love. Glimpses of my mother on her wedding day allowed me to see a slightly older version of myself. Her brown eyes were soft, pleasant and human, without that glint of the beast that seemed to dull mine. Her hair was a deep cinnamon with the same barely tamable waves. They formed a beautiful mane around a deep olive-toned face. My father's muted golden brown hair was almost a direct contrast to my mother's. His skin was terribly fair and could never tan to the color of my olive tone. The only feature that I seemed to inherit was his emerald eyes that held the same animal glimmer as mine. On that day, my mother became Senna Bask, and a year later, they created a child who would be known as Skylar.

Maya continued presenting me with pieces of my mother's life and stopped abruptly as Emmanuel approached my mother and father.

"Your mother remained my host for twelve years. A beautiful life ended so tragically. I grieve less often these days but the sorrow still remains. Skylar, you've been asleep for a while. It is never good to remain in this state long."

"Is it because of you that I can hold magic?" I asked hastily. I wasn't ready to leave her. There were so many questions I needed answered.

"Yes."

"I thought you didn't have any abilities and that you can only live through your hosts."

"Without a body I have no power. Within a body I have no control. I am indeed at the mercy of my host, but I possess magic that mirrors their own. Those without gifts will remain that way; however, those with gifts are indeed enhanced because of my presence."

"Nathan wanted me dead. It wasn't me that he wanted dead. It was you. Why is your existence such a threat?"

"At one time, I was destined to have great power. I possessed power over the dead, were-animals, the undead, and all magical beings. I was destined to be an unstoppable force and a danger to most. That is the reason I was murdered. Now that power can no longer exist."

"Murdered? I thought you died."

She laughed softly, finding a level of absurdity to my statement. "Yes, the story of my death has been told so many times that the truth becomes tales and lies become legend. The Tre'ase knew of my power, and that is the reason she left me in this state. I was a threat to her as well."

"Who murdered you?"

"That I don't know."

"Now all that power is gone?"

"No, not gone, just unable to be used. There isn't a body that I can inhabit that can contain such power. I can only mirror the power of the body I host."

I was silent for a long time, organizing the many questions bombarding my mind.

"Skylar, you need to wake up now. In this state, you are very vulnerable to all who have come in contact with you. Ethos will come to you if you stay in this state, and you will not be able to resist," she warned.

When I didn't make an effort to awake, she called my name. "Skylar, the warlock is calling for my exit. You have to leave now. He asks now, but soon he will use force. He believes that I am going to take my gift from you and end your life. His emotions fill the room. Do you feel it?"

Too focused on her, I hadn't sensed or felt a thing, but now I heard Josh calling. I couldn't feel his emotions—or perhaps I just chose to ignore them. If I knew how panicked he was, I would feel guilty about wanting to stay. Oddly enough, I just felt cold and absent, the way I felt when I gave in to death. There didn't seem like enough time to ask all the questions I needed answered. I needed more time with her.

"Can you do that?"

"Yes. But I won't. During this cursed existence, I have acquired few obligations to others, but your life is my obligation and gift on behalf of your mother. A gift I will never ask to be returned."

"What happens now?"

"I answer Josh's call to leave, and you wake up and live the remaining years of your life."

"Then what will happen to you?"

She answered me with silence.

"Do you die?" I asked impatiently.

"My dying occurred long ago. Twenty-three years to be exact. Your birth was my death."

"Can you find another host?" I asked.

"That is no longer an option."

"You don't have to leave. You can stay. This life you can continue to have. We can share it as we have done before," I stated hastily. Now I could sense Josh's familiar magic. His voice echoed in the distance. He was performing a spell. I could feel it tugging at me.

I had known of her existence for only a matter of weeks and yet I couldn't end it. My mother never would have hosted her nor given her to me if she were bad. She was the only connection I had to my mother. Maybe I was the worst type of fool, but I couldn't end her existence.

"Maya, this life you may have," I repeated.

An uncertain silence filled the space. I thought she would have accepted quickly with appreciation, but she remained hesitant.

"No. I wish things to end here," she stated kindly, leaving me in a state of confusion. She was choosing a life of nonexistence over a life with me. The level of offense was immeasurable.

"You choose death over my life?" I was unable to hide my disbelief and disappointment.

"No, I choose the memories of a good life over what you will offer me. As my host, I experience your life, your thoughts and heart desires as though they were mine. You consider yourself a monster, and at some point, your actions will reflect your beliefs. I've lived in the bodies of monsters, killers, and people who were human in name only. Those experiences brought me no joy. It was a torturous existence that I could not escape, my very own personal hell. Given the choice, I would choose nonexistence over the life I shared with them.

"I've experienced your torment and your perception of the thing that you believe you are. Knowing that I existed in you brought you further grief. Your life will not bring me joy because it doesn't seem to bring you any. You live this existence begrudgingly, the foundation of a monstrous life. I don't want that."

Her voice held a level of sorrow that made me feel a little guilt for all my thoughts and feelings, but it quickly turned to anger. *Why should I feel guilty? I don't owe her anything!*

"Are you a monster?" she asked me.

I didn't know how to answer that. Once a month, I turned into an animal that I failed to identify with. A monster I may not be, but I had no idea what I was. Daily, I battled with a desire to be wholly human—something that would never be attainable. What did she expect from me? Was I supposed to change a belief that I have held for eight years overnight?

"I've been in a house full of were-animals, some I've grown fond of, others I downright dislike, but not one of them I would consider a monster. I can never say that I will truly embrace the animal that dwells in me, but I don't consider myself a monster. This life I offer to you with its fair share of problems, flaws, and insecurities."

There was another uncomfortable silence. I was quickly getting tired of that.

"Josh is going to force me from you. You have to wake up and you need to do it now."

"Are you coming?"

"If you don't wake up now, I won't have that option," she cautioned, her voice remaining a soothing timbre in my head.

"Are you coming?" I repeated. It was important that she remained with me because she was the only link I had to my mother. I very much wanted to be connected.

"Don't make it a decision of regret."

I opened my eyes to a dim overhead light, lying on an uncomfortable hospital bed in Dr. Baker's office. He shifted forward; placing his face inches from mine, staring at me in sheer bewilderment. He moved just enough to allow me to sit up. Restricted by IV lines, I began to pull at them, trying to free myself. He shook his head, moved my hands away, and unhooked them.

My lips were rough like gravel and my throat was so dry that it hurt every time I swallowed. It was hard to speak. "Thirsty," I mumbled, eyeing the brace on my ankle, while ignoring the were-animals standing around gawking at me.

I quickly emptied the glass of water Dr. Baker handed me. I tried to move the ankle that was restricted in the brace.

"You really did a number on it. Two breaks. It should be

healed by now," he stated, taking it off. I moved my ankle back and forth. It felt stiff, but it wasn't painful.

"How long have I been out?" I asked. My joints creaked as though they hadn't moved in weeks.

"You were clinically dead for three minutes." He shined a bright light in my eyes. He had me follow the light a few times.

"Two lives down. Do I have seven more?" I forced a smile to hide the anxiety.

"Not likely, you barely held on to this one. But you did much better than I anticipated,"

Dr. Baker stated solemnly, his face obscured by a frown. "You, little wolf, are simply amazing."

"Which type of amazing? The good kind or the bad?"

He chuckled. "She's fine. I am done here"—he turned to Sebastian—"she's your problem now." Then he walked out the door.

Ethan stood in the corner. His eyes wavered, barely making contact with mine. When I didn't avert my eyes from him, they met mine with full intensity. Ethan was always hard to read. Before, he seemed to hold remorse, but now he held none.

"You killed me," I accused, looking directly at him. His response: a cold distant stare.

"He had to," Josh responded coolly, walking into the room. "Your bond with the Gem could not be broken. You wouldn't let us destroy it—"

"So you destroyed *me*."

"Something like that." He shrugged. "It was quite the task. I had this made especially for you." He handed me the odd-colored knife that Ethan had used on me. The blade with a lilac hue was made from Trincet. A knife made for a pleasant death.

"Did you know that would happen?"

"Ethan suspected it. So we were prepared for the worst-case scenario. It's hard to kill a were-animal in any other manner but brutally. We tried to make it as gentle as possible. We stopped your heart and prevented the osinine from reviving it so that you would die."

"If you knew that would happen, why did you give me the Gem?"

With a pensive look on his face, he shot furtive glances in his brother's direction. "We needed to see how strong the connection was between you and it," he admitted.

It wasn't the things that he said that resonated with me, but what he left unsaid. They wanted to see if I could control it and wield its power for my own use. The Gem of Levage meant a great deal not only to the vampires; I suspected it meant a great deal to the were-animals as well. However, it controlled me to the point that I was no use to them, so they severed the bond.

He stepped closer, his voice dropping to a low serious tone. "It's good that you died. All those who have been bound to you think you no longer exist. Neither Caleb nor Ethos can sense your presence. Now you are free of all bindings, including mine."

"You were dead for three minutes but out for four days. Where were you?" Ethan asked brusquely, pushing himself up from the wall, studying me. "Jeremy said you were alive but in a state that you refused to leave."

I glanced at him briefly, "Asleep, I guess."

Josh looked at Ethan, Sebastian, and Steven, giving them an expectant look before directing his gaze to the door. Reluctantly, they complied. Sebastian lingered longer, watching me for a long time before directing his attention to Josh. Josh nodded once, and whatever it meant, it was enough to ease Sebastian's troubled mind. He backed out, keeping a sharp gaze on me before he disappeared from the room.

Josh crossed his arms over his chest. It seemed to be his turn to study me, and he did so with clinical intensity. "You never asked Maya to leave, and I am confident you heard my request."

I nodded once, waiting for his response. Waiting for him to

say something—anything. To tell me it was the wisest thing I had done or essentially the most foolish. The indecipherable and intense impregnated silence made me think the latter.

His lips curved into a limpid half-smile. Content, amused eyes stared back at me. "Good," he finally stated.

I told Josh everything. I didn't have anyone else to share this information with. He knew far more than I could ever hope to about her life, magic, and this world. "I was with her. I spoke to her."

"And still, you allowed her to remain." He seemed surprised.

"She's been part of my life for twenty-three years. She hasn't bothered me, so why should I bother her?"

Josh remained silent, his eyes intense with avid curiosity as he waited for me to continue. "She was murdered."

His mood became uncharacteristically withdrawn. He didn't seem surprised by the information, as though it were something he already knew.

"I am curious about her. I need to know about the people who hosted her and the horrors she lived through. I have to know what powers she possessed that would cause someone to kill a child." I met his intrigued gaze. "But I don't know where to start. I need your help."

Josh smiled and attempted to look innocuous, but I could see the hunger in his eyes and the thirst for power just shy of his grasp. He hid it well. With all that I had been through, my senses and observations were keener, my perception heightened. Before I came to the retreat, I would have missed it. Josh had a thirst for power and knowledge, but I couldn't determine if it was his strength or a weakness. Did he crave it to be better at his job, to be feared, or just to satisfy a lust for power? I didn't have an answer, yet I still trusted him.

He pondered the request for some time. After careful consideration, he smiled. "I guess we can barter. We explore your effect on magic, and I will agree to help you."

"Why is the idea of me exploring my abilities so important to you?" I inquired pensively.

His smile dimmed. "You are such the cynical woman."

I tracked his movements, attempting to interpret them as I waited patiently for an answer.

"Would it make you feel better if my motives were selfish?"

I considered the question thoroughly. "Yes, it would. I don't believe you are selfish or would do anything that would hurt me, but you are a magic junkie. Your recent discovery of my abilities is your new fix. You seem to crave something in it and I don't know what."

He grinned ruefully, taking a long time to respond. "I want to learn how to use your ability to control dark magic," he finally admitted.

Just as I figured, although he had substantial magical ability, he didn't like feeling powerless when it came to other forms of magic. That is when the similarities between him and his brother were the most apparent. Control was something they desired to a fault and without apology.

Frowning at his proposal, I considered if it was worth it. I hated dark magic and didn't want any part of it. But Josh had proven himself to be a good source, and I trusted him. Was it worth the trade? I considered things for a long time, and Josh was patient as I decided. "Fine. But you unlock any doors to things I don't like, you'd better very well know how to close them. If you break me, you damn well better be able to fix me. If Ethos or anyone else of his sort comes for me, then you need to be the one that answers. I trust you because you've earned it, but if you—"

"Skylar, I give you my word that I won't put you in direct danger. Not to say we may not have some turbulent moments because we are about to embark on unexplored grounds, but your safety will always be my first priority. That is a promise I will never break." He sighed wistfully. "I wish you knew the possibilities. Then you would be just as curious and interested."

I doubted that sincerely. I didn't care about the possibilities when it came to dark magic. I hated the idea and everything about it. Being bound to it or the source of it didn't make me want to do a happy dance. But magic gave me power that was far better than what was offered by turning into a four-legged animal when the moon called. Super-strength hadn't worked in my favor so far. In fact, the only time I was useful was when I used magic.

"If you are going to experiment with me and use me for dark magic, then it's only fair that you share your magic with me and teach me to use it. Will you agree to that?" I suggested.

His smile widened as he extended his hand to me. I shook it.

CHAPTER 17

The next day, I stood in the library between Josh and Ethan, with the Gem of Levage lying on the table and the *Symbols of Death* next to it. When I asked Josh if I could be there when he destroyed it, he was hesitant. In fact, he said no, but either I wore him down with my excessive pleading or he believed me when I told him that I needed to see it destroyed. He had to understand the need. It was something that had irreparably changed my life and had a strange hold on me, and I needed to see its destruction to know that it was really over.

I didn't realize that Ethan's presence came with the agreement. Josh stood close to me, and I could feel the wave of power coming off him. It was different for me now—more intense. I had a new appreciation for it. The purity of it, the calmness and the untainted energy it held.

When he started with the incantation, my skin prickled, the hairs on my arms raised slightly, and warmth crept up my arms. I looked at Ethan, who had stepped to the side, his gaze placed intently on Josh. I tried not to show how the magic was affecting me, but my face was flushed, my skin warmed, and sweat pooled around my temple. My fingers inched closer to Josh's, resting on top of his hands as he continued.

When he stopped reciting the incantation, the Gem just lay there. Then it trembled rapturously for a few minutes, dwindling down to just light thumps against the table. The room temperature dropped to nearly freezing. The Gem crystallized from the inside as icicles formed around its sharp edges.

Josh had released me from my binding. I was killed again to do so. Why did I feel such sharp wrenching pain and emptiness that it made me nauseous? I gripped the table, my nails digging into the solid wood.

"Are you okay?" Josh asked, splitting his attention between me and the spell as he destroyed the Gem of Levage. I held on to the table with all I had because I knew if didn't I would have tried to grab the Gem. It didn't affect me the way it had in the basement, but still, I hated seeing it destroyed.

Josh waved his hand over it and it burst into flames. I felt like I had been set aflame as well, holding on firmly to the dense wood I thought I would crush my fingers. When it was finished, all that was left was a vapor that cast itself over the book, covering it. It hovered there for minutes before settling on it, and then vanished.

The room returned to a normal temperature. The pain disappeared and so did the nausea. The only thing that remained was the odd emptiness that settled in me.

Josh's full attention was on me as he stood in front of me. Pushing away the hair that had fallen over my face, he studied me without saying anything. His hands rested on either side of the table, enclosing me.

"That was intense," I stated casually.

"Yeah, it was." But he wasn't casual. He looked concerned.

"Can I see the book?" I tried to turn my head toward the book but he took hold of my face; his hand cupped my chin returning my focus to him. "What happened to you?" he asked, closing whatever distance there was between us.

I backed up to the table, taking up any remaining space between me and it. "It was just intense. I seem more sensitive to magic. That's all." I didn't know any other way to explain it.

"Okay." He looked unconvinced. Briefly directing his attention to Ethan who was watching us from the other side of the room he asked him to put the book away. Ethan hesitated, his gaze bouncing between me and his brother as his lips tightened. I twisted, watching him as he took the book off the table. Instead of putting it away, he brought it over to me.

"Put it away," Josh urged.

"You wanted her here. Don't cheat her out of this. She should be allowed to see it all—from beginning to end."

"I don't think—"

Before he could finish, Ethan had handed me the book. Nearly snatching it from him, I pulled it close to me and held it. I wanted to keep it close to me and cradle it in my arms. Strangely, I felt a protective urge rise in me, but instead of keeping it linked to me, I flipped through the pages and found where the Gem of Levage had bled into it. Aware that they were watching me, waiting for a response and scrutinizing my reaction, I glanced at it quickly and handed it back to him. They looked surprised.

As Ethan grabbed the book, Josh's hands slid behind my back and under the edge of my jeans. His fingers pressed into my skin. "What are you doing?" I snapped, pulling away.

He smiled. "It's gone. The mark—it's gone."

They both looked relieved, as if at some point through all of this they expected it not to happen. If it hadn't, what would that have meant?

Josh left before I had the chance to ask. Ethan lingered, waiting for me to exit the library. As soon as I did, he locked it.

"Sky."

"-lar" I added. "Sky-lar," I repeated when he gave me a strange, confused look.

I think that was a smile he gave me, but it was rigid, barely curved. He moved closer to me. Ethan's intensity was hard to get used to. It jabbed at you, and then recoiled so fast that it left you awestruck, shaken, and even perplexed.

"You intrigue him," he admitted, the intensity of his gaze boring into me.

"He likes magic. It's what he is."

Ethan stepped closer to me, and the odd way he made me feel after he kissed me forced its way to the surface. A long intense gaze swept over me, roving over my face, to my hands that were clasped in front of me, and then to every place in between.

His tongue slid slowly across his lips, moistening them. My thoughts went to the animal channel right after the poor prey met its unsuspecting demise. The predator always stands over its mutilated carcass, licking the remains of its spoils from his lips with an ominous pleasure on its face. "But it's not what you are. My brother can be very persuasive. He's quite talented that way. You don't have to do everything he asks. If you don't want to explore *magic*, or anything else with him—then don't."

I smiled. "I know how to say 'no,' Ethan. I got that little education when my mother taught me the difference between boys and girls." I started backing away from him. Grinning, I slowly turned around and headed for the stairs. "Riley Fisher kissed me on the playground when I was twelve. He asked. I said no. But he did it anyway. I punched him in the kisser. That day, he learned that 'no means no.' Warn your brother. If I say no, and he doesn't listen to me, he's going to end up like Riley Fisher." I heard Ethan laugh as I headed up the stairs.

I had started packing my things the moment I walked through the door after my conversation with Ethan. I hoped to be home before nightfall. I looked up to find Sebastian leaning against the door.

"Stay until tomorrow." Like everything that came out of Sebastian's mouth, it sounded like a command.

"Is that a request or a command?" I asked politely.

His face relaxed, then he forced a smile. "It's a request. Ethan and Steven can stay with you tonight. I'll have someone perform another sweep of your home to ensure that Demetrius is taking the loss well. I doubt there will be any problems." He went farther into the room.

Sebastian, even in his seemingly relaxed state, still managed to intimidate me. He languidly paced the floor. "It's not good to live as a lone were-animal," he advised in his rich deep voice.

"I know," I acknowledged, my face contemplative.

"Lone wolves don't live long nor fare well in this world, and one with your abilities may be at greater risk. We've saved your life, and it is my understanding that you incurred a debt because of that." I nodded cautiously. Turning to face me, his soft brown eyes lifted to meet mine. "The debt is forgiven."

"Sebastian, I …"

"You saved one of ours, and you were invaluable in finding the Gem. As far as I am concerned, we are even."

"Thank you," I fumbled out, shocked that he would be capable of such benevolence.

He nodded once. "Skylar, I don't necessarily like you, but I respect your tenacity and values. I am extending an offer to join the Midwest Pack." I started to speak, but he raised his hand to stop me. "I don't expect an answer now. You feel obligated to us. I don't want you to accept under that pretense. Take the time you need to make an educated decision because it is quite a commitment. If I don't hear from you, I'll assume it is a declination, and I won't hold any ill feelings toward your decision. But understand that if you don't, and trouble finds you again, my pack will never help, because you have chosen the life of a lone wolf."

I smiled, watching him as he left the room. I chose to be a lone wolf. Essentially, Sebastian just informed me that if I declined pack membership and ever found myself in trouble, they would turn a blind eye to it. And if I were ever a risk to them, I would be handled as most risks are.

~

"Want to go for a run?" Ethan asked from behind me as I stood on the back porch of the house. It was the same spot I had been for the past fifteen minutes as I contemplated going for a jog. It was hard letting go of the constant expectation of vampire attacks.

Ethan wasn't speaking of running in human form. He wanted to run in the way he loved. I was prepared to decline, but when I turned to face him, I ended up nodding in agreement. The way he looked out toward the woods with an inexplicable yearning, I couldn't resist.

I followed him off the porch and when he started to take off his shirt, I took that as my cue to go to the other side of the house to change. I crouched, naked, and wished for my wolf to emerge. Cool fall air whisked against my skin, making me regret that I didn't decline the offer. Becoming increasingly frustrated when the change didn't come easily, I tried to force it. Still, nothing happened.

After several minutes, Ethan padded around the corner in animal form. He looked at me, tilted his head and pulled back his lips. I think he was grinning. He sauntered over and rested his face against the crease of my neck. As I stroked the scruff of his neck, I could feel the pricks running up my arm, the surge of energy through me as my change started. Ethan had run into the woods by the time I had fully changed. He submersed himself so deep into the forest that I had to track him by his scent.

When I found him, he howled playfully, then licked my face. *Ugh.* I turned away quickly, letting him know I didn't like that. He nudged me and did it again. This time, I growled at him. When he pulled back his lips to smile, it was as warm and inviting as if he were in human form. He gently ran his nose along my face and then darted further into the woods. I chased behind him, staying close.

We ran through the woods for almost two hours until we were exhausted. When we neared the house, Ethan changed while walking toward it. I waited near my clothes for him to help me change back. Coming around the corner, he looked surprised that I was still in wolf form. He knelt down. "You need to do this on your own. I won't always be around to help." He spoke slowly, making it easier for me to discern his words. Once he stood and headed for the door, I snapped at him, barely missing nipping his hand. I couldn't believe he was going to leave me like this. He responded with a wry smile.

I flopped down on my paws. I can do this. I closed my eyes, coercing myself to relax into my natural form. But it couldn't. I tried for nearly a half hour as Ethan stood inside watching me from the door. When he started toward me, I growled, baring my teeth. A warning that if he didn't help me, I wasn't going to miss this time. His lips flattened into a thin line, suppressing a grin. He knelt in front of me. "It shouldn't be hard, not for you. Human form, you want it. Just relax into it, Skylar," he stated softly.

I spent a good five minutes glaring at Ethan until he finally left. A long time later, I was finally in human form. I dressed and scurried quickly to the house. The alluring smell of food met me at the entrance.

"Hungry?" Ethan asked when I walked into the kitchen.

I nodded. Starving was more like it.

We ate mostly in silence. Periodically he would ask me questions about my plans. That didn't lead to very good dialogue because I had no idea what I would do. I planned to sell the house. Even if I could learn to walk past my mother's room without having an emotional breakdown, the house was too large for one person.

"Sebastian asked you to join our pack," he acknowledged as he took our empty plates to the sink and cleaned them. He kept his back to me for a while, his breathing slow and rhythmic as though he were considering something.

I remained quiet. I knew there had to be some ulterior motive to Ethan being here with me at this moment. Their actions were rarely selfless.

"Is that what the run and dinner were all about? Are you here to influence my decision to join the pack?" I realized it was being petty and irrational, but I couldn't help my aggravation. No matter how I tried to push the feelings aside, they wouldn't budge.

He looked stunned by my accusation, which he soon traded for a look of pure offense. "No. I was going for a run anyway. I thought you could use a little escape from the house. Perhaps it was a poor decision on my part."

He stared past me, engrossed by his thoughts. He quickly redirected his attention to me. Speaking slowly, his words seemed weighted by his thoughts. "Pack life is all that I know. It's the way I was raised, and if it weren't, I doubt I would choose otherwise. But it's not for everyone. Not all people who join the pack are assets. Some become complications and others … acceptable liabilities. Sebastian seems to think you would be an asset to the pack and your unique qualities an acceptable liability." He looked at me perceptively. "I disagree."

"You don't want me to join this pack?" I asked, failing miserably at hiding my hurt and disappointment.

"I think the life of a lone wolf would be best suited for you," He didn't give the question a second thought.

I had a hard time finding the words to respond. The immature brat in me wanted to call Sebastian right then and accept his invitation, just to annoy Ethan. The rejection stung.

"Why don't you want me ..." The words came too quickly to be censored. "In your pack?" I added awkwardly.

"Do the reasons really matter?"

"I guess not." I tried to sound just as aloof as I stood up to leave.

He reached out to grasp my hand, but I quickly withdrew before he could touch me. "Skylar, it's not that I dislike you. Quite the contrary, I actually find you quite tolerable. You are a chaotic mess, and it's ... endearing."

Seriously, is that supposed to be a compliment? "And you're an ass. We're quite the pair, aren't we?" I snapped back.

He held a look of casual indifference, the insult rolling off him. "I will always want what is best for my pack, and you aren't good for us."

"Message received," I responded in a curt voice as I stood to leave. "Thanks for the run and dinner." I headed back to the room and as far from Ethan as I could possibly get.

"You're quite welcome."

He was a smug one. Before I could close the door, Ethan called to me from the bottom of the stairs. I didn't answer initially, but when I heard him coming up, I poked my head out. I figured if I kept him downstairs, he would just leave me alone.

"It has been quite *interesting* knowing you." There was such finality to his words that I was sure I wasn't going to see him again, if he had anything to do with it.

"Same here," I declared through tightly clenched teeth, wishing I possessed the skill to make my words come off as cold as he did. I closed the door firmly behind me.

. . .

Steven waited patiently as I gathered the remainder of my things. During the drive home, he promised to visit me in a week, to see how things were going. I hoped he would, though I found it highly unlikely. Between school and pack obligations, Steven was a very busy person. Life was going to get in the way, and I doubted he would have time to visit or stay in touch with the "enigmatic mess" of a werewolf.

"Do you think the vampires will retaliate?" I asked once he pulled up in front of the house.

He shook his head. "Once they realize you are alive—which they will—they will assume you are still under our protection. A war between the were-animals and the vampires would leave them with too great of a loss. Demetrius isn't willing to accept that with nothing more to gain than revenge or to make an idle point. He's aware there is power in numbers, and he has already lost several powerful members to this. For now, you are safe from vampire attacks."

I let out a sigh of relief. He smiled modestly. "However, don't be complacent. You have enemies now. Michaela won't soon forget how amusing she found you. Gabriella will begrudge your existence because of what you did to Chase. It would be wise if you were careful," he cautioned. He looked out the window for a long time. When he spoke, his voice was weighted with concern. "The things you can do with magic, keep it to yourself. Gavin's not the only one who hates abnormalities. The Creed really doesn't like it. They're not like Josh. He's kind. Things like that don't bother him." I wasn't sure if he could elaborate, but the look on his face was enough of a warning to keep my mouth shut.

I nodded. Before getting out the car, I hugged him. "Be careful, Sky."

When I walked into the house, I dropped my bags inside, next to the front door. I stayed at the window until he drove away. I had a lot to think about regarding my life, including joining the pack. My life had definitely changed. My existence was known. I had piqued the interest of too many people—the wrong people. I was pulled into a world that I didn't know existed, and there wasn't a rabbit hole in sight for me to jump out of.

There were so many questions I needed answered, and I didn't know where to start. Who killed Maya, and why? What was it about me that made it so easy for me to be bound to something as dark as the Gem of Levage? And Claudia, who was she, really? Like everything else in this world, there seemed to be more to her than just being Ethan and Josh's godmother. The odd painting that commanded my attention seemed to offer more than mere aesthetics. There was something ominous about it, and I felt like I had missed something in it, and it was haunting me at this very moment. Finally, what did it say about me that I had the ability to expunge the most powerful purveyor of dark magic?

I grabbed my bags and started toward my room when I noticed a figurine of *Fantasia*'s Mickey apprentice placed on the side table in the living room with a note:

Here's to dancing brooms and shooting stars. Josh

MESSAGE TO THE READER

~

Thank you for choosing *Moon Tortured* from the many titles available to you. My goal is to create an engaging world, compelling characters, and an interesting experience for you. I hope I've accomplished that. Reviews are very important to authors and help other readers discover our books. Please take a moment to leave a review. I'd love to know your thoughts about the book.

For notifications about new releases, *exclusive* contests and giveaways, and cover reveals, please sign up for my mailing list at McKenzieHunter.com.

Made in United States
Troutdale, OR
11/23/2023

14838800R00222